BULLETS OF '71

A FREEDOM FIGHTER'S STORY

BULLETS OF '71

A FREEDOM FIGHTER'S STORY

CITI OF BOOKS

DR. NURAN NABI

with MUSH NABI

CITIOFBOOKS, INC.
3736 Eubank NE Suite A1
Albuquerque, NM 87111-3579
www.citiofbooks.com
Hotline: 1 (877) 389-2759
Fax: 1 (505) 930-7244

Ordering Information:
Quantity Sales. Special discounts are available on quantity purchases by corporations, associations, and others. For details, contact the publisher at the address above.

Printed in the United States of America.

ISBN-13   Paperback   978-1-960952-61-5

Library of Congress Control Number: 2023911857

Table Of Contents

Acclaim

"Thank you for your contribution to enriching the history of our independence. I think this book is a rare document of our political history. I am confident that it would educate many people about the true story of the Bangladesh Liberation war."

His Excellency Mr. Md. Zillur Rahman,
Honorable President of the People's
Republic of Bangladesh

"The book is a must read for the present generation of Bangladesh as it narrates the events leading to the Liberation War and Independence of their country. It is of immense value for other readers as it describes the role played by other countries in the crucial period of the Liberation of Bangladesh and covers various actions taken by the Mukti Bahini against a much stronger and well-equipped Pakistan Army. The book is a tribute to the people of Bangladesh, all the freedom fighters, and especially to Sheikh Mujibur Rahman, whose leadership inspired the Bengali population."

Lt Gen (Retd) Y M Bammi, PhD, India.
A Veteran of Bangladesh Liberation war '71

"Bullets of '71: A Freedom Fighter's Story enriches our understanding of the liberation of Bangladesh, with its careful description, almost day-by-day, of what the freedom fighter's group did, placed in the context of a balanced yet committed appraisal of the events of 1971. Dr Nabi's "bottom-up" perspective adds a very valuable piece, often ignored in studies that focus on the international dimensions of the war."

***Philip Oldenburg, author of India, Pakistan,
and Democracy: Solving the Puzzle of
Divergent Paths; and former faculty of
Columbia University, New York, USA***

"Even though it is an amazing personal saga, equally fascinating about the book are the political and historical data about a place and an era that were barely on my radar screen. Dr. Nabi in his book seemed less eager to talk about his personal trials and tribulations and more intent on relating the effects of the war on his people and the political ramifications."

***Pam Hersh, Special Writer, The Princeton
Packet, NJ, USA***

"It has taken decades for us to learn what our parents went through in World War II. Dr. Nuran Nabi takes us to a more recent civilian battlefront sharing his terrifying experience while a university student in a distant land. We should be grateful and read his first-person account of Bangladesh's first days toward independence – from raising the flag to mourning the loss of fellow students. We all share a common bond and Dr. Nabi's book should be required reading."
Thomas T. Keating Esq., White Plains, New York, USA

"Ultimately, *Bullets of '71-A Freedom Fighter's Story* is a bold piece of literature written by a man who was not only a part of that generation but was labeled as the brain of the Freedom Fighter forces, a true warrior. This is a must read for history and war buffs, or for anyone who appreciates the truth being told many years after the events have taken place."

Todd Rutherford, AskthePublishingGuru.com, USA

"Stating his own experiences on the political front and as an activist, he tells a compelling story about the triumphs and tragedies of this great conflict that consumed the entire country. "Bullets of '71" is a thoughtful and very highly recommended read, not to be missed."

Midwest Book Review, Oregon, WI USA

Bullets of '71: A Freedom Fighter's Story

"From his vantage point in Tangail, freedom fighter Dr. Nuran Nabi experienced Bangladesh's liberation war firsthand at many levels. Dr. Nabi meticulously, yet dispassionately documents the horrendous events as they unfold. As a trusted emissary of the Tangail freedom fighters, Dr. Nabi's secret conferences with Indian generals make for an intriguing read. Written excellently, Bullets of '71 is the most authentic version of what really transpired in Bangladesh in those dark days of 1971. The book is so poignant and captivating that readers will find it impossible to put it down."

Dr. Fakhruddin Ahmed, Princeton, NJ, USA

"Dr. Nabi's book is a rare document of our political history."

The Daily Star

"I was fascinated by the memory and the style of Dr. Nabi's writing. Both books contain true history. It will educate many people about the true story of the Bangladesh liberation war."

Anwar-ul Alam, Former Bangladesh Ambassador to Spain

"During the last 40 hours or so, I finished reading both books. That only shows how absorbed I was in going through your writings. Your life and activities are a testament of how the spirit of genuine nationalism and fellow feeling enhance one's courage and ability to even offer their lives in times of need."

Professor Bilayet Hossain, Oklahoma, USA

"Bullets of '71 is a rare document of the Bangladesh Liberation War. As a historical thriller and real-life chronicle, this book is a passionate tale of survival."

Belal Beg, Journalist and Columnist, New York, USA

"Although hundreds of thousands of young people fought to sacrifice their lives, it is the few young people like Dr. Nuran Nabi who played pivotal roles in shaping the course of the war towards victory. It is fascinating to see that a young man barely in his twenties, with no recognized uniform, is negotiating with veteran Generals of the Indian Army! Young people should find the book fascinating in that how imposed situations can defy the age barrier in providing leadership. With the aging of our Freedom Fighter population, authentic firsthand accounts of the war are diminishing fast. Bullets of '71 will serve to fill up that need."

Dr. Syed Ashraf Ahmed, Maryland, USA

"Dr. Nabi's 'Bullets of '71,' whether via the life lessons of each and every anecdote or through the rich and vividly detailed dialogues and descriptions of people, places and events- awakens, captivates, enriches and inspires its reader, in this case me, to the core of my being. And that motivational aspect and universal appeal of Dr. Nabi's 'Bullets of '71' that pours out of every page and into the hearts and souls of its reader, is the accomplishment and success of the book and its writers."

Shemonti Wahed, New York, USA

"From the first few pages, I was captivated by the story. Feeling much like an exciting novel, with each turning page, I was deeply saddened to realize time and time again, that the content before me were true events."

Dr. Ivan Khan, New York, USA

"--- I have yet to recover from the indescribably poignant and anguish filled journey, for journey it was that Dr Nabi takes us, in his inimitable style. It was a journey that took us through some of the blackest pages of human history of man's violence to man. Although a free Bangladesh was born as the fruit of this untold violence, the price extracted from her poor but indomitable people was terrible. It is a heart-warming story of a people's undaunting spirit in fighting for their freedom in the face of relentless oppression of a mindless regime. --- And I recommend this book to everyone in this world who value freedom above all else so that they comprehend how that freedom is obtained!"

Ramasubramanian Ranganath, PhD
Toronto, Canada

Foreword

It was a cold February morning in 2004. My family and I were on our way to the Dhaka Club, a Bangladeshi owned banquet hall in Queens, NY. My father had just published two Bangla-language books. The Dhaka Club was the venue for his book release ceremony.

I dropped off my parents at the door as I circled the block for the first parking spot I could find. There was little time to spare. In less than an hour the venue would be bustling with Bangladeshis from all over the Northeast.

Reluctantly, I had given up my weekend to volunteer at the reception desk. As I registered the guests and took down their emails, I couldn't help but notice the excitement on their faces. It wasn't long before the hall was brimming with hundreds of people eager for an autographed copy of my dad's book.

I didn't get it. After all, it was just my dad. I continued toiling away at the reception desk when I finally began seeing some familiar faces. My family friends from New Jersey began pouring through the doorway. After we got through the formalities of how big I had gotten (I was twenty-three), my aunties and uncles began explaining why they were so excited about my dad's book.

For the first time, someone had written a book about the Bangladesh Liberation War that not only captured the freedom fighter's experience, but their experience as a generation. That's when it occurred to me, this wasn't just my dad's book - this was their book. It was their moment to be recognized. I was happy to see that my father was able to make this happen.

I began thinking. There has always been a divide between my parent's generation and mine. My parent's grew up in a corner of the world where the only thing that separated them from abject poverty was getting an education. On the other hand, my life was one where such things were granted.

In college, I had the luxury of spending less time in class, and more time on starting a non-profit for the homeless. Although a worthy cause, my dad still trumped me. He spent his university days starting a revolution. Sadly, that was about as much as I knew of his contribution at the time.

As I mulled through my guilty thoughts, a face in the crowd caught my attention. It was my former finance professor from Rutgers University, Dr. Mahmud Hassan.

Always, enthusiastic to see me, Dr. Hassan approached me saying, "Mushfik, I need to talk to you. You have a very important job to do. You need to write this book in English!"

Leave it to Dr. Hassan to assign homework even after I had graduated from college. But, as we ended our chat, I began to notice why Dr. Hassan was so enthusiastic about getting this book into English. Scattered around the tables at the Dhaka Club were bored Bangladeshi-American kids glued to their I-Pods and cell phones. Like me, these were kids who had little use for a book that they could not read. These were kids who knew only half of their personal history.

As the event wound down, my father approached me. He too had gotten the same adamant feedback - this book had to be translated. Looking at each other, we knew we had no choice. We owed it to our community to accept the challenge. And what a challenge it would be.

A few weeks later we sat down, to begin work on the book. As my father went through his stories with me, the generational disconnect that I had recognized growing up had become prevalent between us again. Historic events and cultural nuances, which my father assumed his original audience understood, were completely foreign to me.

Initially this was frustrating, but we eventually took this opportunity to expand the scope of our narrative. As my father traversed his memories and the pages of his first two books, I prodded him with the inquisitive nature of a young boy. These were simple moments of a young man listening to his father's stories. But, it was through these moments that we would stumble upon valuable anecdotes that my father had never written about before. It was through these simple father-son moments that the book had taken on a new identity.

After more than six years of countless nights of writing, the book had become greater than the sum of its Bangla-language counterparts.

The book had become more than an eye-opening look into the psyche of the man I called dad. It had become an anthology of South Asian history, capturing a first-person account of one of the greatest underdog tales of all time. The book had become a collection of an entire generation's experiences, forgotten amidst the pages of discontinued magazines from the seventies and the fading scars of genocide.

But for me, this book had become a compilation of moments where I-Pods and cell phones could be shut off, where my family could come together to share our unifying-pedigree, where I, the individual in search of identity and introspective reflection could meditate on the unifying thread that connects all of mankind – the struggle for freedom.

By preserving the stories of our generations, we empower our children with the tools and motivation to preserve democracy. We activate the ingredients within ourselves to not only bring justice to those wronged in the past, but to protect future generations, not yet born. There were more than three million people who were killed during the Bangladesh liberation war and genocide. There were more than two hundred thousand women who were raped. It is up to us, to ensure that our children do not bear the sins and sacrifices of our forefathers.

Writing this book with my father, particularly the genocide section was the single most difficult thing I have ever done. I cannot imagine how painful it was for my parents, both of whom had to relive their experiences in order to help me through the writing process.

The sense of generational disconnect that I once felt has finally been replaced with a sense of compassion for all those who suffered in Bangladesh and for those who still suffer throughout the world today.

The liberation war ended more than nine years before I was born, and yet, reexamining the pages of this book, knowing both the profound good and unimaginable evil that humanity is capable of, I cannot help but feel that this story is as integral to who I am as a person, as it is to anyone.

It's more than likely that I will never have the opportunity to impact the world in the same way my father has. However, I hope that through this book his spirit and the spirit of freedom fighter's everywhere can live on forever. Joy Bangla!

Mush Nabi
New Jersey, USA
mush.nabi@gmail.com

Introduction

I was born and raised at the crossroads of Bangladesh history during 1949-1970. My childhood and early years were wonderful and happy amidst the glorious nature of Bengal and the aesthetics of her village. Yet, as time passed, I saw a rapid decline in the socio-economic conditions of Bengal (East Pakistan).

At the threshold of the dreams and promises of my youth, I discovered the volatile state of my motherland. At an early age, I realized that for being a distinct people, we Bengalis were looked down upon by our Pakistani rulers. They exploited us politically, economically, socially and culturally. They treated us as second-class citizens of Pakistan.

People desperately looked for a way out and I was no different. Finally, a man named Sheikh Mujibur Rahman appeared through the clouds of desperation and stood before the nation as he showed us a new path, a path to freedom.

The Liberation Movement was initiated by events such as the 1952 Language Movement. It gained momentum with the 1954 General Election and the Education Movement of 1962. The Liberation Movement finally shifted into high gear with the launch of Sheikh Mujibur Rahman's Six-Point Movement for autonomy in 1966.

In retaliation, Pakistani military rulers accused Sheik Mujibur Rahman of treason and put him behind bars. This trial was known as the Agartola Conspiracy Case. Pakistan's actions were responded to with a tremendous student protest movement in 1968 that reached every stretch of Bengal. The events lead to the people's uprising in 1969, manifested by the Student's 11-Point Movement against Pakistani military rule.

Yielding to the mounting unrest, the military junta was forced to release Sheikh Mujibur Rahman. This was a victory for Bengali nationalism. From that day on, Sheikh Mujibur Rahman became known as "Bangabandhu" – Friend of Bengal.

Bangabandhu won a landslide victory in the 1970 National Assembly and East Pakistan Assembly elections, giving a mandate to his Awami League Party to implement their Six-Point Charter for East Pakistan's autonomy.

These chain of events propelled Bengalis towards the inevitable. We were forced into the liberation war. If not for these events, the Pakistani Army would not have cowardly launched an attack on innocent Bengalis, and we would not have had to take arms in defense.

Shamefully, the history of the Liberation Movement has not been accurately recorded, nor has it been properly evaluated. The turn of events had moved so quickly that before thoughts could settle in the public mind, the war of liberation had taken center stage.

The 1971 liberation war was the defining period of Bangladesh's glorious history. It was an eruption that had been raging inside the belly of the nation for years. So the prospect of freedom and independence made all other national glories and pride look mundane.

However, the world must be told in full about the liberation movement and the liberation war. They must know the fascinating stories of how the student community, under the guidance of their leader, Sheikh Mujibur Rahman, propelled the liberation movement step-by-step towards the liberation war.

Future generations need to understand how the momentum of the liberation movement enveloped ordinary students like me. I hope that my experience, as captured in Born in Bengal, does just that.

There is no hyperbole in stating that Dhaka University was the birthplace of an independent Bangladesh. I am proud to say that I witnessed this moment.

This book covers two of my Bangla-language books. The first is "Born in Bengal" which tells the story of my experiences in the Liberation Movement.

The second book, Bullets of '71 starts with the night of March 25th, 1971, the start of the liberation war, and tells my experiences in the war.

Bullets of '71: A Freedom Fighter's Story

I joined the Bangladesh Liberation War in 1971 at the call of Bangabandhu Sheikh Mujibur Rahman, the father of our nation. During the war, all I thought about was defeating the Pakistani Army and gaining independence for my motherland. I hadn't even put much thought to my survival, let alone writing a memoir. This book was beyond my imagination.

After the war, I said goodbye to the hottest political stage in Bangladesh and returned to a private life. I had confidence that Bangladesh would be built as a modern country based on the basic ideals of the Bangladesh Liberation War. I expected that the heroic account of the liberation war would be written and taught to new generations.

Unfortunately, in 1975, anti-liberation forces killed Bangabandhu and his family and reversed the course of the nation. The history of the Bangladesh Liberation War should have been the driving force to build the nation. Instead, anti-liberation forces attempted to convert an independent Bangladesh into a mini-Pakistan. They not only distorted the history of the liberation war, but also conspired to completely wipe it out.

But, for those of us who were part of the experience, the liberation war was the most honorable and significant chapter of Bangladesh's national history. To forget it would be to forget our identity.

We have no alternative, but to use the spirit of the liberation war to inspire new generations to become more patriotic citizens, not just of Bangladesh, but also of the world.

During the nine-months of the liberation war, Pakistani occupation forces and their Bengali collaborators, such as Razakars and Al Badars, committed war crimes against our people. More than three million people were killed and hundreds of thousands of our women lost their honor.

However, these war criminals were never put on trial for their crimes against humanity. Rather, some were even rewarded and made ministers and members of the parliament by the military rulers of Bangladesh.

The Bangladesh genocide is the least known and least researched genocide. World leaders had turned their eyes from one of the worst genocides in modern history. It has since become the forgotten genocide.

However, we cannot forget the sacrifices made by the people of Bangladesh. We cannot forgive the crimes committed against humanity. To do so would be to sanction a pattern of genocide to continue on throughout history.

It is because of this desire and sense of responsibility that I have decided, after more than thirty-years, to write my memoir on the Bangladesh Liberation War.

The liberation war was a people's war. Bengali people of all walks of life - young, old, men, women, students, farmers, labors, intellectuals, and members of the armed forces, participated in the war.

We fought against great odds and defeated a much stronger army, even though they were supported by two super powers - America and China.

However, there is no romance in war. Rather in war, there is only killing, destruction, cruelty, patriotism, treachery, the disgrace of defeat, and the joys of victory. This book is a collage of those events during the war.

I make no attempt here to write a complete history of the liberation war. I merely penned my experiences and shared an eyewitness account of the war.

Nor did I depend solely on my memory to write this book. I have crosschecked some facts with the Bengali-language book, Shadhinata '71 written by my wartime commander and a legendary war-hero, Kader Siddiqui.

There is a certain risk in writing something from memory after more than three decades. After all, science has yet to uncover the mystery of how memory is sorted in the human brain. But, what we do know is that there is limited space for storage within brain cells. When space for memory is filled, other memories, often those less important, are lost, and accounts of new important events take their place. This theory suggests that the memories still stored in my mind reflect those most important to my life.

While writing these books, I encountered some rather interesting memory games. In spite of trying for days, I had a great deal of difficulty recollecting some of the events or names of the past. Then suddenly, these memories would resurface. And with each recollected thought, came a slew of other related memories that would, eventually, find their way into these pages.

Many of my friends encouraged me to write these books. However, Mr. Belal Beg, a national award-winning television producer, writer, and journalist, took a hands-on approach with helping me with the manuscript for Born in Bengal.

Syed Mohammad Ullah, one of my closest friends and the founding editor of the Weekly Probashi, a New York based Bengali-language newspaper, first inspired me to write Bullets of '71.

By the time I began working on the book, I had lost my collection of wartime photos having moved from Bangladesh, to Japan, and finally to the United States. However, Anowar-ul Alam Shaheed, my co-freedom fighter and the former Ambassador of Bangladesh, helped me by providing rare photos from his private collection.

Mr. Osman Ghani of Agami Prokashani, Dhaka, took the responsibility of publishing the Bengali versions of these books. I thank all of them for their help.

However, there were three people who have always been influential in the works of my expatriate life and this project was no exception. They are my wife Dr. Zeenat Nabi and our two sons, Mushfik and Adnan. My sons were a major source of inspiration in writing these books, as I was determined to share my story with them. I give special thanks to my wife Zeenat for being my best friend and partner in life. I'm not sure how much I could have accomplished in my journey without her.

Upon publication of the Bengali version of these books, I received an overwhelming number of requests to republish the books in English for non-Bengali readers. I agreed, and felt the importance of sharing this story with a wider audience.

In this difficult task, my son Mushfik stepped forward and worked diligently, many days and many nights, to co-author the English version of these books. My special thanks to Mushfik.

Mr. Shameem Chowdhury of Scholars Publications, Dhaka, Bangladesh took the responsibility of publishing the first edition of "Born in Bengal". Also Professor Shafi Ahmed, Mr. Razeeb Hossain,

Dr. Farrukh Mohsen and Dr. Fakaruddin Ahmed were a tremendous help in the proofreading process. I thank all of them for their help.

I put forth a great deal of time and effort in writing these books. However, I would consider it all worthwhile, if the spirit and ideals of the liberation movement and war inspires even a single reader. At the very least, I am content in knowing that my work has brought to light, even for just a moment, the patriotism, heroism, sacrifices, commitment, and determination of the freedom fighters of the Bangladesh Liberation War. Joy Bangla!

Nuran Nabi, PhD
Plainsboro, New Jersey, USA
E-mail: nabi@nurannabi.com
Website: http://www.nurannabi.com

Book One:

Born in Bengal

Dedication

This book is dedicated to the loving memory of my mother Anowara Begam and my father Afaz Uddin who taught me to love the people, families, and communities of this beautiful world.

Chapter 1

Growing Up

Joy around! Joy forever!

Regaining consciousness, I found myself in my mother's lap. I opened my eyes trying to make sense of what had happened. A worried crowd looking down at me and chanting prayers had surrounded me. All I could remember was that I was shivering with a burning fever and severe headache before I collapsed.

The incident took place at the residence of my eldest aunt. We went there to attend the wedding of her daughter. It was the rainy season. The rainwater flooded the banks of the nearby river, swallowing the whole village.

The accumulated water in the open space in front of the house was about two to three feet deep. The water, which came through the paddy fields, was so transparent under the sunny azure sky that you could see everything, even the occasional fish darting off from one side to the other.

Everyone in the house was busy with the wedding. We children took this opportunity to sneak out and play in the water. However, after so many hours of fun, it was clear that my rambunctious activity in the water caused my high fever. As a result, I was sick throughout the night. My mother scolded me for being an added headache to the already hectic wedding preparations. This episode marked the beginning of the 1950s for me. I was about five or six at that time.

The grand wedding was over without me. My mother was embarrassed by the stress I caused, but my aunt consoled her and told her that there was nothing to feel guilty about. Falling sick was natural and we were all susceptible to illness at anytime.

The next day, my aunt bade us farewell with kisses and hugs, as we set out for home by boat. The rainwater had not let up over the last few days. Floods had ravaged the whole area.

Just one week ago, our journey to my aunt's house was time consuming, as our boat had to hug each and every bend of the river. But by the time we departed, the boundaries between land and water had blended. Our boatmen could now save time by sailing over the short footpath that was recently ingested by the river. There were two boatmen with us who were sailing our boat.

My father sat in the front of the boat. From there, he enjoyed exchanging greetings with the passing travelers and villagers. My mother and I were inside the covered shelter of the boat. I heard the world outside and longed to come out and sit by my father's side. But, my mother would not let me out from under the canopy. She was afraid that if I was exposed to the open air that I might get sick again.

Her fear was not without reason. Her first child, my eldest brother Nazrul died of such a fever at the age of six. My parents were still deeply affected by his death. At one point, I started crying to come out of the covered shelter. My father said that as my fever had gone away, there was no danger from the open air; I could come out. And so, I leapt out and sat on my father's lap.

It was an afternoon in the month of Aashar (mid-June to mid-July). The sun was falling. The houses in the area were built on raised land, in order to protect against floods. These houses now resembled islands, as the roads and fields surrounding them had melted into the water. The people here were in desperate need of a boat just to travel from house to house. Nonetheless, life went on normally.

In the front courtyard of every house, I could see the bull and oxen driven milling of paddy from stalks. The animals yoked were forced to move in circles on the heaps of wet paddy stalks, but they never missed a chance to bite away a healthy mouthful of paddy plants. As punishment, the farm worker immediately thrashed a bamboo cane on their wide backs.

After passing a number of villages, we came to a point in our journey where we had to take a direct route across a wide waterway to get to our village. The long pole used by the chief boatman to push the boat forward was now useless. He had no choice, but to raise the sail.

The once small lake, east of our village, now appeared larger than the widest ocean. The villages on the north and south sides were hardly visible. Each corner of the area; from Falda in the south, to Bornigram in the north, to Comilla and Belua in the east, and to Fulbari and Khamarpara in the west, was now a vast expanse of water. There was water everywhere. I had never seen so much water. It seemed as if the sky and water met at the horizon like two old friends frolicking to embrace.

The evening slowly crept in. The reddish glow of the setting sun danced on the rippling surface of the water. It was as if nature had cast a mystical spell over my body.

It was time for evening prayer. The sound of conch shells made before the evening prayer by the Hindus of Falda Village mixed with the Azaan of the Maghreb prayer by the Muslims of the western villages. An eternal bliss settled on the water, sky, and air. My father began his Maghreb prayer.

At this point in our journey, the treetops of our village had become visible, but there still was no sight of any houses. As it got darker and the night befell, fear skulked into my heart.

The head boatman kindled a kerosene lamp, which radiated a dim reddish glow. Images of Kana Bhoot, the fabled one-eyed ghost as described by my elder brother, were haunting my mind. This was the place where Kana Bhoot lived. Kana Bhoot took control of the minds of boatmen who traveled by night. And under its spell, boatmen would ply their boats throughout the night, only to find themselves back at the point from which they started.

I thought that I would ask my father about the story, but before I could open my mouth, my mother ushered me back under the canopy. She had already made my bed. It was getting cold so I slipped under the cotton quilt and drifted into sleep with the lullaby of the boatman's song. Exhausted, I wouldn't remember falling asleep.

Boat Ride

The next morning, as I awoke, I found that the floodwater around our house had swelled up even more. The residential part of our small village circled a big pond. The farmland around the village was mostly for rice and jute, but was now buried under knee-deep waters. Amidst the gaps of the rice fields, villagers set up fishing nets to catch fish.

Fishing nets often trapped the abundant Koi fish. Hot rice with fried Koi fish was a delightful meal at both noon and in the evening. The Koi became thick, fatty, and tasty after getting plenty of nourishment thriving in the floodwaters.

We also often used fishing hooks to catch fish. It was always great fun. Pabda fish was particularly foolish. It used to swallow the bait almost immediately. However, the same was not so with Puti fish. This clever fish would take its time sniffing before it ever took the bait, constantly teasing you. It was so annoying how this fish tested one's patience.

Fishing pleasures came to an end within a few days. The Jamuna River was only ten miles west of our village. The floodwaters from the Jamuna rushed towards our village and inundated the entire area. Our house now stood just inches above water level. The water had already entered some other homes in the village. The affected people came to our house for shelter. The rice and jute were already submerged. My father told me that this was the most devastating flood of his lifetime.

We were now engulfed in the water. The sky was bright and blue. The hot wind began to blow. My mind wandered aimlessly, as my thoughts drifted like dust through the winds. Merchants went about on boats hawking hot Jilapi, Khaja, Goja, Batasha, and other tasty sweets. We would often rush to the banks of our pond to buy these delicious snacks. In addition to the hawkers of fun foods, gypsies brought silver and glass bangles to sell to the women of our village.

Our days passed happily, but I could see the shadow of gloom in the faces of my elders. The floods had destroyed the crops, yet the villagers somehow knew that the worst was still to come.

Winter arrived and the season of homemade pitas (cakes) set on. Pitas were made throughout the night in our house. We used to stay awake late at night to devour the fresh hot cakes before going to bed. When we woke up the first thing on our mind was, yet again, to eat some more cake.

My favorite was the puli pita made with crushed and fried coconut filling. My mother's "puli" was the best. For making the "puli", sugar or molasses was added to shreds of coconut. This mixture was then fried. Next, rice dough was rolled flat and thin, making the cover for the puli. To this, a pinch of fried coconut mixture was placed on the rice sheet at one side. This was done in such a way that the end part could be pulled over the mixture and pressed into a half-moon pattern with the tips of one's fingers. Then it was cut out and fried again before serving.

Winter was pita season in our village. Each household would take its turn in making pitas and then invite their neighbors to share.

Grandfather's House

All of my mother's sisters visited their parents during the winter. Including my mother, they were five sisters. There were about twenty of us cousins, and we raised hell with joyful thunder. Our grandmother used to make a variety of pitas. Every morning, we sat side-by-side on small wooden stools, as my grandmother served us pitas to eat.

There was a swarm of geese at my grandfather's house. I remember, on one occasion, they were chasing me. Before I could run away, one male goose stretched his neck and pecked me on my head. I don't think I had ever been that scared in my life.

Another time, fireworks were arranged to celebrate the circumcision of one of my cousins. To share the joy of the event, my grandfather started letting off firecrackers. Suddenly three fire crackers exploded in his hand and the celebration came to a screeching halt. All five of his fingers were blown away. A few months passed, but his wounds did not heal. Ultimately, the infected wounds spread and he died. The images of this tragedy impacted me throughout my childhood.

Although, my grandmother was in good health, my grandfather's death was such a shock to her that just six months later she followed him to the grave. My grandparents truly were soul mates, two bodies unified by one spirit.

Clash of the Bearded and the Clean Shaved

My father was a student of the Madrasa. He had an expansive collection of religious books. He read regularly for his own enlightenment. On one particular day, men from throughout the area had gathered for a religious discussion. A moulana, a bearded Islamic scholar wearing a sherwani, a long flowing coat, and a cap was speaking on various Islamic issues in a bellowing voice. Suddenly, a clean-shaven gentleman stood up and challenged one of his sermons, claiming that the moulana was misleading the audience.

This was an unthinkable situation. No one could imagine that this religious pundit would ever be challenged by anyone, least of all by a person whose head was uncovered and who did not adorn a beard. It was unheard of. The moulana was visibly shaken by the challenge. Who would be so bold as to dispute him?

As expected, the moulana demanded that his challenger cite the sources for his claim. My grandfather who was hosting the meeting was visibly annoyed. He announced in the meeting that the challenger was none other than his own son-in-law, my father. He, then, turned to my father and asked him to name the book on which he based his challenge.

My father cited the book and also the page in which the truths were given. From my father's example, I had come to learn that in order to hold ground in any confrontation, one must know the sources on which he stands.

Eid and Mosque

Eid is the most celebrated religious festival in Islam. It was on this day that our joys knew no bounds. New clothing would be bought for this occasion. On the morning of Eid, we would be woken up early by the sounds of religious music blasting from my uncle's radio. We would bathe in the pond and then wear our new garments. After that, we scented our bodies and clothing with attar. We would, then, run off to the mosque to say our Eid prayers. After the prayers, the imam would deliver a long sermon and lead the Monajat. We would join the Monajat by cupping our palms in front of our faces, but the imam's Monajat would continue for so long that our arms would begin to ache.

After the prayers, we would all embrace one another and then rush from house to house tasting shemai, a special holiday dessert.

Although, ours was a small village, we had two mosques. They were situated on the southern side of the village within fifty yards of each other on the bank of a small pond. One of the mosques, a tin shed, was believed to have stood by the grave of a pir, or saint. There were remnants of some old structures, which were believed to be the foundation of an ancient mosque. There was an unusually long cement covered graveyard by the foundation's side, which was believed to belong to the pir. The remaining smaller graves were thought to be of his followers.

The few families who believed in the pir used to say their prayers in the old mosque. But, the majority of the villagers went to a new mosque, which they built with brick-walls and a tin roof. Many years later, conflicts among the congregation of the second mosque developed, and so, a third mosque was built, leading to even further segregation.

Though the teaching of Islam advises its followers to join together in a large congregation under a single roof, the politics of the village prevented such fellowship.

Playgroup

My older brother Manan and his friends ran together in a very tight-knit crew. They preferred hanging around and having fun to spending time on their studies. They formed their own playgroup and staged an annual drama every winter. My older cousins Heera and Kamola were the leaders of this group. However, my uncles Matiur and Rahim, my elder brother, and my cousins Khaja and Abu Bakar were the backbone of the playgroup. Gaslights and marching bands from town were hired to publicize the play. The band would go out to adjacent villages playing film songs enticing the village's interest in the play.

On the day of the play, audience members would come in droves of five to six hundred and sit in the open fields in front of the stage. They would bring homemade quilts called kathas to wrap around their bodies, as they sat on straw beds.

Wooden cots were manipulated to set the base for the stage under a small canopy. The playgroup often rented backdrops from town, but most of the time these backdrop themes were completely unrelated to the play. The marching band would also accompany the playgroup in between scenes and during intermission, but their songs were also unrelated to the theme of the play.

My first opportunity to act came when a popular drama, *Nababh Sirajuddoula* was staged. It was the story of the last Nawab of Bengal.

I played one of the soldiers who ran from battle following his defeated general. In that role, I merely ran from one side of the stage to the other. There was no dialogue and my stint in the spotlight lasted only for a few seconds. Nonetheless, it was a moment I wouldn't soon forget.

The man who played my defeated general and whom I followed on to the stage was not only an actor, but also the prompter of the play. He got his makeup early in the evening and then continued prompting till his very short role came up in the end. He never once had any complaints. Such was his passion for theater.

While the dedication of my fellow actor was inspiring, this was not why my experience in this play was so unforgettable. My uncle Matiur played a character killed during a battle scene. His five-year-old daughter, Bokul, anxiously watched the drama unfold from the front row. Suddenly, as she saw her father fall to the stage, she screamed, "They killed my father! Help! Help! Someone please help!"

We would never let her live this down, and teased her about this incident for many years to come.

Primary School

I started reading books after my father introduced me to the alphabet. My father also accompanied me on my first day at school. I attended Sanokboyra Primary School. My father introduced me to the teachers. My first day in school was a little uncomfortable, as is the case for most children, but in time, I adjusted.

One afternoon, we were playing with a patched-up football in a field near our house. A man, in a lungi and plaid shirt with an umbrella in hand, stopped by our makeshift football field. He wanted to know how far it was to our headmaster's house. It was pretty far. He wouldn't have made it by nightfall, so I suggested that he stay the night at our house. He agreed. As it turned out, he was our new headmaster. The next morning, our new headmaster and I went to the school together.

The new headmaster, Mr. Aziz replaced Mr. Atiar. The newly implemented government rules required that all headmasters have certified training from the Department of Education. Under this new ordinance, Mr. Atiar was no longer qualified. He could have gotten the training had he desired, but he was already a wealthy man and enjoyed teaching locally near his home. Had he gotten the training to be headmaster, after a few years, he would have undoubtedly gotten transferred to somewhere far away, just as Mr. Aziz was transferred to us. Mr. Atiar opted to remain in the same school as assistant headmaster so that the two men could join together to run the school harmoniously.

Mr. Atiar used to smoke *Capstan* cigarettes. Whenever he came near, I would smell the cigarette smoke permeate from his clothes. The smell was so satisfying. I remember thinking to myself how great it would be to grow up and smoke *Capstan* cigarettes myself.

Mr. Aziz, the new headmaster had a rough temper, but he loved his students. He had a deep respect for discipline and perseverance. He sincerely wished every student to strictly follow those ideals.

Bokul, the niece of our teacher Mr. Quamrul, came from the city and joined us in the fifth grade. She wore a tiny golden locket around her neck. No other girl at our school wore such ornaments. She was a beautiful girl from the city. It was quite a sensation in the beginning, but as time passed, she too, became one of us. Ever since the first grade, I had been at the top of my class. Bokul, despite her efforts and her city-upbringing could not displace me. Regardless, we both secured scholarships. Bokul would eventually grow up to be a pediatrician in Dhaka.

I remember my days in primary school fondly, with only one exception. Everyday, we had to lineup and sing the Pakistani national anthem, "Pak sar jamin shadbad..."

I disliked singing in Urdu, but nonetheless, we had no choice. One time during the anthem, I snuck away and slipped into the back of the school just to dribble a soccer ball by myself. Soccer was my passion. I would take a soccer ball in solitude over singing in Urdu any day. But before my excitement could settle, I was caught red-handed by the headmaster.

Caning was the inevitable punishment. The headmaster forced me to stretch out my palm and hit me hard with the cane. This kind of caning was supposed to be very painful. However, I felt more humiliation than pain. Imagine the top student in class being punished with cane hits in front of everyone, including the girls. I was ashamed, but the headmaster could not have cared less.

Mr. Aziz was a firm believer in discipline. Despite the caning, I must admit his advice bore me many fruits throughout my life.

General Ayub Khan

One morning, my classmates and I were on our way to school. Suddenly, we saw a helicopter hovering over our heads. It was the first time I had seen a helicopter in my life. I was both excited and frightened by the sight. We began running in every directions as leaflets rained from the helicopter. They scattered all over the place.

The year was 1958. In a military coup d'état, General Ayub Khan seized power in Pakistan and imposed martial law. Most of the people in the villages of East Pakistan were without radio. So, in order to quickly inform the masses, a helicopter was used to disseminate fliers. The people had a new master.

Doctor Hook

There were only a handful of doctors for the hundreds of thousands of people in our region. Dr. Najibur Rahman was the only doctor in the area with a government certified medical degree. The rest were unlicensed self-made doctors. There were also a few homeopathic doctors.

Sick people suffered endlessly. The poor could not afford to go to the doctor. Due to lack of treatment, simple diseases would escalate and people would die. Opportunists took advantage of this situation and began practicing medicine without any knowledge or certification.

There was a Hindu gentleman at the Village Jamtoil. He was known for his interest in acting and sports. He, too, became a doctor overnight. He went around visiting his patients by bicycle. A man in trousers with a brown hat and a medicine bag on a bicycle – he became his own trademark. Patients would come to see him at his house, as well.

Very soon, his practice expanded. However, his fortune also brought him his share of enemies. An influential man once manhandled the doctor trying to force him to part with some of his property. The doctor sent a telegram to Sub-divisional Officer (SDO) stating that his life was in danger and that he desperately sought police protection. The SDO asked the local police officer to investigate the allegation.

However, the local officer took offense that the matter was not directly reported to him in the first place. Rather than giving the doctor peace of mind, he gave him a piece of his mind. However, the doctor did not lose heart. He continued his practice and soon became famous by earning the title "Doctor Hook".

The incident that brought him the title of "Doctor Hook" took place in our village. A poor farmer's wife of Darga house was expecting. Her labor pain had set in for a few days, but the baby still could not be delivered. The woman had been crying out in great pains for several days. This was a matter of great anguish for the villagers. An experienced elderly woman inspected the woman's swelling belly and came to the conclusion that the fetus inside the farmer's wife had died.

The doctor from Jamtoil was called in. He examined the woman and agreed that the fetus inside was indeed dead. An operation was crucial at this moment to remove the dead fetus and save the mother. He was not a surgeon, but the doctor was willing to give it a try. Unfortunately, the act was too dangerous and its success could not be guaranteed. The patient's life was greatly at risk. The doctor would try, but only if he was absolved of any responsibility of the outcome. There was no other alternative and so a contract was signed safeguarding him from any unfavorable consequence. The elders of the village signed the contract as witnesses.

It was a tense moment. The doctor took out a large black angling hook from his bag. The hook was about three inches long and was boiled for a few minutes for sanitation. He then probed into the uterus and hooked onto the shoulders of the dead fetus. He started pulling the dead fetus out slowly. Shrill wails echoed through the village. The woman screamed with agony, before eventually passing out from the pain. And yet, the doctor's focus remained unaffected. He pulled out the lifeless fetus and the woman's life was saved.

The dead child was given a religious burial. Every one expressed their respect and gratitude to the doctor.

However, one night Dr. Hook's home was burglarized. While trying to protect his family and home, this village hero was shot dead by some good-for-nothing bandits.

Hemnagar High School

My father was concerned with the influences of my brother and his playgroup. He felt that the village environment was no longer conducive for my education. He thought that my high school education would be hampered if I continued staying at home. I had to leave. I had to go to a hostel.

Hemnagar, the high school I attended, was only a mile away from my home. Nonetheless, the thought of leaving home was frightening. How could I live so far away from my mother? How could she live without me! I was sure my mother would strongly oppose my father's decision. She could never allow her youngest child to live alone.

However, I would soon learn that I could not have been more wrong! It was my mother, herself, who proposed that I leave for the hostel.

My days at the high school hostel were wonderful. I had so many opportunities for games and sports. Our school was situated on a bank of a big pond in Hemnagar Bazaar. It was within the premises of the Hemnagar Zamindar's palace.

The high school was a one story white-brick building. Our hostel was located just adjacent in a newer building connected to the school. We had a big football field in the vicinity. Facilities for volleyball and badminton were also available in the schoolyard.

I participated in all games and sports. Nonetheless, I gave my parents no reason to worry because I didn't allow my love for sports to interfere with my academics.

My Teachers at the High School

Mahiuddin Talukdar was our headmaster. Every morning, he would ride his bicycle to school. He was intelligent and wise, but was best known for being a strict disciplinarian. He enforced his rules and expectations on both students and teachers.

Once, an assistant teacher was late for attendance, but wanted permission from the headmaster to sign in, as if he were on time. The headmaster told him to ask his conscience. The teacher got the message immediately and marked himself late.

Another time, while our headmaster was away, two school orderlies got into a bitter confrontation, which hindered the day-to-day running of the school. The assistant headmaster and other teachers tried to mediate, but failed. As he returned to the school, the headmaster heard the story and suspended both orderlies for a week. Needless to say, this approach got some results. The next day, they settled their fight and returned for duty.

Our assistant headmaster Nazrul Islam taught English and was also in charge of sports and activities. He played football, volleyball, and badminton with us. Another teacher named Mr. Nazirul Islam taught us mathematics, while Mr. Jainal Abedin taught us science. Mr. Hayet Ali and Mr. Ameer Ali taught history and Bangla respectively. Mr. Rajab Ali taught us Islamic studies. As for my other teachers, Danesh Ali and Mohsin Ali also come to mind, but sadly the other names have escaped me.

Our teachers would always encourage us to study hard. They particularly treated me with special attention. Their interests in my success affected me in many ways and undoubtedly lead to my future successes in life.

Mr. Hayet Ali, and later, Mr. Idris were our hostel superintendents. They were fresh out of college. They would tell us stories of their college life that inspired us to grow and achieve. Our science teacher, Jainal Abedin was the younger brother of Mr. Idris. Despite their relation, they were polar opposites. Mr. Abedin was a strict disciplinarian, while his brother was an easy-going individual.

Mr. Abedin went out of his way to tutor us for free one month before our final national exams. The fruits of his dedication and my hard work paid off. I ranked "first division" with distinction, an honor that had not graced the halls of our school in many years. We showed Mr. Abedin our gratitude with a package of chom-choms and rosho gollas, specialty sweets.

Mr. Hayet Ali and Mr. Idris paid particular attention to our studies in the hostel at night and through the holidays. They would especially encourage us to learn about international affairs. For this, we were required to discuss the editorial contents of such newspapers as the Ittefaq, the Azad, and the Morning News. I remember reading one editorial in the Ittefaq that analyzed the criticism surrounding President Kennedy from his right-wing opposition. Unfortunately, in an ironic twist of fate, President Kennedy was tragically assassinated a few short days after the publication.

In addition to being our Bangla teacher, Mr. Amir Ali was also in charge of the school library. He gave us books on different subjects and encouraged us to discuss different topics with him.

While we were in high school, there was a system of taking elective subjects supplementary to our mandatory classes. Each teacher would compete to win over the brightest students and try to get them to enroll in their class. Mr. Rajab Ali, our Islamic teacher, wanted me to take his class while Mr. Abedin strongly suggested that I took advanced mathematics. I remember having to eventually disappoint Mr. Rajab Ali.

First Girl Student

Ours was an all-boys high school, with no female students, or even teachers. Monowara was the first girl to walk our halls and was admitted in the 8th grade. She was in our class.

Monowara came from the Bhuapur region, about ten miles south of our school. Special arrangements were made and she was given a room at the residence of the school cashier. She was a very bright student and earned her place in our school. However, I remained at the top of the class through graduation. Nonetheless, Monowara successfully dislodged my cousin Latif and held rank in second place through the 10th grade. After Monowara, a few other girls namely Renu and Minu, the daughters of the new postmaster, and Bokul, my cousin got admitted into lower classes. The girls were eventually given a separate common room. The addition of females to the student body added to the richness of the school.

My Cousin Latif

I was born just six hours after my cousin Latif. This made our mothers the topic of many jokes amongst the ladies of our family. Latif and I were like two peas in a pod. Growing up, we shadowed each other and through the 10th grade, that is how we remained.

Latif was light and skinny and I was healthy and stocky. While in the 5th grade, Latif fell to a serious fever. After the fever, he started to grow like a banana plant, and within two years, passed me in both height and girth. Later during hostel life in high school, Latif's physical presence became very reassuring to me.

However, I would often envy Latif. My smaller stature and frame prevented me from overcoming stronger defenders on the soccer field. This often made me resent that I hadn't caught Latif's illness and grown taller and stronger than I was.

Zamindar's Palace at Hemnagar

Hemnagar was named after a zamindar named Mr. Hemchandra. A zamindar was a British-appointed noble, responsible for collecting taxes on behalf of the British Empire.

He was a powerful Hindu zamindar who reigned over predominantly Muslim subjects. In 1947, British Imperialism ended in the Indian subcontinent, and thus, an independent Pakistan and India were born. Zamindar Hemchandra abandoned everything and left for Calcutta to settle in India. He was a legendary figure in our area. We had heard many stories about him.

The zamindar's estate consisted of about two square miles. Seven big ponds clustered the palace. Blanketing the shores of these ponds, various buildings were built to accommodate the zamindar's staff and their families.

The *jalshaghar* stood on one side of the palace. It was a theatre hall where the zamindar attended to indulge in dance and music. Professional singers and dancers were brought from Calcutta. There were stories that once Zamindar Hemchandra took fancy to a beautiful baizee. He held her captive inside his palace. The family of the baizee went to court to free the young girl. However, the zamindar's men provided fabricated details with false witnesses to suggest that the baizee was seen leaving the zamindar's palace after the function in a car. Then, another witness claimed that she was seen taking the train at Jagannathganj Train Station bound for Calcutta. Lastly, another false witness testified that the baizee was seen alighting from the train at Shialdah Station in Calcutta.

The zamindar's own escape to Calcutta was also an interesting tale. As the story goes, on one particular night during the independence movement of 1947, a group of men intentionally slaughtered a cow in front of the palace. The zamindar being a man of the Hindu faith was surely threatened and insulted by this crime as cows were considered to be sacred to the Hindu religion. By morning, the zamindar had come to know about the event and immediately packed and left Hemnagar for good.

The zamindar's palace court was intentionally built to intimidate outsiders. The ceiling of the palace court was forty feet high. Even the most giant of men were dwarfed by the grandness of the zamindar's court. The outside walls and the enormous interior of the court were adorned with exhibits of rare glass and marble. The court was, undoubtedly, a reflection of the zamindar's power and prestige.

Nevertheless, the grandeur of the palace was already blurred by the time we were students at Hemnagar high school. It was as if the whole palace wore the fading beauty of an aging queen. Barring a few, most of the Hindu families had slowly migrated to India. One of the nephews of the Zamindar remained behind. He embraced Islam and took the last name, Khan. He sold properties for a living.

The memory of the zamindar's nephew embracing Islam incidentally reminds me that there were no mosques in all of Hemnagar.

Hemnagar Bazaar

Hemnagar Bazaar, the main market place of Hemnagar, was just a short walk from behind our school. The community market was held every Wednesday. The list of the permanent shops of the market included two groceries, two sweet shops, two jewelers, and one each of tobacco, quilts, and laundry. There was also a licensed shop for hashish. On the day of the community market, about three hundred villagers from the surrounding area would gather together to buy or sell rice, vegetables, poultry, fish, meats, and fruits. The owners of these shops were Hindu except for one Bengali-Muslim and one Bihari-Muslim.

Most of the professional class in our area such as the artisans, carpenters, fishermen, and basket weavers were also Hindu. The majority of the customers, however, were Muslim farmers. In spite of the differences in faith between the classes, the people of the land lived in peaceful coexistence.

This was exemplified at the market. Every Wednesday, Hemnagar became the essence of communal harmony, where Hindus and Muslims came together as brothers and sisters of the human race.

The Laundry Man of Hemnagar

A mother and her son operated the laundry shop of Hemnagar. The son was about 40-years-old, but no one could guess the age of the mother. She could be seen sometimes walking along the road with a huge load of laundry on her head, or at a small basin between the market place and the school where she washed her laundries.

The clothes were boiled with soda or soap. The woman would then take them out and beat them on a black wooden plank at the foot of the basin. The muscles of her sun-blackened hands would swell, as the percussion of her rhythmic beating would resonate through the air. The laundry was thrashed on the wooden plank, so fast and so hard, that the dirt would appear to flee for dear life from the fabric. The clothes were then starched and dried.

Her son, the laundry man, was responsible for the ironing of the clothing. He first sprinkled water on the dry starched clothing. Then he used an iron heated by glowing charcoal embers to press the clothes neatly. As he pressed the fabric, vapor would rise into the air and the gleaming white clothing would reappear under the passing waves of the hot iron.

I would watch the laundry man work steadily, ironing and folding his customers' clothes. On cold days, when I went to pick up our garments, I would bide my time, so as to relish in the cozy warmth inside his laundry shop.

Credit Card

The credit card is a driving force in most market economies. However, it wasn't until my days at Hemnagar Bazaar that I was first introduced to this modern marvel. In order to meet my laundry and other expenses, my father arranged a credit system with the shopkeepers. They received weekly, or monthly payments, from my father at Wednesday's community market.

I was very fond of sweets. I was particularly addicted to the sweets from one of the two shops. The shopkeeper of this storefront often asked me to check the taste of his sweets, which he made the previous night. I remember thinking that I was getting the sweets for free and saving on my breakfast expenses. Years later, I was surprised to learn that the sweet shopkeeper, like the other shopkeepers, got paid for his tasty products every Wednesday at the community market. Despite this revelation, my regard for the sweet shopkeeper never faded.

My favorite sweet maker never forgot me, either. As recently as 1998, my wife returned from a trip to Bangladesh with a suspiciously familiar box. She had received it only days before her scheduled return to the United States. After more than thirty-five years, my favorite sweet maker sent a box of his famous rosho golla, chom-chom, and shondesh for his best customer.

The Dark Shadow of the Crimson Krishnochura

Like the thorns of a rose, Hemnagar had its shortcomings. There was a house on the south side of the bazaar across from the canal. It was densely forested so no one could see the people who visited. Nonetheless, every one knew what went on there. It was a brothel. It was set up in the era of zamindar for the pleasure of men. There was a tall Krishnochura tree that draped the sky above the house. Its gorgeous crimson flowers encrusted its branches like jewels on a scepter. On summer days, its canopy could be seen from miles away. It was undoubtedly the icon of Hemnagar.

This magnificent vista often captured the spirit of the passerby, making him forget about the ugly things that dwelled below its shadow.

Charak Festival

The fishermen and artisans lived in Shimlapara Village, on the western side of Hemnagar. Every year during Charak puja, fishermen would arrange the religious rituals and put on a carnival in front of the zamindar's house, adjacent to the pond. All people, irrespective of Hindu or Muslim, would participate in the carnival.

Children would throng to see the monkeys dance. Statues of deities were mounted inside the court of the palace. At the end of religious rituals, the statues were immersed into the pond as the crowd cheered. In a group, my friends and I would go to the festival and sit on the bank of the pond to watch the immersion of the deities.

Often times, the fishermen of Shimlapara would arrange kirton singing performances that would go on late into the night. My friends and I enjoyed listening to the kirton songs.

Roopban Jatra

Once, our school administration invited the famous Roopban Jatra to perform at Hemnagar to raise funds for the school. Roopban Jatra was one of the most famous Bengali operas. It was based on a mythical love story about a beautiful young princess who was married to a child and later exiled to live in a forest.

The troop had many actresses. This was an added incentive for patrons because during those days, there were very few women who acted on stage for the public.

The zamindar's palace was surrounded from all sides by an enormous wall. Within these walls was the palace garden where a tent was raised. It was under the center of this tent that a stage was constructed for the performance. An audience of about five thousand sat in full circle around the stage.

Our teachers sat by the gate and sold tickets for the show. Our headmaster organized everything under his supervision.

The sound of music and dance under the playful flickering of the gaslights resonated within the walls of the palace and brought back the memory of the zamindar era. Men, women, and children, all enjoyed the show long into the early morning.

The event was a great success and the songs of the opera hummed across the lips of Hemnagar for many years to come.

Seven Rounded Walks

One of the jewelers of Hemnagar Bazaar had a daughter. She was gorgeous. Her beauty mirrored that of a porcelain doll. She was getting married to a groom from Dhaka.

At that point, I had only heard of the beauty of a traditional Hindu wedding. Typically, during a Hindu wedding, the couple would walk around an open flame seven times, while knotted together by their clothing. Finally, I would have an opportunity to experience a wedding for myself and I was not going to miss it - even if the ceremony was during school hours.

During recess, I led my fellow 7th graders to see the marriage ceremony. The father of the bride warmly welcomed us. We enjoyed the whole ceremony as he entertained us with sweets.

When we returned to class, we were ten minutes late. Our teacher was an elderly man. He was so old, in fact, that he had once been the teacher of our school's headmaster. He had just returned from Hajj. We used to call him Hajji Sir. He was due to retire in about two years.

On finding us absent, he became furious and rushed to the headmaster to complain. In the meantime, we returned to class and quickly sat down. The headmaster came and peeped into our class. He found us sitting and quietly left.

Our Hajji Sir came back and wanted to know why we were late. He was shivering with rage and announced mass punishment – a cane hit for everyone! He had the cane in his hand ready. I was the first boy in line and the punishment of the group began with me. I stretched out my left hand as he struck me forcefully in the center of my palm. Even before half the class could receive its punishment, the cane had broken into pieces. The rest of the class narrowly escaped their punishment.

My classmates later jeered, saying that I had paid the price for sitting in the privileged front row.

14th August, Independence Day

Pakistan Bazaar was a mile away from Hemnagar Bazaar. Hatem Ali Khan, an anti-British leftist leader established the Pakistan Bazaar as the rival of Hemnagar Bazaar.

The 14th of August marked the Independence of Pakistan. Every year on this day, the Pakistan Bazaar celebrated the occasion with many festivities. The Union Council sponsored the events.

Amongst the fanfare, the games and boat race were the most popular. About ten to fifteen boats from different villages would come to the canal, by the side of the bazaar. They were each colorfully decorated just for the event. Every boat had a drummer and an impromptu singer to cheer the captain and the boatmen. Crowds would line up along the banks of the canal and would root for the boats from their respective villages.

Games such as soccer, ha-dudu, and lathi khela (stick fighting) were also popular amongst the spectators. Ha-dudu was a game that consisted of two teams of seven players each. The game was played on a small twenty-by-twenty court, which was divided in half for the two teams. One at a time, a player from each team would run holding his breath from his side of the court to the other. This player could score a point by tagging anyone from the opposing team and running back to his team's side. However, if the opposing team caught the player, he would be eliminated from the game. The winning team was determined, either by the number of points scored, or by the team with the most players remaining.

Lathi khela was similar to fencing. In place of an actual sword, each player used a thin bamboo stick. The player, who hit his opponent the most number of times during the match, was declared the winner.

Two brothers of Banipara Village were famous for their excellence in this sport. They reached a level of such skill that they claimed to be able pinpoint the smallest freckle of white lime on an opponent's body with their sticks. It was thrilling to watch them circle and eye each other down. They were like two ferocious cocks, waiting for just the right moment to strike. When suddenly, one would jump up into the air screaming, before attacking the other. Like the crowds of the Roman Coliseum, their fans would throng around the players and cheer on these favored gladiators.

For me, the soccer matches were my most vivid memories. However, one particular soccer match seems to standout most, the father-son game. One team consisted of fathers and the other team consisted of their sons. My father was a soccer player in his younger years. In the father-son match, he was the fullback for his team, while I was the center forward for the sons' team. I tried to figure out how to score against my father, but I was apprehensive about inadvertently kicking him. Though it was all part of the game, culturally the idea of a son kicking his father was something that was incredibly disrespectful.

Thinking back, I am not sure whether it was my father's defense or my hesitation, which played the greater factor, but the game ended in a scoreless draw.

Hatem Ali Khan, Leftist Peasant Leader

Occasionally, I would see Mr. Hatem Ali Khan addressing public meetings at the Pakistan Bazaar. He was born into an aristocratic family of Belua Village. He graduated from Calcutta University in the early 1920's, where he came in touch with Marxist ideology.

Instead of having a highly paid government job and living a comfortable life, Mr. Khan chose to devote himself to the causes of poor peasants. He returned to his village and established Belua Bazaar High School, where he became the headmaster. Perhaps this return to his village was part of a greater social strategy to stay close to his people and organize underground socialist movements.

After the creation of Pakistan in 1947, East Bengal, then East Pakistan, was politically and economically exploited by its corrupt West Pakistani rulers. Since its inception, a rightist political party, known as the Muslim League, ruled Pakistan. In 1954, the opposition in East Pakistan formed the United Front to contest the Muslim League in the general election. The United Front leaned just left of center and was lead by the three great leaders of East Bengal: Mr. Shere Bangla Fazlul Haque, Mr. Hussain Shaheed Suhrawardy, and Mr. Moulana Abdul Hamid Khan Bhashani. Mr. Hatem Ali Khan was a candidate of the United Front against the Muslim League candidate, Principal Ibrahim Khan. It was a fight between David and Goliath.

While Mr. Hatem Ali Khan was the founder of a high school, Mr. Ibrahim Khan was the founder of Bhuapur College and moreover, a very wealthy man. As if the odds weren't stacked enough, Mr. Ibrahim Khan was a candidate of the ruling party. Principal Ibrahim Khan also dramatically outspent and out-campaigned Mr. Hatem Ali Khan.

On Election Day, Principal Ibrahim Khan rented a fleet of buses to transport his voters to the polls. In those days, riding a bus for the people of such a rural and remote area was an exhilarating experience, in itself. Meanwhile, Hatem Ali Khan could only rely on grassroots tactics of door-to-door campaigning with his foot soldiers. My father and uncles were amongst those foot soldiers.

The earliest returns of the vote counts could not have looked worse for Mr. Hatem Ali Khan. Despite this early disappointment, my father and the people of our village stayed up through the sleepless night, praying for a miracle. As the official ballot counting went on late through the night, a decision finally became clear. Mr. Hatem Ali Khan was declared the victor! At last, he was elected member of the East Pakistan Assembly. Our joys, however, did not end there. We would very quickly discover that Mr. Hatem Ali Khan would not be alone. The people had spoken; the tyranny of the Muslim League was over. The United Front gained control of the East Pakistan Assembly.

However, the excitement of this victory was short lived. In 1958, General Ayub Khan in a coup d'état imposed martial law, dismissed the civilian government, and dissolved both the Central and Provincial Parliament. Democracy in Pakistan was left for dead. Mr. Hatem Ali Khan was arrested under this martial law.

A year later, after Gen. Ayub Khan had consolidated his power, Mr. Hatem Ali Khan, along with a few of his fellow United Front leaders, was finally released from prison. General Ayub's oppression of the United Front only added to Mr. Hatem Ali Khan's resolve. He became more determined than ever to mobilize the agrarian people against the subjugation of the Pakistani military junta.

Mr. Hatem Ali Khan held public meetings at the Pakistan Bazaar on Fridays, after the community market. The people would finish buying or selling merchandise and then attend the meeting. In those days, the luxury of a microphone was considered rare and too expensive.

I once had the opportunity to accompany my father and attend one such meeting. This particular meeting was presided over by my uncle Meer Amjad Ali, who was chairman of the Union Council.

Mr. Khan delivered a fiery speech inspiring the people to stand up against injustice and oppression. He also emphasized the importance of the farmer's right to achieve prosperity through struggle. Although, I expected to hear my uncle give a verbose speech, I was amused to see that he who presided over the meeting stood up only to thank everybody and declare the meeting over.

Once, during another such meeting, Mr. Hatem Ali Khan called upon the farmers to stop paying taxes to the government. Under cover of night, a battalion of police surrounded his home and arrested him in the early morning. There was no doubt that General Ayub Khan's military intelligence was well networked. Mr. Hatem Ali Khan was jailed several times in his life for his political beliefs.

Hatem Ali Khan was also a great orator. He could speak on for hours and hours without losing your attention. He used to quote verses from the Koran and the Hadhis to strengthen his points.

As a young boy, I was often fascinated by his speeches. In my mind, I considered him my hero. I dreamt that when I grew up I would be like him and fight for the causes of the peasant class. If needed, I too would go to jail.

I wondered why Mr. Khan held his public meetings on market days. Eventually, I saw the wisdom behind his strategy – cost effectiveness and convenience. First, he did not have to put any effort into gathering an audience. The crowds were already there to shop. Secondly, with the market place and the meeting place being at one and the same location, people were content with finishing their errands at the market and casually sitting down for the meeting.

Mr. Hatem Ali Khan devoted his whole life to fighting for the rights of the farming class. Nonetheless, his services and sacrifices were not duly recognized in the political history of Bangladesh.

A Fight for Prestige

Once, the Sub-divisional Officer of Tangail visited our school. He was the ex-officio president of the school managing committee. His name was Quaderi and he was a non-Bengali officer.

There was an air of excitement all around. Every effort was taken to give the best impression. The premises of the school were cleaned and the walls were repaired. A goat was slaughtered for meat for the luncheon party. Khorshed Alam, the cook of our hostel could not believe that the SDO could eat a whole goat. He assumed it was sensible to buy a few pounds of meat from the butcher. However, later Khorshed Alam discovered that SDOs, or similar high-ranking government officers, were never alone. An entourage of government officials and local elites always accompanied them.

Mr. Quaderi did not speak Bangla. He was an ill-tempered man. On one occasion, Mr. Quaderi scolded one of our teachers in public because while introducing himself, the teacher referred to his own educational qualification as "BA failed". This incited the SDO's outrage. Infuriated, Mr. Quaderi rebuked the teacher for his shameless declaration of his educational qualification. Warning him, the SDO said, "From now on introduce yourself as Intermediate Passed – NOT BA FAILED!" The behavior of the SDO stunned everyone.

Later in the meeting of the managing committee, he was abusive towards our headmaster, while discussing a dispute over financial audits. We knew our headmaster to be a very honorable man who valued his dignity. He was not one to tolerate such abuse. He responded to the SDO's incendiary comments accordingly. This confrontation spawned animosity between the two men. The SDO threatened our headmaster and promised to retaliate. He abruptly left Hemnagar and returned to Tangail.

A Different Taste of Fried Fish

The petty interests of local politics often spilled into the affairs of our school. One morning, I awoke to pandemonium outside. I came to find about two hundred people who had gone down to the pond, next to my hostel. They were busy catching fish with a variety of equipment.

The people had come from the nearby village. The students of the hostel enjoyed watching the people delight as they caught their fish. Within a few hours, they amassed a bounty of fish. Our cook, Khorshed Alam, negotiated a large fish for the students. We were treated to an unexpected feast that night. We dined on carp - both fried and curried.

However, the next morning, we got some bad news. We heard that the nayeb, the local tax collector, filed a criminal case for illegally catching fish from a government pond. The list of alleged offenders included our headmaster, our hostel's superintendent, ten students of the hostel including myself, a local homeopathy doctor Biren Banerjee, and only three actual culprits. What a ridiculous accusation! The locals from the village caught the fish, yet, we were the ones accused. Our only crime was watching as onlookers and tasting a single donated fish.

The false case was dragged on for about nine months. Over the course of these nine months, we were obligated to travel to Tangail for our court hearing. In those days, getting to Tangail meant taking an arduous journey by both foot and bus. This trip could easily cost us our whole day. Thus, just for a single court hearing we would have to waste nearly three days.

I remember one such trip to Tangail that was particularly miserable. In those days, in order to get to Tangail by bus, we would have to cross a river near Pungli by ferryboat. On this particular day, just as we arrived at the river, the sky opened up and a severe storm rained down on us. The ferryboat closed. Along with a fleet of other buses, we spent the entire night trapped in a cold and damp bus.

The next morning, we rushed to court with no time to stop or freshen up. Luckily, we made it to our hearing just by the skin of our teeth.

The irony of such journeys was that on this day, and most other occasions, our appearances in court only lead to rescheduling the hearing for a later date. The court proceedings were clearly a deliberate attempt to harass us. And the court did well to prolong our misery. After nine months of harassment, we were finally acquitted of all charges.

It soon became clear to us that the root of our suffering was the SDO, Mr. Quaderi. On the night of the fishing incident, the nayeb sent an honest report of the event to the SDO and stated the names of the real culprits. The SDO utilized this opportunity. He sent back the report with instruction to include Mahiuddin Talukdar, the headmaster of the school, as the ringleader of the alleged offenders. The students' names were strategically used as well. Without accusing some of his students, it would be very difficult to implicate the headmaster into the plot.

The SDO made good on his promise. He took his revenge against the headmaster. The whole trial process was simply a reaction to the bruised ego of the pompous SDO. The headmaster paid a great price to maintain his dignity and self-respect.

Dr. Banerjee was implicated by the nayeb for a different reason. The residential accommodation allotted to Dr. Banerjee was in the palace of the Zamindar. The nayeb, who lived in a tin shed, thought if he could send him to jail, he would be able to occupy his abandoned residence in the palace. But, the wishes of the greedy nayeb were not fulfilled.

The men from the nearby village had a reason to loot the fish. A few days prior to the incident, a man from that village tried to catch some fish from the pond, but the nayeb insulted him and turned him away. So the villagers looked for vindication and united to plunder the fish.

"Sopital"

During the trial, our parents and guardians were worried that our future careers would be jeopardized should the court find us guilty in the fishing case. But for us students, it was great fun to go to Tangail once a month despite having to attend court.

We made a habit of catching a movie every time we went to Tangail. After arriving in Tangail, our routine was to find a hotel, check in, grab some dinner, and then go off to the movies. However, by the time we reached Tangail, it was often already evening. In those days, tickets were usually scalped, and so in order to watch a movie, we would have to arrange to buy the tickets ahead of time. The possibility of arriving so late in Tangail meant that we risked missing a chance to see a movie. To prevent this misfortune, we decided that whoever got to Tangail first, would buy the tickets for everyone.

On one trip, a group of friends and I were late to reach Tangail. Our other friends, who had already arrived, waited for us at the bus station. As our bus pulled in, we rushed out to see if they had gotten the tickets for the movie. One of my friends told us that he bought tickets for us to see "Sopital". I was disappointed.

I had been looking forward to watching a Bengali film with the most romantic couple of the time, Uttom Kumar and Shuchitra Sen, but would now have to settle for some rotten Urdu film by the name of "Sopital".

Nonetheless, we rushed directly to the theatre and took our seats, just as the seating music came on. It was common practice for the cinema hall to play the contemporary Bangla songs of the day from singers like Protima, Shondhya, Hemonta and others, before a movie began. As the songs faded and the movie started, I was pleasantly surprised to see that we were going to watch the famous Bangla film "Hospital" starring Ashoke Kumar and Shuchitra Sen.

Why then, did my friend make such a stupid mistake in reading the name on the big billboard in front of the cinema hall? I quickly realized that the letter H ("Ha" in Bangla) was written in a light color blending in with the background, while the rest of the word was painted in a bolder dark color, which read to my friend as "Sopital". From that day on we jokingly nicknamed my friend "Sopital".

Doctor Ghee

Not everyone who was implicated in the court hearings had as much fun as we did. The homeopath Dr. Banerjee, who was implicated by the nayeb, had a much more difficult time.

Dr. Banerjee was a descendent of the Brahmin caste. As such he would not touch any food other than that which was prepared by himself or his family. This meant that he had few culinary options while visiting Tangail. Worse yet, he had a big body with an even bigger appetite. Going without food was unbearable for him, but he found a solution to mitigate his hunger.

He brought with him a bottle of pure butter oil, which he made himself at home. Whenever he got hungry, he took a little butter oil and washed it down with water. This is how he survived his three days in Tangail.

Postmaster

The postmaster of Hemnagar was a nice, liberal man with a cultured background. He recently transferred to Hemnagar from the city. He and his wife had two young teenage daughters and a boy. Very soon, they became friendly with the teachers of the school and all of us in the hostel. This clique of friends became known as the cultural elite of Hemnagar.

The postmaster took up a number of programs. He organized a reading club, which arranged regular discussions on current affairs and literary works. He also took the initiative to start a drama group. Additionally, he started a badminton tournament. All such activities were open to both students and faculty, alike.

The nayeb and the doctor of the local medical center, by virtue of being government staff, wanted to join our group. But, as their public image was not clean, we turned them a cold shoulder. Looking back, this might have been another reason why the nayeb had been so quick to implicate us in the events of the fishing case.

The Untouchable of Hemnagar

The man who cleaned the latrines of the Zamindar's palace was a tall elderly fellow. He was the only descendent of the Schedule caste known as the "Untouchables".

When I first saw him, I noticed that his body came to resemble a crescent. As he walked hunched down, his head would hover just above his knees. Watching him walk from a distance, he moved like a rolling bicycle tire.

One day, I realized that I had not seen him in public for a long time. I wondered what had happened to this old man. Finally, I heard news that he had become very ill. This poor man was alone with no family and no one to take care of him.

I couldn't help but to feel sympathy for this icon of Hemnagar. I took some food from the hostel and went off to see him. He lived in a small shack behind the nayeb's office. When I arrived, I found him huddled up, semi-conscious amidst the darkness of the room. It seemed as if no living soul had stepped foot into the dwelling for ages. There was just a lonely old man, slowly withering on his deathbed. I nearly choked on the sadness in the air as I saw a man patiently waiting for his last breath. There was nothing I could do.

I noticed through the corner of my eyes that someone had left a little water in an earthenware bowl. I gently placed my food next to the water and silently left the room with a heavy heart.

A few days later, his waiting was over as he quietly passed from this life to the next.

A Classmate

We had a classmate who was from another very low caste of Hindus called the "Dome". Much like the elderly man of the Schedule caste, the people of the Dome caste were obligated to handle the less desirable services of society. The people from the Dome caste were left to manage the dead carcasses of livestock and other animals.

Our classmate was the first of his family to attend school. He was given free tuition as an incentive for continuing his education. Unfortunately, he had little interest in studying. He was not doing too well in class.

School was merely an opportunity for him to play sports, and in this, he truly excelled. Our school team was incomplete without him. He loved soccer and proved to be a very dependable goalkeeper. As teammates, we got to know each other very well and eventually became friends.

However, despite our friendship, my good study habits had not rubbed off. As the school year came to a close, my classmate found that he had not qualified to take the final national exam. All play and no work forced this gifted athlete to leave school forever. He left his dreams of playing soccer behind him and returned to his family's business.

Hakim the Creditor

A Bihari family lived in Hemnagar. The head of the family was a mail carrier. After his retirement, his eldest son took over the service. Every morning, he left Hemnagar and set for Gopalpur with the day's mail. In his hand, he always carried a spear, which had jingling bells tied to it at the top. The sound of the bell reminded the public of his duty.

Such postal employees were known as "runners". They were very poorly paid, but their faithful duties were always appreciated. There was even a very famous song written about them. Whenever I saw the mail-runner, the song would play in my head.

The youngest son of that Bihari family, Hakim, was my classmate. He dropped out of school in the 7th grade to set up a small roadside grocery store near the pond. Hakim was a good soccer player. However, he stopped coming to the soccer field after he opened the grocery store. Hakim used to sell his products to many of the students on credit.

One day, several students complained that Hakim was exaggerating his records on the books and was overcharging them. When we made our accusations against him, he confessed frankly and explained why he did it. He said he was a businessman.

However, when he bought goods with cash and sold them on credit, he had no liquid assets to run his business. The only way for him to make a profit would be to charge them interest on their purchases. His argument was sound. Unknowingly, Hakim had introduced the foundations of capitalism into his own business.

School Soccer

Back when I was in school, soccer was a very popular game in the villages. There were tournaments all over. Hiring famous players from the city to play for just the semi-final and final matches had become a custom.

Thousands of spectators would gather around the field to enjoy the game. There were no stadium seats for our soccer matches. However, the standing crowd surrounding the field resembled four walls on each side. It was great fun to play soccer in such a setting. The crowed especially enjoyed it when the games were played in the rain.

Meanwhile, I became well known as an under-teen soccer player. Requests came for me to play in tournaments and I started to play on both junior and adult teams.

My short soccer career was full of dramatic stories. Once, while playing for a team on hire, I found that one of my best friends was playing for the opposition. It was my goal that defeated my friend's team. He was so upset by his team's loss that he stopped talking to me after that match.

Another time, I remember having to go up against an enormous fullback. It became impossible for me to get passed his gigantic body. I failed to score a single goal in that match and we lost. The people who hired me were disappointed and made no secret of it.

I was supposed to stay with my hosts for the remainder of the evening, but I decided I had enough. I packed my things and set off for the hostel. I walked down the lonely village road, as darkness fell upon the night sky. Before I could lift my head, the rain began to pour down heavily.

Tired and exhausted, I finally reached the school hostel just before dawn. My older brother, who had escorted me to and from the tournament, was still very furious about the way the team manager treated us. He scolded me for going there and forbade me from playing soccer on hire again. That was the end of my short pro-soccer career. Nonetheless, I continued to play with my friends.

During one of these friendly matches, I tried to head a goal in, but my head collided with the head of the defender as we competed for the ball. As I hit the ground, blood began gushing from my head. The other player was unconscious for a few moments. It was a frightening moment. It would also be the last soccer match I played in at school, at least for a while.

Floods of 1962

The floods returned in 1962. The waters rose so quickly that no one could prepare. Our school was surrounded by floodwater. We were marooned, helpless, and without a boat. Authorities closed down the school. Our cook and five students from the hostel, including myself, were stranded. We spent our listless afternoons on the roof of the hostel watching the floods.

Water had engulfed the villages surrounding Hemnagar. Paddy and jute fields had vanished under the water. Only the trees and some houses were still visible. Occasionally, we saw boats passing by. With no means of escape, we became prisoners of the water. We could not go out for our supplies. So our cook Khorshed Alam rationed our food.

The floodwaters came from the Jamuna River. The aftermath of the floods were felt for months. Crops were destroyed. Food became scarce.

I went back to my village to find that both rich and poor were eating from the same government rations. Every home was eating coarse rice and flour roti. Although the consumption of flattened rice bread was traditionally reserved for special occasions such as Eid, the flour roti was a meal normally unpalatable for the average Bengali. Their typical tasty dishes of fish and rice were replaced with bland servings of tasteless flour roti.

Our hostel was not spared from the effects of the flood. At least one meal a day was replaced by just flour roti.

This experience knocked me off balance, as I had not expected the flood to provoke such consequences. I saw the spirit of the villagers vanish away. The staging of plays in the village came to a stop. The grand festivals of Eid, Puja, and Mela had lost their sheen.

Cooperative Society

I established a cooperative society to balance the potential scarcity of food in the future. My cousins Hashmat, Latif, and Kazeem respectively became the vice-president, secretary, and treasurer of the committee. I was the president. Fifteen other school students were elected as committee members and joined us.

Our first objective was to establish a fund from membership dues. We would, then, use the fund to buy rice during harvest time when prices were very low. Our aim was to hold onto the rice and sell it during times of scarcity when prices soared. We made sure always to sell our rice at cheaper prices to the poor, and to the members of the cooperative, so as to mitigate their sufferings. We also decided to buy homeopathic medicine for my uncle Mukhles, who could then administer his medical services to the poor for free.

Our enterprise had a great start, but would cease to function after I left for college.

The Basic Democracy of General Ayub Khan

Military dictator, General Ayub Khan, had introduced a new form of democracy: Basic Democracy. According to his system, instead of being directly elected by the people, the ward members would select the chairman of the Union Council. This system now enabled a candidate to become chairman by simply gaining the support of a simple majority of ward members, which was no more than seven of twelve votes.

In order to attain such favor, the aspiring candidates would hold no bounds to please the newly elected Union Council Ward Members. They would vie with one another in throwing lavish parties in the ward member's honor and would invite them to their houses to stay over as VIPs.

However, this practice led to holding ward members captive for as long as one month's time. As VIPs, ward members were entertained and treated like royalty, but not permitted to leave until Election Day. On this day, they were escorted by their hosts to the polling centers, where they were expected to cast votes in their favor. It was only after this, that the ward members were free to go home. What a free and fair election under the wisdom of "Basic Democracy!"

In Basic Democracy, the chairmen of the Union Council were no longer accountable to the people. The chairmen were no longer elected by the masses. This enabled them to plunder relief money and material sent for the flood victims. Instead of serving the people, these basic Democrats built their own fortunes. Thus began, the never-ending corruption and exploitation of the common people.

Bullets of '71: A Freedom Fighter's Story

Community Hotel

I won the county championship in the interschool athletics competition for the sprint and long jump. I was selected to compete in the sub-divisional meet. Our assistant headmaster and games teacher, Nazrul Islam, accompanied me to Tangail, the sub-divisional headquarters.

At night, we made arrangements to check into a hotel. Though by name it was called a hotel, it was really more of a room with a giant commune bed. Strangers sat side-by-side on this huge wooden bed and ate supper together. We were served a delicious dinner of steamy rice, hilsha fish, mutton curry, fried vegetables, and split-pea soup.

When it came time to sleep, each hotel guest lied down on the bed, shoulder to shoulder. The hotel boy blanketed the rows of boarders with giant quilts. Each quilt accommodated three to four people at a time. Often times, bedfellows were complete strangers.

I had never fathomed sleeping in such conditions before. Fortunately, there was another room in the back of the hotel, where individual beds were available at higher prices. We were fortunate enough to be able to afford two beds in those quarters.

These low-cost sleeping arrangements were affordable to the poor rural people who frequented Tangail for business and government matters - particularly court appearances.

Dr. Aleem Al Razi

Tangail was the center for the Secondary School Certificate (SSC) Final Examination. I needed to find myself a place to live during the exam. We had some distant relatives there, but I preferred to contact Badsha. Badsha was a very close friend of mine, who lived nearby and was studying at Kagmari College on the outskirts of Tangail. Badsha arranged accommodation for me in the house next door to his uncle's home.

It was a beautiful building on the Mymensingh Highway. It was rented out as the election office for Dr. Aleem Al Razi. Contesting as an independent candidate, he defeated the Pakistan Convention Muslim League Party in the National Elections of 1965 and became a Member of the National Parliament of Pakistan. His election assistant, a young barrister, was still living in the house at the time. The tenancy of the house would continue for another month. This seemed to be the best arrangement for me. It was a decent place, quiet and suitable for studying.

The SSC Examinations had started and was spread out over the course of one week. During the exam, Dr. Razi returned to Tangail to attend a reception arranged in his honor. I had an examination scheduled the next day that required lots of reading. In spite of it, I went to the reception meeting anyway. His assistant introduced me to him. This was the first time in my life that I would meet someone with a PhD.

As we shook hands, my body filled with excitement and hope. Although it wasn't for many years later that I would attain my own PhD, in many ways, I think it was that moment that may have most influenced my decision to pursue such an ambitious goal.

During the reception, Dr. Razi said, "I have heard the legends of General Ayub Khan, the iron man. However, I have no fear of fighting this iron man to secure the interests of East Pakistan".

Dr. Aleem Al Razi started his education in a madrasa and earned the highest degree in religious education called "Title". He then pursued general education. Eventually, he became a barrister and earned his doctorate in law from England. He was a great orator with an infinite sense of humor. His debates in the Parliament were lively and full of information. He commanded a great deal of respect from his fellow members in the Parliament and was always addressed as the "learned" member.

I eagerly tuned into special bulletins of Radio Pakistan on the proceedings of the Pakistan National Parliament debates. Dr. Razi made headlines almost daily and hearing his quotes repeated over the radio inspired me. Someone I knew was fighting for East Pakistan. It was so unfortunate that his contributions to Bangladeshi politics had not received due appreciation in his lifetime.

Relatives
My cousin Latif arrived in Tangail a day ahead of me and stayed with one of our distant relatives in Adalatpara, a residential section in Tangail. Soon after I checked into my accommodation at Dr. Razi's campaign headquarters, I went to see Latif.

I had never met these relatives of ours before. I knocked on the door of the residence. An older man answered. Before I could utter a word, the man asked, "What do you want?"

I simply introduced myself anticipating a warm welcome. Instead, I felt the cold slam of the door on my face. His voice trailed behind the door stating that he "had no room for another guest."

I was shocked. I hadn't even mentioned any desire to stay there. I merely wanted to meet Latif and see how he was doing. This taught me a great lesson. From that day on, I knew that although blood could make someone your relative – it was far from enough to make someone your family. My friend Badsha shared neither blood, nor family name, but he was more my family than this distant uncle would ever be.

Successful Man

High school is a very important part of a child's life. This pivotal moment sets the blueprint for the rest of one's life. The educational contents, environment, and advice have deep and lasting impressions on a young mind. I, too, grew up under these same circumstances.

My grades and other activities earned me special treatment from my teachers. Many of them wanted me to pursue higher education in each of their distinct subjects, or in the subject that they deemed most important.

For instance, Mr. Nazrul Islam wanted me to go for English literature, while Mr. Hayat Ali preferred history. Mr. Zainal Abedin wanted me to follow science.

However, Mr. Rajab Ali, the religion teacher wanted something very special. He wanted me to become a doctor and would pray that I would one day come back to Hemnagar to practice as an MBBS doctor and treat the poor.

The most exceptional suggestion came from my Bangla teacher, Mr. Ameer Ali. He stated that under no circumstances should I further my studies in Bengali Literature. Based on my performance in his class, he had absolutely no faith in my potential for Bengali Literature.

My teachers instilled in me a clear idea that I was not an ordinary student, but rather, an exceptional one. They believed that I had the potential to grow into an extraordinary man. My parents also felt that way, but I never understood what they meant by becoming a "successful man". Nonetheless, by the end of high school, I no longer felt like a "boy". I grew confident, as I became a young man. In my mind I began mapping the outline for my future.

My parents were not the only people who believed in my future. My teachers entrusted this vision and looked forward to my continuing success.

With this frame of mind, I set sail into the uncharted seas of college and took with me this wonderful feeling.

Chapter 2

The World: 101

Ananda Mohan College

It was time for me to move away from the village and to go to college. I wanted to go to Dhaka College, but my parents preferred that I attended Ananda Mohan College in Mymensingh. They felt Dhaka was too far. However, this was not their real reasoning. The real reason was that they had known Mymensingh for ages and felt more closely connected to it. I was admitted to Ananda Mohan College to study.

Ananda Mohan College was a large red brick building. In front, there was a road draped with large trees on each side. On the other side of the road was the soccer field.

The Principal's residence stood alongside the field. Behind the college was a pond. Dormitories and a cottage for the superintendent of the dormitories were built surrounding this pond.

Dormitories for higher secondary students were one-story buildings, situated on both the north and south banks of the pond. Dormitories for undergraduate students were three-story buildings on the east bank of the pond, opposite the superintendent's residence.

Culture Shock

Four students crammed into each room of the dormitory. Three of us arrived on the first day. Of the three, the other two were from the Muktagachha area and were meritorious students. A week later, our fourth roommate finally arrived with his father.

His father was a fair-skinned, six and a half foot giant of a man. He was a police sub-inspector. He looked more like a Punjabi general in the army than a mere police officer.

Meanwhile, our new roommate looked like a handsome prince. On the first night, just before bed, he pulled out an ironed shirt, put it on and slipped under the quilt. The rest of us were amused and exchanged our curious glances.

This was a culture shock for us. The rest of us wore one ironed shirt all week long. To maintain its cleanliness and ironed condition, we took it off as soon as we came back from class and wore it again the next day.

This wasn't his only unusual behavior. Our new roommate did not eat in our dining hall. Every night, he would return late after eating dinner at a restaurant.

However, on one particular night, he returned with bleeding wounds. He tried to keep a tight lip about the matter, but on our insistence, he narrated the story. On his way back to the hostel, he saw a beautiful girl riding a rickshaw and tried to pull on her scarf to get her attention. Unfortunately for him, her guardian was right behind her in a second rickshaw. As his hand reached for the scarf, the guardian trounced on our roommate and gave him a good beating.

This friend of ours was normally polite and decent in his behavior. We would only come to understand the cause for his split personality much later. He had a stepmother who controlled his family. And for this reason, he did not have much respect for his father. His undisciplined lifestyle was an expression of his teenage anger against his father. After only a year, he dropped out of college. I felt bad that he had wasted his opportunity.

Hujur

Both the superintendent and assistant superintendent of the hostel were teachers in the Arabic department. The "super" as we called him, used to live in his quarters, alongside the dormitory. He was a distant relative of mine. My father told me to introduce myself as such because, in times of need, he might be helpful. However, in the two years I spent at the dormitory, I never bothered to reveal this information to the super.

This was, in part, because I couldn't forget the treatment I received in my last interaction with a "distant relative". If this man was anything like the man from Tangail, during my final examinations, I had no interest in letting him know we were related.

We were forbidden to address the super and his assistant as "sir". Instead, we were asked to address them as hujur. This was the title commonly used to address Islamic religious leaders. The assistant super was my next-door neighbor at the dormitory. We were assigned to the room next to his, so that he could maintain a close watch over one of my roommates, who happened to be his nephew. This, of course, brought all of us under his close supervision. He had written off our forth roommate, accepting that he was beyond any control.

On our hujur's insistence, we had to pray five times a day. In particular, we could not escape Fajar prayers at dawn and Esha prayers in the late evening, since he would lead these prayers himself. There was a precondition for Fajar prayers. We had to take a bath before we said our prayers. So, the three of us would get up very early in the morning and jump into the waters of the pond with our eyes half-closed. There were no bathrooms to shower in at the dorm.

Our hujur was a thrifty person and lived a very simple life. He hand washed his clothes. He was a vegetarian, whose meals consisted of rice with smashed green banana and lentil soup. He would often stroll up and down the corridors of the hostel building in his wooden sandals making noise. Actually, this was his technique to keeping us awake and engaged in preparing for our lessons.

A railway track passed by the side of our hostel. In the beginning, the noise of the passing train was tortuous for me. But after a month, I got used to it.

Hujur used to go for walks to the Agricultural University Campus over this track and return. Sometimes we were asked to accompany him. For Jumma Prayers every Friday, he would join the biggest congregation in Mymensingh. He would go to the largest mosque in town. The mosque was far away, and so, he would get there by taking the riverside road. We, too, would accompany him regularly.

Our hujur believed that by praying amongst a larger congregation in a mosque further away, we would bring more blessings into our lives. Moreover, the walking wasn't bad for our health, either.

The First Day of Class

In the classroom on my first day at the college, I found everyone to be a stranger. Some of the students were from Mymensingh, but the rest were from out of town, like me. It was an English class and our teacher was Mr. Jalil.

He started by asking us to introduce ourselves by stating our names, the schools we came from, and our examination results. Most of the students had passed the upper tier, denoting them as first division. Ironically, most of the students pronounced "first" as "fast" and Mr. Jalil grew visibly annoyed. He reminded us to always pronounce the letter "R" in the word "first".

Principal Kabir Choudhury

Just before I enrolled, Ananda Mohan College had been taken over by the government from private management. For this reason, new teachers replaced many of the old teachers. This is how Kabir Choudhury became our new principal. He immediately introduced a new set of rules.

For all dramatic production, the college was no longer allowed to bring in hired professional actresses from outside of the school. This rule change was in response to a scandal, which ensued from an incident surrounding a hired actress from Dhaka. Principal Choudhury declared that if a suitable female student were not found from within the college, the dramatic performance would be suspended for that year.

This was possibly, Principal Choudhury's strategy to encourage female students to act in the play. Principal Choudhury was known to have a very progressive mind.

It was also during his tenure that "Annual Cultural Week" was introduced. In addition, to cultural activities, Principal Choudhury introduced a lecture series based on his foreign experiences. He talked about his exploits in various countries to expose his students to the world and its abundance of different cultures. The presence of this imminent scholar and dynamic educator reshaped the culture and environment of the college. He sparked excitement and enthusiasm in the hearts of his pupils.

Kabir Choudhury was also a man who incorporated routine into his daily life. Every evening, without fail, Principal Choudhury could be found pacing the lawn of his house, sometimes accompanied by his wife Meher, or his daughters. Sometimes, he was even seen holding his wife's hand. Such public displays of affection were highly uncommon at that time.

Bolt Sir

During the first few days in college, I found myself in hot water in my chemistry lab. One of my classmates told me that the person who conducted this class was known as "Bolt Sir". I didn't think much of the nickname, so when I needed to ask him a question, I addressed my teacher as Bolt Sir.

Immediately his temper flared up. I was taken aback, frightened and embarrassed. The lab assistant understood my dilemma. He immediately realized that a prankster classmate, knowing the consequences of calling the professor Bolt Sir, had tricked me.

Our professor was known for being a strict disciplinarian and so his students dubbed him "Bolt Sir", in jest. He clamped down on his students like a bolt in a vice. The lab assistant walked up to the professor and explained the situation. Luckily, I escaped his wrath with a simple apology.

Two years later, during the oral examination for chemistry, I encountered Bolt Sir, one more time. Professor Nurul Hoque Bhuiyan of Dhaka University was the appointed external examiner. As an examiner, he was a terror to the students.

When my turn came, I nervously entered the room. Professor Bhuiyan was meditating on the pages of a book, nearly ignoring my presence. Sitting by his side was Bolt Sir. Immediately, I was taken back again, as his presence shocked me. I knew right away, if he recalled the incident that occurred between us back in the beginning of college, he was sure to fail me.

My fear was proven wrong. He asked me fair questions and I answered them all. After he was finished with me, he invited Prof. Hoque to question me further. Without raising his head from his book, Professor Hoque asked me if I had intensions of studying chemistry at Dhaka University.

Without even thinking, I instantly replied, "Yes, that's my plan".

Professor Hoque responded, "That's a good plan".

Fortunately, my answer would come true, at least partially.

Sub-Assistant Engineer

After starting my first semester, one of my friends said he was going to drop out of college. He decided that he wanted to go to a vocational-engineering school to get an associate degree and a job somewhere as a sub-assistant engineer.

He wanted to make money within two years, rather than waste so much time in school. This particular job was laden with corruption and bribes. He figured that he would take some bribes, and in no time, he would be living comfortably in a lavish home with a car.

This friend of ours was a first division student. His candid statement about his aim in life had shocked us. The other students and I had mixed feelings after learning of the corrupt aspirations of such a meritorious young man. It was unimaginable for any of us to contemplate such unethical ambitions.

Profile of an Islamic Student Activist

By rotation, everyone in the dorm was expected to serve as manager of the dorm-dining hall for a month. Serious students did not revere this chore. They would do anything to avoid it.

One of the students in our dorm was a leader of the Islamic student party, "Chatra Shongha". Sometimes he would lead the dorm in prayer, supporting his righteous facade.

This Islamic student leader was the one exception when it came to managing the dorm-dining hall. Not only did he actively request the responsibility, once he got it, he refrained from stepping down from the position.

Pahloan, a friend of mine from Dewanganj, thought this was a little suspicious. He would ask, "Why would anyone want to continue taking on this thankless responsibility, and why would he never want to quit?"

Pahloan asked for my help in unraveling the mystery. The word Pahloan is in reference to Adonis, and Pahloan stayed true to his nomenclature.

One day, we went to the flea market to check the prices of chickens and vegetables. Upon cross checking prices with shoppers in the market, we were certain that this Islamic Chatra Shongha leader, the champion of religion, was stealing money by inflating the daily expense accounts of the dining hall.

We reported the matter to the assistant superintendent. He had reason to believe us because I was his nephew's roommate and regularly prayed with him. The assistant-super rushed to the flea market and verified the prices himself.

The Islamic activist leader was found guilty and was expelled from the dorm. I was glad to see that Pahalon's initiative unmasked the true face of the Islamic Chatra Shongha leader.

Our search for justice enhanced our reputation amongst our fellow students.

Black Marketers of Movie Tickets

Mymensingh had two movie theaters – Aloka and Chayabani. Whenever a good film was scheduled, the black marketers would buy up all the tickets forcing everyone to pay their higher prices. This upset many moviegoers.

Once, in front of Chayabani, the black marketers started a fight with one of the students from our dorm and beat him up badly. This news agitated the students in our dorm.

It was decided that the residents of the dorm would join the college students living in the Sheorapara neighborhood and would take suitable action in teaching the culprits a lesson.

The plan was immediately set into action. The next evening, students from our dorm rushed towards Chayabani Hall with hockey sticks in hand. Our roommate, the son of the police sub-inspector joined the mob. My other roommate, the nephew of the superintendent, would not join the group because he knew his uncle would disapprove.

Our other roommate was quiet and somewhat timid in nature, and so he too would not go and join the fight. Personally, I was against taking the law into our own hands, and so the three of us had nothing else to do. We simply waited for news of vindication.

The victorious students came back around eleven at night. They taught the black marketers a lesson and left many of them bloodied and injured. The students of Sheorapara earned the respect and admiration of those in our dorm for their help in this incident. All over Mymensingh, they became known as the protectors of the dorm. From that day on, no college student in Mymensingh was ever required to approach a black marketer for a movie ticket.

The Odd Couple

There was a funny pair of friends in the undergraduate dorm. One of them was about six and half feet tall and had fair skin. The other was short, less than five feet, had dark skin, and was very scrawny in stature. Their physical differences were so striking that no one could miss them.

Every evening, they used to go out wearing white synthetic shirts, tight pants, and black goggles. Their shoes would clatter as they passed through the corridors of our hostel on their way into town. They probably never realized that they were such oddities.

Dressed up for Friday

There was another interesting character in the degree hostel. Every day of the week, he would wear ordinary clothes, but on Fridays he would put on his best attire.

It was nice to see him pass through our corridors on his way to his village, Fulbaria, wearing white laundered linens and a panjabi.

His head was adorned with a Jinnah cap. He walked with a stick in his hand and a bag under his arm. His name was Shamsher Ali.

Many years later, I came across a Muslim cleric in New York conducting a marriage ceremony. He had a long flowing beard and was wearing a beige sherwani and a turban on his head.

At first, I could not recognize him, but when I heard his voice, I immediately realized it was the one and only, Shamsher Ali. Dr. Shamsher Ali is now the imam of a mosque in New York.

Chatra League Leader Masud Parvez

Early on in my first year of college, the Chatra League drew me to student politics. The Chatra League was a pro-Bengali nationalist student organization that fought against the military dictatorship of President General Ayub Khan and East Pakistan Governor Monayem Khan.

Masud Parvez was a Chatra League leader at our college. He was the son of a sub-inspector of the Ghatail Police Station.

One night, the news spread that the gangsters belonging to the National Student Federation (NSF), an organization supporting Governor Monayem Khan attacked and repeatedly stabbed Masud Parvez. The attack was intended to intimidate the Chatra League and left Masud critically wounded.

We, the members of the Chatra League, went to see him in the hospital. Once at the hospital, we did all we could by donating blood. Fortunately, Masud recovered.

After college, Masud Parvez became a famous film hero and went on to direct many films, as well.

Ashraf of NSF

Ashraf, a resident of the undergraduate dorm, was a leader of the infamous student political body, the NSF. He had built a reputation as a skilled boxer.

However, one day, a mutinous faction of the NSF made an attempt to kill him. Ashraf was from Dhaka, not from Mymensingh. There was a conflict between him and the local NSF leaders regarding the sharing of privileges bestowed by the government.

In an attempt to kill Ashraf, the local NSF leaders stabbed him repeatedly in the abdomen. His condition was very serious. He only survived because as a boxer, he was able to resist the attack initially. We, the students of the hostel, went to see him in the hospital. Ashraf was bleeding profusely and needed a lot of blood. And so, yet again, we donated blood generously.

Despite being a leader of the NSF, politics took a back seat to his health. To us, Ashraf was still a fellow resident of the hostel. So, an attack on him was considered an attack on everyone.

Election of the Student's Union

It was election time for the college's Student Union. The main contesting parties were the NSF, the Chatra Union, and the Chatra League.

The NSF was the student wing of the Ayub-Monayem regime. Governor Monayem Khan was from Mymensingh and practiced as a lawyer in town. For his mediocrity in his profession, he was derogatively called "Bot tolar ukil" meaning cheap sidewalk lawyer.

However, because of his patronage, the NSF, infamous for hooliganism, was very notorious and powerful. They started their election campaign vigorously. The younger brother of our physics teacher, Mr. Kalam was nominated to run against the NSF candidate for Vice President of the Student Union. He was a Chatra Union leader, but in order to defeat the NSF, the Charta League and Chatra Union joined hands.

However, we had to campaign in secrecy in fear that the NSF gangsters might attack us.

The campaign manager for the NSF panel was Mr. Wasim. He was a popular body builder and later became a famous film hero in Bangladesh. Though the NSF had full government support behind them, we won the election and took over the executive body of the college's student union.

India-Pakistan War of 1965

A war between India and Pakistan broke out in 1965. When the news of the war came to our college, there was a protest rally at our soccer field. Principal Kabir Chowdhury and representatives of the student body and faculty made angry speeches denouncing India. Our English teacher Mr. Bari said in his speech, "the enemy does not know whom they have taken on."

Sometime after the meeting, President Ayub Khan addressed the nation over the radio. At one point in his speech, he too said, "The enemy does not know whom they have taken on". I was taken back by the similarity of their speeches.

All of us at the hostel enrolled ourselves in the volunteer force. Our main job was to spread out in groups in the town and oversee the enforcement of a blackout program at night.

Mymensingh was a small quiet town at night. When the city blacked out, the air grew cold and eerie. It was now a ghost town.

Sheikh Mujibur Rahman at Mymensingh

Early in 1966, Mr. Sheikh Mujibur Rahman, the President of the Awami League, came to Mymensingh to address a public meeting. That was the first time I had ever seen Sheikh Mujibur Rahman in person.

In the early 1950's, the Awami Muslim League was formed under the leadership of Moulana Bhashani, Shamsul Haque, and Sheikh Mujibur Rahman as the president, general secretary, and assistant general secretary, respectively. The aim of the party was to fight for and protect the interests of the people of East Pakistan against the oppression of the Muslim League government.

In 1954, the Awami Muslim League formed a coalition with other political parties known as the "United Front". The United Front won the election and took over in East Pakistan and the Central Government.

Awami Muslim League leader, Mr. Hussain Shahid Suhrawardy became the Prime Minister of Pakistan and Mr. Ataur Rahman Khan became the Chief Minister of East Pakistan. Sheikh Mujibur Rahman became a minister in the government of East Pakistan.

Later, when Mr. Shamsul Haque grew mentally ill and disappeared, Sheikh Mujibur Rahman became the General Secretary of the Awami Muslim League.

In 1957, at the Kagmari convention, the word "Muslim" was deleted from Awami Muslim League to reflect the secular nature of the party and it became known simply as the "Awami League". However, in the convention, a sharp difference of opinions surfaced between the communist and nationalist members regarding the policies of both, the provincial and central governments of their party.

In addition, another interesting polarization appeared in the convention. Both, the rightist and leftist groups united and conspired against Sheik Mujibur Rahman. They wanted to oust Sheikh Mujibur Rahman as the general secretary of the party. They passed a resolution that no one could hold both party leadership and a ministerial position at the same time. An elected individual would have to choose to serve only one office.

They anticipated that Sheikh Mujibur Rahman would opt for the more prestigious ministerial position and resign from party leadership. It was generally considered that the ministerial position was more attractive for aspiring young politicians.

But to their dismay, they were surprised to find that Sheikh Mujibur Rahman chose to remain the party general secretary over the minister-ship and resigned from the government office. It was an unprecedented event in political history.

Sheikh Mujibur Rahman had grander plans in mind!

A few days later, Moulana Bhashani and his communist and leftist followers quit the Awami League, accusing the Central Government of following pro-American foreign policies and accusing the East Pakistani Government of not fulfilling its election promises. They later formed a new political party under the leadership of Moulana Bhashani by the name of the "National Awami Party".

When Moulana Bhashani resigned, Moulana Abdur Rashid Tarkabagish became acting-president and Sheikh Mujibur Rahman remained the general secretary of the Awami League.

In 1958, when General Ayub Khan came to power by imposing marshal law, he banned all political parties and their activities. He placed many political leaders, including Sheikh Mujibur Rahman and Hossain Shahid Suhrawardy, former Prime Minister of Pakistan, behind bars.

In the early 1960's, when the ban was finally lifted and the prisoners were freed, Sheikh Mujibur Rahman revived the Awami League. In 1964, Sheikh Mujibur Rahman and Tajuddin Ahmed became the president and general secretary of the Awami League, respectively.

There was a growing economic and political disparity between East and West Pakistan. In essence, East Pakistan had become more of a colony of West Pakistan than an equal partner.

In response to this situation, in 1966 Sheikh Mujibur Rahman launched a Six-Point Charter for the autonomy of East Pakistan. Among his list of demands, the most important was that the Central Government would only have control of defense and foreign policy and that the East Pakistan Government would have its own currency and the power to impose and collect its own taxes. Mujib's Six-Point Charter, in fact, was really a one-point charter – the independence of Bangladesh. The Pakistani ruling junta saw right through this.

They claimed that the Six-Point Charter was a threat to the integrity of the Central Government. The Ayub-Monayem regime felt threatened. However, the six-point demands were becoming increasingly more popular, day-by-day.

During the 1965 war between Pakistan and India, it was revealed that East Pakistan had no defense mechanism. During the war, not only had East Pakistan lost communication with the west wing of Pakistan, but also had become completely isolated from the rest of the world.

Prices of essential commodities rose after the war creating pressure on East Pakistan's economy, which was already burdened by the step-motherly attitude imposed by West Pakistan. It was now evident that East Pakistan desperately needed autonomy in economic management and defense.

On this basis, Sheikh Mujibur Rahman drew up his historic Six-Point Charter of autonomy for East Pakistan. Initially, in February 1966, Sheikh Mujibur Rahman raised this Six-Point Charter in a national press conference in Lahore, West Pakistan.

Soon after, he formally raised his Six-Point Charter at the East Pakistan Awami League's central committee meeting for their endorsement. Surprisingly, some of the senior conservative leaders, like Salam Khan and others, opposed the Six-Point Charter.

However, young and progressive leaders, like Tajuddin Ahmed, Syed Nazrul Islam, and others, supported the Six-Point Charter and the Awami League soon overwhelmingly endorsed it.

After the Six-Point Charter became a party mandate, Sheikh Mujibur Rahman undertook a countrywide campaign to enlist the people's support. It was this Six-Point Charter that brought Sheikh Mujibur Rahman to Mymensingh. It was here that he addressed a meeting.

The meeting was held in a small open ground along the side of the United States Information Service Center. The meeting was conducted by Rafiquddin Bhuiyan and was presided over by Syeed Nazrul Islam. About five hundred people were in attendance at this meeting.

In the public meeting, Sheikh Mujibur Rahman, in his loud and clear voice, roared, "Look, Mr. Ayub Khan, I have no personal grudge against you. I am fighting for the cause of the people of East Pakistan. The fate of East Pakistan can only be solved through the implementation of this Six-Point Charter!"

Sheikh Mujibur Rahman was arrested in Dhaka the next day. This was followed by the relentless harassment of him and his Awami League.

Ayub Khan and Monayem Khan proclaimed that the Six-Point Charter was nothing more than a mechanism intended to dismantle

Pakistan. They believed that it would lead to civil war in Pakistan. They threatened to use force against Sheikh Mujibur Rahman and his Six-Point Charter campaign in order to preserve the unity of Pakistan.

Meanwhile, I was drawn deeper into Chatra League and Awami League politics. I could personally attest to the picture that Sheikh Mujibur Rahman painted of East Pakistan as I visited my village. The economic condition and standard of living were deteriorating each day.

Though I was a politically conscious young man, I could not see a viable resolution to this epidemic. And just then, Sheikh Mujibur Rahman appeared with his six-point resolution like a glimmering light of hope at the end of a dark tunnel.

I was attracted by Sheikh Mujibur Rahman's vision and was magnetically drawn to his bold leadership. I slowly grew more familiar with Sheikh Mujibur Rahman and the Awami League leaders of Mymensingh.

Awami League President Sheikh Mujibur Rahman

In the afternoons, my friends and I would go out on our daily walks around town. The Awami League leaders Syed Nazrul Islam and Syed Sultan Ahmed lived near our hostel.

In addition to their work in politics, they were also well known and respected lawyers. On occasion, we would pass by their homes. In those days, newspapers arrived in Mymensingh from Dhaka in the late afternoon. We would find the two men drowning in a heap of newspapers on their porch.

Missing My Mother

My mother would always expect me to come home and I, too, would seize any opportunity to visit her.

During a three-day vacation, I took the opportunity to return home. On the way, our bus had stalled, delaying the journey by a few hours. It was almost evening when I reached Gopalpur. Here, I found that the floodwater had risen significantly and was about to overflow onto the main road.

By the time I reached Hemnagar, the night was already consumed in darkness. Unfortunately, I still needed to cross two canals to reach my home. There was no sign of life, nor could I find a single boat to help me cross.

The furious sounds of the rushing floodwaters echoed against the emptiness of the dark sky, heightening the ghostly mood of the night. I waited for a long time in hopes that some form of help would arrive, but sadly nothing came.

I started cursing myself for making this hasty journey without checking the flood situation. Streams of thought were crisscrossing in my mind. What would happen if I were swayed away by the strong currents? What about the snakes? I would be helpless and lost without a prayer.

Nonetheless, it was too late for me to turn back. So I searched deep within the pit of my stomach, looking for any ounce of courage. I decided to swim across the canal. The little ray of hope that lead me into action was the fact that the canal was narrow and I had no luggage. By the grace of God, I made it across.

Waiting by the door, my mother saw a ghost-like figure drudging through the darkness of the night. With each step, the thrashing of wet fabric against the ground could be heard. However, this was no ghost. It was merely I, her son, returning home. I was cold, drenched, and missing my mother.

Mangos and Lychees

My mother knew that I was coming home for summer vacation. She saved the short lasting summer fruits – the mangoes and lychees.

It so happened that one summer, I was a few weeks late arriving home. My share of the ripening mangos and lychees began to rot. Yet, my mother would not give them away to anyone because she was sure that I would be home soon.

The day I was supposed to come home, she spent hour after hour, staring at the walkway, hoping that at any moment my figure would appear approaching the door.

My vacation ended and it became time for me to bid farewell. I would say my Salaam, by touching my mother's feet.

Nonetheless, even after I said my goodbyes, she would walk me out of the house to the dirt road. She would stand at the edge of the road, watching me walk slowly into the distance until I disappeared into the horizon.

I, too, could not help but look back while I walked with beads of tears rolling down my cheeks.

The Ominous Sign

I had mixed feelings about coming home during summer vacations. Although, seeing my parents and my family was a great pleasure, the growing poverty of the villagers started to cast a shadow over my visit.

The happiness of the villagers I knew of as a child had faded away with each passing day. The signs of poverty were everywhere. The tradition of staging dramas had ceased long ago.

Hira Bhai, the director of dramas, had gotten a job with the police department and eventually left the village. Kamala Bhai had also left for Dhaka to look for a job. Lebu and Sohrab Bhai had become primary school teachers and moved far away to north Bengal.

My elder brother, Mannan had gotten a job in the Karnafuli Paper Mill of Chittagong with some help from one of my uncle's connections. However, he had trouble adjusting to the job and soon quit to return home. My father insisted that he go back out and find something new. So he had left for Dhaka, where he lived with Komala Bhai, while looking for a job.

Just a few days ago, those families in the village who were solvent, now began selling their lands to make ends meet. The buyers were part of a newly emerging class of village ration dealers and members and chairs from the Union Council. The broken fences of homes were left without repair. The bamboo bridge near the pond that fell years ago was still left in shambles.

Before, our villagers shared the fish from our pond with the people from the adjacent village. However, these tremulous times compelled the villagers to change their generous ways.

They decided not to allow the people from the other villages to catch fish in their pond. The people from other villages had been enjoying this privilege for a long time.

They now refused to give up their privilege. A clash became imminent.

One day, neighboring villagers came down to catch fish in a mob. Our villagers resisted them. A few people from both sides were injured. Both sides filed criminal cases. The police, infamous for taking bribes, took advantage of the situation, but the problem was never resolved.

Neighboring villagers took the law into their own hands and enforced a blockade around our village. They blocked the road to the markets, the Union Council, and the police station. Life in our village became miserable and so they accepted their defeat.

Fishing was once again made open to all.

I was also bewildered by something my mother said. She told me that a man from the Bhuiyan house, on the eastern side of our village, had become a beggar. This was unthinkable.

The farmers with smallholdings, who had some how managed to survive, were now forced to sell off their properties and become landless laborers. In the past, farm laborers came from the poorer areas around the Jamuna River looking for work in our village.

The old man from Bhuiyan house who took to begging was initially dependent on his eldest son. However, one night, for reasons unknown, the son killed his wife and fled away into the darkness.

The old man tried to survive by working as a day laborer, but he was too old to work and no one would hire him. Finding no other means for survival, he resorted to begging. However, he could not bear to beg in his own village. To avoid public disgrace, he left the village in the early morning hours to beg in distant villages and wouldn't return till the late evening.

This sense of pride was common amongst the villagers, even though poverty affected them all. The story of the old man begging brought a dark cloud of shame over all of the villagers. They could neither accept, nor do anything about it. This marked the ominous turn of village life.

Sheikh Mujibur Rahman, My Leader

I was on a full scholarship throughout college. In addition to those finances, my father gave me some extra cash for my sundry expenses. My life was pretty comfortable.

But soon, my father's contributions started to shrink. Now, even I could feel the affects of the despairing economy. It hurt me to see my village in these dire circumstances. The village of peace, love, and happiness from my childhood days had slowly slipped away with each turn of the calendar's pages. The village I saw before me was no longer my own.

I have noticed that the poverty that plagued my village had spread throughout East Pakistan. I found that West Pakistanis were rapidly progressing. While we, the Bengalis, were falling behind. We needed to do something as a nation, and for that, I looked for a leader. At this crossroad of my national identity, Sheik Mujib appeared like the sun on the horizon. He did not look for me as a supporter. Rather, it was I, who found him as my leader. I got myself seriously involved into Chatra League and Awami League politics.

Chapter 3

On to Dhaka

My First Train Journey

It was 1967. I had just passed the Higher Secondary School examination in the first division with distinction. I had to leave Mymensingh and go to Dhaka to enroll in the university.

My parents wanted me to study at the engineering university. So for the first time in my life, I boarded a train and set out for the capital city.

There were no trains in our district, so until now I had relied on riding a bus to get around. A few of my friends had some experience riding trains and they gave me some pointers. Despite their tips, I was overwhelmed with anxiety. I could feel tension accumulating on the crux of my brow.

The train stopped at Gofargaon Station at night. Some passengers left our car and got off the train, while others boarded. The train started to move again slowly.

Suddenly, a man jumped off the moving train and vanished into the shadows. Moments later the passenger, who had sat next to the mysterious man, cried out, "Pickpocket! Pickpocket! Oh my God, I have been robbed. I am ruined. All my money is gone!"

Before we made sense of what had happened, the train had picked up full speed. The man who was crying aloud was a businessman. He was going to Dhaka with cash for investment purposes.

The gang of pickpockets marked him at Mymensingh Station and one of them took the seat by his side. The thief was able to take advantage of the busy flow of passengers at Gofargaon Station and made off with the money.

Gofargaon Station was notorious for these kinds of crimes. I had heard several stories about Gofargaon Station before, but I never thought I would witness such a crime in front of my very own eyes.

I, too, was carrying a significant sum of cash to pay my admission fee at the university. Immediately after the businessman's outcry, I checked my wallet to make sure that I had not fallen victim, as well. Luckily, my money was safe. However, I remained vigilant until I arrived in Dhaka the next morning.

The Fuming Magistrate

After I arrived in Dhaka, I met up with my cousin, Khaja. I stayed with him and his roommate at their residence on New Elephant Road. Khaja and his roommate were both bachelors. Khaja's roommate was a magistrate.

Their house sat alongside a rail line. Just on the other side of the rail line were two famous Dhaka University dormitories – Jinnah Hall and Mohsin Hall.

The next afternoon, we sat in the living room sipping tea and shooting the breeze. Just at that moment, a few men came to see my cousin's roommate, the magistrate. He was a taciturn man, but I guess that is the nature of most magistrates.

One of the visitors was a lawyer. The lawyer complained that it took them a great deal of time to locate the house. He requested some of the magistrate's time in private.

Khaja and I obliged and went to another room. All of a sudden, we heard the bellowing voice of the typically soft-spoken magistrate. He was shouting at them. He wanted them to leave right then and there. My cousin and I were surprised by this outburst. We couldn't figure out what was going on, but one thing was certain – the magistrate was fuming.

As the confrontation captured our attention, we heard the magistrate shout, " How dare you offer me a bribe! Unless you leave right now, I will call the police!"

As the visitors left, we returned to the living room and found the magistrate still quaking in his rage.

Apparently the men thought they could influence a case in the magistrate's court. Clearly, they were wrong.

A Girl

As my parents wanted, I applied for admission into the engineering university. Most diligent students had applied for admission into Dhaka University to study economics, physics, and biochemistry. I decided to give biochemistry a shot, as well. In those days, students were required to submit admissions applications to the respective dean's offices. The Office of the Dean of Science was in Curzon Hall.

I was on my way to submit my application. With no conventional traffic signals, the road was congested with cars and rickshaws. People had no choice, but to wait till the roads were safe to cross.

I was waiting across the road from Curzon Hall, in front of the High Court building. Within minutes, admission aspirants and their guardians surrounded me.

As soon as the traffic thinned, we rushed to cross the road. At that very moment, my eyes grew fixated on a sight.

An elderly man with a white beard, dressed from head to toe in white Islamic linens, was crossing the road. Holding firmly, he gripped the fair hand of a delicate young girl. The beautiful girl was calm and quietly attached to her father's side and followed him across the road.

I immediately assumed that the she was a young schoolgirl, on her way to visit her older brother or sister at Curzon Hall.

I did not know it then, but this simple moment would mean so much to me later in life.

Destiny

In addition to past transcripts, a written admissions test was required for admittance into the engineering university. On the day of the test, I got on a rickshaw headed towards the engineering university. My rickshaw driver decided to cut through Dhaka University.

I don't know why, but while passing the Registrar's Office of Dhaka University, I decided to stop. I got down from the rickshaw and went into the Registrar's Office.

There, I saw a list of the students selected for admission into the Biochemistry Department. Scanning through the list I found my name.

The engineering university was just across the road, and in minutes, the admissions test would start. I never made it across the road. I didn't even give it a second thought. I simply deposited my admissions fee and got admitted into the Biochemistry Department right away.

It was my parent's sole desire that I enroll at the engineering university. However, it seemed destiny had her own plans.

Perhaps my parents were disappointed that their son never became an engineer. Now, when I look back, I am amazed at how whimsically I had chosen my profession.

Students of the Biochemistry Department

The Department of Biochemistry was housed on the 2nd and 3rd floors of a red three-storied building, situated on the east side of Curzon Hall. The Pharmacy Department occupied the ground floor of the same building.

On the first day of class, the students introduced themselves to one another. They gathered here from different parts of the country. Among the crowd, I only knew two students, my classmates from Ananda Mohan College.

Except for one girl, everyone else was a stranger to me. It was the girl who had caught my eye a few days ago crossing the road in front of Curzon Hall. She was Zeenat Ferdous, my new classmate. My classmates and I would later know her as Bokul.

There were thirty-two students in our class. Of the thirty-two, twenty-five were male and only seven were female. But soon, one of those seven females, Rosy married and left for England. Soon after, Quamrunn, a new girl from Karachi, enrolled and the numbers readjusted. However, when Motashim Billah transferred from another department, the ratio tilted even further in favor of the males.

I still remember most of my classmates, but do not know of all of their whereabouts. The ones I can locate today are Dr. Zeenat Ferdous Nabi (Bokul), research scientist (USA); Dr. Motashim Billah, research scientist (USA); Dr. Towfiq (USA); Syeeda (Canada); Atia (USA); Dilruba (UK); Dr. Ishtiaq Mahmood, Dr. Anwar Hossain, Dr. Kazi Salamatulla – all professors of Dhaka University; Solaiman Khan, deputy secretary, Government of Bangladesh; Mohammed Sharif, Brigadier General, Bangladesh Army; Amin, businessman; Safdar, businessman; Aziz, executive in a pharmaceutical company; Huda, a bank executive; Nilufar and Masud Reza – professors at Agricultural

University; Zulekha, professor, Holly Cross College; Hadis uddin, Inspector General of Bangladesh Police; Zahiruddin Prodhan, businessman; Abul Hashem Khan, Executive of a corporation; Shaheed Hassan, a singer of Shadheen Bangla Betar Kendra - Liberation war radio, currently living in New York; Rezaul Karim, owner of a pharmaceutical company; Sohrab Hossain, Currently Bangladesh Ambassador to Islamabad, Pakistan; and Minhaz whose whereabouts are unknown to me.

Recently, three of my classmates passed away prematurely: Huda – from heart attack; Solaiman – from cancer; and Salamattullah – from a mysterious death.

The Teachers of the Biochemistry Department

All of our teachers were PhDs from American or European universities. Professor Kamal Ahmed was the founding chairman of our department.

In those days, biochemistry was the leading branch of science. It seemed as if almost everyday, researchers were making groundbreaking discoveries. The double helix and the genetic code were sensational and far-reaching discoveries.

These discoveries regularly came out in scientific journals and textbooks. Beyond the glamour of the subject, the departmental laboratory was also the most modern, equipped with state of the art instruments. All of this made our department a new center of knowledge and a source of jealousy for others.

As I said earlier, most of our teachers had PhDs. I still remember them. They were: Dr. Kamal Ahmed, Dr. Nurul Hoq, Dr. Matiur Rahman, Dr. Anwar-ul Azim Choudhury, Dr. Gomez, Parvez Ahmed, Dr. Ashraful Alam (now in North Carolina, USA), Dr. Abdul Mannan, Dr. Nurul Alam and Dr. Rita Alam (now in Texas, USA). Dr. Yusuf was a part-time teacher. Later, Dr. Khairul Bashar, Dr. Ekramuddoula (now in Canada) and Dr. Rafiqul Islam joined our department as teachers.

Sadly, Dr. Anwar-ul Azim Choudhury and Dr. Kamal Ahmed passed away.

Shukumar Barua, the Rhymester

Rats and monkeys were used for research in biochemistry. They were housed in a small building adjacent to the Biochemistry Department Building. Golam Hossain used to look after these animals as if they were his own children. From January to December and even through the holidays, Golam Hossain was there to care for them.

The laboratory assistant of the Biochemistry Department was a soft-spoken simple man. However, we did not know about his other talent. Until one day, when he received the Bangla Academy Award for Literature. He was the famous lyricist and bard, Shukumar Barua.

Neither title nor rank is a measure of one's true talents or abilities. Shukumar, our soft-spoken lab assistant spoke more powerfully and passionately with a just few lines from his soul, than a thousand voices could bellow in a lifetime.

Today, his name and lyrics ring across the ears and hearts of Bengal.

Fazlul Hoque Muslim Hall (F. H. Hall)

In those days, like most science students, I became a resident at F. H. Hall. This was a three-story redbrick rectangular building behind Curzon Hall, on the eastern bank of a pond. Dhaka Hall stood on the other side of the pond.

There was a Language Movement Memorial Sculpture in front of F. H. Hall. This was an architectural novelty, in that it consisted of a huge black marble stone with a dedicatory statement engraved on it.

Professor Meer Faqruzzaman was the provost of the hall at the time. Our house tutors were Khairul Anam, Shahadat Ali, and a lecturer from the Biochemistry Department. The errand boys and watchmen were both Bengali and Bihari.

My Roommate

I was placed in room 142 which sat in the middle of the ground floor in the east wing of the hall. My roommate was Hasnat, a meritorious physics student. He was senior to me by one year. He stood at the top of the Higher Secondary School Certificate Examinations. Slim and slender, but good-looking, Hasnat Bhai had a Sylheti accent. He always addressed me as "roommate" and never by name. I was very happy to get a studious roommate like him.

In those days, no one would go out bare-bodied, or in a lungi, outside of their living area. However, tradition started to give way as some students started to violate this tradition by going out to the dinning hall in lungis. As the casual culture spread through the hall, students were seen sitting on the watchmen's bench, indulging in gossip and trivial chitchat.

Soon, there was a whispering resentment against this behavior. Hasnat Bhai, for instance, always wore a shirt while going to and from the common bath area. I decided to follow his lead.

In F. H. Hall, second-year students would get a single room based on academic achievement. In accordance with this criterion, Hasnat Bhai moved out of our room and was replaced by a new roommate. His name was Monayem Faruk, a first-year chemistry student from Sylhet with a heavy Sylheti accent. Monayem was a very polite and friendly young man.

Monayem Faruk is now the head of a pharmaceutical company in Dhaka. Hasnat, who is now Dr. Hasnat, lives in England and holds a senior position at the Public Education Department. Recently, the Queen of England honored him with a national award in recognition of his service.

Feast

My first dinner at the dining hall was a big surprise. The menu consisted of half a roasted chicken, polau (buttered rice with saffron), yogurt, sweets, and various other items one would expect at a royal feast.

In contrast, dinner at Ananda Mohan College consisted of lentil soup, which was no better than hot water, and a piece of chicken. I considered myself lucky to be a university student, let alone, to be able to feast like this everyday.

Sadly, however, my roommate burst my bubble when he informed me that this kind of food was only served twice a month. Nevertheless, I was happy. I got an entire month's worth of meals and two feasts of roasted chicken and polau for only 40 takas (about 67 cents). I couldn't have asked for more.

Bullets of '71: A Freedom Fighter's Story

Student Politics

Never before in history, had a group of students shaped the history of their nation the way the students of Bangladesh did. The students were more informed and active than the average citizen.

Unlike the farmers, workers, government employees, and businessmen, the students were free from the burden of dependents. As a matter of fact, most of them had nothing to loose and were willing to take risks.

These advantages enabled the students to plunge headstrong into the belly of political movements. Before launching any major movement, political parties would throw the issue as a trial balloon to the student body to test the reaction of the public and the government. This made student politics the barometer for the nation's politics.

In those days, the active student organizations in East Pakistan were: the Chatra League, the student front for the Awami League; the Chatra Union - Motia Group (the student front of the National Awami Party, pro-Russia), the Chatra Union - Menon Group (the student front of the National Awami Party, pro-China), the NSF (the student front of the Convention Muslim League, pro-government), and the Islami Chatra Shongha (the student front of Jamaat-e-Islami, an Islamic fundamentalist party).

In general, the belief was that the brightest students belonged to the Chatra Union and the mediocre would go to the Chatra League. The goons and scoundrels were believed to be members of the NSF. Islami Chatra Shongha members were known as the religious types. However, these generalizations were not necessarily true.

Many Chatra League activists were bright students, as well. As a matter of fact, there were good and bad students in every organization. Further more, the success of student politics depended both, on the quality of their followers, as well as, on the relevance of their ideology and goals.

The first impact of student politics on the Bangladesh Liberation Movement was the Bengali language movement of 1952. On the 21st of March 1948, Governor General of Pakistan, Mohammed Ali Jinnah, declared in a public meeting at Dhaka Race Course Maidan that Urdu, and only Urdu, would be the national language of Pakistan.

This was despite the fact that the Bengalis in East Pakistan constituted the majority of Pakistan's population.

Three days later, Jinnah repeated the same unjust statement in a meeting at Curzon Hall. The student body roared in protest and said to his face, "NO! NO! NO!" They demanded that Bangla also be the national language of Pakistan.

The student body intensified the language movement to establish Bangla as a national language of Pakistan along side Urdu. The Muslim League government in East Pakistan, headed by Chief Minister Nurul Amin, under the instruction of the Central Government, decided to suppress the movement at any cost.

On February 20, 1952, the government imposed a curfew and enacted "penal code 144" throughout the district of Dhaka. The student body was not intimidated. They accepted the challenge. They refused to compromise with their mother language, Bangla.

The next day, on February 21st, 1952, the student body assembled at Dhaka University Campus. They decided to defy penal code 144 and launch a procession in support of establishing Bangla as the national language.

Police fired on the procession. Four students, Salam, Barkat, Rafique, and Jabbar were killed on the spot and many more were injured and arrested. Those four young men were the first ever martyrs to die for their mother language in the history of the world.

No other nation had to shed blood for the right to speak their native language.

The 21st of February was a turning point in the Bangladesh Liberation Movement. On that day, the seeds of Bengali nationalism were sown deep into the soil of Bangladesh. Many student leaders including, Gaziul Haque, Abdul Matin, Toha, Oli Ahad, Abdus Samad Azad, Zahir Raihan, Habibur Rahman, and others played important roles on that day.

In the early 1960's, the student body first challenged General Ayub Khan and his military dictatorship. They began a movement for education reform and restoration of democracy.

They demonstrated against General Ayub Khan during his visit to East Pakistan. They even burnt General Ayub Khan's effigy on the streets of Dhaka during his visit. The student body dared to put a garland of shoes on a life-sized poster of Ayub Khan and paraded it down the streets.

This was unthinkable in military rule because wearing shoes around someone's neck was considered an insult in the cultures of the Indian Subcontinent. Though many students were arrested and put behind bars, they still continued their movement against the autocratic rule of General Ayub Khan. They would stop at nothing to restore democracy in Pakistan.

Many student leaders played an important role in the early 1960's anti-Ayub movement. Among them were: Sheikh Fazlul Haque Moni, Sirajul Alam Khan, Sheikh Obaidur Rahman, Ferdous Ahmed Quoreshi, and Abdur Razzaque of Chatra League and Mohammed Farhad, Rashed Khan Menon, Hayder Akbar Khan Rono, Pankaj Battacharge, and Motia Choudhury of Chatra Union.

In the early 1960's, political leaders were put behind bars, their parties were in disarray, and political activities waned. Nevertheless, these student leaders and their followers challenged the so-called iron man - General Ayub Khan. The 1952 Bengali Language Movement and 1962's anti-Ayub movement were important milestones in the Liberation Movement of Bangladesh.

The Monju-Makhon Cabinet

The elections of the Dhaka University Central Student Union (DUCSU) and those of the residential halls were significant factors in the politics of East Pakistan in 1967.

It was election time in F. H. Hall. The government-backed NSF was very powerful. They were at the height of their high handedness. In the last election, the NSF was defeated and so to avenge their loss the NSF harassed the Chatra League students.

They ransacked the rooms of the Chatra League members. Among the victims were Shahjahan, a brilliant student of Physics (now lives in New Jersey, USA), Mahmud Hasan (now a famous internet activist against the rise of Islamic fundamentalism who writes under the penname of Fatemolla, lives in Canada) and a fellow from Nilfamari.

This young man from Nilfamari had won in the previous election. The NSF goons forced him to walk around the hall grounds in just his underwear. Not being satisfied with that, they trapped him on the roof of the hall building.

From these horror stories, there was no wonder why many were scared of contesting the NSF in the coming election. The question remained, who was brave enough to contest on behalf of the Chatra League.

Chatra League leaders Ziaul Hoque, Riaz Uddin, and Mushtaq Elahi sat down to choose Chatra League nominees. Someone proposed the name of Anwar Hossain Monju, the youngest son of the powerful editor of the Daly Ittefaq, Manik Mia.

Manik Mia had a great following among old Dhaka residents, who were famous for their unity and bravery. If needed, his followers could easily take care of those NSF thugs. It seemed very unlikely that the NSF would even consider laying a hand on Monju just because he was the son of Manik Mia.

In view of these considerations, Anwar Hossain Monju was nominated for the vice-president post of the Student Union of F. H. Hall, while Abdul Quddus Makhon was nominated as the general secretary.

After choosing the panel of nominees, a problem arose regarding submission of the nomination papers to the Provost Office.

The NSF thugs, who had seated themselves in front of the Provost Office, forcibly took away the nomination papers from the candidates who went there to deposit them.

They took this step to prevent Chatra League from taking part in the election and winning it. They knew it was inevitable because they could see the rise in popularity of Sheikh Mujibur Rahman's six-point movement and mounting hatred against the Ayub-Monayem government.

How would we overcome this hurdle? We were perplexed. Suddenly, someone hit on an idea that an unknown first-year student should be the courier of the nomination papers. Amin and I were selected for this mission. We had fears about Amin being caught because, while still very new, he had already gained some recognition as an activist for the Chatra League.

However, since I was yet to be known as an activist, it was decided that I would carry the nomination papers on my back hidden inside my undershirt. I approached the Provost's office timidly.

At the gate, the NSF ruffians were chatting, while keeping watch for any Chatra League activists coming with nomination papers. As I approached the office, I was questioned by one of the thugs who wanted to know why I was there.

Luckily, I was ready with an answer. I told him that my monthly dining hall fees were overdue and today was the last day for me to make good on my payments. Otherwise, I wouldn't be allowed to eat.

One of the ruffians was a student of the Biochemistry Department. He recognized me as a new student of the department and told the others to let me in. Thus, I entered the Provost Office with the nomination papers of the Chatra League candidates.

In the elections that followed, the Monju-Makhon panel came out victorious. This win, along with other victories for the Chatra League in different student halls, played a significant role in boosting the campaign of Sheikh Mujibur Rahman against the military rule of Ayub Khan.

A 12 Goal Defeat

The chairman of the Biochemistry Department, Dr. Kamal Ahmed had only one condition for admission into his department: merit. However, other departments would relax the rules to attract some players in order to promote departmental athletic teams.

While in my first year, I got a chance to play on our departmental soccer team in inter-departmental competition. Our team had good students, but no good players. Our opponent's team, on the other hand, had some great players.

The match began. However, our team was no match at all. It was such a one-sided game that in spite of the full-throated support of our friends and teachers, we suffered a humiliating twelve-goal defeat.

After the game, some of the fans mocked us and joked that the goals were "judiciously distributed" – two goals for the captain and one each for the other ten players. As for me, I hadn't played very well, as I had been out of practice.

However, this shameful defeat did not have any effect on the Biochemistry Department's strict admission policy. The merit-based admission criterion remained in effect and most good athletes were deterred from joining the department.

Captain Piaru

During my second year at the university, I was allotted a single room based on my academic performance. It was on the second floor on the north side of the hall. My neighbor to one side was Piaru, the captain of the Public Works Department (PWD) Team of the National Soccer League. On the other side was Sharif Ahmed, one of my classmates from the Biochemistry Department.

I was really happy to be Piaru's neighbor. He had a polite, friendly and jovial personality. Although he was a student of statistics, soccer was his passion, addiction, and dream. It was his life.

At a relatively young age, he was lucky to become the captain of a first-class club of the National Soccer League.

Aside from studies and politics, soccer was one of my passions. It didn't take much time for Piaru and me to become good friends. He had a collection of posters of famous world players like Brazilian superstar, Pelé and many others, which he used to show me. His club regularly provided him with nutritionally balanced meals. Needless to say, I too got to share in some of these luxuries, from time to time.

Later Piaru became the President of the PWD club, but sadly, in 2004 an unknown assailant gunned him down in front of his club. What a tremendous loss to the nation's soccer institution.

F. H. Hall had a tradition of housing great soccer players. Famous national players like Zakaria Pintu and Major Hafiz were residents of our hall. Piaru himself brought a young goalkeeper named Fazlur Rahman from Rajshahi University and got him a seat in the hall.

Sharif Ahmed, my other next-door neighbor eventually went on to become the Brigadier General in the Bangladesh Army. In early 2000, while stationed as a military attaché in the Bangladesh Embassy in Madrid, his military orderly attacked him. He was seriously wounded, but sadly, his wife and child were both killed.

Such were the tragic fates of my two neighbors at F. H. Hall.

Dhaka Stadium, which was the venue of first class matches for the Dhaka League, was not very far from the hall. It was not long before I became a regular spectator, especially for all the matches of Mohammedan Sporting Club. The right forward of Mohammedan was Musa from West Pakistan, while the left forward was Protap of Dhaka. Musa was a hotheaded rough player. He sometimes committed very hard fouls and for this he was nicknamed "Pagla Musa" or Crazy Musa.

Noni Bosak, the father of a famous actress, Shabnam was a regular referee. Sometimes, if his calling did not please the spectators, pandemonium would ensue and many times the police had to rush in to keep the situation under control. On many of these occasions, when things did get out of hand and the audience rushed the field, the referees, and players would have to be escorted out by the police.

During my F. H. Hall days, I enjoyed another form of entertainment, going to evening cinemas at the Naz Theatre, which was located on the upper floor of Gulistan Cinema Hall. Often times, Habibullah, Amin, and I went to the cinema. On many occasions we would run into the famous "Dada" Sirajul Alam Khan, the prevailing senior leader of the Chatra League.

The three of us also used to frequent Chinese restaurants. Habibullah would encourage us to go to a new place every time we ate, so that by the end of the year, we would have tasted every menu of every Chinese restaurant around campus. We also enjoyed Hajji Biriani of old Dhaka, mughlai parata at the stadium shopping arcade, and the Morog Polau of the Gulistan area.

Humayun Ahmed, the Magician

The early days of my first semester were full of curiosity, excitement, and joy. At the hall and at campus, it was thrilling to meet new faces – students and teachers, alike. The Teacher Student Center, the TSC, hummed with activities like shows, seminars, meetings, and the like. The TSC was also the meeting venue of students from the arts and science departments.

The cultural show that was staged to welcome the new students was gorgeous. Dr. Osman Ghani, the Vice Chancellor of Dhaka

University, welcomed us with a speech in English. His tone was clear and his pronunciation was excellent.

In the talent show part of the function, new students performed recitations, songs, dances, the guitar and other morsels of entertainment.

Humayun Ahmed, a first year student of chemistry, showed excellent feats of magic. However, his stage performance was a little nervy. Possibly, all great people make their start like that.

The real power of this student-magician was unknown at the time. It was much later that Dr. Humayun Ahmed was acknowledged as a great novelist and dramatist. He enjoys unparalleled popularity for his works in film and television to this day.

Dr. G. C. Dev and Dr. Mohammed Shahidullah

Dr. G. C. Dev was a professor and Chairman of the Department of Philosophy. He was a philosopher in the truest sense of the term. With his long gray hair and white attire, he even looked like a philosopher. Dr. Dev would come to our hall to see our provost, Dr. Mir Fakruzzaman.

On his arrival, Dr, Dev would sit down on the lawn with the students and begin discussing philosophy and life. From his smiling face, radiated a certain child-like simplicity and sense of happiness. It was contagious. And yet, even the brightest young minds were humbled in the presence of this philosopher.

F. H. Hall Mosque was on the second floor of the indoor recreation center of the hall. Occasionally, Dr. Mohammed Shahidullah would come to this mosque to say his Friday prayers.

He was, then, a Professor Emeritus of the Bangla Department. He was very old and lived a kind of retired life. After the prayers, he would take up serious Islamic topics for general discussions. A good number of students would always crowd around this Professor of Bangla to listen to his scholarly discourse on Islam.

Dr. Shahidullah was a renowned linguistic scholar of the subcontinent. He had learned eighteen languages of the world including Bangla, Urdu, Arabic, Farsi, Sanskrit, English, German, French and many others. He obtained a doctorate degree in phonetics from France.

Though he had learned a lot on Islam because of his proficiency in the Arabic language, he was a true secularist. He believed in Bengali nationalism. He propagated the philosophy that Muslims, Hindu, Buddhist living in Bengal were all - Bengali.

He was proud of the Bengali language and culture. He campaigned for the celebration of the Bengali New Year, which he thought to be a part of the Bengali culture. As the result of his campaign, the Bengali New Year celebration began in the cities.

He was one of the pioneering minds, who inspired the movement for the recognition of Bangla as a state language.

Principal Ibrahim Khan, Prof. Syed Ali Ahsan and Professor Abdul Hai

Rabindranath Tagore was taboo in Pakistan as he was the embodiment of Bengali nationalism. After the war with India in 1965, the Pakistan Government came to believe Bangla culture was a threat to Pakistan. So the government felt it necessary to eradicate the importance of the Bangla language and culture. In essence, they wanted to eliminate the influence of Nobel-winning poet Tagore from the social, political, and cultural arena of East Pakistan. They banned Tagore's songs from radio and television.

To ridicule the ignorance of the anti-Rabindranath people, there was a joke circulated at the time. It was about East Pakistan Governor Monayem Khan, the stooge of military dictator Ayub Khan.

It was said that he was so annoyed with the popularity of Tagore's songs that he ordered Professor Abdul Hai of the Bangla Department to write Tagore songs of his own.

Professor Hai replied, "Sir, if I write songs, they will be Hai songs, not Tagore Songs".

This was, in fact, a form of communalism. To drive their message deep, they branded Rabindranath a Hindu and Kazi Nazrul a Muslim poet. The communalism went to such a ludicrous extent that even the words of Nazrul and Tagore's poems were changed.

Thus, poetic references to Bhagban (a Hindu god) became Rahman (one of the many names of Allah) and Mohashashan (Hindu graveyard) became Gorosthan (Muslim graveyard), and the like. A few Bengali poets and writers went out of their way to help the government in this unholy mission.

Principal Ibrahim Khan and Syed Ali Ahsan were alleged to have supported the government's bid to introduce Roman writing in place of Bangla letters.

On one occasion, the idea was being discussed in an open meeting, held under the famous Banyan tree of the Bangla Academy. As soon as Principal Ibrahim Khan appeared on stage, the students sitting in front burst into protest.

The old man, standing with the support of his cane, did not understand the situation and so he started to make his speech. This time, the students started shouting slogans condemning those who wanted to replace Bangla letters with Roman letters.

The old man stood there puzzled, before the organizers took him away from the rostrum and seated him on the stage with the others. After him, Syed Ali Ahsan tried to make his speech. But he, too, was booed. At this point, the organizers had no choice, but to help the men down from the stage.

I saw all of this happen from my seat in the back row. I was especially sad for Principal Ibrahim Khan. He was an influential man from my area. He was the founder of Bhuapur College, which heralded educational progress in the region.

Earlier to that, he had established Korotia Shahadat College and continued educational leadership through his service to the college as a principal for many years.

He did not deserve the booing after making such a significant contribution to society. Nevertheless, the people could not help themselves. He did not understand the need of the hour, nor could he read the writing on the wall. It is unfortunate that Principal Ibrahim Khan made himself into lesser personality in the eyes of the new generation.

The Chatra League of F. H. Hall

F. H. Hall bares the rare distinction of being the birthplace of the Chatra League. Illustrious national leaders, such as Tajuddin Ahmed and Abdur Razzaque, among many others, lived in this hall.

Tajuddin Ahmed was the General Secretary of the Awami League and later became the first Prime Minister of Bangladesh, who led the nation during war.

In 1967, Abdur Razzaque was the General Secretary of the Chatra League and led the movement against the Ayub-Monayem government from F. H. Hall.

However, there was another Chatra League leader by the name of Mushtaq Elahi, who traveled all the way from Rangpur in North Bengal to meet with Razzaque. It was the evening of August 2, 1967, when Mushtaq had arrived at Razzaque's dormitory room.

Just as the two men had commenced an exchange of greetings, a swarm of police officers had charged into the room and arrested Abdul Razzaque. His role in the anti-government movement led to this arrest. This may have been the most frightening experience in the life of the young provincial leader, Mushtaq Elahi.

Another central leader of the Chatra League, who also lived in F. H. Hall, was Fazlur Rahman Khan. We called him Faruk. This student leader from Tangail was the Joint Secretary of the Chatra League Central Committee. At that time, Abdur Rauf and Mohammed Ali were president and secretary of the Central Committee, respectively.

Faruk lived on the first floor in the northeast corner of the hall. He was just down the corridor from my room. He encouraged me to become more active in Chatra League politics. Since we were both from Tangail, I felt he had higher expectations for me than he did of the other students in the hall.

Anowar Hossain Monju and Abdul Koddus Makhon, vice-president and general secretary of F. H. Hall Student Union, were also recognized as central leaders of the Chatra League. Monju was a bit out of touch with the resident students of the Chatra League, as he was not a resident of the hall himself.

Makhon, on the other hand, was a resident of F. H. Hall and lived on the third floor at the southeast corner. He maintained a close personal relation with the activists of the Chatra League.

Mushtaque Elahi, central leader of the Chatra League, President of Dhaka University Chatra League branch and Literary Secretary of Dhaka University Student's Union, was also a non-resident student of this hall.

The Chatra League activists whose names I still remember are: Abdur Razzaque - a freedom fighter, Awami League leader, and former minister; Anowar Hossain Monju - a Jatiyo Party leader and former minister; Fazlur Rahman Khan - a freedom fighter, Awami League leader, and former member of the Parliament; Dr. Mushtaque Elahi - a freedom fighter and professor of Mass Communication in the USA; Rashidul Alam - a freedom fighter and secretary of the Bangladesh Government; Habibullah - a freedom fighter and senior officer of the Civil Aviation Department of the Bangladesh Government; Amin - a businessman and leader of the Jatiyo Shamajtantrik Dal (JSD); Solaiman Khan - a freedom fighter and deputy Secretary of the Bangladesh Government; Dr. Alauddin - a freedom fighter, former Vice Chancellor of Jahangir Nagor University, and currently an advisor to Sheikh Hasina, the Prime Minister of Bangladesh; Nurul Islam Milon - a freedom fighter and leader of the Jatiyo Party, Nazrul Islam - a valiant freedom fighter and martyr of the Bangladesh Liberation War; Obaidul Hoque Babul - a freedom fighter and later a businessman who was sadly gunned down around the turn of the millennium; Nurul Islam - a freedom fighter and professor of Dhaka University; Dr. Imamul Hoque Emu - a professor of Dhaka University, Gias Uddin - a freedom fighter and officer of the Bangladesh Government; Zulfiquer Ali - a freedom fighter and magistrate of the Bangladesh Government; Kaisar - a college professor; and Sadeque, Mushtaque and Faruque who ultimately settled in the USA working and doing business in the pharmaceutical industry. There were so many other student activists, classmates, and friends, but sadly, many of their names escape me.

Dhaka University Students demonstrated in support of the Six-Point Movement

National Students Federation (NSF)

General Ayub Khan came to power after a military coup. He then formed his own political party known as the Convention Muslim League Party. Ayub Khan introduced a limited form of democracy known as 'Basic Democracy' and implemented a system of Governor-rule in East and West Pakistan. Ayub Khan then appointed Monayem Khan, a mediocre lawyer from Mymensingh, as Governor of East Pakistan.

The Chatra League and Chatra Union had already launched an anti-government campaign for democratic rule in Pakistan. To counter them and also to popularize his government, Monayem Khan formed a student front named the National Students Federation (NSF).

The party was comprised of opportunistic students from elitist families. The NSF recruits were the sons of members of the Convention Muslim League Party and bureaucrats. With the direct support of the government, the NSF's job was to harass and frighten the activists of the Chatra League and Chatra Union from participating in anti-government activities.

The NSF spawned terror groups in the residential halls of Dhaka University and other educational institutes of Dhaka to mobilize this effort. Pachpattu who lived in F. H. Hall and Khoka who lived in Dhaka Hall, were the NSF's top two leaders.

NSF Bullying

One day, after class I was returning to the hall walking along the bank of the pond. As I walked, I saw a couple of NSF thugs taking turns beating up another student. The student was crying in agony. Their leader, Pachpattu, was smoking a cigarette, while enjoying the action.

This crime happened in broad daylight, but no one dared to do anything about it. I, too, was afraid. I couldn't even look at the scene directly, so I kept walking, but out of the corner of my eye, I saw the transgression unfold. Later, the hall gatekeeper told me exactly what had happened.

The victim was a non-resident student from old Dhaka. It was alleged that his only crime was falling in love with the sister of an NSF member. What a price to pay for young love!

Another incident of NSF bullying occurred one evening after dinner. My roommate, Monayem, and I were deeply engrossed in our studies. Suddenly, we heard pandemonium coming from the corridor outside. We came out of our dorm room to see what was going on.

We saw a number of NSF thugs with daggers and sticks in hand, screaming in the hallway, hurling abusive words towards Chatra League followers and frantically hunting for their rooms. Frightened, my roommate shut our door. We could hear the thugs coming closer, kicking down our neighbors' doors.

Before we could collect our thoughts, we heard violent kicks at our door. They were screaming at us and threatened to shoot the door down if we didn't open it. Not knowing what to do, we panicked and opened the door.

They rushed in and asked, point blank, who between us was a Chatra League activist. Before I could answer, Abdul Hoque, one of the attackers and a student from the Biochemistry Department, recognized me. He told the others that I was a student from his department. He told them to leave us alone and luckily they did. They left our room, but instructed us to leave our door open.

It was just a few days before that Abdul Hoque and I were on the soccer field playing side-by-side. He was our department's team captain. It was this common passion for soccer that spared me in this incident.

Under the police protection, the thugs of NSF make their way to attack supporters of the 6-Point Movement

Killing of Pachpattu

The pillaging by the NSF at F. H. Hall was in response to another serious incident that happened earlier in the evening. The notorious leader of the NSF, Pachpattu was struggling for his life after he was stabbed at Salimullah Muslim Hall (S. M. Hall). He was a student of F. H. Hall.

On that fateful evening, a group of NSF thugs, lead by Pachpattu, went to S. M. Hall to enjoy the monthly "feast". NSF thugs commonly crashed the monthly feasts of various dormitories, despite not being residents of the hall and not paying for the food.

That evening, as they feasted, the thugs took a scene right out of a Bollywood film. Typical of villains in a movie, they began fooling around and roughhousing, tossing food at one another.

After their stomachs were plump and full, they headed off to room 116 to relax and shoot the breeze. This was the room of the S. M.

Hall NSF branch president. It was just the day before that this room belonged to Mosleh Uddin Ahmed, a third year student of Physics. He had another month before his final exams. Until then, he was to live in room 116. Unfortunately, the NSF president had other plans. He told Mosleh Uddin to vacate the room, immediately. Out of fear of retaliation, Mosleh obliged.

As Pachpattu and his group made their way to room 116, an unknown group of young men entered the S. M. Hall dining room. They were looking for Pachpattu and upon some brief questioning, the men made their way to room 116, as well. Pachpattu and his men were relaxing in the room. The group of unknown men swarmed into the room and stabbed Pachpattu repeatedly in the chest and stomach. The rest of his men had no choice, but to flee, some of which even jumped out of the window to save their lives.

Apparently, Pachpattu's assailants were a group of young men from Old Dhaka. They were known Chatra Union supporters. It was alleged that there had been some prior conflict between these young men of Old Dhaka and Pachpattu.

Moments after the incident, the assailants had left S. M. Hall and Pachpattu was taken to the hospital where he eventually died. The NSF thugs of F. H. Hall went berserk with the news of the attack on Pachpattu, their leader; and sought revenge on the residents of F. H. Hall.

Luckily, most of the known activists and leaders of the Chatra League were not in the hall that night. They fortunately escaped any form of retributive attack. We, too, were fortunate as we were still new and not yet known as Chatra League activists.

The Last Days of the NSF

Despite the loss of a fellow student, the student body felt a sigh of relief with news of Pachpattu's passing. A few days after Pachpattu's death, the bullet-ridden body of Khoka, another notorious leader of the NSF, was found just outside the university at the Race Course Ground.

With the removal of these two nefarious leaders, the harassment and torture of students became less frequent. We had even noticed that the incident triggered a sense of insecurity and fear in the hearts of NSF cadres.

Encouraged by this change, the Chatra League and Chatra Union pushed their anti-government movement forward without any fear. The death of Pachpattu and Khoka signaled the beginning of the end for the Ayub-Monayem regime.

Pachpattu hailed from the district of Barishal. Before he came to Dhaka, he was known as a handsome, polite, and friendly young man. It was Governor Monayem Khan and his leadership who turned this young gentleman into a monster.

One of his sisters was a student of Rokeya Hall. There had never been a more decent, polite, and simple girl than Pachpattu's sister. However, as sweet and simple as she was, no one ever knew of her relation to Pachpattu, as she never told anyone that they were brother and sister.

The NSF was as hated by people as Razakars were hated by those in the post-liberation era. Razakars were the Benedict Arnolds of Bangladesh. They were fellow Bengalis and the cadre of the Jamaat-e-Islami Party who opposed the liberation war. They collaborated with Pakistani occupation forces leading to the death of millions of innocent civilians.

Islami Chatra Shongha

Islami Chatra Shongha was the student wing of the Jamaat-e-Islami Party. Moulana Moududi was the chief of the Jamaat-e-Islami of Pakistan, while Golam Azam was the provincial chief in East Pakistan.

Matiur Rahman Nizami was the chief of the Islami Chatra Shongha in East Pakistan. The aim of Jamaat-e-Islami was to establish Islamic rule in Pakistan. During the late 1960's, Islami Chatra Shongha was busy strengthening their organization.

However, the party covertly worked against Bengali nationalism and Bengali culture, while propagating their so-called "Islamic culture." Speaking in the name of religion, they attempted to cover their promotion of West Pakistani interests.

Two students of the Biochemistry Department, Abdul Malek and Masud, were the leaders of Islami Chatra Shongha. They were both from North Bengal. Malek was a very talented student and was at the top his class. Polite, friendly, and soft-spoken, Malek was the central leader of Islami Chatra Shongha and a man to be followed. With his charm and magnetic charisma, he would often try to reel in new students.

Meanwhile, it was known that the Islami Chatra Shongha did not support the anti-government movement for democratic rule and an autonomous East Pakistan. This particular stance led to a clash with the anti-government student body.

One day, there was a confrontation between the Islami Chatra Shongha and the opposing student body at the TSC. This confrontation quickly erupted into violence and mayhem. Men from both sides pulled out hockey sticks and repeatedly whaled on one another.

However, one such blow during the fight struck Malek in the head. He was killed. The incident left the Biochemistry Department riddled with grief. This was an unwarranted demise of a brilliant student of Biochemistry.

Most students of the Islami Chatra Shongha wore a guise of passivity and grace. Who could have imagined that these seemingly peaceful figures would one day transform into such ravenous monsters?

In 1971, during the Liberation War, the Islami Chatra Shongha evolved into the killing squads known as Razakar, the Al-Badar, and the Al-Shams. These killing squads of the Islami Chatra Shongha were responsible for the murder of pro-liberation intellectuals, many of who were their own beloved teachers.

Student Activists of Biochemistry

Aside from me, there were quite a number of student activists in my department. Amin, Solaiman, Hadis Uddin, Mokbul, Mahmud Hassan, and I belonged to the Chatra League. Safdar and Sharif belonged to the Chatra Union Menon group. Bokul and Atia belonged to the Chatra Union – Motia group. Abdul Hoque, Sirajul Islam Mazumdar, and Faruk belonged to the NSF. Anwar and Huda belonged to extreme leftist camps.

Desperate Times for the Awami League

The Awami League became the target of oppression by the Ayub-Monayem regime as soon as its leader, Sheikh Mujibur Rahman, launched his six-point movement for the autonomy of East Pakistan. The leaders of the Awami League were hunted down by police and arrested. Even Sheikh Mujibur Rahman, himself, was repeatedly detained.

At one stage, almost all the top leaders of the party were put behind bars. This included most of the central and local leaders, including Tajuddin Ahmed, Kamruzzaman, Mizanur Rahman Choudhury, and many others. During this crisis, Mrs. Amena Begum was the acting-General Secretary of Awami League.

As a result of such extreme oppressive measures by the government, anti-government movements were attenuated to a great extent. The strength of the movement approached nil. It was during these desperate times that the participation of Dhaka University students in Awami League activities became crucial. It was only through a significant student involvement that the anti-government movement was kept alive. We the students of F. H. Hall led the way in this regard.

By Candle Light

The Awami League office was located in a small house at Purano Paltan. Mohammad Ullah, an Awami Leader from Noakhali, was, then, the office secretary of the Awami League. During these desperate times, the office was usually barren. Most of the leaders were in jail.

Government spies kept a vigil on those coming in and out of the office. It was mostly the Chatra League activists who went to the Awami League office. The close vicinity of F. H. Hall to Purana Paltan, allowed us to visit the Awami League office almost every evening. We usually found Mohammad Ullah sitting alone in the office.

One particular evening, we found Mohammad Ullah doing some work by candlelight. He glanced at us and asked us to have a seat. He read our minds and started explaining why he was using a candle. He told us that the electricity had been cut off due to a nonpayment of bills.

Businessmen, who once generously donated to the party, ceased all financial contributions, in fear of government persecution. Making things worse, even the landlord was pressured by the government to evict the Awami League.

In spite of these hardships and obstacles, the leaders and activists of the Chatra League and Awami League continued the struggle for the emancipation of our people.

Suhrawardy and Shere Bangla

The Awami League had arranged a seminar to observe the death anniversary of Hossain Shahid Suhrawardy at his Mausoleum near Curzon Hall. Since Mizanur Rahman Choudhury, the acting-General Secretary of the Awami League, was arrested and detained, Mrs. Amena Begum was appointed to his position. She coordinated the function.

Student leader, Abdul Koddus Makhon, played a very important role in organizing the meeting. There were about one hundred guests in attendance, of which, at least half were students from F. H. Hall.

Dr. Kamal Hossain, an eminent lawyer and an Awami League leader, was the chief guest. Prof. Afsaruddin of Dhaka University was the keynote speaker.

In those days, Dr. Kamal Hossain was not fluent in Bangla, and so, he used to rely on speaking broken-Bangla. However, he made his address at the meeting in English.

He greeted the audience with "My dear friends…" and then paused and said, "There is a lady amongst us, but when I say friend, I think I can refer to her as well".

Coincidently, the only lady at the meeting was Mrs. Hossain, his wife. In those days, female students and women activists tended to avoid such meetings in fear of harassment by NSF thugs and police.

Actually, in those days, people in general avoided attending anti-government and Bengali cultural programs. Once, on the death anniversary of Shere Bangla A. K. Fazlul Hoque, the Krishok Sramik Party organized a meeting. Krishok Sramik Party president, Mr. Solaiman had specially requested us to attend the meeting.

We were a little late getting to the meeting. However, upon our arrival, we saw that the meeting had started without us, but more importantly, was in front of an audience of no more than thirty people. Luckily, we brought with us an entourage from F. H. Hall of about just as many, doubling the audience size. The meeting turned out to be a success.

In those times of struggle, one of our most important responsibilities was to ensure the success of meetings like this.

Agartala Conspiracy Case

It was January 1968. The Ayub-Monayem administration brought forth a case against Sheikh Mujibur Rahman, accusing him of treason. It was known as the Agartala Conspiracy Case. In addition to Sheikh Mujibur Rahman, there were about thirty others, who were also implicated in the case.

The allegations claimed that Sheikh Mujibur Rahman was engaged in a conspiracy with India to make East Pakistan an independent state. It was further alleged that Sheikh Mujibur Rahman met with Indian intelligence officers in Agartala, India. Hence, the case came to be known as the Agartala Conspiracy.

After the Indo-Pak war of 1965, Sheikh Mujibur Rahman raised a strong voice for provincial autonomy and prepared a charter, pinpointing six demands necessary in attaining this goal.

The six-point demands included that the provincial government should have an independent currency and the power to impose and collect taxes.

In 1966, in a round-table conference in Lahore, West Pakistan, national leaders from various political parties came together. Sheikh Mujibur Rahman presented his six-point plan for autonomy of East Pakistan. It was rejected almost instantaneously. They considered it a formula and means for destroying Pakistan.

Right after that meeting, Sheik Mujib and the Awami League became the target of government forces. Sheikh Mujibur Rahman was taken to prison.

Many of his followers were also in prison. Under these circumstances, people realized that the Agartala Conspiracy Case was nothing but a false and fabricated attempt at undermining and oppressing an anti-government movement. Its aim was to destroy Sheikh Mujibur Rahman and the Awami League.

In June of 1968, a special military tribunal was set up to hear the case. Under tight security, the hearing began at the Dhaka Cantonment. Sheikh Mujibur Rahman addressed the court in a written statement.

A confident and fearless voice bellowed from his body as he read his statement aloud. He denied all charges filed against him and said that the case was nothing more than a response to his Six-Point Charter for the autonomy of East Pakistan. It was a calculated plan to destroy him and the efforts of the Awami League Party.

This abuse of state power was clearly a means of harassing and intimidating political opponents. Of the accused co-conspirators, he personally only knew two. They were Ruhul Quddus and Shamsur Rahman Khan, two civil servants whom he met during his tenure as a minister of Pakistan. As for the other accused co-conspirators, not only were they not connected to him, he proclaimed that he had never even met them before. This went for Lt. Commander Moazzem Hossain of the Navy, as well, who was accused of being a key player in the conspiracy.

The proceedings of the tribunal were open to the press, so they received wide publicity. What was initially, an attempt to exploit and victimize Sheikh Mujibur Rahman and his followers inadvertently became an opportunity for Sheikh Mujibur Rahman to reach out to the people of Bengal. His powerful statements and declaration of innocence awoke the beast that lay sleeping in the hearts of Bengalis.

The student community and the people at large were overwhelmingly drawn to Sheikh Mujibur Rahman and his six-point movement. Their temples now swelled in rage as they directed their anger against the regime of Ayub and Monayem.

**Police escorted Sheikh Mujibur Rahman to the
Special Tribunal Court for the Agartala Conspiracy
Case, January 1969**

The Attorney's Handshake

Many famous lawyers took the side of Sheikh Mujibur Rahman
and the other defendants. Salam Khan, Ataur Rahman Khan, Khan
Bahadur Mohammad Ismail, and Mirza Golam Hafiz were among the
notable attorneys. A host of young lawyers also assisted the defense
cases. The most distinguished of these young lawyers were Barrister

Amirul Islam, Barrister Moudud Ahmed, and Advocate Aminul Hoque.

The famous Thomas Williams, a lawyer from England, was brought to defend Sheikh Mujibur Rahman and the others. Many people participated in funding this historical case.

Special mention must be made regarding Abdul Mannan, an Awami League leader from Tangail. As a reputed income tax lawyer in Dhaka, he was well connected amongst the business community. Mr. Mannan actively solicited donations from these businessmen and raised a considerable fund for the legal fight.

I was fortunate to see Thomas Williams up close. It was at a marriage ceremony at the Hotel Purbani. The bride was the elder sister of my roommate Monayem Faruk.

Barrister Moudud Ahmed was assisting Thomas Williams during the trial. However, Barrister Ahmed also happened to be the brother-in-law of Monayem. He invited Thomas Williams to the wedding as his special guest.

After the marriage ceremony was over, the guests lined up to congratulate the newlywed couple. When his turn came, Thomas wanted to know if he could congratulate the bride by kissing her on the cheek. Some people from the bride's side politely declined his request, as it was against Bengali custom.

So, Thomas Williams congratulated the new couple by simply shaking hands.

The Eleven-Point Movement

The Agartala Conspiracy Case made the student community and particularly, the Chatra League more rebellious and resilient in their cause. Nonetheless, most of the leaders and activists of the Awami League were still behind bars. It was the student community who filled this void and kept the movement alive and vigorous.

Three student parties, namely the Chatra League, the Chatra Union (Motia Group), and the Chatra Union (Menon Group), joined hands and intensified the anti-government movement. With the polarization of student groups, even a faction of the NSF was inspired to detach itself and join the anti-government movement. By November 1968, the movement had turned into a full-fledged student revolution.

In January 1969, an all-party student body known as the Central Student's Action Committee was formed to push the movement further. The Central Student's Action Committee consisted of representatives from each student organization. The committee was comprised of: Tofael Ahmed, Vice-President of DUCSU and a Chatra League leader; Nazim Kaman Chowdhury, Secretary of DUCSU and a NSF rebellious faction leader; Abdur Rauf, President of the Chatra League; Mohammad Ali, Secretary of the Chatra League; Shamsuddoha and Saifuddin Manik from the Chatra Union (Motia Group); and Mustafa Jamal Haider from the Chatra Union (Menon Group).

Within a week after forming the Central Student's Action Committee, the famous Eleven-Point Charter was drawn up. It included the demands mentioned in the Awami League's Six-Point Charter. This charter became the mandate for the national emancipation of Bengalis. Although the students created it, the impact of the Eleven-Point Charter spilled over and through the entire Bengali population.

Tofael Ahmed, as a proponent of the eleven-point movement, was recognized as an inspiring student leader amongst both students and the general people.

Tofael Ahmed, leader of the 11-Point Movement addresses a huge public meeting at Paltan Maidan, Feb 9, 1969

People's Uprising of 1969

Ever since the Agartola Conspiracy Case, we became more involved in the movement, dedicating all of our efforts into being full-time activists. The hotbeds for politics, such as Bot Tola, Shahid Minar, Race Course, and Paltan Maidan were in the vicinity of F. H. Hall and Dhaka Hall. It was this close proximity, which made F. H. Hall and Dhaka Hall centers for all political action.

The first significant program launched to achieve the Eleven-Point Charter was a strike on the 17th of January, followed by a student rally at Bot Tola of the Arts Campus. To stop the event from occurring, the government imposed a ban on public assembly by enacting Penal Code 144. We violated the order and avoided getting arrested by splitting ourselves into smaller groups and reconvening at Bot Tola.

The police patrolled the arts campus the way ravenous tigers circled pray. However, the leaders of the Central Student's Action Committee managed to reach the venue by wearing different disguises.

As the small groups converged into a body of a thousand students, the rally commenced. Tofael Ahmed presided over the meeting and he and his fellow leaders unanimously decided to challenge the government ruling and violate penal code 144.

Thus, we rallied together and marched out of the campus in a procession. Instantaneously, we were met with police reprisal. The police attacked us with tear gas, water canons, and batons. Many students were arrested and even more were wounded. Ultimately, we were forced to disperse into different directions.

In protest of the police brutality of January 17th, a general strike and demonstration were called into effect on January 18th and 19th. However, these events were no different than the previous day and we clashed with police again. The events of these three days, coupled with the excitement in the air, pushed the movement beyond the student community and deep within the hearts of the general public.

Public support for the Eleven-Point Charter spread like wildfire, as masses across the country spontaneously participated in strikes and demonstrations against the government.

The Central Student's Action Committee called for another strike and protest rally on January 20th. This time, the administration took even tougher actions. The Pakistani Army was deployed to suppress the movement. They completely cordoned off Dhaka University. Penal Code 144 was still in effect, but now it was being enforced with machine guns.

Nevertheless, we set out from our dorm in a procession towards Bot Tola. On our way, near the Bangla Academy, police armed with batons and tear gas attacked us. We were prevented from arriving at our destination.

Meanwhile, a large body of protesters from various directions managed to assemble at Bot Tola. Repeatedly, they attempted to rise in a procession to violate Penal Code 144, but all efforts were futile. The police violently attacked with baton charges, tear gas, and water cannons to confine them to the campus.

A sea of livid demonstrators, raising their sticks and fists into the air, demand the release of Sheikh Mujibur Rahman from the Dhaka Cantonment, 1969

Asad, the Martyr

After being attacked near the Bangla Academy, we turned around and headed towards Dhaka Medical College, chanting anti-government slogans. However, the police attacked us once again on the road between Dhaka Hall and the Medical College. Many of us jumped the fences at the Dhaka Medical College and took shelter. Others, to save themselves, managed to make it back to Dhaka Hall.

Once inside the Medical College, we regrouped and discussed amongst ourselves what we should do next. Suddenly, amidst our conversation, we were startled by the screeching sounds of police gunfire.

There was another procession passing through the road in front of the Medical College. The police had confronted the protestors. A student leader of Chatra Union named Asad was in the forefront of the procession. A police officer approached Asad and brandished his gun at point blank range. He fired. Asad's lifeless body fell to the street.

We couldn't believe what we had just seen. Anger filled our blood as we charged to the site. The police, overwhelmed by our cries, retreated. Asad's body was recovered and brought inside the Medical College.

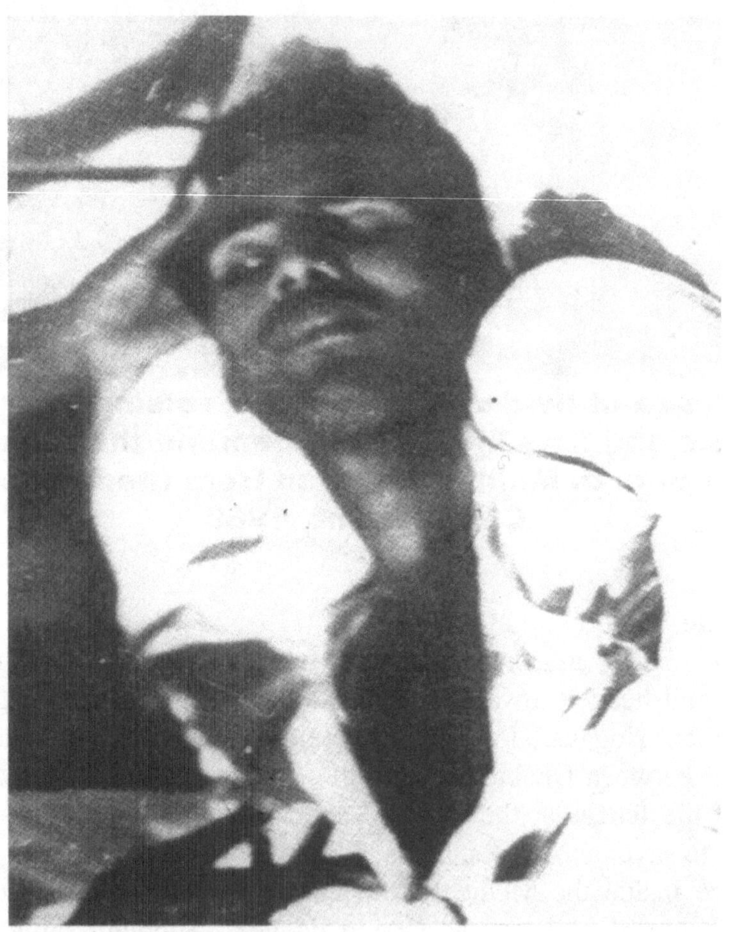

Asad, a student leader, killed at point blank by police during a demonstration in Dhaka, 20th January 1969

As word of Asad's death spread through the city, the passivity of protestors was lost and pockets of confrontation with police and protestors exploded into battle.

In the evening, political and student leaders assembled with us at the Medical College. Among the student leaders were Tofael Ahmed, Saifuddin Manik, Shamsuddoha, and many others.

Joining the students, were political leaders: Professor Muzaffar Ahmed, Mohiuddin Ahmed, Rashed Khan Menon, and other. They reviewed the situation and mapped out the next steps.

In reaction to Asad's murder, the leaders launched a three-day protest program from January 21st to January 23rd, which included a strike, a demonstration, and a torched vigil. Much like the fiery torches they carried, the whole country burned with rage.

On the 24th of January, military forces were called in to aid police. And once again, the police and military forces opened fire upon unarmed protesting crowds. Several people were killed across the country.

One such protest procession was held in front of the secretariat building. The police fired upon the protestors. Matiur Rahman, a young schoolboy, was killed on the spot. The protestors were angered by the injustice. They turned their fury onto the office of the government-controlled daily newspaper, The Morning News, which was conveniently located adjacent to the secretariat's building. The pro-government news office was set on fire. Within a few moments, it had been reduced to ashes.

On the 24th of January, the revolution had truly begun. People from all walks of life rose up and took to the streets. Young and old, men and women, poor and wealthy, farmers and laborers, peasants and civil servants, all rallied together with students and occupied the streets. Student leaders, Tofael Ahmed, Saifudin Manik, Mahbubullah, and others addressed the crowd and lead the processions.

The ocean of enraged faces was armed with bamboo sticks, swords, hammers, and rocks. The people's army adorned black flags. They were not ready to back down.

Throughout the city, brigades of civilian forces confronted and swarmed the military and police. Wave after wave, the police tried to intimidate the masses, but the people would not give in. Overwhelmed by their resilience, the police and military were forced to retreat to their barracks for the day. Knowing that the war had only just begun, this initial success gave us a taste of what victories may lay ahead.

The next day, the Central Student's Action Committee called for another nation-wide strike. Confrontation between protestors and military forces again ensued. The military opened fire once again on the crowd.

The enraged people and the brute military forces come face to face in Dhaka

Away from protestors, a young mother named Monwara sat on the veranda of her home as she breast-fed her child. A stray military bullet pierced her body as she cupped her child and fell dead to the floor. Another innocent life lost became just another reason for the crusaders to push the anti-government movement further.

Over the course of the past week, I along with thirty or forty student activists of both, the Chatra League and Chatra Union from F.H. Hall worked day and night as frontline soldiers for the anti-government movement. Through this exhilarating experience, we developed a deep and enthusiastic brotherhood. We felt as if we were fighting a war and with every passing day, we had won another battle.

In this kind of movement there was a certain risk to life. However, I never felt it for a moment. Rather, the romance and excitement spawned by a youthful mind gave me courage.

The Case Dropped – Sheikh Mujibur Rahman Released!

The tyrannical regime of Ayub and Monayem Khan was already quivering. A section of the pro-government student organization, the NSF had already joined the movement. The government was running out of allies. They could only depend on the military and the police. Meanwhile, the anti-government movement of the Eleven-Point Charter was picking up steam. On the 9th of February, a public meeting was held demanding the release of Sheikh Mujibur Rahman.

Following the lead of student organizations, the anti-government political parties: Awami League, NAP, and others, formed a coalition named the Democratic Action Committee (DAC).

Muslim League leaders like Nurul Amin and Mahmud Ali and others, who were still on the fence, reluctantly joined the DAC. The DAC called a protest meeting on February 14th to support the eleven-point demand for provincial autonomy and the release of Sheikh Mujibur Rahman.

As this movement pushed forward, Tajuddin Ahmed, the General Secretary of the Awami League and some of the other detained Awami League leaders, were set free. The Central Student's Action Committee endorsed the February 14th meeting.

We went to the meeting in a procession from F. H. Hall. Once again, it was another huge gathering. The speakers, one-by-one, took to the podium demanding the release of Sheikh Mujibur Rahman and the immediate resignation of General Ayub Khan.

Each political leader was given time on stage. Eagerly, the people listened to the Awami League's Tajuddin Ahmed, National Awami Party's (Pro-Russia) Professor Mozaffar Ahmed, and student leader Tofael Ahmed.

However, when Nurul Amin and Mahmud Ali approached the podium to speak, the crowd met their voices with such booing that the men found it impossible to speak. The masses had finally distinguished their friends from their enemies.

On the 15th of February, Sgt. Zahurul Hoque, one of the accused from the Agartola Conspiracy Case, was shot to death by the army while in custody. The next day, after the funeral services, the masses exploded into anger and organized an enormous anti-government procession. The angry protestors attacked the residences of ministers, setting many of them on fire.

Students protest on the streets in support of the autonomy of East Pakistan during the people's Uprising, 1969

Although his voice was heard later than expected, Moulana Bhashani, the President of the National Awami Party (Pro-China), finally announced his support for the eleven-point demands and asked for the immediate release of Sheikh Mujibur Rahman.

On this same day, another small, but significant incident took place. We were marching in a volatile procession near Bangla Academy. Suddenly, a splinter group of protestors broke away from us and attacked the residence of the presiding judge of the Agartala Conspiracy Case. His mansion was set ablaze. In a desperate attempt to save his life, the judge looked for a disguise.

With his Bengali cook's Lungi wrapped around his waste, he attempted to pass for a commoner and fled through the backdoor. With no judge to preside over the case, Sheikh Mujibur Rahman's impending freedom became just a matter of time.

With each day, we achieved another victory for the movement, while the government only appeared to lose more and more ground.

During a strike on February 18th at Rajshahi University, the army attacked a crowd of protestors. After a barrage of bayonet charges, Dr. Zoha, a professor from Rajshahi University, was left for dead.

News of his tragic death was received in Dhaka at night, which led to a nation-wide protest. In Dhaka, anti-government processions rose to the streets violating the government-imposed curfew. Military forces fired on protestors through the night. As the smoke melted into the dark sky, hundreds of souls drifted to heaven.

With rocks, bamboo sticks, and clenched fist, angry students take on the armed military forces

Giving into the demands of the people, the government declared February 21st as a national holiday in honor of those who were killed in the Bengali Language Movement of 1952. This was a historic victory for the Bengali people. The nation observed Language Martyr Day with unprecedented enthusiasm and sprit.

On that same day, General Ayub Khan announced that he would not run for reelection for the presidency of Pakistan. This, too, was another moral victory for the people. The man acclaimed by his supporters as the "Iron Man", finally showed weakness and began to melt from the heat and pressure of the Bengali people.

The Agartala Conspiracy Case was dropped the next day, on February 22. The government bowed down to the people's will and released Sheikh Mujibur Rahman and all other political prisoners. There was a wave of celebration across the country.

In Dhaka, people flooded the streets. We organized a procession from F. H. Hall to the Shahid Minar, where Sheikh Mujibur Rahman was scheduled to arrive.

Shahid Minar, which symbolized the unity of the Bengali people, was now the symbol of a nation united behind a single national leader. His name was Sheikh Mujibur Rahman. The country he left, before going off to jail, was no more. A free man, Sheikh Mujibur Rahman found himself in a new Bengal with the strength of an entire nation roaring behind him.

The dictatorial regime now began falling to the floor like a house of cards. Over the last few months, we had shouted slogans proclaiming, "We will break the locks of this prison and free our leader!" Now that slogan had finally come to fruition. Our joy knew no bounds.

Sheikh Mujibur Rahman Becomes Bangabandhu – A Friend of Bengal

At Shahid Minar, we learned that Sheikh Mujibur Rahman was heading towards Paltan Maidan, where people had gathered impulsively expecting him to come and speak. We, too, followed the crowd and reached Paltan Maidan.

By the time we arrived, there was already an unbelievable sea of people awaiting the arrival of their leader. Some people were still skeptical regarding Sheikh Mujibur Rahman's release from jail. Nonetheless, they eagerly waited to see him for themselves.

Moments later, Tofael Ahmed stood up before the crowd and said, "I have just come from a meeting with our leader. He is free, but very tired. He needs his rest. We will hold a public reception for him tomorrow at the Race Course grounds".

The crowd then burst into thunderous cheering.

The next day was February 23rd, 1969. In addition to the citizens of Dhaka, people from across the country came on foot, by bus, by train, and even by steamboat to assemble at the Race Course grounds.

Our contingent from F. H. Hall was lost amongst the crowd. There was vast ocean of faces that gathered, which patiently waited to see Sheikh Mujibur Rahman.

With the sun glimmering behind him, an outstretched hand reached into the sky greeting the audience. He was a broad figure with a commanding presence. His shoulders adorned a black vest, as his hand clenched a tobacco pipe. The electricity resonated through the crowd to the outer limits of the horizon. The masses greeted Sheikh Mujibur Rahman, as they chanted the thunderous slogans of "Joy Bangla!"

The meeting began with Tofael Ahmed presiding over it. All the leaders of the Central Students Action Committee were present on stage. Khaled Mohammed Ali, General Secretary of the Chatra League, Saifuddin Manik of the Chatra Union (Motia Group), Mahbubullah of the Chatra Union (Menon Group), and Mahbubul Hoq Dolon from the rebellious faction of the NSF, each made welcome speeches.

Tofael Ahmed stood before the crowd to give his presidential address preceding the speech of Sheikh Mujibur Rahman. The people welcomed their beloved student leader with applause. Many of who saw him, now, for the first time.

Tofael Ahmed exuberantly praised the leadership of Sheikh Mujibur Rahman. He said, "This is the man who spent the best years of his youth in jail, fighting for the greater good of Bengal. This is the man who stood fearlessly before death in the name of his people, and this is the uncompromising man who selflessly fought for our nation. How do we address such a man? I, on behalf of the people and the student body, do herby bestow upon him the title – Bangabandhu," friend of Bengal.

And with this decree, a thunderous clamor of applause filled the air. They approved with a roaring chant, "Joy Bangabandhu! Joy Bangabandhu! Joy Bangla!" (Victory to Bangabandhu! Victory to Bangabandhu! Victory to Bangabandhu! Victory to Bengal!)

From that day on, Sheikh Mujibur Rahman took his place in the hearts of Bengalis everywhere as Bangabandhu.

I was too deep into the crowd to read the reaction of Bangabandhu as the masses cheered.

Tofael Ahmed, then, invited him to speak. He stood up and greeted the crowd, but the slogans did not cease. In a deep bellowing voice, he spoke from the depths of his heart. He paid respect to those who were killed in the continuing struggle for democracy and autonomy. He thanked the students and the people for driving the anti-government movement and getting him out of jail.

He announced his staunch support for the Eleven-Point Charter of the students and expressed his promise to implement them. Finally, before he finished, he called upon the people and the student body to maintain their unity under any circumstance.

From that day forth, a new chapter had begun in the political arena of Bangladesh.

Farmers' Leaders: Moni Singh and Hatem Ali Khan

The previous day, we had marched in a procession from Shahid Minar to Paltan Maidan. Slogans were chanted from the procession without pause. Some of the slogans shouted, "Padma, Megna, Jamuna, is our national address! We broke down the prison doors and freed Sheikh Mujibur Rahman! Ayub-Monayem Regime, go to hell!"

There was a small group marching ahead of us. When we got near, I found an old man shouting slogans softly, but with every slogan voiced, he clinched his hand and forced it to the sky. Four or five students surrounded him. Among them was Al Mujaheedi, a Chatra League leader hailing from Tangail. He was an acquaintance of mine.

Upon getting closer, I found that the old man was none other than Hatem Ali Khan. He, too, was freed on that same day. Al Mujaheedi told me that they were going to Paltan Maidan, where all the freed political leaders including, Moni Singh and Hatem Ali Khan, were to be honored.

I went up to Hatem Ali Khan and introduced myself by referring to my father. This was a great moment for me. This was the man who inspired me with his speeches when I was a young boy. I used to dream about becoming a leader like him when I grew up. It felt good to see him marching amongst the masses. From the look of it, he was also pleased to recognize me in reference to my father's name. Then, he said he was proud to see that I was working for the nation. He added that my father must have been proud of me.

However, I wasn't so sure if this was true. Since the scholarship I earned was not enough, my father supplemented my studies with an allowance. However, the national turmoil had already affected my studies. I already lost one academic year. My father would have to support me for at least an extra year in order for me to finish. I couldn't imagine that he would have been too thrilled with my activities. My only hope was that as a politically conscious man and an activist for Hatem Ali Khan, he would understand.

Our march ended at Paltan Maidan. It was a huge gathering. People were in a festive mood. Their leaders were released from jail. There on the stage, I saw for the first time, Moni Singh, a legendary communist leader of Bengal.

Moni Singh spent most of his political life either underground or in jail. He was born of a Zamindar family. Moni Singh was wealthy and highly educated. However, the plight of the poor farmers and laborers moved him. He left his past and decided to start a new life as an advocate for farmers and laborers.

He joined the communist party and became a party figurehead. Back then; he was a source of inspiration for young men and women. There was a certain romantic appeal of taking sides with the have-nots.

Each of the freed leaders, including Moni Singh and Hatem Ali Khan, were given a warm reception. Regardless of party affiliation – the nation was united. The speakers demanded that the government accept the Eleven-Point Charter and resign immediately.

One General Out, Another General In

In reaction to the events in East Pakistan, General Ayub Khan made a last attempt to salvage his regime. On March 10th, General Ayub Khan invited leaders from all the major political parties to attend a round table conference in Rawalpindi, West Pakistan. His alleged goal was to find a political solution to the situations in the country.

Bangabandhu Sheikh Mujibur Rahman accepted the invitation to attend the roundtable conference. However, Moulana Bhashani rejected it.

It was said that one day, Bangabandhu met Moulana Bhashani, secretly, in Dhaka to discuss the issue. Moulana Bhasani reiterated his position and said, "Mujib, don't go to Rawalpindi to attend the round table conference, General Ayub Khan's regime is already dead". Bangabandhu replied, "Hujur, you are right, Auyb's regime is dead. However, I have given my word to the people. I have to attend the meeting. I am going to attend the regime's funeral".

Bangabandhu, along with his Awami League leaders, attended the conference. Bangabandhu presented the Six and Eleven-Point Charters and insisted that the implementation of these programs, alone, would satisfy the people of East Pakistan.

The West Pakistani leaders rejected the proposal. So, Bangabandhu walked out from the conference and returned to Dhaka on March 13th.

Despite the regime's unity on rejecting the six and eleven-point charters, the round table conference didn't do much in terms of regaining ground. The events in East Pakistan, coupled with the withdrawal of the Agartala Conspiracy Case and ultimate release of Sheikh Mujibur Rahman, proved to be more than enough to stifle General Ayub Khan's stronghold over the country.

Until now, General Ayub Khan's powerbase was built on the support of the army. However, this would now change. The Chief of Staff of the Pakistani Army, General Yahya Khan had been waiting for this day.

On March 25th, General Yahya Khan kicked out Ayub Khan from office and seized power. Immediately, he imposed martial law. There was a new tyrannical dictator in Pakistan.

It's ironic that just a year ago; General Ayub Khan celebrated ten years of iron-fisted rule over Pakistan. The yearlong celebration was titled "A Decade of Development". And yet, hundreds of thousands in government money and other resources were wasted to publicize the celebration itself.

Posters and advertisements in newspapers, radio, and television were used to praise Ayub's Regime. His sycophants boasted that General Ayub Khan had the support of the military, bureaucracy, and the business community. Above all, he had the support of the major super powers: America and China.

Additionally, they claimed that General Ayub enjoyed the support of the Islamic and Arab Nations. He was the ruler of Pakistan, and he had come to stay. Ayub's supporters further mocked Sheikh Mujibur Rahman's anti-Ayub campaign, by claiming the movement was "suicidal and destined for failure".

However, they completely miscalculated the political consciousness of the Bengali people and their resolve to take control of their own destiny. The regime failed to realize the people's power. Within a year after the "Decade of Development" celebration, this so-called "Field Marshal", "Iron Man", and "President for life", Ayub Khan was unceremoniously ousted from the political scene of Pakistan forever.

The effects of the round table conference proved to be much different for Bangabandhu. His unwavering commitment to the six and eleven-point charters at the conference was heard through out the nation.

Once again, Bangabandhu Sheikh Mujibur Rahman showed his bold leadership. Upon his return to East Pakistan, Bangabandhu only solidified his place in the hearts of his fellow Bengalis.

Under pressure from the masses, General Yahya Khan was forced to announce that elections to the national and provincial parliaments were to be held during the months of October and November of 1970.

He proclaimed that the newly elected National Assembly would write a new constitution for Pakistan. At which point, he would return power to the civilian government and retreat with his army to the barracks.

While Moulana Bhashani and other leftist parties chose to boycott the election, the Awami League decided to participate. The Awami League was regaining its political strength and Sheikh Mujibur Rahman's popularity was on the rise.

The Awami League hoped to get a mandate for the six and eleven-point charters through this election. The Awami League started a vigorous campaign with their recognizable election symbol, "The Boat" and set sail through the whole country.

With this political development, I was relieved that I could redirect my attention from the streets, back to the classroom. It was time for me to focus, once again, on my studies and prepare for my Final Honors Examination scheduled for January of 1971.

Tofael joins Awami League

After the charges from the Agartola Case were dropped and Bangabandhu was released, the Awami League office at Purana Paltan, once again, hummed with life. Evenings were filled with bustling crowds. Visitors from far and near flocked to the office.

On occasion, we would head out from F. H. Hall for an evening stroll. After we rounded the Stadium and Baitul Mokarram Shopping Market, we would stop by the Awami League office.

One evening at the Awami League office, we found a press conference being held for the announcement of Tofael Ahmed's joining of the Awami League. Bangabandhu, himself, was there in person. Tofael Ahmed presented a written statement expressing his firm commitment to the Six-Point Charter and his loyalty to Bangabandhu's leadership. After Tofael Ahmed had finished, the journalists requested Bangabandhu to make some comments.

In response Bangabandhu said, "Today is Tofael's day to speak. If I say something, you might be tempted to make it a headline, neglecting the importance of Tofael's announcement. This is why I am not going to say anything today. It is his day!"

During another visit to the Awami League office, I found Abdul Mannan, the Publicity Secretary of the Awami League, toiling away in his office.

I knew him from before, as he hailed from Tangail. I stopped by his office and exchanged greetings.

Our attention was then averted to a small crowd in front of Bangabandhu's office. I made my way into the crowd and found Bangabandhu talking to an Awami League delegation from Noakhali. They were requesting Bangabandhu to attend a general meeting at Noakhali to kick off the election campaign in their area.

The Awami League was in the midst of preparing for the upcoming general election. There was a great deal of excitement amongst the Awami League campaign workers.

The delegation from Noakhali expected Bangabandhu to accept their request. Bangabandhu replied by saying, "Tajuddin Ahmed is in charge of coordinating my schedules. See him and make your request".

Unfortunately, for the men from Noakhali, they had already done so and Tajuddin Ahmed told them that there was no slot for a meeting this month. In response to this news, Bangabandhu said, "Tajuddin is the Party Secretary. His word is final in this matter. But, I will be sure to give you time later."

This incident revealed the unique qualities of Bangabandhu's leadership. His adherence to the party hierarchy showed his faith in the democratic system. Despite his authority, he kept his trust with his colleagues.

Vice Chancellor Justice Abu Sayeed Choudhury

After the mass uprising of 1969, Justice Abu Sayeed Choudhury was appointed the Vice Chancellor of Dhaka University. My first reaction was negative as he was the son of Abdul Hamid Choudhury, a leader of Ayub Khan's Convention Muslim League and a former speaker of the East Pakistan Assembly.

Upon accepting his new responsibility, Justice Choudhury began meeting with various student groups and members of the faculty. This soft-spoken, polite man of small stature soon won over the hearts of many students, and eventually even my own.

He was in the newspaper almost daily. When invited, he would attend any meeting possible, and delivered speeches filled with knowledge and wisdom.

He was invited as the chief guest to the annual dinner at F. H. Hall. It was a huge arrangement under a canopy covering the entire courtyard. Loud speakers were blaring out Bangla songs throughout the day.

When Justice Choudhury arrived in the evening, the party was already in full swing. There was a festive mood that wafted through the air. The tone for the evening was set just as Rabindranath Tagore's famous song came on, "My heart is dancing like the peacock".

After the sumptuous dinner, the vice chancellor made his way visiting the dormitory rooms of his students. He wanted to see, first hand, how his students lived. As he passed from room to room, he spent a moment exchanging greetings with his students.

He stopped at my room, and upon discovering that we were both from Tangail, he opted to stay for a few more moments to talk.

Justice Choudhury will always be remembered as an affectionate and loving person.

General Secretary of the Biochemistry Department

The departments of Dhaka University each had an elected student committee to organize extracurricular activities. The head of our department was the president of the student committee. The general secretary of the student committee was elected from amongst the students.

In my 3rd year, I was elected as the General Secretary, while my classmate Motassim Billah was elected the editor of the department magazine.

The Scientist's Seven-Point Charter

The scientific community adapted a Seven-Point Charter demanding the improvement of their status and professional opportunities. This campaign began after I was elected general secretary of the biochemistry department.

In this capacity, I was elected a member of the Seven-Point Campaign Steering Committee. Kaiser, a senior student of the Soil Science Department and also a Chatra League leader, was the president of the steering committee.

Kaiser lived in F. H. Hall. One day, I went to his room to run an errand. There in his room, I happened to run into some of the leading scientists from the National Science Laboratory.

No one knew it then, but these were, in fact, the people behind the Scientist's Movement. In addition to their behind-the-scenes support, these scientists also provided some funding for the campaign.

The main purposes of the Scientist's Movement were to create job opportunities for science students and to attain an equal status, salary, and benefits to those of the civil servants.

In an attempt to realize the seven-point demands of the scientists, we organized protest meetings and marches on Curzon Hall campus. I don't quite remember, but we might have even called a one-day strike.

With General Ayub Khan gone, Governor Monayem Khan was also booted out of power. The new dictator of Pakistan, General Yahya Khan appointed Admiral Ahsan as the Governor of East Pakistan.

The Governor came to Dhaka University for the groundbreaking ceremony of the Science Annex Building. Justice Abu Sayeed Choudhury, the Vice-Chancellor, was sympathetic to the Scientist's Seven-Point Charter. He arranged a meeting for the leaders of the campaign with the governor.

Admiral Ahsan expressed his support for the Seven-Point Charter. He, himself, was a former student of science. He spoke very eloquently about the essential role played by scientists in developing the country. Justice Abu Sayeed was present in our meeting and facilitated the discussion.

The F. H. Hall Elections of 1970: The Mushtaq-Rashid Cabinet

We ran into a problem nominating candidates for the vice-president and general secretary posts for the ensuing hall elections. Anwar Hossain Manju and Abdul Kaddus Makhon were the vice-president and general secretary of the hall during the previous term.

Sheikh Fazlul Hoque Moni, the central leader of Chatra League indicated that he wanted his younger brother Sheikh Selim to be nominated, either as a candidate for vice-president, or general secretary of the Dhaka University Central Students Union (DUCSU). Abdul Rab, a Chatra League leader was nominated for vice president of DUCSU.

Meanwhile, Makhon had his eyes set on the general secretary post for himself and so, he was also nominated for DUCSU.

We nominated one of our senior students, Rashidul Alam, a fellow from Kushtia for the post of general secretary. Selim was left with only one other choice, to run for vice-president of F. H. Hall.

However, a problem arose concerning the nomination for the post of vice-president. Most of the Chatra League activists wanted someone well known on Curzon Hall Campus to run. We, the nomination committee, were in a dilemma regarding whom to nominate. On one hand, we had the desires of central leader, Sheikh Moni, and on the other, the wishes of the Chatra League activists of F. H. Hall.

After a long brainstorming session, Mushtaq Elahi was nominated for the post of Vice-President of F. H. Hall. He was a student of the Zoology Department on Curzon Hall Campus, a leader of the central committee of the Chatra League, and the Literary Secretary of DUCSU.

Mushtaq Elahi was popular amongst the students of north Bengal for his leadership against the Ayub-Monem government. He was expelled from the Medical College of North Bengal as punishment for his activities against the tyrannical regime. He had just finished his M. Sc. Degree in Zoology.

Mushtaq Elahi was a non-resident student of F. H. Hall. No one knew where he lived. We were sent out on a mission to find him. We needed to get his consent for the nomination and deposit the paperwork the next day at the Provost Office of F. H. Hall.

Mushtaq Elahi had just gotten married and was living with his sister at the time. Amin, Rashid, Habibullah, and I were finally able to locate him. When we reached his home, it was already past one in the morning.

We were hesitant to knock on the door so late at night. It crossed our minds, for a moment, to just turn around and head back, but then we realized that tomorrow was the last day to submit the nomination papers. We were determined to take his consent, before the night was over.

I mustered up some courage and knocked on the door. There was no response. After waiting for a few moments, we decided to introduce ourselves in a loud voice. This approach worked. Mushtaq Elahi opened the door. He greeted us and said, "After all these years of successfully dodging NSF thugs, I was almost certain that your knocking meant that they had finally found me."

We couldn't gauge whether Mushtaq Elahi was pleased or just annoyed by our late night visit. We explained to him why we were there. He said that he had just recently gotten married, and it was finally time to say goodbye to politics. His goal was to simply find a job and support his new family.

We apologized for disturbing him at such a late hour, but requested that he give our proposal a second thought before we left. We told him that we would come back for an answer later in the morning.

Thankfully, after a good night's sleep and undoubtedly much deliberation, Mushtaq Elahi accepted our proposal and signed the nomination papers. I guess once an activist – always an activist.

Mushtaq Elahi used to work for the weekly Banglar Bani, owned and founded by Sheikh Fazlul Hoque Moni. After depositing his nomination papers, he went to work at the newspaper office.

Sheikh Moni teased Mushtaq Elahi by saying that "If you were so eager to become the vice-president of F. H. Hall, why didn't you just tell me so before?"

We launched campaigns for the Rab-Makhon panel for DUCSU and the Mushtaq-Rashid panel for F.H. Hall in full force.

In addition to Amin, Habibullah, and myself, our campaign team consisted of Julfiqqar, Babul, Gias, Majid, Nazrul, Milon, and many others.

Amin, Habibullah, and I were dubbed the "Three Jewels of the Chatra League" of F. H. Hall. Had the French expression the "Three Musketeers" or the Chinese expression the "Gang of Three" gotten currency at that time, we would have undoubtedly been referred to as such.

Often, we would dispatch into groups to reach out to the non-residential student voters throughout Dhaka city.

One day, Chatra League President Noore Alam Siddiqui came down to F. H. Hall to campaign for our election. He made a fiery speech in support of the Rab-Makhon and Mushtaq-Rashid panels. He had a poetic control of the Bangla language. He manipulated beautiful prose and imagery to compose a lengthy speech. However, his message could have been summarized in just a few stanzas. Nonetheless, the students listened to him with rapturous attention and exploded in applause after he finished.

In contrast, Makhon spoke rather simply. After the meeting, Noore Alam Siddiqui gave me a few hundred takas to help with the election campaign costs. I distributed this money among the campaign workers for their rickshaw fare and other expenses.

Abdur Razzaque, a senior student of the Physics Department and a Chatra League worker, spent a lot of time at the hall working for the party. However, he was a non-resident student.

One day, I gave him some money to campaign among the non-resident students. The next day, he returned half of the money to me, stating that he campaigned door to door on foot. Therefore, he had no rickshaw expenses. He asked me to give this money to another worker.

My heart was filled with admiration for his honesty and dedication. It was because of the efforts of thousands of activists like Razzaque that the Chatra League could make such a historical contribution to the causes of Bengali nationalism and the Liberation Movement.

Nabi and Bokul, Face to Face

Rokeya Hall was Dhaka University's female student's dormitory. In the Rokeya Hall elections of that year, Rafia Akhter Dolly and Hashi were heading the Chatra League Panel.

The opposition was lead by the Maleka-Ayesha Panel of the Chatra Union. The Chatra Union always won elections in Rokeya Hall. However, that year the Chatra League was expected to win, riding the coattails of the People's Uprising of 1969. To ensure our victory, we launched a very strong campaign for the Dolly-Hashi Panel on Curzon Hall Campus.

One day, while carrying out my campaign duties on Curzon Hall Campus, I ran into my classmates Bokul and Atia, who were residents of Rokeya Hall. They were Chatra Union campaign workers. Almost immediately, we began arguing.

At one point, they alleged that in anticipation of the smashing defeat, the Dolly-Hashi panel was trying to buy votes. I didn't know how to respond to the absurd allegation.

There is a saying "It is where there is fear of tigers that darkness is likely to fall." Right at that moment, Dolly was campaigning on Curzon Hall Campus and stopped to greet us.

I immediately reported to her the allegations raised by Bokul and Atia. They were caught off guard. They couldn't believe that I was so quick to report to Dolly. I myself was a little embarrassed that I couldn't hold my tongue. However, Dolly took the claim with a grain of salt and replied, "Regardless of what you might say against me now, I know that come polling time, you two will be sure to cast your votes for me."

The two Chatra Union campaign workers were put at ease by her response and said, "We were just teasing one of your diehard supporters."

The Rab-Makhon panel won the 1970 DUCSU Elections. In F. H. Hall the Mustaq-Rashid Panel won by a landslide. However, The Dolly-Hashi panel lost by a narrow margin in the Rokeya Hall election.

In the S. M. Hall election, Syed Ahmed and Anwar-ul Alam Shaheed of the Chatra League, were elected vice-president and general secretary, respectively. Shaheed was a student leader from Tangail.

The Chatra League went on to win elections in other halls, as well. The landslide victory of the Chatra League in this election had strengthened Bangabandhu's grip on national politics.

Chatra League Rivalries

Ever since its birth, Chatra League participated in various movements for democratic rule and autonomy in East Pakistan. They challenged the autocratic rule of the Ayub-Monayem regime. Sheikh Fazlul Hoque Moni, Sirajul Alam Khan, Abdur Razzaque, Tofael Ahmed, and many others led Chatra League in these movements.

In 1967, Ferdous Ahmed Quoreshi and Abdur Razzaque were the president and general secretary of the Chatra League, respectively.

In the following year, at a national conference at the Engineers' Institute, Abdur Rauf and Khaled Mohammad Ali were elected the president and general secretary of the Chatra League.

Ferdous Quereshi and Al Mujahedi formed a rival committee. However, this committee failed to get recognition from either the Chatra League or the Awami League.

During the conference, F. H. Hall was selected as the resting place for delegates from Tangail. Fazlur Rahman Khan Faruk, a central Chatra League leader from Tangail made these arrangements. A few of these delegates were accommodated in my room.

One of the guests was a student leader from Tangail. He was tall and fair in complexion. His friends had introduced him to me as the younger brother of Latif Siddiqui, a student leader of Tangail. The name of this polite and soft-spoken student leader was Abdul Kader Siddiqui. Kader Siddiqui would one day go on to become one of the most legendary figures in Bangladeshi history. However, on that day in 1968, this tall fair skinned young man looked like nothing more than your average Chatra League activist.

Chatra League became a strong organization during the Agartola Conspiracy Case and the Eleven-Point Movement. During this time, Tofael Ahmed, then vice-president of DUCSU emerged as the undisputed leader of not only the Chatra League, but also the student community as a whole. By then, he was making headlines in both national and international press.

In 1970, Noore Alam Siddiqui and Shahjahan Siraj were president and general secretary of the Chatra League, respectively. At the same time, Abdur Rab and Abdul Quddus Makhon were vice-president and general secretary of the Dhaka University Central Students Union. Later, these four student leaders became fondly known as the "Char Khalifa" (the four Kalifs).

The student leaders of the early 1960s: Fazlul Hoque Moni, Sirajul Alam Khan, and Abdur Razzaque became youth Awami League leaders by the end of the decade. As youth leaders, they coordinated activities between the Chatra League and the Awami League.

However, there was a subtle rivalry, which soon arose among these three leaders. Questions came to surface that spawned this rivalry. How much control would each leader have over the Chatra League? Who would pick the next leader of the Chatra League?

Sirajul Alam Khan was the most active in group-politics. He resided with a student named Rumi in S. M. Hall, though Sirajul Alam Khan himself was no longer a student of Dhaka University. He could be often seen riding around in the backseat of Rumi's motorcycle.

Sirajul Alam Khan was known as "Dada" in the Chatra League circle. From time to time, he used to come to F. H. Hall and was often found chatting with students loyal to him. Sometimes, he was also seen during the evening shows at the Naz Cinema Hall, where only English films were shown.

He always sat in the same seat in the last row of the movie theatre. Among his associates in F. H. Hall, Amin, Habibullah, Julfiqqar, and Gias later joined the Jatiyo Shomajtantrik Dal (JSD) of Sirajul Alam Khan.

The grouping and lobbying between Abdul Razzaque and Sheikh Moni were not as active as Sirajul Alam Khan's. Within the Chatra League, all three were also distinguished with their ideological differences.

Sirajul Alam Khan was known as a leftist, Moni a rightist and Razzaque walked along the middle of the road. Whatever their differences were, they were united in their commitment to Bengali nationalism and their allegiance to Bangabandhu Sheikh Mujibur Rahman.

The Power of the Slogan

Between 1967 and 1970, the anti-government rallies and processions utilized slogans to encourage and excite student activists. These slogans were short scripts that rolled rhythmically off of one's tongue. Authors of the slogans were usually anonymous. However, these slogans were well planned and well written to express the ideals and objectives of the movement succinctly.

In 1968, the Chatra League Convention was held at the Engineers Institute. For the first time at this conference, a few students raised the slogan "Joy Bangla!" (Victory to Bengal!)

At that time, members and leaders of Chatra League were not yet ready for the slogan. As a result, a few angered students attacked those initiating the slogan. Some of these chanting students were even left wounded.

The message was premature for leaders and activists of the Chatra League. However, only one year later, "Joy Bangla!" would be chanted by every Bengali and became the war cry for the Bangladesh Liberation Movement.

The history of "Joy Bangla", its propagation, and acceptance proved that there were a few people in society, who would always be ahead of their time. Soon, the masses would accept this cry and follow them.

These days were filled with many exciting and rousing slogans. Translated, some of the slogans read as followed:

"Your country, my country – Bangladesh! Bangladesh!"

"Yours address, my address - Padma, Meghna, Jamuna!"

"We will break down the prison doors and free Sheikh Mujibur Rahman!"

"Ayub and Monayem are brothers – hang them from the same rope!"

"Your leader, my leader – Sheikh Mujib! Sheikh Mujib!"

"Scrap the Agartala Case! – Scrap it! Scrap it!"

"Liberation's true name is struggle!"

"Eleven-Points! Eleven-Points! – Grant it! Accept it!"

"Down with the Ayub regime!"

In those days, folk songs found a place in public meetings, too. Aside from providing entertainment, these songs carried political messages. There was a popular song sung by Apel Mahmood, which said, "O Bengali tui hishab shikh-re!" (Oh Bengali, learn how to protect your interests).

Another song by Abdul Jabbar sang: "O Mujib baiya jao-re" (Oh Mujib, march forward!) also gained huge popularity.

There were a few talented individuals who specialized in firing up rallies and marches with slogans. One would start by giving out the first line of the slogan at the top of his lungs and then the crowd would respond in rhyme with the next line electrifying the atmosphere.

Some of the Chatra League activists became experts in the art of slogan chanting. No one could match their emotion and zeal. It seemed as if these slogans spewed from their hearts.

There were many such great slogan-artists, but I can only remember a few. The ones I still remember today are: Chishti and Nazrul (killed in the Liberation War), Mahboob, Aftab, and Rabiul. Among the female activists, Momtaz was the most famous.

In those days, these slogans ignited fire in our blood, as we marched in rallies and processions for the Liberation Movement.

Graffiti (Chika Mara)

Various innovative methods were used to propagate the aims and objectives of the movement among the masses. One of these measures was to utilize mobile public address systems, which were mounted on the tops of rickshaws.

Activists rented these systems and publicized schedules for meetings and processions. The primary supplier of this service was a company by the name of "Call-Ready". Any newspaper report covering a rally or demonstration was sure to have a photograph with a shot of a "CALL-READY" microphone right in front of the speakers.

Mounting posters on the walls was another method of publicity. No one knew where these posters were made or printed. However, they always managed to reach the halls of the university and the rest of Dhaka, just in the nick of time.

The management of the movement mirrored that of wartimes. Responsibilities and posts were all pre-assigned. There was a complex web of networks, which allowed for information and messages to pass freely amongst activists. This resulted in an efficient execution of programs. Our central leaders would coordinate these tasks. Throughout the mass uprising of 1969 and the Non-Cooperation Movement of 1970, our group in F. H. Hall, along with several others, executed these tasks.

Writing slogans and programs on walls and roads was known as "Chika Mara" (rat killing), which was Bengali slang for graffiti. When one was given the task of writing graffiti on the walls, they had to do so at night without getting caught by the police. How this task came to be known as Chika Mara is unclear, but one could probably make a guess.

The prevailing story of the day went as follows: One day, an activist was just about to write on a wall when a police officer spotted him in the distance. The officer shouted out, "Hey, what's going on?" To this, the activist innocently replied, "Nothing. I am just trying to kill a rat."

During the Liberation Movement, Dhaka was blanketed with posters and slogans. Unfortunately, Chika Mara had no effect on the rat population and they continued to proliferate happily.

In addition to me, the F. H. Hall's chika mara squad included Rashidul Alam, Amin, Habibullah, Julfiqqar, Gias, Nazrul and others. We would work all night long. At the end of the night, tired and hungry, we would go to restaurants on Topekhana Road for tea and snacks. Some of these restaurants were open through the night.

The waiters of the restaurants cordially received us as their regular midnight customers. Our other option was to go to a restaurant on the east side of F. H. Hall in the shanty area. However, the food there was never any good. In contrast, the parata and mutton curry of the Topekhana Road restaurants were unrivaled.

The restaurants on Topekhana Road also played music on loudspeakers all through the night. Deep into the night, the silence of the slumbering city was embalmed with these songs.

Tired and listless, I truly enjoyed listening to those songs, as I sipped my spiced-sweet milk tea. The voices of popular artists like Hemonta, Shandhya, Manna De, and others still ring in my ears. One of my favorite songs was a parody that went, "My three teenage sister-in-laws are never up to any good, they fool around, and I get complaints everyday from the neighborhood…"

The Cyclone and Tidal Waves of November 1970

On November 12th, 1970, a devastating cyclone and its resulting tidal waves hit the East Pakistan islands of Hatia, Sandwip, Ramgoti, Potuakhali, Moheshkhali, Bhola, and Southern Chittagong.

Hundreds of thousands of people and cattle were killed in this natural disaster. The National Weather Department failed to warn the masses of the coming storm. The West Pakistani officer in charge of the department did not feel that it was necessary to broadcast any such warning.

As a result, thousands of people were washed away, while they were still asleep. The cyclone bore tidal waves, which rose as high as thirty to forty feet, washing away cattle, property, and everything else in between.

The news of the catastrophic destruction and loss of lives reached Dhaka after two days. Those who survived the devastation of the cyclone could have been saved had news of the disaster reached Dhaka in time. All of East Pakistan was in shock from the loss, as well as the irresponsibility of the National Weather Department.

Pakistan's military dictator, General Yahya Khan stopped in Dhaka on his way back from China to West Pakistan. His first point of order was to attend a party at the residence of a Bengali businesswoman that evening.

After the party was over, he flew directly back to West Pakistan. The President of Pakistan, General Yahya Khan, did not feel it necessary to visit the people of his country who had fallen victim to the cyclone. Apparently, even the Governor of East Pakistan was too preoccupied to tend to the matter.

Bengalis were shocked and enraged by this step-motherly treatment meted out by the provincial and central governments of Pakistan. If the people didn't already feel it before, this was surely a wake-up call. The autonomy of East Pakistan was essential for the survival of the Bengali people.

The student community of Dhaka University organized a massive effort to gather relief for the victims. We, the students of the Biochemistry Department, broke into groups and set out to collect relief material from the citizens of Dhaka. I went door to door at

Azimpur Residential Colony with a group. People donated generously to meet their needs.

The Central Government of Pakistan failed to come to the rescue of the victims of the 1970 cyclone in the coastal districts of East Pakistan. Instead, vultures preyed on the corpses of cyclone victims.

Bangabandhu postponed his election campaign and made a trip to the devastated areas with relief supplies. Moulana Bhashani, after a similar trip to the cyclone ravaged areas, called a public meeting at Poltan Maidan in Dhaka. He criticized the Central Government for a lack of relief efforts. However, he stressed the need for poverty alleviation, before the elections.

He questioned the ethics of election campaigns at a time when people needed succor. Moulana Bhashani had already boycotted the election. The tragedy of the cyclone only provided an excuse for his preexisting stance against the election.

A famous Bengali poet, Shamsur Rahman, was so moved by the tragedy and Bhashani's speech that it inspired him to write the poem "Sofed Panjabi" (White Panjabi). It was in reference to the white clothing adorned by Moulana Bhashani as he delivered his speech.

Press Conference of Bangabandhu

Coming back from his trip to the cyclone-torn areas, Bangabandhu called a press conference at Hotel Shahbag on November 26th. Amin, Habibullah, and I were selected as volunteers at the press conference.

We arrived long before the press conference started. It was an average sized hall, but became packed with national and international journalists, before Bangabandhu and his associates arrived.

Bangabandhu came in and sat on the seat reserved for him, flanked by Taj Uddin and Syed Nazrul Islam to his right and left. Dr. Kamal Hossain and other leaders were seated in the back row. We stood just behind them.

As Bangabandhu greeted his audience and began speaking, a storm of flash bulbs went off against the constant clicking of cameras. Bangabandhu expressed his grief for the loss of hundreds of thousands of people and their properties. He went on with great pain, as he described the miserable plight of those who were still alive.

He scathingly criticized the neglect and apathy of the human crisis by the central and provincial governments of Pakistan. He then explained how the Six-Point Charter, drawn by the Awami League, was essential and could have helped the people during such a tragedy. He stressed that if there was autonomy in East Pakistan, this kind of calamity could have been better managed. We wouldn't have to look for help from a Central Government that rests peacefully thousands of miles away.

A number of journalists repeatedly shot questions at Bangabandhu: "Does this catastrophe indicate that East Pakistan will become independent? Is the Six-Point Charter a precursor to independence? Will you follow Moulana Bhashani's appeal to postpone the election?" Bangabandhu cautiously replied to all of the questions.

At one point, a journalist nagged him with the question: "Is East Pakistan's independence a hidden agenda for the Six-Point Charter?"

To this, Dr. Kamal Hossain stood up from his seat and replied in English, "Gentlemen, Bangabandhu has answered all of your questions. I hope you are all satisfied. This is the end of press conference. Thank you very much."

This was a very smart move. As if Bangabandhu had heaved a sigh of relief, he stood up to leave. Even then, the journalists followed him and continued bombarding him with questions. Nonetheless, Bangabandhu remained silent.

The press conference was attended by a host of foreign journalists. Eloquently, Bangabandhu replied to all of their questions in fluent English.

This was the first time I had ever seen Bangabandhu up-close. I was amazed to see how skillfully and diplomatically he managed the barrage of questions at the press conference. I thought to myself that under his leadership, I would do anything for my country.

I also appreciated the timely interception by Dr. Kamal Hossain at the end of the press conference. It seemed to me that Dr. Hossain was very adept at reading the mind of Bangabandhu.

Hunger Strike

The families of many students hailing from the southern parts of the country suffered losses because of the cyclone and tidal waves. Many students had to rush to the aid of their families. These students were unable to sit for final examinations. They needed more time to study.

To press their demand, they resorted to a hunger strike under the banyan tree at the Arts Building. Solaiman from our class took part in the hunger strike. With one of our own involved, we had no choice, but to attend. Justice Abu Sayeed Choudhury was sympathetic to the cause. Ultimately, he deferred the examination and ended the hunger strike by feeding the strikers with his own hand.

The indescribable suffering of the cyclone victims, once again, showed that we were being treated as second-class citizens of Pakistan. It was now clear to all of us that the Central Government had no concern for us. Our future lied in our own hands.

American Journalist

Foreign journalists swarmed through Dhaka to cover the election of 1970. One morning, a few weeks before the election, I had finished eating breakfast at the cafeteria.

As I was returning to my room, a taxi pulled up to the hall gate. In those days, taxis were only available in front of the Hotel Intercontinental (now the Sheraton). The taxis provided services to hotel guests traveling to and from the airport.

Before I knew it, a white man got out of the taxi and said hello to me. He was a reporter. I think he said he was from the Washington Post. Nonetheless, I am sure he was an American. He was looking for an interpreter to communicate with villagers about their views on the upcoming election. He asked if I could help him and offered me an honorarium. I did not want to miss this opportunity. I rushed to my room, changed clothes, and returned to the taxi.

We went to Savar, a village not far from Dhaka. After leaving the paved road, we drove along the dirt road as far as it would take us. The two of us went around from door-to-door through the village, talking to the villagers.

By the time we had gotten to the village, I had already told him that I was a Chatra League Activist and a diehard follower of Bangabandhu. This news made him a little concerned. He was worried that my affiliation would bias the translation. He made me promise that I would merely translate the villager's statement, as it was, without interjecting any of my own opinions. And so, I gave him my word.

The villages we visited were scattered far from the paved road. The villagers were poor farmers. In some yards, we could see men milking cows, while in others, they were thrashing paddy. Young children ran around naked, playing in the grass.

This area was a part of the constituency of Ataur Rahman Khan, the former Chief Minister of East Pakistan. He was contesting in the election as an independent candidate. The American was a very professional reporter. I expected him to carry a camera, but he only carried with him a paper and pen. I thought pictures of villages would be more helpful for him. However, as a veteran war correspondent in Vietnam, he thought otherwise.

Primarily, he put three questions to the villagers. Whether they support Sheikh Mujibur Rahman, who they will vote for in the Provincial Assembly, and who they will vote for in the National Assembly.

In response to the questions, they said they supported Sheikh Mujibur Rahman and that they would all vote for the Awami League in the National Assembly. However, they all intended to vote for Atuar Rahman Khan for the Provincial Assembly, as he was the former Chief Minister of East Pakistan. As the election results later proved, these villagers stood true to their word.

In the evening, the foreign journalist dropped me of at F. H. Hall. Before leaving, he thanked me and shoved a hundred dollar bill in my hand. My jaw dropped. In those days, it was a dream to earn such a huge amount of money in a single day. For the first time in my life, I knew the smell of a dollar.

My Mother

It was December 1970. I was preparing for the Honors Final Examination. Because I was preoccupied by my involvement with the Eleven-Point Charter and the people's uprising, I fell behind with my studies. This hampered my progress.

To make up for the lost time, I was working extra hard. Just at this critical moment, I received a disheartening message. My mother had fallen ill. I dropped everything and rushed home.

When I saw my mother, I could not believe my eyes. My mother was a rather small woman. She was a beautiful lady with a fair complexion and rosy cheeks. It was the hue of her cheeks that brought her the nickname "Lal" (red). Her face had a charm that was very calming.

Now, she was lying in her bed, sick for a month, as her body had atrophied. She was reduced to half the woman she once was. Her belly was swollen and water had accumulated in her legs.

Our local doctor was looking after her, but the treatment showed no results, as he could not diagnose the disease. My mother knew the news of her illness would affect my studies. So, she asked that I be left in the dark about her condition.

However, now that the situation had deteriorated beyond control, I had to be informed. I wasted no time and brought my mother to Dhaka by bus. That six-hour journey was very painful for my mother.

I guessed my mother had cancer. I decided to get her admitted into the Post-Graduate Hospital. However, it was difficult to get admission directly into the hospital. A friend of mine suggested that I take my mother to the private clinic of Dr. Nurul Islam, the director of the P. G. Hospital. If he examined my mother and recommended her for admission, it would not be hard getting her into the hospital. I followed my friend's advice.

Dr. Islam examined my mother for five or six minutes and came to the conclusion that she might, indeed, have cancer of the liver. He gave me a note for her admission into P. G. Hospital.

P. G. Hospital occupied the southern part of Dhaka Medical College, close to F. H. Hall. My mother was admitted there.

Dr. Nurul Islam carried out various tests for about two weeks and disclosed to me that the cancer affecting my mother had taken a turn for the worse. There was no use treating her any longer. The few days she had left needed to be spent amongst her loved ones. He asked me to take her home, as soon as possible.

In the two weeks she was at the hospital, her health had further deteriorated. She could not eat the hospital food at all. During the day, I had to go to class. However, I spent my nights by my mother's side in the hospital.

In the evening, when I returned to her side, she would complain to me about the nurses. They did not respond to her calls, and even when they did, they tended to misbehave with her. I found this news to be infuriating, but alas, there was nothing I could do. I could not afford to confront the nurses, as I relied on them to be with her during the day. My mother's life lay in their hands.

Since F. H. Hall was in close proximity to P. G. Hospital, I was able to manage both the responsibilities of caring for my ill mother and attending to my studies at the university.

Now, I had a dilemma. How could I take my mother back to Tangail? She was so sick that it was impossible to travel by bus. She could not even sit. The cancer had caused her belly to further swell, while water continued to accumulate in her legs. In pain, her groans cried through the air. I could no longer bear the sufferings of my mother. I felt helpless.

I had faced the thugs of Monayem Khan and fought to bring down the autocratic rule of the "Iron-Man", Ayub Khan, and yet, I fell helpless in the face of my own mother's sufferings. I could do nothing to alleviate her pains. I could not take it any more.

When together, my mother would take my hands into hers and hold them for hours. I too, could not keep her out of my thoughts. The problem of taking my mother to Tangail was haunting me.

Deeply engrossed in my thoughts, I was walking along the bank of the pond. I was on my way back to F. H. Hall, when I met Abul Fazal at the hall gate. He was my friend and classmate. He could see the worry in my face. Immediately, he inquired about my troubles.

I told him about my mother and my present quandary. He paused for a moment, and said to give him some time. He suggested that I return to my room, eat something, and wait for him.

Fazal returned after sometime with a smile running from cheek to cheek. He looked at me and said, "I have arranged a car to take aunty home". Fazal told me that his uncle, Khondker Mushtaque Ahmed just happened to have an extra car. He had acquired the car during the recent election campaign. Mr. Ahmed was away visiting his constituency in Comilla for the evening and would be gone till the following day. He took his own car with him, leaving this one lying idle. The car was at his residence at Agamoshi Lane awaiting his return. As a relative of Khondker Mushtaque, Fazal took this opportunity to make an arrangement with the driver. Under the circumstances, I was able to use the car from night till noon the next day.

I still cannot find the words to thank him for this unforgettable service. I finally understood the phrase, "A friend in need is a friend indeed".

I immediately set out for Gopalpur via Tangail with my mother and reached my cousin Bokul's house at night. My mother was lying semi-conscious on my lap in the back seat of the car. Despite being half-awake, my mother did not let go of my hand for a moment. There truly is a special bond between a mother and her child.

I realized that if I took the car all the way to my village, it would not return to Dhaka before noon. I had no intention of getting my friend in trouble, and so, we decided to stay at Bokul's and told the driver to take the car back in the morning.

Early in the morning, Bokul's husband left for the village to inform my family of our arrival. In the morning, my father and elder brother arrived, along with some other relatives.

Everyone burst into tears at the sight of my mother's condition. Meanwhile, my mother had already lost the ability to speak.

Over the last two weeks, I was overwhelmed with taking care of my mother. I watched as she slowly crept towards death. I became conditioned. My senses were dulled and my emotions grew numb. I forgot how to cry. Deep within me, I knew these were my last moments with my mother. I was not willing to leave her side.

Nonetheless, my father and brother insisted on my return to Dhaka to take the Honors Final Examination, which was now only a few days away. I couldn't help it. I didn't want to leave my mother's side. I thought to myself, I could always take the exam next year, but if my mother were to pass, I would never see her again. I spent the whole morning with these thoughts running through my mind.

My father sat down with me again. He explained to me that life and death fall only at the hands of our Creator. Miraculously, people have survived even graver conditions than that from which my mother suffered. He told me to be strong and keep my faith in God. He asked me to continuously pray for my mother reciting "Sura Yunus", a verse from the Koran. After much consoling, he persuaded me to get into the car and return to Dhaka.

Before I got in the car, I took one last look at my mother.

Once inside the car, something happened to me. The emotion that sat dormant for so long, suddenly overpowered me. I began to bawl. Torrents of tears rolled down my cheeks. I was completely unable to control my emotions.

The driver of the car stopped many times to console me. In spite of the depressive mood, I could not forget the act of kindness my friend and the driver had shown to me by enabling me to take my mother home. I asked him to stop at the bus station in Tangail for a brief moment.

Despite his reluctance, I bought the famous Porabari chom-chom sweets, a specialty of Tangail for the driver to take home.

I would receive a letter every week with the news that mother's condition continued to stay the same. Under the influence of painkillers, she would sleep all day. With every letter, I was assured that if the situation got worse, my family would inform me.

At long last, the Honors Final Examination was over. The Liberation Movement of 1968-69 and my mother's illness just before the examination had effected my studies. I didn't do as well as I had hoped.

At noon, the very next day, my father showed up at my dorm. He embraced me with a big hug. Immediately, I knew what had happened. He hadn't hugged me since the first day I moved to the student dormitory in the sixth grade. That was nearly ten years ago.

Holding each other, we cried. My mother had died in her sleep last week. She was buried that same day. Since I was right in the middle of my exams, my family chose not to inform me. My future and education were more important to my parents, than was a final moment with my ailing mother. This was possibly the cruelest virtue of middle class values.

While consoling me, my father said that if I had dropped the examination, I would have fallen a year behind. The scholarship money would have stopped, resulting in monetary hardships.

Additionally, there was no way of predicting, which way my mother's condition would turn. Suppose I dropped the examination and did return home. Then suppose she survived. I would have dropped the examination for nothing. Considering all of these factors and the importance of the honors examination, my father waited till now to inform me of my mother's death.

My father looked at me and said, "You are a grown up now. You have worked for the country. You must now take into consideration your own interests."

My father spoke more about the sense of responsibility than the sorrow of the loss.

During my first three years away from home, I had visited my family every vacation. In the last three, while I was engulfed in the movement, I had only visited my family once or twice.

My mother used to complain about my lack of visits, while I pointed to my studies as my excuse. However, I don't think she bought it. Though I wasn't with her physically, she was always in my thoughts. I could always feel her love and affection around me, as if she was sitting awake by my side.

After my mother's death, I felt as if I had been uprooted from the earth. I felt detached and alone in the world.

1970 Election

Chatra League activists were instructed to go to their respective electoral constituency and work for Awami League candidates. In those days, university students were received as honorable and respectable members of society. Their presence would help Awami League candidates.

With this belief, I went to my constituency of Gopalpur and Bhuapur to work for Awami League candidate, Hatem Ali Talukdar. I met the Awami League candidate at the office of the president of the Gopalpur District Awami League, Dr. Najibur Rahman.

I explained to Mr. Talukdar the purpose of my visit. He told me that he understood my intentions, but my help was not needed. He was confident that the election would fall in his favor. His words carried a subtle condescending undertone. Mr. Talukdar was not an educated man.

I don't know whether he was threatened by my higher education, or just carried the burden of some other inferiority complex, but he refused to welcome my assistance. So, I went home, rested for two days, and then returned to Dhaka.

We, the student activists of F. H. Hall were given the responsibility to campaign for Bangabandhu Sheikh Mujibur Rahman and Advocate Zahiruddin, for the National Assembly. We were also given the task of campaigning for Gazi Golam Mostafa, a candidate for the Provincial Assembly.

We organized ourselves into several groups and went out to campaign door-to-door. We paid special attention to voters in Old Dhaka so that they did not vote for Khawza Khoiruddin. Khawza Khoiruddin was a member of Dhaka's Nawbab Family and a Muslim League candidate. His family had a great deal of influence in Old Dhaka.

Khawza Khoiruddin told the people of Old Dhaka that votes for Sheikh Mujibur Rahman and his Six-Point Charter would be votes for the end of Pakistan.

During our door-to-door visits with the voters, almost everyone told us that Sheikh Kamal, the eldest son of Bangabandhu, had already visited them. Sheikh Kamal was a Chatra League activist. He was a young and energetic man with an extraordinary organizing capacity. In search of votes for Awami League candidates, Sheikh Kamal and his friends had already combed the streets of Dhaka city.

Election Day

A number of student leaders received Awami League nominations in the General Election of 1970. Two student leaders were nominated for the Provincial Assembly in Tangail, Fazlur Rahman Khan and Abdul Latif Siddiqui. Fazlur Rahman Faruk was nominated for the Mirjapur constituency and Abdul Latif Siddiqui was nominated for the Kalihati constituency.

Faruk was also a leader from F. H. Hall. On Election Day, Faruk requested that we visit his polling centers as observers. Accordingly Rashid, Amin, Habibullah, and I reached Mirjapur early in the morning by bus. Since Faruk was busy traveling from one polling center to the next, he could not meet us at the bus station. However, he did provide us with a chauffeured car for the day.

Faruk left a message with the driver instructing us to visit each and every polling center. He asked us to stay at each center for sometime, so that we could talk to the people, before we moved on. I wasn't quite sure how our presence was going to make a difference exactly. I assume that because we were Dhaka University student leaders that our presence would be able to draw some support for the Awami League.

We spent the whole day visiting polling centers, talking to Awami League activists and voters. At the end of the day, we became sure of an Awami League victory in Tangail. That evening we had dinner in Tangail. We especially enjoyed Tangail's famous Porabari chom-chom.

After our bellies were full and our appetites satisfied, we set out for Dhaka by car. Once we arrived to Dhaka we made our way directly to the Awami League office, instead of going to F. H. Hall.

It was midnight. Election results were coming in. The early results hinted at a landslide victory for Awami League. There was an excitement in the office. The smell of victory wafted through the air. Nonetheless, for the four of us, it had been quite a long and arduous day.

We were tired, and so, we returned to F. H. Hall to retire for the night. However, when we got back to the dorms, sleep was the farthest thing from our minds. We found that Provost Dr. Fakruzzaman was watching the live election results on television at his residence. We decided to join him.

Like flies on honey, we were glued to the television set till the mid-afternoon. By this point, we had no doubt that the Awami League boat had set sail and was pushing full-steam ahead.

The Awami League captured 167 out of the 169 seats in the National Assembly and 305 out of 310 seats in the Provincial Assembly. This emphatically made it clear to the world at large that Bengalis were totally united in their demand for autonomous rule.

Bangabandhu and his colleagues in a happy mood after the Awami League's overwhelming victory in the general election of 1970

My Mother, My Land, and Me

I was lost in a trance in the four years between 1967 and 1970. The tyrannical rule of Ayub-Monayem, the Agartala Conspiracy Case, the eleven-point movement, the People's Uprising, the Election of 1970, and other such momentous events tore my life from its normal course. I was a lone island, amidst an unforgiving tempest. Waves of political commotion, brutal police and military action thrashed upon my shores.

My life became circumscribed within a small segment of Dhaka centering on F. H. Hall. Each of the other halls of the university namely, Iqbal Hall, S. M. Hall, Rokeya Hall, Jinnah Hall, Mohsin Hall, and Dhaka Hall, had made equally important contribution to the mass movements.

As Tofael Ahmed, leader of the eleven-point movement, lived in Iqbal Hall, it was known as the center of student politics. However, as I was a resident of F. H. Hall, the majority of my recollections centered on this dormitory.

Just as a single tree can block the view of an entire forest, the student movement detached me from reality and the rest of the world around me. One day, as if a curtain was removed from over my eyes, I could suddenly see things beyond my segment of Dhaka. It was December of 1970.

After hearing news of my mother's sickness, I found myself aboard a bus heading towards Tangail. The only thought on my mind was that of my mother's illness. Nothing else seemed to matter. The mere thought of this woman would inspire heavenly feelings from deep within my soul and the whole world would seem so sweet. It was she, my mother, who was now sick. With a disengaged mind, I tried to browse over a mental picture of my mother's present condition.

Slowly, my eyes drifted across the faces, dresses, and conversations of my fellow travelers. Reality finally hit me. By every bus stop on the Dhaka-Tangail Highway, by every front yard that we passed, I was shocked to see the sunken faces of the poverty-stricken people and their malnourished children. What a strange and different world I was in now. This was no Dhaka. This was not what I was used to.

Having been within the confines of the capital, I was unprepared to see how much the country had deteriorated. This deterioration was magnified further, when I reached my village.

The name of my village was Khamarpara. It was a small village that grew around a big pond with its dwelling houses. This is where I was born. This is where I spent the most wonderful days of my childhood. In those days, one could see this joy and happiness gleaming from every household. But, as the years passed, this happiness had started to fade away. In the last four years, the situation had completely worsened.

I was surrounded by miserable faces. Roads and ways fell in disrepair. Bamboo fences surrounding homes were left in shambles. Many of these people were living in dilapidated houses. Others were forced to sell their homes just to feed their families. More and more, farmers were becoming day laborers. Many children were going about without clothing. There was no doctor at Hemnagar Medical Center. No doctor had returned after the last government doctor left. Even the pharmacy was closed. Instead, cattle grazed the medical center compound.

The symbol of pride and self-respect of the middle class rested on their ownership of land and home. The selling of their property to escape hunger bore serious blows to their family name and honor. They felt belittled.

I was terribly upset at the sight of my sick mother. But, I was doubly shocked to learn that my father had to sell portions of our land to meet the cost of my mother's treatment. My elder brother was still out of work.

The prices of goods, which had shot up during the 1965 war with India, had not yet come down. To top it all off, there were repeated floods that ravaged the countryside over the last few years. Half of our land was dedicated to cultivating jute. However, the price of jute had fallen significantly.

Given all of these factors, my father was short on cash. He had no choice, but to sell his land. My mother vehemently protested, "I just have a simple fever! It will eventually go away on its own. There is no need to sell any land!"

I was bitter. I felt guilty and helpless. I could do nothing to protect my father's honor and dignity. To complete my honors course studies it took me four years instead of three. Had there not been a movement, I could have certainly finished sooner.

My sense of helplessness only intensified when I took my mother with me back to Dhaka for treatment. It was too late. Even the best medical care could not help. In spite of having been surrounded by the most loving and caring people, my mother had to suffer excruciating pain before she left this beautiful world.

I couldn't make sense of what was going on. In one hand, I held my personal interests. In the other, I held national interests. Though, I could not fulfill my personal responsibilities, I had consolation in knowing that I had done my part in the national liberation movement.

In the course of human civilization, there comes a time when youth gladly make the supreme sacrifice for their motherland. My concern for self-interest was overshadowed by the call of Bangabandhu and Bangladesh. The thunderous voice of Bangabandhu instilled in me an ironclad resolve. We had to liberate Bengalis from Pakistani exploitation and misrule.

I had rediscovered that individual happiness lied in the collective wellbeing and achievement. This newfound realization inspired me to further dedicate myself to the Liberation Movement.

Moulana Abdul Hamid Khan Bhashani

In the early 1960s, after the passing of two popular Bengali national leaders, Hossain Shahid Suhrawardy and Shere Bangla Fazlul Haque, only two popular leaders remained, Moulana Bhashani and Bangabandhu Sheik Mujibur Rahman.

In 1949, Moulana Bhashani, Shamsul Haque, Sheikh Mujibur Rahman, and others formed the East Pakistan Awami Muslim League as an opposition political party against the ruling Muslim League. Later H. S. Suhrawardy joined the Awami Muslim League.

In fact, the Awami Muslim League was a coalition of Bengali nationalist, communist, and leftist forces. The communist party was banned at that time in Pakistan. Therefore, the communist and leftist politicians took shelter under the Awami Muslim League.

In 1954, Moulana Bhashani, H. S. Suhrawardy, Shere Bangla Fazlul Haque, Sheikh Mujibur Rahman, and others formed a broad based coalition known as the "United Front" and won the election in East Pakistan. Unlike Fazlul Haque, Suhrawardy, Ataur Rahman Khan, and Sheikh Mujibur Rahman, Moulana Bhashani did not join the government. Rather, he continued to serve as the president of Awami Muslim League.

In 1957, in the Awami League's National Convention at Kagmari, Tangail, there was a sharp division in the convention between the communist/leftist faction and the Bengali nationalist faction.

Moulana Bhashani led the communist/leftist faction and accused their own government, led by Ataur Rahman Khan in East Pakistan and H. S. Suhrawardy in the Central Government, of being "soft on the autonomy for East Pakistan".

He further accused that the Central Government was following a pro-American foreign policy. Sheikh Mujibur Rahman led the Bengali nationalist faction and defended the government.

Moulana Bhashani and his communist/leftist followers resigned from the Awami League and later formed a new party named the "National Awami Party" (NAP) with a socialistic slogan.

While the Awami League, under the leadership of Sheikh Mujibur Rahman, was fighting against the autocratic and dictatorial rule of General Ayub Khan, demanding the restoration of democracy and autonomy for East Pakistan, Moulana Bhashani supported General Ayub Khan.

Moulana Bhashani led a government delegation to visit China and met Chinese supreme leader Mao Tse Tung. After that visit, Moulana Bhashani declared his infamous policy statement, "Don't disturb Ayub". Bengali people were stunned. That was the biggest mistake of Moulana Bhashani's political career.

There was another set back for Moulana Bhashani. The effect of the Russia-China adversary in global politics spilled over into NAP politics. As a result, the NAP was split into a Pro-China group, led by Moulana Bhashani, and a pro-Moscow group, led by Professor Muzaffar Ahmed. The NAP Muzaffar group also criticized Moulana Bhashani for his support of the Ayub regime.

After the passing of H. S. Suhrawardy and Fazlul Haque, Sheikh Mujibur Rahman was left to lead the anti-Ayub movement by himself. While Sheikh Mujibur Rahman and other leaders of his party were behind bars, the people expected Moulana Bhashani to take a stand. However, Moulana Bhashani stayed on the fence.

The student body filled the void and came forward. They led the movement and launched the Eleven-Point Charter. Leaders of the Central Student's Action Committee met Moulana Bhashani and sought his support for the Eleven-Point Charter. But, Moulana Bhashani disappointed the nation once again.

Under pressure from the ultra-leftist faction of his party, he refused to endorse the Eleven-Point Charter. He claimed that he could not make an endorsement without the approval of the party's central committee, which was scheduled to convene in Khulna in a few weeks. However, in such times, each moment and decision carried with it a hefty historical significance.

Despite his failure to act, Moulana Bhashani himself realized the situation. He had seen the writing on the wall. The people had spoken. It was only a matter of time before the Ayub regime had to go.

Finally, on the 16th of February at a Paltan Maidan public meeting, Moulana Bhashani, in his typical thunderous voice, rendered his unequivocal support of the Eleven-Point Charter. He demanded the immediate release of Bangabandhu Sheikh Mujibur Rahman. Otherwise, he was prepared to march to the cantonment himself and break down the prison walls.

In spite of some misunderstanding, Moulana Bhashani was a great patriot. He led a very simple personal life. He lived in a small cottage with his wife in a village in Kagmari, about sixty-five miles away from Dhaka city. There was no sofa, or even a living room, in his cottage. His visitors were entertained in an open corridor on wooden chairs. His trademark attire was a lungi and panjabi, traditional commoner's clothing, topped with a straw cap on his head. He was the epitome of a simple man.

However, he was also a shrewd politician, who worked under tremendous constraint and managed a very complex balance within his party. Some of his communist followers alleged that Sheikh Mujibur Rahman's Six-Point Charter was nothing but a CIA conspiracy to sabotage their socialistic agenda. They further alleged that Sheikh Mujibur Rahman was a pro-American politician.

History proved that they were wrong. Sheikh Mujibur Rahman was a pro-Bangladeshi politician. He was not pro-America, nor pro-Russia, nor pro-China. He was his own man, a true people's leader. Moulana Bhashani realized this long before his fellow party members did.

Moulana Bhashani was not a communist, but a practicing Muslim, who prayed five times a day and went on a pilgrimage to Mecca. His followers were divided into various groups ranging from leftists to ultra-revolutionary communists. The communists thought that they were using him for their own communistic purposes. However, it can also be perceived that Moulana Bhashani was using the communists for his own goals.

There was a very special personal relationship between Moulana Bhashani and Sheik Mujibur Rahman since they were once president and general secretary of the Awami League. Though they parted ways and led two competing political parties, their personal relationship remained cordial and respectful to each other.

In the 1970 general election, Moulana Bhashani declared "food before vote" and boycotted the election. His ultra communist followers in the party were happy.

However, many people believed that Moulana Bhashani had a hidden agenda. He boycotted the election to help Sheikh Mujibur Rahman. By withdrawing his party from the election, he ensured Sheikh Mujibur Rahman's victory.

There would be no split of progressive votes in East Pakistan. The Awami League won the election with absolute majority, both in East Pakistani and in the Pakistan National Assembly. Moulana Bhashani knew Sheikh Mujibur Rahman needed a mandate to implement his Six-Point Charter.

Moulana Bhashani declares his full support for Bangabandhu in a public meeting at Paltan Maidan, 9th January 1971

Once again, Moulana Bhashani rose above the occasion. During the 1971 Liberation War, ultra-leftist party leaders Abdul Haque, Toha, Motin, Alauddin, Moshiur Rahman, and others opposed the liberation movement. However, Moulana Bhashani opposed them and eventually abandoned them.

He even expelled his party's general secretary, Moshiur Rahman. He supported the liberation war wholeheartedly. While Bangabandhu was in a Pakistani jail, Moulana Bhashani embraced the liberation war by becoming the Chairman of the Advisory Council of the Provisional Bangladesh Government.

Moulana Bhashani started his life as a self-taught religious leader and had thousands of followers. However, he started his political career in the Assam Province of India to fight for the rights of the local Bengali Muslims in Assam.

In 1947, after the independence of the Indian subcontinent, he came to East Pakistan and settled in a small village in Kagmari, near Tangail.

Moulana Bhashani introduced innovative tactics in the agitation movement, such as sit-in-strikes, human barricades against government offices, hunger strikes, etc.

Once, during a procession, while violating curfew, the police confronted Moulana Bhashani. He then started praying on the street in front of the police forces. The police could not arrest a man while in prayer.

The western media characterized Moulana Bhashani as the prophet of violence. However, to the millions of laborers, framers and common people in Bengal, he was known as their "Mozlum Jananeta", the leader of the oppressed. He was a true friend and a patriot. He brought the plight of poor people in the forefront of politics in Pakistan.

Chapter 4

The Thunders of Joy Bangla!

Conspiracy Once Again…

Finally, six months past schedule, the written portion of the Honors Final Examination was over. Now we waited for the laboratory examination. I felt a sense of relief. I thought to myself, that during my time at Dhaka University, my studies ran parallel to my dedication to the country. I was actively involved with a movement against a tyrannical government, for the Eleven-Point Charter, for the withdrawal of the Agartala Conspiracy Case, for the release of Bangabandhu, and the Election of 1970. Now, it was time for me to dedicate myself to graduation and establishing my career. It was time to take responsibility for my family and relieve my father of the burden.

But alas! Destiny had something else in store for me. The Pakistani rulers were hatching a conspiracy to deny power to Bangabandhu, in spite of the Awami League's majority in the National Assembly.

Moreover, in the Provincial Assembly, the Awami League bagged 305 seats out of 310. On January 3rd, in a mammoth public rally, the elected public representative belonging to the Awami League took a public oath to frame a new constitution on the basis of the six and eleven-point charters.

In the middle of February, General Yahya declared March 3rd as the date on which the newly elected National Assembly would sit in Dhaka. This assured us of a peaceful transfer of power.

However, just before the end of February, Zulfikar Ali Bhutto declared his plans to boycott the National Assembly that was to be held in Dhaka. It was a part of a bigger conspiracy.

General Yahya, based on his military intelligence report, expected that Sheikh Mujibur Rahman's Awami League would not win a majority in the Pakistan National Assembly. They expected there to be an anti-Awami League majority under the leadership of Bhutto.

Bhutto's life long ambition to become the prime minister of Pakistan was shattered by the victory of Bangabandhu. He was determined, at any cost, to resist Bangabandhu and become the prime minister of Pakistan.

Under the guise of going bird hunting in Larkana, President Yahya Khan met with Zulfikar Ali Bhutto at his residence. Political observers saw this visit as very controversial because while, President Yahya Khan was willing to go out of his way to meet with Zulfikar Ali Bhutto, the leader of the minority party, he was not willing to extend this same courtesy to Bangabandhu.

Instead, Bangabandhu had to go to the Banga Bhavan, the Presidential Palace in Dhaka, just to meet with President Yahya Khan.

As it turns out, the worries of the political observers were justified. In fact, amidst their hunting expedition, ZulfiKar Ali Bhutto and General Yahya Khan decided to join hands in a conspiracy to deny power to Bangabandhu.

In the meantime, Bhutto declared that in addition to his People's Party of Pakistan and Bangabandhu's Awami League, the Pakistani Army should have an equal say in determining the future of Pakistan. However, this contradicted General Yahya Khan's promise to the nation when he first took power. General Yahya Khan promised that he would hand over power to the leader of the majority party after the election and would have his army retreat to the barracks.

Bhutto's statement finally confirmed the people's fears. He had conspired with the army to foil the outcome of the election.

ZulfiKar Ali Bhutto

Mr. Bhutto was the youngest foreign minister in General Ayub Khan's cabinet. He was known as the general's protégée. Bhutto was the western-educated, young, handsome, and flamboyant minister of General Ayub Khan's military regime. However, Bhutto was also an over-ambitious politician.

After the 1965 India-Pakistan War, Pakistan was forced to sign a ceasefire agreement with India in Tashkhant, USSR, under the sponsorship of Soviet Union. Mr. Bhutto seized this opportunity.

Based on the anti-Indian sentiment in Pakistan, he opposed the Tashkhant Agreement. He resigned from the cabinet and formed a political party named the "People's Party of Pakistan".

He launched socialistic slogans for his party demanding "Food, clothes, and shelter for the poor". His slogans were attractive to the masses of West Pakistani people. From the inception of Pakistan, the people were ruled by a coalition of military, bureaucratic, and feudalistic forces who ignored the plight of the common man.

I had the opportunity to attend Bhutto's meeting at the Engineer's Institute in Dhaka. That was his first visit and public meeting in Dhaka, after he had launched his political party. He came to Dhaka to mobilize support for his party in East Pakistan.

Most of the attendees in the meeting were students like me. He addressed the audience in eloquent English. He sounded very confident and charismatic. He tried to portray himself as a champion of democracy and a friend to the poor. However, we were skeptical of him because of his past connection with the Ayub regime.

He measurably failed to recruit any support in East Pakistan for his party. However, he gained popularity in West Pakistan with his popular socialistic slogans and eventually won majority of the seats in West Pakistan, becoming leader of the minority party in the Pakistan National Assembly.

It was expected that Mr. Bhutto would respect the democratic verdict of the Bengalis and support the handing-over of power to Bangabandhu Sheikh Mujibur Rahman, the majority leader in the Pakistan National Assembly. But unfortunately, Bhutto had no respect for democracy.

He joined General Yahya Khan in a conspiracy to deny power to Bangabandhu. He even suggested that rule over East Pakistan and West Pakistan should be split. He demanded that he rule West Pakistan, while Bangabandhu rule over East Pakistan.

It was a preposterous demand to break Pakistan. Many political circles considered this to be treasonous because Pakistan was still one country and should be ruled by only one government.

Later, it was proved that Bhutto was an excessively self-serving and opportunistic politician. He did every thing possible to gain power. It was this selfishness, which later served as a catalyst to break Pakistan.

Non-Cooperation Movement

It was the first day of March 1971. We were in the midst of the practical test for the B.Sc. Honors Final Examination. It was the last day of testing. We were taking the exam in the laboratory of the Biochemistry Department, situated on the third floor in the northeast side of Curzon Hall. From that room, we could peer over the entire street bellow. However, no one had time to lift their heads from their work to peek at the road. We were all deeply involved in the laboratory test. It was noon.

Suddenly, thunderous slogans ripped through the lab and shattered our silence. We looked out the window to the street. Thousands of angry people were marching through the street with bamboo sticks in hand.

This was quite a surprise. Such a militant procession had not been seen since the mass uprising of 1969. Someone had informed us that at the advice of Zulfikar Ali Bhutto, Yahya Khan had postponed the sitting of the National Assembly, indefinitely.

This declaration by Yahya Khan was illegal and dictatorial. According to the law, he could not take such action without consulting Bangabandhu, the leader of the majority party. This was a clear attempt to snub the will of the people.

Meanwhile, on that day, Bangabandhu was presiding over the meeting of the Awami League Parliamentary Party at the Purbani Hotel in Dhaka. Upon hearing the announcement, Bangabandhu realized the intention of the conspirators.

He roared in anger and said, "I can't let the postponement of the National Assembly session go unchallenged".

He took up the challenge and called a general strike. The students were furious and rallied behind him. Within no time, angry people from all over the city flooded the streets with bamboo sticks and iron rods.

Clearly, General Yahya Khan had underestimated the resolve of the Bengali people. The revolution may not have been televised, but it was clearly unfolding before us.

Bangabandhu protests the postponement of the National Assembly Session by General Yahya Khan

The Defining Moment...

As a politically conscious activist of the liberation movement, things immediately became clear to me. I felt an urgency rush through my body. The defining moment had finally arrived. It was time for me to make a decision.

Immediately, I decided to boycott the exam and join the demonstration. Out of the thirty-five examinees, only four of us: Amin, Solaiman, Bokul, and I were political activists.

I told Amin and Solaiman, "Let's Boycott the Exam!" Instantaneously, they both leaped into the air. However, Solaiman said that the three of us should not boycott the exam alone. Rather, we should invite everyone to join us. Otherwise, everyone else would complete the exam and we three alone, would fail.

He further said that this was the last day of the examination and it would be over in just a few hours. Others might not respond to our call. We saw his point.

Regardless, we decided to appeal to all the examinees to boycott the examination. If no one responded to our call, we would report the matter to DUCSU and seek their advice.

While the three of us discussed the matter, the attention of the other students remained fixated on the noisy demonstration outside. Some of our classmates even went out to the balcony to get a closer look at what was going on. We called upon everyone to boycott the exam. Many of them agreed. Only a few remained hesitant. They told us that there were only a few hours left till the end of the exam, and that maybe we should just finish before joining the processions.

As we were discussing the situation, word got out that the university was officially declared closed. Bangabandhu had called for a strike throughout Dhaka. Amin, Solaiman, and, I left the classroom and headed straight to the demonstration. We got the news that the whole country had gone on strike spontaneously, just as we had.

Our procession was heading for Hotel Purbani, where Bangabandhu was still presiding over the Awami League Parliamentary Party meeting. Spontaneous processions, much like our own, headed to Purbani from each corner of the city. Even an international cricket match at the stadium had been completely abandoned. The spectators of the game came down from the stands to join the procession. Motijheel District soon became flooded with people. Our procession could not even make its way to Purbani.

There wasn't an inch of road on which we could proceed. The roads were completely flooded with demonstrators. It was a resurrection of the 1969 People's Uprising.

Meanwhile, thousands of people had thronged to Paltan Maidan because it was rumored that a meeting would be held there and Bangabandhu would speak. Our procession started to move towards Paltan Maidan, which by the time we arrived, had already turned into a vast ocean of faces.

Here we heard Tofael Ahmed and four other student leaders: Abdur Rob, Shahjahan Siraj, Noore Alam Siddiqui, and Abdul Quddus Makhon addressed the meeting. They explained the future actions declared by Bangabandhu for the non-cooperation movement. It was declared that there would be a strike in Dhaka on March 2nd and in the whole country on March 3rd.

Tofael Ahmed said, "From now on, our struggle is not for the six or eleven-point charters, but rather, for a one-point charter: The Independence of Bangladesh". The audience intensely applauded Tofael Ahmed.

For the first time, people in the processions and the speakers in the public meeting demanded the independence of Bangladesh.

It was further announced that Bangabandhu would address a public meeting on March 7th and would make a historic declaration. The meeting ended with a roaring approval of Bangabandhu.

Female students demonstrate in a public meeting with bamboo sticks during the Non-Cooperation Movement

The Chatra Union (Motia group) also organized a protest meeting near the Baitul Mokaram. Motia Choudhury, known as the "Ogni Konna" (Fiery Woman), vehemently criticized General Yahya Khan for postponing the National Assembly session. She demanded the independence of Bangladesh.

Student leaders, Nurul Islam Nahid, Shamsuddoha, and others, also addressed the gathering.

The Flag

On March 1st, student leaders met Bangabandhu at the Purbani Hotel. Bangabandhu instructed them to from a student action committee. Under the leadership of DUCSU, the student body formed the Independent Bangladesh Student Action Committee. On the same night, a historic meeting took place at Iqbal Hall.

Four youth leaders: Sheikh Fazlul Haque Moni, Serajul Alam Khan, Abdul Razzaque, and Tofael Ahmed; and four student leaders: Noore Alam Siddiqui, Shahjahan Siraj, Abdur Rab, and Abdul Quddus Makhan, met at Iqbal Hall. That was their first, and possibly, last meeting together.

They decided to select poet Rabindranath Tagore's song "Amar Sonar Bangla" as the National Anthem of Bangladesh and designed a national flag for independent Bangladesh. The flag consisted of the silhouette of Bangladesh in the Center of a fiery red sun, which rose over a green backdrop. It was further decided that a resolution for independent Bangladesh would be read at the meeting the next day.

In support of the March 2nd strike in Dhaka city, the Independent Bangladesh Student Action Committee organized a protest meeting at Dhaka University Arts Faculty Campus.

From F. H. Hall, we joined the meeting in a procession. It was one of the largest gatherings ever on the campus. While the meeting was going on, a large procession from Iqbal Hall joined the meeting.

A student in the front of the procession carried the flag of Bangladesh from the top of a long pole. At the sight of the flag, the student body roared in a thunderous slogan - "JOY BANGLA!" (VICTORY TO BENGAL!)

Immediately, Nazrul Islam, a fellow activist from F. H. Hall standing next to me, grabbed the flag and handed it over to the stage and student leaders hoisted the national flag of Bangladesh in the air. Students at the meeting saw for the first time ever, the Bangladesh National Flag.

Until now, we had only dreamt of this moment. At last, the prospects of an independent nation were coming true. What a feeling!

As planned, M. A. Rashid, the office secretary of the Student League, read the resolution for an independent Bangladesh. There was a certain romantic thrill that captivated me during that meeting.

Students demonstrate with the Bangladesh Flag during the Non-Cooperation Movement, March 3, 1971

March 3rd

On the 3rd of March, the Student League and Sramik (labor) League jointly organized a protest meeting at Paltan Maidan. We joined the meeting in a procession from F. H. Hall. It was a huge meeting.

The killing of several innocent people by the Pakistani Army over the last two days had agitated people. They came to the meeting brandishing bamboo sticks and iron rods. A significant number of industrial workers from Tejgaon and Narayanganj came to the meeting with scarlet bandanas wrapped around their heads.

Bangabandhu was the chief guest and student leader, Nore Alam Siddiqui, presided over the meeting. Tofael Ahmed, labor leader Abdul Mannan, and other student leaders, spoke at the meeting as well.

Bangabandhu condemned the killing of innocent people by the Pakistani Army. He demanded General Yahya Khan withdraw his army to the barracks. Once again, he criticized Bhutto and General Yahya Khan for pushing the country into a confrontation. He warned them of the consequences.

He told Bhutto "If you don't want one constitution for Pakistan, adopted according to the democratic process, then you can adopt one for your West Pakistan. We will adopt our own constitution for Bangladesh".

Once again, a resolution for independent Bangladesh was read in the meeting. But this time, it was a moment of historic consequence. It was done in the presence of Bangabandhu.

It was further declared in the resolution that Bangabandhu was the father of independent Bangladesh and all Bengalis were required to fight for their liberation.

On that day, for the first time, many female students came to the meeting with bamboo sticks in their hands. It was another gratifying day for me. I witnessed the unfolding of a new chapter in the creation of independent Bangladesh.

March 7th – A Moment In History

The students of F. H. Hall had left for home. However, about fifteen of us, belonging to the Chatra League and Chatra Union, stayed behind to work for the Non-Cooperation Movement. We had been working in preparation for the March 7th rally. We were determined to make the event a success.

March 7th, 1971. We were assigned to work as volunteers at the event. The route from Bangabandhu's residence to the Race Course had to be secured. It was rumored that the army would assassinate him, while on his way to the Race Course.

We were positioned on the corner of Mirpur Road and Science Laboratory Road, right in front of the Science Laboratory Building. For his safety, Bangabandhu's actual route was kept a secret.

We could see a flood of people heading for the Race Course from every direction. We were impatiently waiting for Bangabandhu to pass by. At that moment, someone informed us that Bangabandhu had already reached Race Course through a different road. On receiving this news, we rushed towards the venue.

Race Course had become a boundless field of faces. In my lifetime, there would be no other event in the world that would bring so many people together, just to hear one man speak.

It was so crowded that we had no chance to make it near the stage. We found standing room in the far end of the gathering, under a loud speaker. Slogans could be heard from all around like the sounds of a storm.

On the stage, student and youth leaders spoke before Bangabandhu. As Bangabandhu came to the podium to speak, hundreds of thousands of voices ripped through the sky as they chanted slogans. "Joy Bangla! Heroic Bengali, take up arms – Liberate Bangladesh! My leader, your leader, Sheikh Mujib, Sheikh Mujib!" and other such slogans were cast into the air like bellowing waves of sound.

When the chanting resided, Bangabandhu took off his thick black-framed spectacles and put them down on the podium. He raised his right hand in the air. Pointing to the sky with his index finger, he addressed the audience, "My brothers". As he uttered these first words, a pin-drop silence fell over the crowd. With his thunderous voice he began to speak:

> I come before you today with a heart, laden with sadness…this sadness remains today in Dhaka, Chittagong, Khulna, Rajshahi, and Rangpur, where the streets are soaked in the blood of my brothers and sisters.

Today, the people of Bengal desire emancipation. The people of Bengal wish to live. The people of Bengal demand that their rights be acknowledged.

What wrong have we committed? Following the elections, the people of Bangladesh entrusted the Awami League and me with totality of their electoral support. It was our expectation that the Parliament would meet. There, we would frame the constitution on which we would develop this land. The people of this country would achieve their economic, political, and cultural freedom. But, it is a matter of grief that today we are constrained to say, in all sadness, that the history of the past twenty-three years has been the history of persecution of the people of Bengal. It has been a history of the bloodshed of the people of Bengal. This history over the past twenty-three years has been one of agonizing cries of men and women.

…What have we gained? The weapons we have bought with our money to defend the country against foreign aggression are being used against the poor and downtrodden of my country today. It is their hearts, which these bullets pierce. We are the majority of Pakistan. Whenever we Bengalis have attempted to ascend to the heights of power, they have swooped down to stop us.

…I do not desire the office of prime minister. I wish to see the rights of the people of this country established. Let me make it clear, without ambiguity, that beginning today, in Bangladesh, all courts, magistracies, government offices, and educational institutions will remain closed for an indefinite period.

Bangabandhu finished his speech by giving his final instructions to the people:

…In every village, every neighborhood set up a Sangram Parishad (Resistance Council) under the leadership of the Awami League. And be prepared with whatever you have. Remember: We have already given blood, and we shall give even more blood, but God willing, we will free the people of this land.

The struggle this time is a struggle for emancipation. The struggle this time is a struggle for independence.

People were overwhelmed with joy and excitement. Such a huge gathering was unimaginable. That scenery and emotion of the day simply could not be described by words. Rather, it could be felt. It could be felt within the deepest pulse of my heart. Those who were there at the meeting were the luckiest people on earth to have witnessed such a historic moment and felt such electricity flowing within them. That day can never be duplicated. Not in the history of Bangladesh. Not in the history of the world.

In my opinion, Bangabandhu had declared the independence of Bangladesh on that day. He had instructed his people to take whatever arms available and be readied to defend their land.

Bangabandhu's address to the people was broadcasted over Dhaka Radio the next day on March 8th. This added more heat to the nationwide agitation.

7th March 1971, Bangabandhu Sheikh Mujibur Rahman declares at Race Course Maidan "The struggle this time is a struggle for independence".

A Secret Meeting

It was the 8th of March. A fellow activist and confidant, Amin told me that we were going on a special mission the next day. He asked me to stay behind in the dorms.

I asked him, "So, what is this special mission about?"

He replied, "Personally, I'm not clear on the details, but I'll find out and give you the story tonight."

Amin was almost a full-time activist and had much more contact with the central leaders than I did. So, I didn't bother to press him for more information.

As he promised, Amin came to my room that night and closed the door. In a low voice, he slowly whispered the details. The plan was exciting with a certain flare of romance. The details read like the pages of a spy novel.

Amin informed me that earlier that morning two men had come to the dorm looking for us. They met Ashraf and left a secret with him. Ashraf then, relayed the information to Amin. Amin spent his day cross-checking the identities of the two men with central leaders. We were not quite sure who else was involved in the plan.

However, the next day at noon, Amin and I had left the hall for our destination. We met Ashraf at the hall gates. Anwar was with him. As we came together, Ashraf whispered, "The four of us can not board the rickshaw together in front of the dormitory. Instead, we have to walk farther away from the dorm and take separate rickshaws."

As Ashraf suggested, we walked quite a distance from the dorm and then broke into pairs boarding two rickshaws. Amin and I were in one rickshaw, while Ashraf and Anwar boarded another. Ashraf's plan went further to suggest that we were not to rely on just these two rickshaws, but rather, we were to stop halfway and hire new rickshaws to finish our journey. This part of the plan would certainly prevent anyone from following us.

Ashraf looked tense and excited. At the Mogbazar Juncture, we got down from our rickshaws and hired new ones.

While on our rickshaw, Amin told me that four more activists were to join us in our mission. Despite all the secretive elements of the plan, I had no feelings of doubt or anxiety in me. Rather, I felt quite pleased knowing that we had taken the utmost caution and security in executing the plan.

Eventually, we came to Kawran Bazaar and got down from the rickshaws. We then walked along the rail line to a two-story house. Upon our arrival, two men received us. Ashraf introduced one of the men, as Kamal Siddiqui, a high-ranking civil servant for the East Pakistani Government. He was then a SDO for a district outside of Dhaka. Ashraf then informed us, it was actually Kamal Siddiqui who had come to F. H. Hall yesterday to invite us to the secret meeting.

There were no other people in the house. However, it was quite enormous with many rooms. We went into a room on the second floor and took our seats. A few minutes later, our comrades Habibullah, Rashidul Alam, Julfiqqar, and Riaz joined us.

After seeing each other in the same room, we were all relieved to know that we were close friends and soldiers fighting for the same ideology. We all longed for the liberation of Bangladesh. Previously, we had taken an oath. We agreed, that by any means, the eight of us would fight together for the liberation of Bangladesh. We repeated this oath, closed the doors, and sat down to begin our secret meeting.

Kamal Siddiqui started by explaining the significance of the Non-Cooperation Movement lead by Bangabandhu. He said, "The Pakistan Army could attack our people at any time. To combat this, we need to organize an armed resistance to defend our people and ourselves. We must prepare immediately."

Our only hope to combat the brutal Pakistani military was to rely on guerrilla warfare. We needed to organize ourselves in small groups and get training in guerrilla tactics.

Finally, after these introductory words, he revealed the identity of the other man who greeted us at the door. He was a trainer of guerilla warfare. He spent the next two hours teaching as much as he could about art of guerilla combat. He then said, "Since you are all tested activists, you should each take it upon yourselves to organize and train your own guerilla units."

The Pakistani military was sure to attack Dhaka. We had to use guerilla warfare to defend ourselves. Since there were many national and international journalists living in Dhaka, they would publicize our armed resistance throughout the country and all over the world. Everyone would know that the people of East Pakistan had begun the war for the independence of Bangladesh.

After the secret meeting, we returned to the dorms, once again, breaking into groups and again changing rickshaws midway.

Later, we came to know that the house where we conducted our meeting actually belonged to renowned actor – Raju Ahmed, elder brother of Aminul Hoque Badsha who was press secretary to Bangabandhu.

The present whereabouts of those who attended the secret meeting are as follows: Dr. Kamal Siddiqui, Freedom fighter, and retired Principal Secretary to the Prime Minister of Bangladesh; Rashidul Alam, freedom fighter, Retired Secretary, Bangladesh Government; Dr. Ashraf Ahmed, scientist, now living in the USA; Dr. Anwar Hossain,

Freedom fighter, professor at Dhaka University; Habibullah, Julfiqqar and Riaz, freedom fighters, high ranking officers of the Bangladesh Government; and Aminul Hoque, a freedom fighter and businessman, involved with JSD, a leftist political party.

Everyday after the secret meeting, the events of the Non-Cooperation Movement took on new and dramatic turns. We had no choice, but to respond to these changes. Before we knew it, we were each individually submerged into our own missions for the Non-Cooperation Movement.

As a result, we had no follow up to our secret meeting. That was the last time that the eight of us would have the opportunity to work together. However, it was the beginning of our lives as dedicated soldiers for liberation.

The Last Days of East Pakistan

Everyday, across Bangladesh, people were dying in clashes with the Pakistani Army. Bangladesh was running under Bangabandhu's leadership. 32 Dhanmondi, the residence of Bangabandhu, became the White House of Bangladesh. The authority of the Central Government was confined only within the Cantonment and the Governor's House. Flags of Independent Bangladesh were fluttering throughout the length and breadth of the country. Student leaders raised the flag over Bangabandhu's home and in his car. Bangabandhu visited Pakistani President Yahya Khan and Minority Leader Bhutto at the Governor's House with the flag of independent Bangladesh flying high from his car.

Meanwhile, under the cloak of negotiations, Pakistan was bringing in soldiers and war equipment to Bangladesh. For the same reason, Lt. General Yakub Khan, a general known for his tougher track record and intellect, replaced Admiral Ahsan who was known for his decency and civility.

From March 1st to March 24th, people wholeheartedly participated in the non-cooperation movement. All political parties supported the call of independent Bangladesh. However, a few ultra-leftist fringe groups, the Jamaat-e Islami party, and the Muslim League opposed the movement.

Moulana Bhashani attended a public meeting at Paltan Maidan on March 9th. I was curious about the meeting. So I, along with a few friends, attended.

Moulana Bhashani spoke in his usual style. He said, "I know Mujib. I love him more than my son. He was my protégée. He was one of the best party secretaries I had in my political career. Do not distrust Mujib".

He supported Bangabandhu unequivocally and urged everybody to unite under the leadership of Bangabandhu. He criticized General Yahya Khan and Bhutto for not respecting the democratic principle of majority rule. The meeting also requested Bangabandhu to form a national government for independent Bangladesh.

On the same day, the Central Committee of the Student League approved their declaration for independent Bangladesh, which they proclaimed on the 2nd of March at Dhaka University Campus. They also approved a resolution requesting Bangabandhu, the father of the nation, to form a national government for an independent Bangladesh.

Meanwhile, the opposition leaders of West Pakistan blamed General Yahya Khan and Bhutto for the postponement of the national assembly session in Dhaka. They were worried about the situation in Bangladesh and the unity of Pakistan. They urged General Yahya Khan to meet Bangabandhu to find a political solution to the crisis. Some of them, such as Wali Khan of the NAP, Air Marshal Asghar Khan, Mia Momtaz Doulatana of the Muslim League, and others arrived in Dhaka to talk to Bangabandhu.

On March 14th, After Bhutto's political bombshell demanding the separate rule of East and West Pakistan, West Pakistani politicians vehemently criticized Bhutto for his irresponsible statement. It was perceived by political circles that Bhutto was desperately seeking power when he realized that his dream to become prime minister of Pakistan was far from reality.

His frustrations heightened, when he realized that he wouldn't even become the deputy prime minister or foreign minister. Rather, he would merely sit in the National Assembly, as minority leader.

General Yahya Khan came to Dhaka on March 15th with his advisors to meet Bangabandhu. There were mixed reactions to his presence in Dhaka. Some thought that there might be a political solution to the problem. Others thought that it might be a ploy to buy time to reinforce military fortification before an all out attack on Bangladesh.

March 15, 1971, President General Yahya Khan arrives in Dhaka for negotiations with Bangabandhu

While Bangabandhu was meeting with General Yahya Khan, the Non-Cooperation Movement was going on in full swing. All of the newspapers were supporting the call for independent Bangladesh. Public meetings and processions were also organized in various parts of Bangladesh.

March 17th was Bangabandhu's birthday. We went to his residence in a procession. Thousands of people arrived there. Moulana Bhashani held a public meeting in Chittagong. Once again, he urged the people to support Bangabandhu. He said that Bangabandhu has already declared the independence of Bangladesh.

On March 19th, a historic incident took place in Joydebpur Cantonment in the outskirts of Dhaka. Pakistani military authority ordered the East Bengal Regiment in Joydebpur to disarm. However, the Bengali soldiers and their officers refused to lay down their arms. Then, a group of West Pakistani solders were sent there to execute the order.

When the news broke out, thousands of local people joined the rebellious Bengali solders and civilians and barricaded the roads to halt the West Pakistani solders. In response, West Pakistani solders indiscriminately fired upon the people. The Bengali soldiers and civilians, in turn, responded with fire. Several villagers were killed and several West Pakistani solders were wounded. West Pakistani solders were forced to retreat to the Dhaka Cantonment.

It was the first armed resistance by the Bengali, and an open rebellion by the Bengali solders, against West Pakistani solders. All over the country, people were blocking the supply of foods and other materials to the cantonment for the West Pakistani solders. The Pakistani military authority issued a stern warning against such actions. However, the Bengalis ignored the warning.

Zulfikr Ali Bhutto came to Dhaka on March 21st with his advisors. He was escorted under a blanket of extraordinary security from the airport to the Hotel Intercontinental. However, the workers of the airport and the hotel had snubbed him. The hotel employees refused to let him use the elevator. When the military escorted him to the elevator, they found it to be "out of order".

March 21, 1971, Z. A. Bhutto, Chief of People's Party of Pakistan arrives at Dhaka, under tight security to meet Bangabandhu

Bangabandhu and his advisors had several meetings with President Yahya Khan and Bhutto. The main point of contention was the Six-Point Charter of the Awami League. Bangabandhu was determined to incorporate the Six-Point Charter into the constitution. Yahya and Bhutto were against it.

They argued that two of the six points of the Six-Point Charter: "separate currencies and the power of imposing, as well as, the collecting of taxes for the two provinces" were threats to the unity of Pakistan. The points were unacceptable to them.

Nonetheless, Bangabandhu was determined to incorporate the Six-Point Charter, as it was, into the constitution. He argued that he campaigned in the election with the Six-Point Charter and the people of Bangladesh, overwhelmingly, gave him the mandate to implement it.

Bangabandhu in a meeting with Z. A. Bhutto at Hotel Intercontinental on March 23, 1971

March 23rd is Pakistan Republic Day. It was tradition to fly the Pakistani flag over the entire country, and particularly, over all government offices. However, in 1971, it was a completely different March 23rd.

Pakistani flags were hoisted in only two places in all of Dhaka city. One was in the military cantonment and the other was over the Governor House. Instead, Bangladeshi flags were hoisted over every house and office throughout Bangladesh.

Even at the Hotel Intercontinental, where Bhutto and General Yahya's advisers were staying, the flag of Bangladesh was proudly adorned. Additionally, the Bangladeshi flag was flying with honor and dignity at each of the foreign embassies and missions in Dhaka.

Bangabandhu, himself, hoisted the Bangladesh flag at his residence in the early morning.

Bangabandhu raises the flag of independent Bangladesh before a jubilant crowd at his residence on 23 March 1971

We attended the flag raising ceremony at the Paltan Maidan at 9 AM. The Independent Bangladesh Student Action Committee organized the event. We sang the Bangladesh National Anthem "Amar Sonar Bangla". The Joy Bangla Battalion marched in formation saluting the flag.

After the meeting, we went to the residence of Bangabandhu in a procession led by the Joy Bangla Battalion. Bangabandhu received us and returned the salute from the Joy Bangla Battalion.

The flag of independent Bangladesh is hoisted at a huge public meeting in Dhaka on March 23, 1971

On this day, Bengali employees at Bangladesh Television refused to take orders from West Pakistani solders, shutting down broadcasting in the evening of March 23rd.

In the meantime, General Yahya Khan had appointed notorious General Tikka Khan as the Governor of East Pakistan, replacing relatively mild-mannered Lt. General Yakub Khan. General Tikka Khan was known for having once brutally crushed a tribal rebellion in West Pakistan.

However, his first official experience in Bangladesh crushed his ego. Chief Justice Siddiqui was supposed to conduct General Tikka Khan's oath to office. However, the chief justice refused to conduct the ceremony without the permission of the Bangabandhu. Without being sworn into office, General Tikka Khan was forced to work as a military administrator, rather than work as a governor. It was a slap to the face of the Pakistani military establishment. The Bengali nation was united against the Pakistani Military Junta.

On March 24th, we went to Bangabandhu's residence with a large procession to show our support. He told the gathering that we should continue our vigilance. This time, the Bengalis will win.

Another historic event took place in Chittagong, the port city of Bangladesh. When it was known that the Pakistani military would unload arms and ammunition from the M. V. Shoat Ship, thousands of people came out to the streets in protest. They constructed barricades along the streets, blocking the cantonment from the port. The Pakistani military fired on the protestors and killed several of them. The dockworkers boycotted the ship. The Pakistani military could not unload their weapons. It was another victory for the Bengali people.

The Non-Cooperation Movement Activist of F. H. Hall

As mentioned earlier, about fifteen student activists remained in the dormitory. Everyone else had left F. H. Hall. Out of those activists and leaders, whose names I still remember are: Abdul Kaddus Makhon, Rashidul Alam, Aminul Hoque, Habibullah, Solaiman, Anwar Hossain, Syed Ashrafuddin Ahmed, Alauddin, Obaidul Hoque Babul, Yahya, Mijanur Rahman, Nurul Absar, Nazrul Islam, Nurul Islam Milon, Nurul Islam of Rangpur, and Mahbubuzzaman of the Chatra Union.

We each went out everyday to work for different programs in the Non-Cooperation Movement. As was in 1969, we became full-time activists. But now, we had much more experience. This time around, we were much more organized and skilled.

What a turn of events! I thought to myself that as soon as my finals were over, I'd be headed straight home. That obviously didn't happen. I guess it's true what they say, "Man proposes. God disposes."

Sustenance for an activist

In the meantime, the dinning hall had closed. My scholarship money had ended. There was no way I could get home to bring money. What would I do now?

The Non-Cooperation Movement was going on in full swing. The life and death of my nation depended on it. Under these circumstances, I could not flee from my post and run back home. My life and the nation's life had merged into one. The liberation of the Bengali nation had become my obsession. It flowed deep within my blood. But, how was I going to survive?

I took my problem to my cousin Khaja who was my first line of support in Dhaka. He suggested that I stay with him, but I did not want to leave F. H. Hall, the center of student activities. So he arranged an alternative.

Khaja had a friend, an eminent income tax lawyer from Mymensingh, who lived next to the USIS Library, which was near F. H. Hall. It was arranged that his servant would bring food for me at noon and in the evening, in lieu of tutoring his daughter, a 5th grade student.

Later, I came to realize that the proposal for tutoring his daughter was merely a plea in case I refused to take the gratuity. In actuality, the lawyer was keen to help an activist of the Non-Cooperation Movement. His servant regularly brought food for me in a lunch box and I did my part by tutoring the girl whenever I had time. Despite my inability to regularly tutor, my food supply never stopped. The last opportunity I had to accept one of these gracious meals was at noon on March 25th, 1971.

The Beginning of the Liberation War

Everyday, from the 1st to the 24th of March, we went to Iqbal Hall to get instructions from the leaders of the Independent Bangladesh Student's Action Committee and executed those plans. Every night during this time period, riffle-training classes were conducted at Iqbal Hall Field.

I participated in the training for a few days. Female students from the Chatra League also participated in this training. Our routine work during the Non-Cooperation Movement was to participate in processions, meetings, putting up posters, and setting up barricades during strikes.

March 25th was a day of confusion and anxiety. Several rumors began flying about in Dhaka. Some were saying that the discussion among Bangabandhu, General Yahya Khan, and Bhutto were going well, and soon, an agreement would be made and power would be transferred to Bangabandhu. However, sources close to Awami League high command indicated that negotiations had failed. General Yahya Khan would leave Dhaka and a military crack down was imminent.

We spent the day with a lot of apprehension and anxiety. As usual, Amin, Habibullah, and I went to Iqbal Hall in the evening. However, the situation on this day looked quite different from the norm. The atmosphere was grim. None of the central student leaders were present at the office. On most days, the office bustled with the sounds of leaders and activists. However, on this day the office seemed eerily vacant and quiet.

Chishti, a student leader from Iqbal Hall broke the news to us. He said, "Talks amongst Bangabandhu, President Yahya Khan, and Mr. Bhutto had broken down. President Yahya Khan had left the Cantonment for Dhaka Airport on his way back to Pakistan. The Pakistani Army would attack East Pakistan tonight."

We were instructed to pick up as much manpower as possible from the slums behind the Foreign Students Dormitory and Jinnah Hall. We had to set up a barricade near Shahbag Hotel to block the army movement towards Dhaka University. We set out from Iqbal Hall to carry out this mission, apprehensive of what would happen next.

Book Two:

Bullets of '71
A Freedom Fighter's Story

Dedication

This book is dedicated to the memory of the three million people who lost their lives and the hundreds of thousands of women who lost their honor during the nine months of liberation war.

Introduction

In 1947, British rule came to an end in the Indian subcontinent. The region was divided into two independent countries, India and Pakistan. However, Pakistan was made of two wings, West Pakistan and East Pakistan. These two wings were separated by more than a thousand miles of Indian Territory, not to mention, two different ethnicities, cultures, languages, and climates.

The destiny of this bizarre state, Pakistan, was written in its creation; it was predestined to break.

From the very beginning, the Bengali people of East Pakistan were victims of economic and political exploitation by their West Pakistani rulers. Bengali people became second-class citizens in their own homes. East Pakistan was nothing more than a colony to West Pakistan. The undemocratic rule and economic hardships combined to create a serious disconnect among the Bengali people of East Pakistan against the central government.

Moreover, as Bengalis were the majority population in all of Pakistan, Bengali (Bangla) was the most commonly spoken language. Despite this, West Pakistani rulers conspired to impose Urdu as the sole-national language of Pakistan. This was a blatant attempt to annihilate Bengali national identity. It was another blow to the integrity of Pakistan.

In the meantime, on February 21st, 1952, the Pakistani police and army fired on a peaceful demonstration of Dhaka University students who demanded that their mother language, "Bangla", be established as the state language. Five students were killed and many more were wounded. The Bengali people of East Pakistan were outraged by this massacre. They revolted against Pakistani authority.

This event unified Bengalis for the first time to rise as a Bengali nation, to rise as Bangladesh. The seeds of Bengali nationalism were sown on the 21st of February 1952.

Bengali nationalism began to solidify against economic and political exploitation by Pakistani rulers. The solidarity of Bengali nationalism first erupted during the 1954 general election of Pakistan. The Muslim League, the party that led to the creation of Pakistan was completely rejected by voters in East Pakistan. The United Front, a coalition of pro-Bengali nationalist political parties, was voted into power in East Pakistan.

However, West Pakistani rulers were taken off-guard by this unexpected result. They conspired against the people's verdict, fired the newly elected-government in East Pakistan and West Pakistan, and imposed military-rule led by General Ayub Khan.

The people were robbed of their democracy. The economic discrepancy between East Pakistan and West Pakistan continued to widen. The Bengali people became further agitated and resolved by this undemocratic political development.

Early on in life, I was perturbed by the effect of this continued downtrend on the social, political and economic conditions of East Pakistan. I became politically conscious and grew rebellious day-by-day. I looked for a new avenue to confront the situation, but could not find one. Nonetheless, I noticed that my people were becoming desperate. We needed a way out.

Finally, a leader named Bangabandhu Sheikh Mujibur Rahman appeared in the horizon and showed the way. I, along with the rest of my people, saw a light at the end of the tunnel.

In 1966, Bangabandhu (Friend of Bengal) launched a six-point charter for the autonomy of East Pakistan to address the grievances of the people of East Pakistan. Instead of a dialogue for a political solution, the Pakistani military junta put Bangabandhu behind bars and conspired to hang him for alleged treason. This was known as the "Trial of Agartala Conspiracy Case".

However, in the meantime, the Bengali people had approved Bangabandhu's six-point charter as their own demand for emancipation.

We, the student community of East Pakistan, launched a movement for an eleven-point charter against military ruler Ayub Khan. We demanded, among others, the release of Bangabandhu, the resignation of Ayub Khan, the restoration of democratic rule, and the granting of autonomy to East Pakistan.

The movement for the six-point and eleven-point charter during 1966 to 1969 marked the climax of our liberation movement. As a student activist, I put my heart and soul into the liberation movement.

In 1969, the student movement for an eleven-point charter had transformed into a people's uprising. Pakistani dictator General Ayub Khan was forced to withdraw the "Agartala Conspiracy" case against Bangabandhu and release him from jail.

Eventually, General Ayub Khan was forced to resign, but before he did, he handed over power to another general, General Yahya Khan. Yielding pressure to the people's demand, General Yahya Khan had arranged a general election in Pakistan in 1970.

Contrary to the expectation of the Pakistani military junta, Bangabandhu's party, the Awami League, won 99% of the seats in the East Pakistan Provincial Assembly and a majority of the seats in the Pakistani National Assembly.

Zulfikar Ali Bhutto's party, the People's Party, became the minority party in the Pakistan National Assembly. These unprecedented election results gave mandate to Bangabandhu to become the prime minister of Pakistan as well as to govern East Pakistan based on his six-point charter for autonomy.

General Yahya Khan promised to hand over power to Bangabandhu Sheikh Mujibur Rahman and convened over the first meeting of the Pakistani National Assembly in Dhaka on March 3rd, 1971.

After the election of 1970, I thought that the country was finally on the right track. I thought that democratic rule would be restored and replace military rule forever. I imagined that Bangabandhu would become the prime minister of Pakistan and write a new constitution implementing autonomy for East Pakistan. My responsibility as a student activist would finally be over. I would now build my career. I went back to the Dhaka University to complete my study.

However, before I had completed my final examination, my destiny once again propelled me into another movement, the Bangladesh Liberation War.

Bullets of '71: A Freedom Fighter's Story

The 1st of March 1971. We were in the midst of our final laboratory examination for our BS honors degree at Curzon Hall campus, Dhaka University. This was the last day of our final examination. There were only two more hours to go before we were done with our examination. We were extremely eager to finish.

Suddenly, our attention was interrupted by the sound of thunderous slogans, which rose from the streets below. We rushed to the window and saw thousands of people marching with bamboo sticks in their hands chanting anti-General Yahya Khan slogans. We came to know that General Yahya Khan had postponed the National Assembly meeting scheduled for March 3rd in Dhaka without consulting Bangabandhu, the leader of the Pakistani National Assembly.

Bangabandhu saw through the consequences of General Yahya Khan's undemocratic and non-parliamentarian actions. It was a conspiracy to disenfranchise the people by negating their verdict. In protest, Bangabandhu called for a non-cooperation movement and a general strike throughout East Pakistan. The people responded to Bangabandhu's call with militant street demonstrations. And now, Bangabandhu's call for a non-cooperation movement had reached the windows outside of our exam-hall. Before we could decide what to do, Dhaka University authority had already announced the closure of the university, sine die.

Before the ink in our exam-books could dry, my fellow activist friends, Solaiman, Amin, and I ran from the laboratory and joined the demonstration without thinking of our future. Once again, we responded to the call for our motherland and jumped right into the non-cooperation movement.

The non-cooperation movement had intensified each day. Bangabandhu addressed a protest meeting at Suhrawardy Park on the 7th of March. It was the largest meeting ever held in all of Pakistan. We, as the activists of the non-cooperation movement, worked day and night to organize the meeting. In that mammoth public rally, Bangabandhu made his historic declaration:

"...you fight the enemy with whatever you have..,

...the struggle this time is for emancipation, the struggle this time is for independence!"

This was received as Bangabandhu's proclamation of independence for Bangladesh and the demise of East Pakistan.

The next day, the non-cooperation movement spread like wildfire across the country. Curfews were enacted to impede the movement's success. Each day, the people confronted the Pakistani military and each day, they were killed for it. However, the people did not back-down.

The days unfolded in this manner until, the fateful night of March 25th when the Pakistani military attacked the innocent and unarmed people of Bangladesh with tanks, mortars and machineguns.

At mid-night, on the 25th of March 1971, Pakistan initiated what would prove to be one of history's most devastating acts of genocide against the people of Bangladesh. We were left with no choice. We had to fight back. The Liberation War of Bangladesh had commenced.

Chapter 1

March, the Rebellious Month

Face to Face with the First Bullets of Genocide

March 25, 1971. We were setting up barricades at the intersection of Mymensingh Road and Elephant Road. We were in front of Shahbag Hotel. It was about a quarter to midnight. A few cars traveled along Mymensingh Road, but we did not notice. We were too busy with the task at hand.

A little tired, I stood apart on the sidewalk for a while. Some cars approached the square and stopped near the fountain. People inside took notice of us. It was probably the clamor we created that struck their curiosities.

One car changed its direction from south to west. The area was half-lit, and half-dark. The headlights of the car fell brightly onto our eyes, blurring our vision. Suddenly, the headlights switched off.

There was no doubt that these were military jeeps.

Before we knew what was going on, the headlights of one jeep were switched on again. Instantly, the occupants of the jeeps opened fire on us with machineguns.

Amidst the roaring sound of machinegun fire, I jumped off the sidewalk and fell into a ditch. As I regained my senses, I ran westward. I could hear the groans of my friends hit by the bullets.

Those who managed to get up also started running. The air was filled with the cries of people and gunfire. For the first time in my life, I knew the sound of gunfire, up close and aimed directly at me.

Arguably, we were face to face with the first bullets of the Bangladesh genocide.

I tried to keep running, but I was losing my will. My legs were becoming rubbery. I felt as if I had been shot.

I was quite lucky. My cousin Khaja lived nearby on Elephant Road. He lived in a house adjacent to the railway tracks.

With my last ounce of energy, I ran to his house drenched in the filth of the ditch. As soon as I entered Khaja's house, I checked my body for bullet-wounds. Luckily, aside from some bruises, I escaped unscathed.

After the running and the horror of the evening, my thirst had finally caught up to me. I had a seemingly unquenchable thirst. I was exhausted.

I quickly drank a tall glass of water. As the water ran against my cheeks, I realized that I was still filthy. I went to the sink and did my best to wash myself clean of the stench of raw sewage.

My heart still pounding, I found it difficult to stand. I went to the living room and stretched my body across the sofa.

Khaja was visibly frightened by the look on my face and in the way I stormed into his home. He began pressing me about what had just happened.

With a deep breath I regained my composure and started narrating the incident to Khaja.

However, before I could finish, I was interrupted by the blasting sounds of gunfire. Khaja and I tried to follow the sounds with our ears.

The sounds were coming from Dhaka University, Peelkhana, and Rajarbag. Iqbal Hall of Dhaka University was the headquarters of the Student's Action Committee. Peelkhana was the headquarters of the East Pakistani Riffles (EPR), the border security force. Rajarbag was the police headquarters.

A few moments later, Khaja and I came out and could see fire and smoke billowing out from those exact directions.

We couldn't figure out exactly what was going on. A mixed feeling of anxiety, fear and depression burdened me.

Had anything happened to our leader Bangabandhu Sheikh Mujibur Rahman? Was it just one-sided firing? Were the Bengali policemen, EPR and soldiers revolting? I had no answers.

Unfortunately, radio Dhaka and the Indian radio stations had no news of what was going on in Dhaka either.

Was the world outside aware of what was happening here? There were still flames rising. All around, there was the ceaseless thunder of intense firing. It was a living hell.

A night of terror, concern, and despair ushered in the dawn. The firing lost its momentum in the morning hours. However, rings of smoke could still be found rising from the horizon. I fell into a daze.

What was going to happen next? What would be our future? While these thoughts raced through my mind, I grew exhausted from my sleepless night.

Finally I drifted into slumber.

March 26: A Terrorized Morning

Khaja woke me up from a deep sleep. He seemed to be excited, and yet, still in a state of shock. I was perplexed and a bit confused. I could not figure out what was going on.

In a whispering voice he asked me to hide in the bathroom. A soldier was moving towards the house with a rifle in his hand. It was scary. Right away, I realized the danger we were in. In seconds, I jumped off the sofa and ran into the bathroom. A little later, I heard knocking at the door. My blood froze. I began praying to Allah.

It seems that people are most inclined to remember God in desperate moments like this. I began to wonder: Is God moved to answer the prayers of those who only choose to remember Him in times of crisis? Such thoughts crept into my head.

Khaja opened the door and greeted the soldier. A conversation followed in Urdu. I couldn't follow the dialogue all the way from the bathroom. I ardently recited my prayers. Several moments passed without any sound. I feared that they had arrested Khaja and taken him away.

Thankfully, soon after, I heard Khaja's voice again. Then I heard steps clanking along the staircase to the roof. I had no clue as to what was going on. I continued my prayers and kept my ears open.

Finally, Khaja had come back. He bolted the door and came close to the bathroom to say, "The danger is over, but stay in there for a little while longer".

I've known Khaja to get riled up easily over petty matters, but surprisingly on this day he remained calm, composed, and careful.

A little later Khaja returned and said, "It's safe. You can come out now. They're gone".

I heartily thanked Allah and came out of the bathroom. I asked Khaja what had happened. Khaja then explained that five armed West Pakistani soldiers had been patrolling the streets with apprehensive steps. With their fingers clenching the triggers of their rifles, they scanned the neighborhood.

They saw the Bangladesh flag waving over our rooftop and asked Khaja to take it down. Khaja was well versed in Urdu.

He put on the guise of a Muslim League supporter and convinced them that it was only under pressure from the students that he was forced to hoist the Bangladeshi flag.

The soldiers bought into his story and let him bring down the flag without any repercussions, and immediately left the house.

As it turned out, the soldiers were scouring the neighborhood in search of the Bengali EPR soldiers and policemen who had revolted and fled from Peelkhana Camp and the police headquarters. It dawned on me that last night, many of the Bengali policemen and EPR personnel might have been killed by the Pakistani Army.

Bangabandhu: Arrested, but Still Alive

A little later, Pakistani military dictator General Yahya Khan addressed the nation over Radio Pakistan, Dhaka. Martial law had been imposed all over East Pakistan.

Khan accused Bangabandhu of anti-state activities and informed the nation of Bangabandhu's arrest. While the news of his detention was of concern, it was a consolation knowing that he was still alive.

Nonetheless, it was only Bangabandhu, who Yahya accused of treason. He termed Bangabandhu as the sole author of "anti-state" activities.

The Pakistani military regime and its advisors thought that Bangabandhu was at the root of all evils. This idea coincided with the doctrine of General Ayub Khan, the former military dictator. The Pakistani military credo became "Annihilate Bangabandhu and his party and all will be set straight".

However, the Bengalis had woken up. They had become engaged in the liberation struggle. They became a unified nation under the leadership of Bangabandhu - the symbol and focal point of the Bengali nation. And yet, the Pakistani rulers failed to comprehend this unequivocal truth.

Imprisoned Under Curfew

March 26th. The public was confined to their homes. Tensions pulled tight through the city. The roads were completely deserted. The shrill cries of crows heightened the nightmarish mood. Every door was bolted. Each window was clamped shut. These unsettling circumstances rekindled images from the hectic events of the past few weeks.

Since March 7th, the central government had no control or authority at all in East Pakistan. From that day on, everything moved under Bangabandhu's directives. Admiral Ahsan, the provincial governor of East Pakistan was known as a mild tempered man. As a military ruler, he was perceived as "not tough enough". General Tikka Khan, known as the notorious "Butcher", replaced him. However, the government employees of Bangladesh ignored Tikka Khan's authority as well. They continued to support the non-cooperation movement declared by Bangabandhu.

Yahya Khan arrived in Dhaka on March 15th for a dialogue with Bangabandhu. Bhutto and other West Pakistani leaders followed him. Bangabandhu set forth his uncompromising demands: drafting a constitution on the basis of the Six-Point Charter, transferring of power to him, and the withdrawal of military rule.

Rumors spread throughout Dhaka. One such rumor was that Yahya was merely biding his time in order to stockpile military material and reinforcements in preparation for a crushing attack on the Bengalis.

On the other hand, contrary rumors suggested that Yahya would hand-over power to Bangabandhu. Those days were filled with anxiety and expectations.

Every evening we visited Iqbal Hall. The Independent Bangladesh Students Action Committee had its office at Iqbal Hall. There we received information from student leaders regarding various developments. They instructed us on what to do next.

March 23rd. It was the national day of Pakistan. Typically, Pakistani flags would be hoisted from every corner of the country.

However, Bangabandhu had a different plan. He gave the call to observe March 23rd as Resistance Day. On this day, there were no Pakistani flags in sight. Pakistani flags were hoisted only at the Governor's house and the establishments within the cantonment.

However, this was not to say that flags were not proudly brandished atop each and every building. In fact, there were two types of flags seen throughout Bangladesh. The first was the black flag of mourning, commemorating those who gave their lives for the Bangladesh Liberation Movement. The second was a flag of deep red and green. These were the flags of the new nation of Bangladesh.

The Student League formally hoisted the Bangladeshi flag in a meeting at Paltan Maidan, while the national anthem of Bangladesh was sung. They went to Bangabandhu's residence and gave him a formal guard of honor and hoisted a Bangladeshi flag at his residence. Crowds were seen spontaneously marching through the streets with sticks clenched in their hands. Some were even armed with rifles and guns.

Yahya Khan was due to address the nation over the radio. This led many to think that a political settlement might have been reached. Instead, Pakistani soldiers opened fire on rallies in Rangpur and Chittagong. Bangabandhu reacted to such atrocities fiercely, and in protest, called for a strike throughout the country on March 24th.

As the next day approached, tension and fear gripped the nation. Uncertainty hung over the outcome of dialogue between Bangabandhu and the military junta.

Sometime in the evening, I had a talk with Abdul Quddus Makhon, a leader of the Students Action Committee and came to know that the dialogue had failed. This made me quite apprehensive.

At around at 8:00 pm, my fellow student activists, Amin and Habibullah, accompanied me to Iqbal Hall as usual. However, this evening was much different than most.

The student office was empty. Typically the office was bustling with many student leaders and activists. Chisti, a die-hard student activist informed us that the dialogue had failed.

Tonight, the army was preparing to crack down on Dhaka. We needed to set up barricades on various roads to prevent them from making their move into the city.

The leaders of the slums adjacent to Mohsin Hall and Jinnah Hall would provide some fifty activists. They assisted us in constructing barricades at the Shahbag Hotel intersection.

It was this group, our group, who faced the first bullets of the Bangladesh genocide in front of Shahbag Hotel.

Radio News

The rest of March 26th was marked with uncertainty and concerns. Khaja and I spent another sleepless night. At noon, we came to know from Akashvani, the Indian Radio station, that the Pakistani military junta had committed genocide throughout Dhaka. Many of the teachers and students of Dhaka University were murdered in cold blood.

The Indian radio further reported that Pakistani soldiers attacked Bengali personnel from EPR and the police department. The Bengali EPR and police personnel were attacked at their headquarters in the middle of the night while they were still asleep. In response, Bengalis had revolted from their respective positions at Peelkhana and Rajarbag. Many of them fought to their deaths. The rest were unable to put up a strong enough resistance and fled from the barracks.

Since the army was on patrol, I tuned into Akashvani, BBC, and the Voice of America and listened at a very low volume. The news of the killings and massacres gradually poured in through the radio. This was the beginning of genocide.

My tension and restlessness started to intensify. What was going on? How were my friends? Where were the Awami League leaders now? Had they been arrested? Could they flee Dhaka? Could a resistance be organized?

I was enraged and grew restless. Meanwhile, Khaja recited the Koran and steadily said his prayers.

Corpses and Ruins Everywhere

On the 27th of March, the curfew was lifted for two hours. Khaja went out to investigate the condition of his office in Old Dhaka. I went towards New Market along Elephant Road. On the streets, frightened people ran frantically in every direction. It wasn't clear where they were headed, but anxiety and fear were visible on their faces.

The flea market that once stood next to New Market was now burnt to ashes. The smoke still billowed out from under the ruins.

As I moved on, I confronted a more terrifying spectacle. It was unimaginable. Corpses were scattered in front of the shops. They dangled from rickshaws, carts, and blanketed the pavement.

It took me a while to come to grips with what had happened. As I regained my senses, I joined the procession of human bodies running in panic.

As I hysterically ran through the streets, I came across the slums adjacent to Iqbal Hall. They too, had been turned to ashes.

Next I entered the hall compound. The carnage of last night's gunfire was present everywhere. I could see one or two individuals inside. I had no idea what they could have been doing inside. Nonetheless, I didn't wait to find out. I went on my way.

While on the way towards Salimullah Muslim Hall (S. M. Hall), I found several corpses lying in a row on the pavement of Iqbal Hall. It seemed as if they were neatly positioned, side-by-side, like the keys of a piano. I presume they must have been killed elsewhere and had been placed there for a reason.

Getting closer, I realized that I could identify one of the bodies. It was Chisti Helalur Rahman, the die-hard activist of the Students League. He was dressed in trousers and just a tank top. I couldn't bear to get any closer to his lifeless body. Not that I was scared, but rather, my senses had escaped me. Without any tinge of emotion, it was as if I was watching these horrifying images through a slow-motion lens.

Eventually, others who came to see the corpses joined me. It was time that I moved on.

Chisti's image haunted me. Only some 36 hours ago, this patriotic young man asked me to construct the barricade. Now he was nothing more than a dead body. He was the first martyr of our liberation war, at least amongst the people that I knew.

He was engulfed in the dream of a librated motherland. The idea pumped through his veins. A young man from Bogra, Chisti chanted passionate slogans, which inspired others. Chisti, Aftab, Mahbub, Rabiul, Mumtaz, Nazrul and other student activists were famous slogan artists. They were specialists in firing up rallies and marches with their thunderous slogans. But Chisti's voice was now silenced forever.

I walked towards Shahid Minar (Language Movement Martyr's Monument) passing S. M. Hall. However, Chisti's memory was still in my head.

Caption: Genocide victims of Pakistani military attack in Dhaka city on March 25, 1971

Shahid Minar and the Marks of Blood

Shahid Minar was crushed to dust by the military junta. This symbol of Bengali nationalism was subjected to the wrath of the

Pakistani military. I was awfully shaken, so much so, that I did not feel any anger.

Originally, I had planned to go to Fazlul Huq Hall to find out what had happened to my friends. But this scene at Shahid Minar exhausted my strength.

I changed my plans and decided to go back to Khaja's house. Turning left, I walked between the Science Annex Building and the University Medical Center. I took a shortcut through Jagannath Hall and came near Rokeya Hall.

People were shuffling along the streets as fast as they could. While a few rickshaws were still in operation, there were no private cars on the road. Frightened, the people were fleeing.

I passed Rokeya Hall and the University Library, and then moved on towards Shahbag Hotel. At that time, I did not know that the Pakistani Army had also committed a massacre at Rokeya and Jagannath Halls.

I could see some military convoys near the hotel. Later, I came to know that they were there to seize the radio station. Ironically, this was the same platoon that had attacked us on the night of the 25th.

I made a left towards Elephant Road. I took a look at where we had constructed the barricade just two nights ago. It was all gone now. As I stood there, an army officer yelled at me from a passing jeep. They were not letting anyone stand idle. We were all asked to move quickly.

Despite his orders, I took a moment to carefully look for any signs of blood. And yes, in still pools, the sacred blood of those martyrs painted the roads crimson. Though, I knew not all of their names, the blood that had spilled was the blood of my fellow comrades.

While walking along, I glanced at the ditch I had jumped into on that fateful night. In broad daylight, the scene had become much more visible. Everything became more real. The filthiness of the ditch was indescribable.

The two-hour break in curfew was almost over. I returned quickly. Khaja too, had returned. He shared with me what he had learned of the brutality of the Pakistani soldiers in Old Dhaka.

Refugee in Jinjira

Khaja decided it was no longer safe to stay at his house. He had talked things over with his business partner and had arranged for us to stay in Jinjira from the next day on.

The curfew was lifted on March 28th. We headed out to move to Jinjira, which was just across the Buriganga River. Despite, having lived in Dhaka since 1967, I had never actually been to this older side of the city. We took a rickshaw for part of the journey. We then traveled by foot the rest of the way.

As we walked, I looked around and thought to myself, "This would be a good place for guerilla warfare". I recollected my encounter with a guerilla-warfare trainer back in early March at Raju Ahmed's home. He had told us about the Russian resistance against the Nazis to protect Leningrad.

The zigzagging narrow lanes and dark alleys of old Dhaka were very tricky. The Pakistani military would never be able to navigate through such a place. I don't know why, but my mind became flooded with fantasies of counterattacks against the Pakistani Army.

We found the Pakistani soldiers patrolling at Sadarghat Ferry Station. As a precautionary measure, we changed our plans and avoided the military. We headed further west where we hired a small boat and crossed the river.

We reached Khaja's friend's house across the Buriganga River in Jinjira. He had been living in Dhaka for a long time. As a staunch supporter of Bangabandhu and the Awami League, he was very happy to see us.

"Stay here as long as you wish", he told us.

There were already, some ten to fifteen refugees taking shelter in his home. Most of these refugees were residents of Old Dhaka city who fled their homes because they no longer felt safe. They shared with us the atrocities committed by the Pakistani military in their part of the city.

In spite of the grim setting, I enjoyed listening to the richness of the Old Dhaka city-accent, the subtle intricacies with which they told their stories, and the dry humor for which they were well known. The company of the other refugees eased my burden a bit.

Announcement of Independence

Arriving at Jinjira we heard something very significant. A Major by the name of Zia had read an announcement proclaiming the independence of Bangladesh in the name of Bangabandhu on March 27th over Swadhin Bangla Betar Kendra (Free Bangla Radio) from Chittagong. When the broadcast was repeated, I heard the announcement for myself.

Major Zia had asked the nations of the world to recognize independent Bangladesh. Bangabandhu was safe. The people of the country were putting up a strong resistance against the Pakistani Army.

This information reminded me of an earlier event. On March 19th, a historic incident took place in Joydebpur Cantonment on the outskirts of Dhaka. The Pakistani military authority ordered the East Bengal Regiment in Joydebpur garrison to disarm.

However, the Bengali soldiers and their officers refused to lay down their arms and fought against the West Pakistani Army.

It was the first open rebellion by the Bengali soldiers against the West Pakistani military. It was the first armed resistance by the Bengali people.

Nevertheless, I was enthused by Zia's announcement. I felt inspired knowing that Bengali soldiers were proceeding towards Dhaka from Chittagong and Comilla.

Everybody in the house was tuned into Zia's announcement and the news bulletins from Free Bangla Radio.

My fellow refugees then asked me what I was going to do next. From their questions I realized that Khaja had exaggerated my stature.

I decided on my next course of action. I told Khaja that I would leave Jinjira to join the fighters in the free zones of Comilla and Chittagong.

I inquired whether anyone could guide me to my destination. Someone enthusiastically volunteered. The plan was to go to Agartala, a town on the other side of the Indian border. We would have to travel on foot and by boat.

I was excited, but Khaja objected. He didn't object to my joining the liberation war. Rather, he insisted that I get my father's consent.

Khaja's suggestion required a visit to my parent's home in Tangail. I was a loving son. My father regarded me as the source of the family's pride and dreamed that one day I would become a minister or a well-respected bureaucrat. Khaja was not ready to shoulder any responsibility if anything happened to me in combat.

Rumors spread that the Pakistani Army would attack Jinjira in search of fleeing Bengali EPR and police personnel from Peelkhana and Rajarbag. Everyone was frightened.

The Pakistani military raided Jinjira that very night. Luckily, they were still quite a distance from our location. Nonetheless, they could attack any day. Jinjira was no longer safe.

We returned to Dhaka the next day, on March 29th.

The question I had to ask myself was - where would I go from here.

The Road Home

I came to know that the Dhaka-Tangail buses were in operation. I proceeded towards Gulistan bus terminal.

Khaja saw me off as I boarded the bus. It was over-crowded. There was no place to sit. I had no choice, so I continued standing.

My fellow passengers all looked awfully tense and terrified. Everyone was silent. People were fleeing with whatever they could carry in hand. This was the pervasive scene on the road. Many of them were moving out with their family members.

In those days, buses to Tangail passed through the cantonment. However, on this day, as the bus approached the cantonment, the soldiers told the driver that the buses were no longer allowed. We had to take a different route.

As the driver made a u-turn, he accidentally got the bus caught on the road divider. It could have been that the driver was a novice. It could have also been that he was just terribly frightened. Regardless, the soldiers became suspicious.

They came over and asked everyone to get down. While we all stood in a row, we prayed to Allah for our lives. After the experiences of the last few days, we were all genuinely horrified. Even the young children began to cry.

The soldiers were particularly scrutinizing the male passengers. They then picked out four individuals who appeared to be stout and strong. I was overlooked, perhaps, because of my small physique.

Thankfully, the rest of us were asked to get onto the bus. Of the four, one of them was traveling with his wife and children. They cried aloud. They refused to get onto the bus without him.

Pain struck deep into the hearts of the passengers. But alas, we were helpless. The sharp knife of death was at everyone's throat. The bus returned towards Gulistan. The four unfortunate souls were left behind.

Only Allah knows what happened to those fellows.

I asked the driver to move towards Aricha through Mirpur. He was so frightened that my words didn't even reach his ears.

We returned to Gulistan. I boarded an Aricha-bound bus. We were all petrified as the bus pulled near Mirpur Bridge. The army might also be stationed at this point. It occurred to me that we might not be able to leave Dhaka.

Fortunately, there was no military post or presence at Mirpur Bridge. The bus driver pressed down hard on the gas pedal as we crossed the bridge. We were all relieved. We were finally out of Dhaka city limits. We had all gained a new lease on life.

We crossed Jahangirnagar University. I got off the bus at Nabinagar Cross Road, which connected to a road to Tangail.

The Caravan

More than a hundred families were waiting at Nabinagar to go to Tangail. However, no transportation was available. I waited for half an hour.

Then a local leader appeared to inform us that there would be no transportation arriving for us here. He told us that if we could walk down to Tangail Road, we might be able to find some means of transportation. We all walked towards Tangail Road.

I had no luggage with me. I only had fifty takas in my pocket, which Khaja had given me before I left. I was walking quickly.

A large procession formed. The women and children found it a little difficult to walk. Some people had been carrying more than one bag. Many of them probably had never walked such a distance before. It was about ten miles, but it felt like a never-ending march.

To protect life, honor, and dignity, we all fled Dhaka to escape the grasp of the Pakistani military beast.

I was walking with a family. They had left their home at Dhanmondi behind. Their new destination was Jamalpur. The head of the family was a public servant. He was carrying his young son in his arms. His wife was carrying a couple of bags. Their daughter would have been about 15 or 16. She was also carrying two bags. I volunteered to take a bag from the mother. She thanked me, but refused.

"It is not too difficult," she said, "but if you could carry my child that would give my husband a much needed break."

I gladly obliged.

It took us four hours to reach Tangail Road.

Free Tangail

The buses were at Tangail Road as we expected. Here, we came to know that Bangabandhu had formally proclaimed the independence of Bangladesh before his arrest by the Pakistani Army on the night of March 25th.

Bangabandhu's proclamation message was distributed by the EPR wireless system to all the cities in Bangladesh.

But to me, Bangabandhu proclaimed the independence of Bangladesh on March 7th at Ramna Race Course (now Suhrawardy Park) when he declared "--the Struggle this time is a struggle for Independence--".

The Free Bangladesh Liberation Council of Tangail had propagated Bangabandhu's proclamation of independence in Tangail by announcing his message through loud speakers and distributing leaflets. They arranged buses for the people fleeing Dhaka.

Everyone was eager to know what was happening in Dhaka. We all gave our stories. We came to know more about the Liberation Council of Tangail. Abdul Latif Siddiqui, a member of the Provincial Assembly had been elected chairman of the council and Khandoker Asaduzzaman, a senior civil servant was the advisor.

We further came to know that the Bengali soldiers, under the leadership of Major Shafiullah, left Joydebpur garrison and were organizing a war of resistance. Moreover, the people of Tangail were planning to arrest the Pakistani soldiers stationed in Tangail. These stories and the formation of the Liberation Council in Tangail inspired me. I felt stronger.

My plan was not to stop in Tangail, but rather, to go straight to my parent's house. Everyone at home was anxious to see me. I took the bus towards Mymensingh en route to Gopalpur. From there, I still had a five-mile walk ahead of me. When I finally reached my Khamarpara home, it was quite late at night.

Chapter 2

Resistance

The Formation of the Bangladesh Government

My father, my older brother, and others were delighted to have me back at home. My father had asked me to come home after the university closed down on March 1st.

Unfortunately, I hadn't been in touch with him since. My family had become extremely worried ever since they heard about the military crackdown on the university during the early hours of March 26th.

It was just a few months ago that we had lost my mother to cancer. Had she been alive, undoubtedly she would have been worried-sick about me.

The news of my arrival spread throughout the region. Herds of people from neighboring villages came to see me. They wished to be updated on the escalating situation in Dhaka.

Inquisitively, they all asked the same questions, "What was going to happen next? Would we languish as the slaves of Pakistan? Would we ever be free? They were all anxious to know.

On April 10th, news of the formation of the Bangladesh government was broadcasted over Free Bangla Radio. A government body was formed in exile in India.

On the 11th, Tajuddin Ahmad, the General Secretary of the Awami League and leader of the exiled Bangladesh government, addressed the nation and asked Bengalis to join the liberation war to fight Pakistan.

He briefed us on the state of the liberation war. His words inspired hope in us all. Tajuddin had answered all of our questions.

The Battle of Kalihati

On the morning of April 13th, we heard fierce blasts of mortar shells coming from the south. News came in that Pakistani forces had already taken over the towns of Tangail and Mymensingh. The Bengali soldiers, EPR forces, the police and freedom fighters tried to put up a resistance. Unfortunately, they were unsuccessful and were forced to retreat towards the Indian border.

Suddenly, I became increasingly more curious about the sound of firing from the south. I became intrigued.

I talked to my cousin Latif. He was a student of Ananda Mohan College. Together, we planned to go and find out more about the firing. However, other young men such as my cousins Hasmat, Kajim, and Manju, and Jainal, a local bank employee decided to join us as well.

Four school students named Mohan, Makhan, Jyotsna and Shahjahan, and Mr. Farhad Ali, an elderly man also joined our group.

We all proceeded south. As we got closer, the sound of gunfire became more intense. By noon, we had heard that the EPR forces had put up a resistance against the Pakistan Army in Kalihati. Abdul Latif Siddiqui, the member of the Provincial Assembly was leading the resistance.

Earlier that morning, the firing began near the Kalihati Bridge. Now, it was evident to us that the fighting had moved north to Ghatail. We decided not to travel any farther and stopped at Garjana.

The villagers at Garjana informed us that the EPR force could not hold its position against the strong offensive of the Pakistani Army. They were forced to flee and dispersed in various directions.

A few minutes later, we saw a Pakistani helicopter land at Ghatail police station. This confirmed our fear that in addition to Kalihati, Ghatail Police Station had fallen to the enemy, as well.

We had traveled a long distance, only to receive this terrible news. We were all heartbroken.

It was almost evening. We headed back north towards our village. After having traveled fifteen miles on foot, we had become very tired and hungry. We decided to take a break and spend the night at a friend's house.

The next day we returned home. We were received with the furious eyes of my father and others. My father scolded that it was wrong of me to take the others. All of my uncles were livid that I took their sons with me and made them spend the night away from home.

The Provisional Government of Independent Bangladesh

On April 17th, Free Bangla Radio broadcasted the swearing-in ceremony of the provisional government of Independent Bangladesh. The inauguration ceremony was held in Mujibnagar, in the liberated area of Kushtia, just outside the Indian border.

Bangabandhu Sheikh Mujibur Rahman was elected President of independent Bangladesh. Since he was imprisoned in Pakistan, Syed Nazrul Islam was elected the acting-President. Tajuddin Ahmed was elected Prime Minister, while the other ministers were Captain Muhammad Mansur Ali, Abul Hasnat Muhammad Qamaruzzaman, and Khondokar Mushtaque Ahmed.

This proclamation marked a new chapter in Bangladesh liberation history. It was an exciting moment for us.

In those days, we ardently listened to news bulletins from foreign radio stations such as, Akashvani, the BBC, and the Voice of America. Free Bangla Radio was broadcasted every evening.

Many households had their own transistor radios, but usually some twenty-five to thirty people would assemble at our compound to listen to the broadcast together.

After the broadcast, we would all discuss the situation till midnight, before going to sleep. I usually spent my day playing cards and chess with my cousins, Latif, Hasmat, and Kajim.

My Comrade, Habibullah

One afternoon, while playing cards, Mohan came running in to say, "Look who has come". As I looked outside, I saw Habibullah, my dear friend and fellow activist from Fazlul Huq Hall at Dhaka University.

I jumped up and gave him a bear hug. I was both amazed and excited.

The last time we were together was on the evening of March 25th. While we were constructing the barricades in front of the Shahbag Hotel, we had become separated trying to save our lives from the shower of Pakistani bullets. Until now, I hadn't been sure if he had survived that evening.

After lunch, Habibullah told us of his horrifying experience. On that very evening when the Pakistani Army started firing, he fled and ran back to Fazlul Huq Hall. The firing went on throughout the night. The Pakistani armed forces went on with their carnage at Iqbal Hall, Jagannath Hall, Rokeya Hall, and then entered Dhaka Hall by morning.

Once in Dhaka Hall, they killed Prof. Khan Khadem, a teacher in the physics department and a large number of students and employees of the hall.

They then invaded Fazlul Huq Hall, which was adjacent to Dhaka Hall. Habibullah along with some twenty-five activists of the non-cooperation movement were still inside the hall. They could smell the impending danger. They divided themselves up into several groups and went into hiding.

There was a West Pakistani guard who had been working at Fazlul Huq Hall for many years. The Pakistani soldiers asked him to open the hall gates and lead them to the students. He swore in the name of Allah that there were no residents inside the hall. He told them that the few who had been there had left the hall the previous evening. The Pakistani soldiers believed their fellow West Pakistani and left the premises.

The humanity of this West Pakistani Pathan guard, and above all, the will of God, saved the lives of these twenty-five students, including that of my good friend, Habibullah.

Habibullah hailed from Netrokona, a town in the Mymensingh District. He could not find any means of transportation to Netrokona from Dhaka, so he decided to head home through Tangail.

Although he knew I was from Tangail, Tangail was a large district with eight counties. He wasn't sure exactly where about Tangail I was from.

It was completely coincidental that he ran into a man in Tangail town, who told him that I lived in a village in Gopalpur. I was really glad to see him.

The three of us, Latif, Habibullah, and I decided that we would go to India to join the liberation forces. However, my father raised an important point. Habibullah should not leave for India directly from our place. He should first go to his parents and seek their approval first. Habibullah agreed.

He rested up for a week and then prepared to leave for Netrokona. By then all the towns and local police headquarters had been taken over by Pakistani forces.

Habibullah was healthy and stout. It would be easy for Pakistani soldiers to suspect him as a Bengali member of the armed forces. So traveling by bus and walking through towns were out of the question.

He decided that he would have to walk through the rural areas. This path would take him about eight to ten days to reach Netrokona. Nonetheless, it was the only way to be safe.

On the day Habibullah was supposed to leave, a family from Pabna stopped by our home. They were on their way from Sirajganj to Netrokona.

The family consisted of a young public servant, his wife and a 2-year old daughter. They told us about what had happened in Pabna and Sirajganj. The Sub-Divisional Officer (SDO) of Sirajganj mobilized a Bengali resistance against the Pakistani forces with a display of extraordinary courage.

However, he was forced to withdraw in the face of a massive air raid. Once again, the Bengali forces fled towards the Indian border and the two towns fell into the enemy's hands.

The SDO of Sirajganj was a courageous and handsome young man. He retreated to the border, along with his forces.

One of the SDO's relatives was a high-ranking Bengali civil servant, who was pro-Pakistani. The civil servant convinced the SDO to return to his job and assured him that he would make sure that nothing would happen to him.

Buying into his story, the SDO trusted his relative and returned to his job. Immediately, the young SDO was captured and taken to Dhaka Cantonment. It was there, where he was mercilessly tortured day-after-day until finally his flesh-torn body fell dead to the floor.

This SDO of Sirajganj was one of many Bengali officers who was tortured and killed in the custody of the Pakistani Army.

After listening to their disheartening tale, we served the public servant and his family lunch. We suggested to the family that they stay with us for a few days before continuing the rest of their journey.

They politely declined and left with Habibullah for Netrokona. Latif and I escorted them across the Tangail-Madhupur Highway towards the Madhupur Forest.

The Way to India

Latif and I decided that we would head to India in early May. We were trying to determine the best way to get across the border. In the first week of May, Imam, paid us an unexpected visit. Imam was the husband of Sufia, Latif's sister. Sufia was staying with us. Imam was working as a member of the EPR in Halishahar, Chittagong.

However, since March 25th, no one knew of his whereabouts. We had heard of a battle in Halishahar between the EPR and Pakistani military forces. We were all worried. Sufia spent many sleepless nights crying and praying for her husband. Now, with Imam's arrival, our home was filled with happiness and relief.

Imam told us about what he had been through in Chittagong. The members of the EPR, the East Bengal Regiment, and the police had each put up a fierce resistance. Halishahar was the EPR headquarters. The EPR's initial strike against the Pakistani forces was successful. However, the EPR, grossly under-armed, was forced to retreat against a superior military strength.

Imam went on to tell us that many members of the EPR, East Bengal Regiment, and the police had regrouped. They had engaged in a battle against Pakistani forces in the territories closest to the border. He himself became detached from his platoon and never made it across the border. So he returned to Tangail. He came partly by boat and partly on foot. His journey took him almost a month.

We told Imam that we planned to go to India. He was happy to hear the news and volunteered to accompany us. Regardless, he knew that his wife Sufia would require some convincing. For that he asked us to give him a week or two. We postponed our plan accordingly.

We set out for India on a sunny morning in mid-May. Sufia and Latif's mother wept bitterly as they said good-bye to Imam and Latif. There was nobody to weep for me. However, I could see my aunt wiping her tears. My father and older brother embraced me to say that God would protect me.

As we left from the southern exit of our home, we headed north to the public road. There, we passed the courtyard on the right side of our property. It was from this spot that my mother used to watch me when I left for school. But on this day, as I turned to the courtyard I could only see my aunts and Sufia standing under the tree. I missed my mother. I wished she could have been there to see me off.

In the past, when I would leave home, first for Ananda Mohan College and then later for Dhaka University, my mother would stand under the tree for as long as she could see me. I wondered whether she would have allowed me to leave for India if she were still alive.

During the liberation movement of 1969, the Pakistani Army killed Asad, a student leader near Dhaka University. When my mother got wind that a student was killed in Dhaka, she became terribly upset as her eyes filled with tears. It was only after she heard Asad's name over the radio that she settled down and stopped crying. News of any incident in Dhaka would upset my mother.

Nonetheless, on this day, her memory haunted me. I missed her very much. I struggled to hold in my tears, but failed. I walked quickly ahead of Imam and Latif to keep them from seeing my eyes. Throughout our walk, I didn't say a word to them. Imam was trying to tease me, "Hey leader, you aren't getting scared, are you? You aren't chickening-out about joining the war?"

I couldn't tell them what was really on my mind.

We spent the night at Imam's place. The next morning we moved north toward Jamalpur. We spent the whole day walking along the coastal areas of the Jamuna River and reached a small village on the west side of Islampur. We needed to find a village that had accommodations for guests. Finally we found one.

The residents of the house greeted us warmly. I have long since forgotten the name of the village, but I remember it was within the constituency of Rashed Musharraf, a member of the Parliament.

We disclosed to the family our plan to cross over to India after dinner. At that time, a bank official working in Jamalpur town was staying in the village. He was one of thousands of Bengali civil servants who remained on-strike in support of the non-cooperation movement. He informed us that two days ago, a group of young men were arrested while trying to cross the border to India.

Apparently, this route was not as safe as we had hoped. This was disappointing. We decided that we would go back to Tangail in the morning and explore an alternate route.

After dinner, we gossiped with the residents of the house. Then as we were preparing to go to sleep, a young boy brought a note for us and said, "Read it, it has been sent by my Apa (older sister)." I unfolded the note and read the message. A student of Mymensingh Girls College had written it. She was an activist of the Student Union. Since the college had been closed for the non-cooperation movement, she had been staying at her village home.

The message confirmed the earlier story of the group arrested by Pakistani forces. However, it also identified a village leader who conspired in the arrest. He was pro-Pakistani. The message further warned that a follower of that man had been spying on us! The girl cautioned that we might be in grave danger. Therefore, she had requested that we leave the village right away.

This piece of paper impacted me in two ways. I came to understand and appreciate the patriotic sentiments of a young woman. However, the presence of a pro-Pakistani village leader angered me greatly.

I showed the message to Imam and Latif. A resident of the house was still with us, making it difficult to discuss the matter openly. However, reading their faces I could tell they were eager to know our next move. At this point we all knew we could not afford to trust anyone.

We thanked our hosts for their hospitality and mentioned that we'd be heading for the border now. At the stroke of midnight we left the house. Immediately we began discussing the contents of the letter. Latif and Imam agreed with me. Crossing the border tonight was too risky with a spy on our heels. We decided to backtrack and started walking southward to Tangail District.

It was a very dark night. We had no flashlight. We couldn't even see the ground on which we walked. It was becoming impossible to move. Finally, after walking for about four hours, we gave up. We were so tired that we needed to look for a place to sleep. Most of the dwellings in this costal area were just one-room shacks. However, we would need to find a place with some sort of guest quarters. Once again, we got lucky.

The night was coming to an end. Very carefully, we awoke the head of the family. We apologized for bothering him and sought his permission to spend the rest of the night in his guest quarters. He happily agreed. However, the guest quarters were actually a one-room shed for his cows. In the corner of the room was a small cot. Nonetheless, we were so tired that we had no trouble sleeping alongside the cows!

At about ten in the morning, our host served us some Chatu (fried wheat powder), salt and water for breakfast. We needed to walk the whole day along the coastal belt and realized that food might be a rare thing to find. So we gratefully accepted his hospitality and ate whatever he could offer. With our stomachs full, we continued our journey.

We did not come home directly. Rather, we stayed at Imam's place for a week. When we finally returned, we noticed that not everyone was pleased with our presence.

The Formation of the Freedom Fighters Group

By then, Pakistani occupation forces had deployed the Pakistani militia and armed forces in every police station in Tangail District. They had started organizing "Peace Committees" and Razakar groups to support Pakistani forces. Razakars were local pro-Pakistani armed militias. They consisted of members from the Jamaat-e-Islami and the Muslim League, two pro-Pakistani political parties.

Under these circumstances, it was unsafe for a family to house one EPR member and two student activists. The three of us had no choice, but to split up. My father arranged a hideout for me. Imam went back to his parent's home, while Latif went to another relative's place to stay. I went to Chargovindabasi, Bhuapur to stay with my older brother's in-laws.

Two days later, on June 2nd, Shamsu, a student of Bhuapur College came to see me. I told him of my plan to join the liberation forces. Shamsu reported that Anwar-ul Alam Shaheed, general secretary of S. M. Hall Student Union was hiding in the neighboring village. I knew him very well at Dhaka University. I asked Shamsu to arrange a meeting with Shaheed.

The next day, Shamsu and I went to the home of Aziz Bangal, another student of Bhuapur College. There I met Shaheed and told him of my plan to join the liberation forces. Shaheed told me that Enayet Karim; president of the Tangail District Student League had also been living underground in a nearby village. Shaheed and I decided to form a group of Mukti Bahini, freedom fighters. I returned to my hideout at Chargovindabasi.

After two days, Shamsu came back to see me. He told me that two more student leaders, namely Sohrab Ali Khan Arzoo and Mohammad Suhrawardi had been hiding in the neighboring village and wanted to see me. They also wanted to form a Mukti Bahini group. Shamsu had mentioned my name to them. They immediately showed their interest in me.

I went to see them right away. They told me that they had gathered some arms left behind by the EPR after the Battle of Kalihati. If we could recruit a dozen policemen, EPR, and Bengal Regiment soldiers, and student activists, we could form a group of freedom fighters. The proposal was quite encouraging. I told them about Imam and a couple of soldiers who had left the EPR. I promised to contact them.

It was decided that on June 18th, some Bengali members of the army, EPR, and police would assemble with their weapons in a village on the west side of Bhuapur. I left for home to prepare.

At this point, Latif had already returned. I had sent a message for Imam. Latif and I went to a village named Banni to meet a policeman, and then to two other villages to meet two soldiers. We requested that they join the liberation forces. It was only in April that these three had last fought against the Pakistanis. They had since withdrawn to their villages in defeat. They questioned whether we had the firepower and ammunition to face the Pakistani military force. We told them about our dozen "303 Rifles". But apparently, that wasn't enough to convince them. The three men did not join us. We came back disappointed.

Imam returned to our place. Imam and I left for Bhuapur to join Arzoo and Suharawardi. Latif did not join us on that day, but a few months later he joined the Mukti Bahini as well.

On June 18th, we met Arzoo and Suhrawardi in a village on the west of Bhuapur. There were about twenty people, but only a dozen rifles. Habibur Rahman, an army soldier was present. Three student activists, Mati, Smriti, and Kalam came from Tangail town. We decided that the military training must begin immediately. Habibur Rahman was appointed our trainer, while Imam was selected as his assistant.

The next day, some more men joined our group. I told them of my failed mission regarding the three individuals who declined our invitation. Habibur underlined the urgent need for army personnel. If they knew that Habibur was working with this group, they might change their minds and join us. I was asked to visit them again.

Training went enthusiastically on the first day. Before we knew it, we were an organized camp of liberation forces. Sentries were deployed on regular shifts around the camp. The next day, we had even more recruits.

To facilitate the recruitment of those three individuals, I returned home on June 22. I would meet them the next day.

Joining Kader Siddiqui

It was the morning of June 23rd. As I was leaving my house to make my visits, eight strangers arrived at the front courtyard. I was a little surprised. The men were dressed in lungis and robed in shawls. It was summertime, so the shawls looked suspicious. They said that they were here to see me. As they took off their shawls, I saw that each was armed with a Sten gun. They were freedom fighters.

They had just received training in India. Their first mission was to blow up the bridges on Dhaka-Tangail Highway and Tangail-Madhupur Highway. It was expected that with the destruction of the bridges, the mobility of the Pakistani forces would be restricted and their morale would be left in the rubble.

After arriving to the area, they had heard of my activities, which prompted them to come to see me. Lutfor Rahman of Sharishabari was their leader. The freedom fighters whose names I remember were Tuku, Rakib, Foyez and Badal. With the exception of Lutfor Rahman, who was a businessman, the others were students from different colleges and schools in the Jamalpur District.

They had arrived at Lutfor's place from Mankachar, India by boat. The freedom fighters carried with them Light Machineguns (LMGs), Sten guns, and explosives. They had left the ammunition at

Sharishabari and came to seek my help in getting the support of the local people.

I was extremely pleased to see them. I told them of my activities over the last few weeks and assured them that I would help. They were encouraged by my accounts.

I arranged for their breakfast. Then quickly, I led them to our camp at Bhuapur. We were a team of nine freedom fighters, eight of us armed with automatic weapons. Every onlooker, young and old, was excited by our presence.

It was nearly mid-day when we reached camp. However, to my surprise, no one was there. The landlord informed us that our Mukti Bahini group had gone to Bhuapur Bazaar to join another Mukti Bahini group led by Kader Siddiqui. We wasted no time and headed straight to Bhuapur.

We arrived at Bhuapur by early afternoon. For us, Bhuapur presented an exciting scenario. Freedom fighters were on guard at every point of entry to Bhuapur Bazaar. A group of guards halted us. We disclosed our identities and then were escorted to Bhuapur Bungalow. Freedom fighters in proper uniforms with LMGs and 303 Rifles were everywhere. It was an unforgettable experience.

Stepping toward the bungalow, I wondered if I knew this commander of freedom fighters, this Kader Siddiqui. Could he be the younger brother of Latif Siddiqui? Was he the same Kader Siddiqui who was once the general secretary of the Tangail Student League?

I recalled that in 1970, during the central conference of the Student League at Dhaka, arrangements were made for the delegates of Tangail to take their mid-day rest at Fazlul Huq Hall. At that time Kader and others came to my dorm-room to rest. I recalled meeting him again in Tangail on another trip returning home from Dhaka. I had been wishfully thinking that this Mukti Bahini commander would be the same man I had known.

My presumption was correct. I saw Kader sitting on a chair in the balcony. He had changed a lot since I last saw him. He had grown his hair and beard. He was wearing a military uniform with a pistol bound to his waist. A freedom fighter introduced me to him. I mentioned to him that we had met before at Fazlul Huq Hall. Then I introduced my companions and explained why they had come to our area. While discussing these matters, I expressed my joy and excitement to meet the freedom fighters under his command. I immediately stated my desire to join his group.

In Kader Siddiqui's book titled Swadhinata '71, he describes our first encounter as follows.

> On June 23rd, a young man of twenty-two or twenty-three years old, named Nuran Nabi came to our camp at noon. He was from Hemnagar of Gopalpur. He was accompanied by a group of eight freedom fighters that had come from India. They wanted to blast the bridges on Dhaka-Tangail or Tangail-Mymensingh Highway.
>
> Nuran Nabi said, 'They seek your cooperation.' He wore spectacles, looked rather short and had round face. He further said, 'the group came to our village. I have escorted them here; I want to join your group. This year I have appeared at the Honors Final Examination in Biochemistry at Dhaka University. Whatever responsibility you assign me, I will do it… and I can do it'.
>
> I looked at the innocent and affectionate face of the young man without a blink and said, 'If you really want to cooperate with us, you can do a lot; there is no doubt about that. Give me some time and I will talk to you in the evening. You have walked a long distance. Have your meals and take some rest.

After lunch, I met with Shaheed, Enayet Karim, Moazzem Hossain Khan, Ali Asgar Khan, Aziz Bangal, Shamsu, Abdul Alim, Quddus, Bhola, Dudu Mia (a local leader), and three middle-aged men named Abdul Bari, Bharat, and Arfan. Like me, they all joined the group that day.

With the presence of Shaheed, Shamsu and Aziz, I felt at home. However, contrary to my expectations, Arzoo and Suhrawardi of our team were not there. Nonetheless, I found Habibur Rahman, Imam and others. I came to learn that Arzoo and Suhrawardi were here yesterday with the group. Previously, they committed to Kader that they would help build up the Mukti Bahini.

However, last week, they had formed a Mukti Bahini group with others and me and began their operations. When our group was initially formed, neither Arzoo, nor Suhrawardi, had mentioned the name of Kader Siddqui.

Apparently, they had a disagreement with Kader. Since Arzoo and Suhrawardi failed to uphold their pledge, Kader did not accept them into his group, claiming that it was in the greater interest of the liberation war.

However, a few months later, these two men would join the Mukti Bahini again under Kader and performed their duties with unparalleled dedication.

Kader Siddiqui

I met Kader again later that evening. He suggested that I work at the Mukti Bahini headquarters. Shaheed and a few others would also be working there. So, I gladly accepted.

On the evenings of June 23rd and 24th, I had conversations with several members of the Mukti Bahini, including close confidants of Kader. They explained when and how Kader had organized this group of freedom fighters.

Kader's father was a well-known lawyer in Tangail. His older brother Abdul Latif Siddiqui was a student leader and was later elected to the East Pakistan Provincial Assembly. After a family incident, Kader left home and joined the Pakistani Army. There, he served for two years, but then left the military to attend college.

As a college student, Kader became very active in students politics. He was elected general secretary of the Tangail District Student League. During the non-cooperation movement of March 1971, Kader played a significant role in Tangail District.

After the 26th of March 1971, the Free Bangladesh Liberation Council of Tangail was formed under the leadership of Latif Siddiqui. Kader was also an active member of the council. He attempted to convince the soldiers of the Bengal Regiment stationed in Tangail to defect for Bangladesh.

After the fall of Tangail under Pakistani military occupation, Kader tried to flee to India. However, he failed and went underground to the hilly areas of Tangail in April 1971. It was then, from amidst the shadows, that Kader secretly planned an intricate network to organize the Mukti Bahini. On May 4th, 1971, the Mukti Bahini formally made its debut with Kader Siddiqui and his trusted associates.

Kader's associates, with whom he founded the Mukti Bahini, were: Manirul Islam, Saidur Rahman, Faruk Ahmad, Abul Malek, Abdur Razzak Siddiqui, Sadrul, Hamidul Haq, Khorshed Alam, Shawkat Momen Shahjahan, Mamunur Rashid, and Moazzem Hossain Khan.

Kader Siddiqui began his operations by stockpiling arms and ammunition left by the EPR. Next, he began training the new recruits of the Mukti Bahini. Then, in need of a headquarters for the Mukti Bahini, he took to the hills of Sakhipur. Sakhipur was just adjacent to Kalihati and Basail. Establishing a base there would later prove to be a significant strategic move.

On June 10th, Kader Siddiqui formally took an oath with his fellow freedom fighters at Bahertali Bazaar in Sakhipur. He organized the Mukti Bahini into several companies. Each company was placed under the leadership of a skilled commander. Each commander took charge of a specific zone. From May 4th to June 19th, the Mukti Bahini was successful in various operations against Pakistani forces and their allies.

Kader Siddiqui himself led operations against the police stations in Kalihati, Ghatail, and Gopalpur. The success of these operations created great enthusiasm amongst the freedom fighters. Gopalpur police station was taken over on June 19th. The next day, Kader Siddiqui moved to Bhuapur Bazaar and established a camp.

I, along with Shaheed and other student leaders, joined Kader at Bhuapur on June 23rd. From that very day, the three of us, Kader, Shaheed, and I, formed a successful team. We were the core leaders and our relationship was built on mutual trust and respect. Each of us was complementary and respectful to one another. The cohesion of this trinity would be the key to the success of the Tangail Mukti Bahini.

Kader possessed extraordinary organizing skills and self-confidence. He was a rare military genius. His knack for strategic-military planning was unparalleled. Shaheed and I were his left and right arms. From these strengths he built the Mukti Bahini comprising of seventeen thousand freedom fighters and fifty thousand volunteers.

In recognition of his heroism, he was popularly known as "Bagha" or "Tiger" Siddiqui. The Bangladesh Government awarded him the gallantry title Bir Uttam, the highest title awarded to living-war heroes. Kader Siddiqui, in my opinion, is the greatest war hero in Bangladesh's history.

Kader Siddiqui, Commander of Tangail Mukti Bahini

On June 25th, Kader went to Falda to visit the company of Fazlur Rahman. I, along with Shaheed, Moazzem, Daud, and Nurul accompanied him. There, I witnessed a great exhibition of discipline by the Mukti Bahini. Fazlur Rahman's company received Kader with a military guard of honor. Thousands of people assembled to watch this ceremony.

Captain Fazlur Rahman carried the demeanor of a very smart and skilled leader. His woolly moustache resembled that of the world-renowned artists, Salvador Dali. Captain Rahman's fluency in English, his neatly pressed military uniform, his pistol and grenade at his waist, all made him stand out as an archetype commander. The freedom fighters in his group demonstrated exceptional athletic feats. Everyone appreciated his accomplishment of building such a disciplined Mukti Bahini unit. In the evening we came back to Bhuapur.

By then, Kader was known as the Commander-in-Chief of Tangail Mukti Bahini. Everyone greeted him with that title and called him "Sir". Without any hesitation, I too, followed suit. Some even referred to the Tangail Mukti Bahini as the Kaderia Bahini.

That evening, Kader called me in for a meeting. He said that contact with the Indian government was of the utmost importance. He entrusted me with this responsibility. I had to go to India. Eagerly, I accepted the assignment. I said, "I hope, I can prove myself worthy of your trust, Sir."

Nurul would be my companion to India. Before the war broke out, he was the chief of Tangail District Volunteer League. He went to India in April and came back in May. Among the eight freedom fighters that had come from India, Lutfor Rahman and four others would join me on my journey to India. The remaining three stayed at camp with the Tangail Mukti Bahini. We left for India on the night of June 26th.

Contact with the Indian Government

By mid-June 1971, the Mukti Bahini was able to liberate large areas of Tangail District from the Pakistani-occupation forces. Tangail was only forty miles from Dhaka. At this point, the Pakistani Army only had control over Tangail town and a few police stations. This was quite embarrassing for the Pakistani military junta.

They tried to mount a counter-strike on the Mukti Bahini to recapture the liberated areas. Initially, the Mukti Bahini strategy was simply "to hit and run". We found some success with this strategy. However, it was essential to have heavy arms and ammunition to maintain the liberated areas and protect our headquarters.

Additionally, in order to counter the attack of the enemy, it was essential that we limit their movement by destroying some bridges. However, there was one major setback to this plan. We didn't have any explosives.

Kader's plan was to make contact with India and the exiled Bangladesh government at Mujibnagar to get supplies of heavy arms and ammunition. This became my responsibility.

Crossing the Border

With this mission, my companions and I left Bhuapur for India on June 26th. We hired a small boat for our voyage. Our first stop was Lutfor's house at Raghunathpur. It was across the Jamuna River to the north of Jagannathganj Ferry Station. Another five freedom fighters joined us there. These five men had come from India with Lutfor, but stayed behind at his house while Lutfor visited me.

After sailing for two days and two nights, we reached Changainarchar, about fifteen miles north of Bahadurabad Ferry Station.

We were truly in a "danger zone", but this had nothing to do with Pakistani forces. This area belonged to pirates! The people here lived in constant fear of attack.

Even though we were armed freedom fighters, we too, were not immune to such raids. In the dark hours of the night as we passed through, pirates tried to attack our boat. They fired at our boat and asked us to stop. The boatmen panicked. However, I asked them to move quickly and try to escape from the pirates.

Lutfor became excited. He wanted to test his training. He wanted to test out his machinegun. He sought my permission to retaliate. This would be his first test as a soldier. This would be my first test as a leader.

I thought for a moment and said to Lutfor, "No, don't shoot".

I explained to him that the sound of gunfire would surely alert our enemies at Bahadurabad Ferry Station and would put us at risk of losing our cover. Moreover, as the Mukti Bahini commonly used this route, we couldn't afford to reveal it to our enemies. If this were to happen, things could really get dangerous, not only for us, but also for every freedom fighter who chose to travel by this route.

It was up to us to discover a secret and safe river passage to India. Until now, this route appeared to be the quickest and safest. But now, I had no choice, but to make a strategic decision. We retreated for about thirty miles and embarked on an alternative route.

This time, we divided ourselves into two groups until we reached the Melandah area of Jamalpur, each group taking a separate path. We had to walk down an additional fifteen miles. The groups were formed with the assumption that if one failed, the other would still fulfill its mission to reach India and inform the governments of Bangladesh and India of our situation.

The first group consisted of Nurul, Lutfor, and I. We were to report at the Indian border check-post in Porakhasia via Islampur. Rakib, Tuku, Foyez, and Badal were in the second group. Their destination was the Mukti Bahini camp at the Mahendraganj-Indian border post via Dewanganj. Both routes were dangerous and filled with peril. But against all odds, we went on.

On the 2nd of July, our team took shelter at the residence of Bashir Master (teacher). Bashir was a fearless and truly patriotic individual. He secretly offered shelter to freedom fighters and was always hospitable.

He knew of the Tangail Mukti Bahini. One of his sons was a correspondent for the Daily Paigam, a newspaper owned by Monem Khan, former pro-Pakistani Governor of East Pakistan. In spite of this, he strongly supported the liberation war.

Incidentally, the chairman of the local council was a Pakistani supporter and also the chairman of the pro-Pakistani Peace Committee. If he ever came to know about our presence, we would be in serious trouble, and Bashir's fate would be no better. Despite these risks, he gave shelter to my team. Other freedom fighters continued to receive similar hospitality from Bashir Master during the war.

On the 3rd of July, we resumed our journey. Hazaribari Railway Station was a strong outpost of the occupation forces. In order to mislead enemy soldiers, Nurul wore the ordinary clothes of a local villager. Lutfor dressed up as an Islamic priest, wearing an Islamic cap and a long white robe. To his advantage, he already had a long beard.

Unfortunately, trying to conceal my identity wasn't quite as simple. I was a young man with glasses and clearly resembled a college student. At that time, there weren't many college students in the area. Most were either in the city, or like me, fighting for independence. Even for the few, who might still be around, they knew better than to come out in public. To do so, would most definitely spell disaster.

So I had to disguise myself. I removed my glasses. I found an umbrella and a shopping bag. With a pen and paper, I made a list. I made a list of groceries. I was a grocery shopper!

We paced ourselves, trying to keep some distance between ourselves. Cautiously, we reached the ferry station, which was just across from the train station.

There were a few boats waiting at the ferry station. However, none of the boatmen were willing to go to Bokshiiganj. Suddenly, an old man came near us and whispered to Lutfor, "Sir, I have figured you out! Board my boat. You can pay me whatever price you deem fair. I often take the Mukti Bahini across…"

I immediately became suspicious of the old boatman. What would we do if he handed us over to the Pakistani forces? We closely scrutinized the old man. Finally, we decided there was nothing mischievous about him. If he wanted to reveal our identity to the enemy, he would have done it by now. He was just an innocent boatman. After all, we really didn't have much choice. Ultimately, we took a risk and boarded his boat.

As the boat neared Bokshiiganj, darkness had already blanketed the landscape. We were hungry and tired. We hadn't eaten all day. Moreover, sailing amidst such darkness in unknown waters was quite dangerous.

Constrained by our circumstances, we sought shelter in a house at Mesherchar. The lord of the house was a kind person. He greeted us warmly. But he also warned us that his neighbor was a politician who contested in the last election on behalf of the pro-Pakistani party. Not only did he bid his allegiance to the Pakistani Army, but was actively collaborating with them against the Mukti Bahini.

This was no place for freedom fighters to stay. So, we filled our stomachs with water and then proceeded towards the Indian border.

It was about midnight. We finally found a house where we could rest till morning. The owner of the house was a former member of the Jamaat-e-Islami, a pro-Pakistani political party. However, the crackdown on March 25th by the Pakistani Army, and the bestial killings and tortures that followed had a major effect on him. He was a changed man and now a staunch supporter of the Mukti Bahini. He was more than willing to help us. At daybreak, he arranged for a woodcutter to lead us to the border.

We waded through waist-high waters and crossed three miles of swamp before we finally reached dry land. While I was walking, I noticed a tingling in my legs. I carefully looked down and saw that my legs were speckled with some sort of black stuff.

I thought it was probably just some algae or muck that I had carried with me from the swamp. However, when I reached down to clean myself off, I felt something slippery and squishy. At the top of my lungs I screamed, "Leeches!"

The woodcutter ran towards me and scrapped them off my legs with the blunt side of his knife. When Nurul, Lutfor, and the woodcutter looked down at their own legs, they realized that their luck hadn't been any better.

Leeches are miraculous creatures. The chemicals in their suckers provide their host with an anesthetic effect. As soon as a leech bites its host, the area becomes numb. The victim does not feel any pain at all. Unnoticed, it is free to suck blood happily until it becomes swollen and spongy. It seems evolution was working against us here. Though, we were fortunate that we were in the water for only a short period of time.

For the woodcutter, this was a trip that he had made several times before. He moved swiftly. We followed behind, thoroughly perspired. We met a few people along the way, who inquired about our identities. Cleverly, the woodcutter introduced us as the traders of tobacco leaves going up the hills for business.

Finally, on the 3rd of July, we crossed the border. From that point on we had to travel uphill. The woodcutter casually said, "The occupation forces used to regularly patrol these parts before, but now they were too scared of the Mukti Bahini. They don't patrol here that often anymore. Most of the time, they don't even come out of their camps."

The sun was rising. We started our journey very early in the morning. We barely had anything for breakfast. Soon we were too hungry to walk uphill. We asked the woodcutter if we could find a place to eat. He changed course and headed towards a tila, a small hill, and asked us to follow him.

It was a steep tila. The woodcutter quickly walked along the spiraling-narrow steps that were cut into the side of the tila. For us, this was a tough act to follow.

The walking path ended at the top of the tila, just in front of a Garo (an indigenous tribe) house. It was a small hut made of straw. There were several trees around the hut. The top of the tila was about one hundred square feet. It resembled a lookout tower. We could see the majesty of the entire valley from here.

The woodcutter explained to us that the Garo family had to live atop the tila in order to protect themselves from the wild animals of the area. This was not the first time that he had visited this family.

The man of the house cordially received us. His wife and young son were out working in the valley. This was the Garo custom. The men stayed at home, while the ladies and children worked in the field.

We couldn't understand his language. However, the woodcutter somehow managed to communicate with him anyway. We sat in the yard on a small stool. The woodcutter asked if the man could provide us with some food. He nodded his head and brought a whole jackfruit and put it in front of us.

Eating an entire jackfruit was no small feat. However, there was no certainty as to when or where we would have our next meal. So, we ate to our heart's content.

He gave us a small glass of water to share amongst the four of us. He apologized, explaining that water was scarce due to a drought during the last few weeks. Rain was their main source of drinking water.

It was time to say good-bye to the woodcutter and our host. We wanted to offer the woodcutter some wages for his service. However, as we tried to give him some money, the man protested, "You are willing to sacrifice your lives for my country. How can I accept money from you?"

Our Garo host reiterated the sentiment.

However, with the woodcutter gone, we needed a new guide. We were going to need help crossing the hilly terrain to reach the Porakhasia camp of the Indian Border Security Forces (BSF). Immediately, the Garo man called on his son, who was still working in the field. He asked him to take us across the hill to the BSF camp. After bidding farewell, we rushed down to the valley following our new guide.

It was afternoon. Our guide crisscrossed the valley. We tried hard to keep up with his pace. Since none of us spoke his language, all we could do was make sure we shadowed him.

The landscape was beautiful. Under a clear blue sky, dark-green hills rose majestically from the base of narrow green valleys. It was a stunning view.

This was the most peaceful leg of our trip. There wasn't a single face that we crossed paths with. Silence prevailed throughout the valley.

After walking about a mile, the stillness of the valley was suddenly broken by music coming from a distance. However, we couldn't pinpoint the source. We asked our guide, but with the language barrier, we got nowhere.

As we moved forward, the sound became more pronounced. It was the ringing of bells. Finally, we found our musicians. It was a herd of cows!

The cows were grazing along the valley. Each cow had a bell on its neck. As the cows ate and their necks swayed side-to-side, a beautiful sound resonated throughout the valley.

We could not see any cowboys watching over the heard. Rather we saw only a group of cowgirls. They were young Garo girls dressed in colorful bottoms, but completely topless. They were not roaming after their cows. Instead, they sat lying on a raised bamboo platform under the shade of trees. They were enjoying the music, soothing afternoon breeze and tranquility of the valley. They did need to keep a close eye on their cows. The sound of the bells told the cowgirls exactly where their herd was.

After several ours of walking, we crossed the hills and arrived at an Indian boarder road. It was time for our guide to return home. We were on our own from this point on. We thanked our guide and said goodbye.

People were walking along the road. We asked one of the pedestrians to show us the way to the Indian BSF camp at Porakhasia. Heading east, we walked towards the camp.

After half an hour, we saw a small village market at the side of the road. There were only about a hundred people gathered at the market. Most of them were Garo men and women doing their weekly shopping.

We were hungry and were in need of something to eat. Bananas, pineapples, rice, and vegetables were on display in the market. However, the dust from the market air blanketed most of the produce. We decided that bananas were the safest way for us to go.

After shopping, we stepped away from the crowd and stood in an open space at the corner of the market.

As I pealed my banana and was about to take my first bite, someone tapped my shoulder and uttered something to me in Hindi. I turned around. Unexpectedly, I found myself face-to-face with an Indian police constable.

At first, I couldn't take him seriously. The constable was wearing shorts and knee-high socks. Atop his head was a tiny-colorful hat. The hat was so small compared to his head that it didn't actually cover his head. Rather, it gently sat on top. I couldn't help but think, "Even the gentlest of breezes could send his hat flying through the air at any moment!"

He was the first policeman I saw in this kind of clothing. However, when I saw his face, I realized that this was a serious matter. Swinging his club, he asked us very stoically, "Who are you and where are you headed?" He demanded to see a form of identification.

We had no passports or documentation. I told him who we were and explained our mission. He was skeptical about my claims and accused, "You are Pakistani spies!"

He threatened that if we failed to show him identification, he would have no choice, but to arrest us.

I was caught completely off-guard. However, I challenged his accusations and asked him to take us to Porakhasia BSF camp. It was a tense situation.

As we were engaged in this sharp exchange, his superior officer arrived at the spot. This made us even more apprehensive. However,

I stuck to my story and explained our mission to him. To our surprise, he smiled and said, "Welcome to India!"

He understood our situation. We were relieved. He even gave us a ride in his jeep to the BSF camp. Later, we found out that it was not uncommon for some stray police constables to harass refugees just to solicit bribes.

Finally, our onerous journey had ended. We reached Porakhasia camp safely. It was just before sunset.

The BSF officers and the freedom fighters were both very keen on making contact with the Tangail Mukti Bahini. Gratitude flowed from every direction.

The pain endured over the past two weeks quickly dissipated from our bodies and minds. The Bangladesh and Indian governments were informed of our arrival.

Dr. Mahmud and Prof. Hannan Khan at Porakhasia Camp

Captain Baljit Singh of the Indian Border Security Forces (BSF) greeted us at Porakhasia Camp. He introduced us to Dr. Mahmud, Prof. Hannan, and Subedar Abdur Rahim, the commanders of the camp. We came to know that Subedar Rahim was involved in the battles against the Pakistani Army at Goran-Satichora and Kalihati of Tangail, which took place in April.

Subedar Rahim was a very hospitable host. As representatives of the Tangail Mukti Bahini, he was happy to have us stay with him. And after such a long and arduous journey, we were more than happy to take a sojourn.

That evening we had the opportunity to talk to Dr. Mahmud. Both, Dr. Mahmud and Professor Hannan were from the Mymensingh District. We learned that Dr. Shahjada Chowdhury, the chief medical officer of our Mukti Bahini group, was a friend of Dr. Mahmud. They were both former-students of Mymensingh Medical College. There we also met a representative of the Bangladesh government.

In March of 1995, I organized a program in Brooklyn, New York in celebration of Bangladesh's Independence Day. The program was held under the banner of the National Coordination Committee for the Trial of Bangladesh War Criminals of 1971. As a Co-convener of that program, my name appeared in the local newspapers frequently.

Coincidently, Dr. Mahmud happened to be in New York for the medical treatment of his brother. He read my name in the Weekly Probashi, and thought to himself that this "Nabi" just might be the same person he knew back in 1971. So he showed up at the function in Brooklyn.

As always, traveling from New Jersey to New York City, I was fashionably late. After I arrived, my fellow organizers informed me that someone named Dr. Mahmud was waiting to see me.

It had been a long twenty-five years, and so, the name didn't immediately ring a bell. I tried hard to recollect, but still could not make the connection. However, as soon as I saw him, there was no denying that I was in the presence of my fellow freedom fighter! It was truly a pleasant surprise. Like two distant-brothers reunited, we embraced.

There were about a thousand people at the function. I introduced Dr. Mahmud to them. As he addressed the meeting, he pulled a card out from his pocket. He said that Abdur Rahman Biswas, President of People's Republic of Bangladesh, had sent it to him. It was an invitation for him to join a reception arranged to celebrate Bangladesh's Independence Day. However, President Biswas was a Razakar, a traitor to Bangladesh.

Dr. Mahmud said, "I, as a freedom fighter, cannot accept the invitation of a Razakar. To do so, would be a great disgrace!"

As he uttered these words, he raised the card to the crowd and tore it apart, piece-by-piece. The audience erupted in applause.

I too, raise my hand and saluted Dr. Mahmud, as his actions embodied the true character and spirit of the Mukti Bahini.

Brigadier Sant Singh

The next afternoon, a Sikh officer of the Indian Army came to see us. He introduced himself as Brigadier Sant Singh and embraced me. I was not at all prepared for such a warm greeting. He told me that he had been trying very hard to establish contact with the Tangail Mukti Bahini. So, he was very relieved to see us.

After an introductory greeting, he said, "You have to go to Tura with me this very day. Tomorrow, Major General Gill will meet with you. Get ready young man".

I had nothing more to prepare. So I said, "I am ready".

It was decided that Nurul and Lutfor would stay behind in Porakhasia and join me later at Mankachar.

I boarded the jeep of Brigadier Sant Singh. We were heading towards Tura, an important town of Meghalaya, an Indian province. From the plains of Porakhasia we had been heading upward to the hilly areas. Brigadier Singh was driving the jeep himself. I was sitting beside him. It was an uphill journey all the way to Tura.

The nature around us was simply breathtaking. Never before had I seen such a beautiful landscape. The curvy roads that stretched through the hills and the speeding jeep made for a beautiful spectacle. Brigadier Singh looked extremely skilled and self-confident as he drove the jeep. At some points of our journey, we would find ourselves with a hill to one side, and a valley of some hundred feet, to the other. It was quite scary. If the car slid down, we would be doomed.

I was enjoying this vista with rapt attention for quite some time. Suddenly, it occurred to me that silence on my part could be deemed impolite. I told Brigadier Singh of the enchantment I had been experiencing. With a smile, he said that he had noticed my captivated state of mind, but was happy to know that my silence had come from my response to the aesthetics of nature, and not from any source of displeasure.

"It gives me great joy to get to know a romantic freedom fighter such as you," he said.

I replied, "I am not a poet or novelist. I have no talent to express the passionate mind. I tend to keep those thoughts inside."

Nonetheless, the conversation moved on. It blossomed into a meaningful dialogue. We discussed several personal details, likes and dislikes, family anecdotes, and so on. And through this communication, we established a relationship of mutual respect. It was the beginning of an extraordinary relationship, one that might prove to hold significant consequence.

It took almost an hour to reach Tura. I conveyed to him the details of the Tangail Mukti Bahini, the personal profile and political philosophy of Kader Siddiqui. This Sikh officer was almost of my father's age, but I was deeply impressed by his sincere and warm demeanor.

Mukti Bahini Training Camp at Tura

The Mukti Bahini training camp was situated in a valley several miles from Tura. We reached the camp just before evening. Major Mukherjee and Captain Bose, two officers of Brigadier Singh's brigade welcomed me.

The camp was half a mile away from the hilly road. Just after the entrance were several rows of tents for the Indian Army. There were about five hundred Indian soldiers stationed there. Just beyond the Indian Army tents was an open field, across from which, were hundreds of tents for the Mukti Bahini. It was on this field between the two campsites that the Indian Army trained these one thousand freedom fighters.

I was having a cup of tea at Brigadier Singh's office. In the distance, I could see hundreds of Mukti Bahini, standing in rows on the field, singing our national anthem. Instinctively, I stood up in salute. Looking at me, Brigadier Singh did the same.

He said, "Come on. Let's go, I'll take you there. I was going to introduce you to them tomorrow anyway". We walked to the field and joined the freedom fighters in their assembly.

With my arms clenched to my sides, I attentively joined them in singing our national anthem. As the singing ended, Brigadier Singh took the microphone and said, "I'd like to introduce you to a very special person. I am sure that you will all be pleased to meet him."

He announced my name and handed me the microphone.

I was completely unprepared. All of a sudden, I found myself standing in front of a thousand freedom fighters. My knees began trembling. Slowly, as I raised the microphone to my mouth, I realized that each and every individual before me was willing to give his life for the liberation of Bangladesh. They were willing to die for my people. They needed to know that they were not alone. It was up to me to tell them.

I told them about the formation of the Tangail Mukti Bahini. I told them about our operations. I told them about the large areas that we had liberated from the Pakistani Army.

"We are only forty miles from Dhaka!" I shouted.

Suddenly, the electricity of the crowd began to hum.

I went on to underline the heroism of Kader Siddiqui and offered them salutary greetings on his behalf. I said that soon we would welcome them across the border to join us in a fight against the enemy. I said, "I hope to see you all in the free zone soon. I hope to see you all in a liberated Bangladesh."

Before I could conclude, I was interrupted by an eruption of slogans "Joy Bangla! Joy Bangabandhu!" I knew at that moment Bangladesh was alive, and that her pulse was at the center of this camp.

It was a bright and sunny afternoon. The passionate slogans chanted by the thousand freedom fighters passed through space creating echoes against the mountains. It was a moment incapable of being captured amongst the commonality of human expression. It was a moment that could only be felt by the depths of one's soul.

Brigadier Singh and I were standing on the platform. Behind us were Major Mukherjee, Captain Bose, and an EPR Subedar. I took the microphone again and led the slogan. "Joy Bangla! Joy Bangabandhu!"

Nothing in my twenty-two years of life had prepared me for such a moment. To say that I was deeply moved by the event was an understatement. I would always remember this moment for the rest of my life.

Those of us on the platform left the freedom fighters and returned to the office of Brigadier Singh. He left me in the care of Major Mukherjee and said that the next morning I would meet with General Gill, the commander of the 101 Communication Zone of the Indian Army.

To the left and rear of the camp, were hills that peered over the range. To the right of the camp was a river with a mountain rising from behind the opposite bank. Interestingly, like most mountain rivers, the banks were encrusted with rocks and gleaming white waters. However, the river was so deep, and the water roared so boisterously that the river took on a personality of its own. It was in the fellowship of this river that many Mukti Bahini found solitude and peace amidst their preparation for war.

My accommodations were arranged in a VIP tent that was situated on the bank of the river between the camps of the Indian Army and our freedom fighters. I didn't understand why my tent was labeled "VIP". It had two beds made of thin bamboo. The mattress of the bed was comprised of a blanket and a thin sheet draped over the bamboo shoots. On top of the mattress were a simple blanket and a pillow. The next day I found that the freedom fighter's camps had almost identical arrangements. The sole difference was that their beds lacked a bed sheet. I knew that this was going to be a no-frills affair, but I never imagined that a single bed sheet could draw the line between VIPs and the rest of the camp. Nonetheless, after several weeks, this was the first restful night's sleep that I had gotten. It felt good to be a VIP.

First thing in the morning, I got ready and reported to Captain Bose's tent. As we ate breakfast, he asked me a series of specific questions about Kader Siddiqui and me. With a small notebook he recorded my responses. He asked me to name the central student and youth leaders that I knew. I mentioned Abdul Quddus Makhon, a student leader of Fazlul Huq Hall. I mentioned the youth leaders Sirajul Alam Khan, Tofael Ahmed, and Abdur Razzak. Lastly, I brought up my connection with Fazlur Rahman Khan, an elected member of the provincial assembly from Tangail. All in all, the discussion took place amidst a very friendly atmosphere.

It wasn't until much later that I learned that Captain Bose was, in fact, an intelligence officer of the Indian Army.

Meeting with Major General Gill

At about ten in the morning, Brigadier Sant Singh came and picked me up in his jeep. We left for the headquarters of the 101 Communication Zone of the Indian Army. It was a couple of miles away on the other side of Tura.

We went straight to the office of Major General Gill. He was expecting us.

A Sikh officer, Major General Gill was a tall man of six and a half feet. His head was adorned with a thick salt-and-pepper beard and a turban. Clenched in his hand was a long cane, the top of which was intricately crafted.

There were two sofas in his office. Brigadier Singh and I sat on one; General Gill took his seat on the other. After the initial greetings, we began our discussion.

He informed me that the Indian Army, through the interception of Pakistani radio messages, had learned that Kader Siddiqui and the Tangail Mukti Bahini had been successful in liberating vast areas of Tangail from Pakistani forces. After this news, it became strategically important that he and the Indian Army make contact with us. Coincidently, it was our independent initiative to seek them out as well. So this was a mutually beneficial meeting.

He asked me what he and the Indian Army could do to further help our efforts. I mentioned that thus far, we have only engaged the enemy in "hit and run" operations. But, in order to protect the free zones, it had become essential that we have sufficient arms and ammunition.

While we discussed the matter, I reached for my sleeve. Folded to my elbows, I slowly unraveled my shirtsleeve to reveal a letter from Kader Siddiqui.

About three weeks earlier, when I left home, I was wearing my usual university dress shirt. In order to disguise myself at Jamalpur, I took off the shirt and borrowed one from Lutfor. He got it from a refugee camp in India. However, this particular shirt had no pockets. Thus, as I unfolded the sleeve, General Gill looked at us and asked Brigadier Singh whether this was a safest way to carry a letter. We looked at each other and neither of us had an answer. For a moment, we both felt a bit uneasy.

The letter was a small piece of paper addressing the Indian government and the exiled government of Bangladesh. Kader had noted that in Tangail the Mukti Bahini had engaged in an all-out-war against the occupation forces. Any assistance would contribute greatly to the war effort. In conclusion, he wrote, "Nuran Nabi is my representative. His word is my word."

The three of us discussed matters for half an hour. General Gill said that the supply of arms and ammunition was not a problem. We could take whatever we were capable of transporting. He instructed Brigadier Singh to make the arrangements. Brigadier Singh mentioned that he too was not worried about providing the supplies, but rather was concerned about how we would transport it all. Nonetheless, he said he'd look into the details.

General Gill said that making the arrangements to transport the arms might take a while. He suggested that in the meantime, I get some rest or maybe, take a trip to Calcutta. He said he could facilitate this as well. I humbly said that the liberation war was rapidly gaining momentum. So the earlier I returned with the supplies, the better it was for us. The better it was for Bangladesh.

He was a bit taken back by my reply. He said, "Many of your leaders come to me for personal favors; some even request that I arrange for more comfortable living accommodations. Your words have touched me deeply. I can see that your favor truly lies with your motherland."

I was extremely gratified with the outcome of the meeting. I thanked the general for the meeting and returned to camp with Brigadier Singh. I retired to my "VIP" tent with a sense of satisfaction.

At lunchtime, Captain Bose took me to their officers' mess hall to eat. As I returned to my tent with a full stomach, I began thinking about the four Indian Army officers I had met over the past few days. I was genuinely impressed with the way they had treated me. There was a certain touch of warmth that I found in all of them. In fact, as I thought about them, I recalled an event from 1967.

I was still a student of Ananda Mohan College at the time. It was a holiday, and I was walking home from Jagannathganj Train Station. Incidentally, I discovered that I had been walking parallel to a private of the Pakistani Army for quite some time without uttering a word. To avoid being rude, I tried to engage him in a conversation. I asked the young soldier his name, where he was from, and where he was stationed. He didn't answer. So, naturally, I asked him again.

He reacted sharply saying, "Can't you see that I am army personnel. We don't talk to civilians unless we have to." I apologized, stating that I wasn't aware of the protocol.

Comparing the warmth of the Indian Army personnel to my earlier experience, it became apparent that the Pakistani military considered themselves to be our rulers and masters. After all, the military had been ruling Pakistan for so many years. Meanwhile, India had always remained a democratic nation, where the Indian Army's role was always to serve a civilian authority. The Indian Army simply had a different mindset.

In the early afternoon, Brigadier Singh asked me to meet him in his office. He told me that all of the arrangements had been made for our supplies. The next night, Major Bindar Singh of the BSF at Mankachar would take care of everything.

I had to sign some papers at the quartermaster's office of Singh's Brigade in order to have the supplies delivered. Boats had been hired from Mankachar to transport the arms and ammunitions. There were only six boats that agreed to go on the two-hundred-mile roundtrip journey from Mankachar. Of course, boats alone weren't enough. We needed experienced boatmen who knew the rivers, as well. Brigadier Singh advised me to be ready to leave for Mankachar in the morning. He embraced me and wished me a safe journey back to Tangail.

Meeting with Mujahidi and Rafia Aktar Dolly at Tura

I returned to the tent with Captain Bose. He suggested that since my business at the camp was complete, I should take a tour of Tura Town in the afternoon. I agreed, but before I could do so, I knew I had to talk to the freedom fighters before I left. I intended to talk to them the previous day, but when I had a chance, they were busy with their training drills. Some of the freedom fighters were probably from Tangail. I'm sure they were curious of the details surrounding their respective families and villages. I might be able to provide them with this information.

Captain Bose agreed to my proposal. We walked over to the camp. The freedom fighters were lying on their cots. They were resting up, before the vigorous training scheduled to come in the evening.

I got the chance to talk to a number of them. Most of the freedom fighters were from Mymensingh, Tangail, and Sylhet. Their training would be complete by the following week. They counted the days to when they could return to their homeland and put their training to use. They were eager to face the enemy. They were eager to free Bangladesh. Before I left, I told them that I would see them next, when we were all in a liberated Bangladesh.

Captain Bose and I took a jeep to Tura, the capital of Meghalaya. Tura was a small town, but it stood several hundred feet above sea level. The original inhabitants of the town belonged to the Garo tribe. The winding roads of Tura crept along the hills like a snake along a tree trunk. One path hung just fifty feet above the other, as the dwellings of the town's people encrusted the space in between.

We cruised around town in our military jeep, before stopping downtown.

Typically, the Garo were short in stature and had flat noses. Suddenly, from amidst the crowds, two familiar faces appeared. A poet and student leader of Tangail, Al Mujahidi was walking with his head high above the pedestrian crowd. Rafia Aktar Dolly, a former student leader and member of the National Assembly was with him. I knew both relatively well. It was a pleasant surprise.

They told me that they had endured a great deal of pain and suffering to reach Tura. They had just arrived a few days ago but would soon be back en route to Calcutta. I told them about my mission to return to Tangail with supplies of arms. Due to time constraints, we kept our conversation brief.

A Strange Reaction from the Subedar

In the evening, Captain Bose proposed that we have dinner at a restaurant in Tura. I thanked him but said, "No, I would rather eat at the camp". Nonetheless, he insisted. His persistence struck my curiosity. I asked if there was something wrong. He hesitantly stumbled over his words. I was shocked at what I had learned. More so, I was disappointed.

The previous day when I arrived at the camp, I was accommodated in a VIP tent and had dinner in the Indian Army officer's mess hall. There was an EPR Subedar who stayed in the tent just adjacent to mine. He assisted the Indian soldiers in the training of our freedom fighters. Though he too was staying in a VIP tent, his meals were arranged through the Mukti Bahini mess hall.

Apparently, my special treatment had wounded his ego. So, he complained to Captain Bose saying that either, as an officer, he get his dinners in the Indian Army officer's mess hall, or I be asked to eat in Mukti Bahini mess hall, as well.

I would be leaving for Mankachar the next day after breakfast with the captain at his tent. By having our dinner at Tura that night, Captain Bose could easily avoid dealing with the Subedar and his complaints.

I had no comments and agreed to have dinner in Tura. Nonetheless, I couldn't get past the complaints that the Subedar had with me. What was wrong with him? Most of us were preoccupied with the thought that if we failed to retaliate against the Pakistani Army, we would be slaves forever. This Subedar, on the other hand, was only concerned with his own self-image.

Then again, what if this man was sincerely hurt? After all, he was the senior-most Bengali Army personnel at the Mukti Bahini camp. It was fair for him to expect some special privileges. With this in mind, I asked Captain Bose if he could arrange for the Subedar to have his meals with the Indian officers.

Captain Bose said that this wasn't the issue. Rather, this was the most politically correct arrangement. It was an opportunity to promote camaraderie amongst the freedom fighters. None of the freedom fighters at the camp were salaried personnel. However, many of them possessed academic qualification and accomplishments superior to that of the Subedar's. Therefore, privileges could not be bestowed on military rank alone.

I had no solution for the Subedar's quandary. Nonetheless, the matter kept swirling in my head. For the first time in my life, I found myself in this situation. Was I the target of jealousy?

How could this be? Could something as small as where we ate bring a man to resent another? I was a guest here for only two days. More importantly, I was a fellow freedom fighter. Surely, I would have extended the same grace to another.

I found the whole situation a bit unsettling. However, as the lessons of my life would unfold, I would come to know first-hand, the extent to which jealousy could lead one Bangladeshi to maliciously attack another.

Supplies of Arms from India

The next morning, I proceeded towards Mankachar in an Indian Army jeep. The driver was a Gurkha soldier of Nepalese origin. During the two hours spent driving to Mankachar, the driver and I did not exchange a single word. Aside from his native language, he had no other means of communication. I spent my time gazing aimlessly out the window. I let the majestic charms of the mountains seep into my mind and mesmerize me.

In the afternoon, we reached the Mankachar BSF camp. Major Bindar Singh, the commander of the camp, cordially received me.

There, I also met my fellow freedom fighter, Nurul. Major Singh told me that the arrangements for my return were finalized.

The warm reception and help that I received in India amazed me. On the evening of July 5th, with six boatloads of arms and ammunition, we set sail for Tangail.

To ensure our security, a platoon of Mukti Bahini trained in India accompanied us. Rezaul Karim, a student of Rajshahi University was the commander of this platoon. His deputy was Amjad Hossain, a student of Dhaka University.

Captain Mahbub of the Mukti Bahini was assigned as our guide. He was responsible to lead our convoy across Bahadurabad Ferry Station. He hailed from the border area and was quite familiar with the local routes.

Captain Mahbub was an interesting character. He had a thick black beard and shoulder length hair. He wore shorts, an army hat and boots. With this outfit, he truly looked like a guerilla fighter.

He called himself a captain, though he had no official rank in the Mukti Bahini. In fact, he was previously a soldier in the tank regiment of the Pakistani Army. After the Pakistani Army crackdown in Dhaka on March 26th, he deserted his unit and joined the liberation war. He dedicated himself to recruiting young refugees who came to Mankachar, into the Mukti Bahini. He helped them with basic military training.

I was unfamiliar with the route ahead, so I asked Captain Mahbub for his recommendation. He suggested that sailing through the Jamuna River via Bahadurabad Ferry Station would be the shortest and quickest path. We would have to navigate through about twenty miles of local waterways to reach the Jamuna River. Nonetheless, he assured me that this would be the shortest route.

Captain Mahbub, Commander Karim, and I were in the lead boat. Commander Karim divided his platoon among six boats. I explained the rules of engagement to Commander Karim and instructed him that no one should open fire without my order.

Captain Mahbub mentioned that though the Bahadurabad route was shorter, there was also a potential risk there. On the east of the Jamuna River was Bahadurabad Ferry Station and on the west was Fulchari Ferry Station. The Pakistani Army had strong garrisons at both locations. These two ferry stations connected the rail communication between Dhaka and northern Bangladesh. Therefore, these stations were important strategic locations for the Pakistani Army.

Captain Mahbub further informed us that the enemy gunboats patrolled the river regularly. At night, a high-powered searchlight routinely swept over the river passages like clockwork. Our only opportunity to cross would come exactly at midnight. Precise timing would be essential.

In spite of the risk, we stuck to our plan and proceeded towards the Jamuna River. Our plan was to cross the river under the cover of night, navigating alongside the river's west bank.

While traveling towards the Jamuna River, Captain Mahbub suddenly ordered a detour. I did not question his decision since he knew this area better than me. After an hour of sailing, we passed through a village. There were dwellings on both sides on the bank. Captain Mahbub ordered the boatmen to slow down and anchor us to the bank near a house.

I was confused by his order. I questioned Captain Mahbub's decision.

With a faint smile under his mustache, he replied, "Let's eat."

The house belonged to a relative of Captain Mahbub. More importantly, his new bride was staying at this residence. Since Captain Mahbub was a freedom fighter, his family was not safe at his home outside of Islampur.

His new wife and family were staying in this remote village near the Bangladesh-India border. Here they were safe.

This respite was a win-win situation. After a long time, Captain Mahbub finally had a chance to see his new bride, while we were pleasantly surprised with a sumptuous dinner of steamed rice and lentil soup.

Consequently, this break added an additional two hours to our trip. Having been ahead of schedule, this stop would bring us to the Jamuna crossing precisely at midnight.

Our appetites satisfied, we embarked on our journey once again. After an hour of sailing, Captain Mahbub cautioned that we were nearing the intersection of the Jamuna River.

Anxiously we waited in the silence of the dark night for about twenty minutes. Suddenly, the mighty roar of the Jamuna welcomed us! Without the ability to hear anything over the thundering current, the presence of darkness became ever more foreboding. We could not see anything around us. The mighty Jamuna had overwhelmed us completely. Now helpless, we were at her mercy. It was a scary moment.

Earlier I had instructed each boat to stay close to one another to prevent any separation. After all, we had no wireless communication sets. With the help of a strong down current, the boats picked up speed. I had to admit that I was pleased with our good fortune to be traveling so quickly. I was confident that we would cross Bahadurabad Ferry Station before the enemy could detect us.

After a few minutes, we saw a dim light on the eastern horizon. Captain Mahbub pointed to the east and said, "That's the Pakistani military position at Bahadurabad Ferry Station."

We turned towards the western bank, moving away from the enemy at Bahadurabad Ferry Station. After a few minutes, the enemy began to scan the river by searchlight. Noises from our convoy might have alerted them.

Though we were out of the searchlight's reach, we did not know the location of their gunboats. They could be hiding anywhere. Moreover, the searchlight was continuously scanning the river as if they were specifically looking for us.

I did not want to take the risk of losing our arms and ammunition to the enemy, nor to the river. I asked Captain Mahbub if we could bypass the enemy position through another route. He replied that there was an alternative passage. However, we would have to retreat near the border, and it would be a much longer journey. I decided that this was what we had to do.

We turned around and began to row our boats towards the north. The strong current that was once our ally, now pushed fiercely against us. It was very tough sailing. It took two hours to retreat the distance upstream that we had just traveled downstream in thirty minutes.

At dawn, we broke our retreat in a village north of Islampur. The muezzin, an Islamic clergyman, was giving Azaan, the Islamic call to prayer, from the mosque for Morning Prayer.

The villagers were still asleep. I consulted with Captain Mahbub, Nurul and Commander Karim about our next move. We decided that we would travel quickly through the local rivers bypassing Bahadurabad Ferry Station and then continue our journey through the Jamuna River to Tangail.

We left the village before the inhabitants ever woke up. We would pass through Islampur. We had to move fast so that we could cross the Patharghata Railway Bridge, which connected the Jamalpur-Bahadurabad rail-lines. We had to do this before sunset.

This route was also very dangerous and difficult. The Razakars were always on guard at the bridge, even at night. Earlier in the month, the Mukti Bahini attempted to blow the bridge up. The enemy responded with reinforced bridge security. Nonetheless, this was our only option. This was a risk that we had to take if the supplies were going to get to Tangail.

Though the river made our retreat quite difficult, lady luck had not left our sides. We still had one advantage. Dharmakura Bazaar was located right next to the bridge.

Typically, village markets were busy only once a week. On market days, hundreds of people from all around would congregate at the market to buy and sell their goods. This day just happened to be Dharmakura Bazaar's market day. Soon swarms of merchant boats would crowd the riverway near the bazaar and we would have no trouble blending in.

Despite our good fortune, we could never presume safety. If our cover got blown, we would have to be prepared to fight.

Though our strategy was sound, I was still a little apprehensive. I had to anticipate that our convoy of six boats was at risk of getting stuck in traffic under the bridge. I prepared a set of contingency plans suitable for any situation.

This time we had no choice. We had to move forward no matter what the consequence. We were determined to successfully complete our mission.

I changed the leadership of the boats. I brought Nurul into my boat and transferred Commander Karim into Nurul's boat just behind us. If our boat came under fire, I knew Commander Karim could lead his platoon and provide us with cover.

Captain Mahbub, Nurul, and I were in the first boat. Commander Karim was in the second. Amjad Hossain was in the third. Rakib was in the fourth. Faiz was in the fifth and Barek followed behind in the last boat.

The Mukti Bahini all stayed under cover of the canopy. Only the commanders sat outside. Nurul and I, dressed as merchants, sat in front of the boat. Meanwhile Captain Mahbub, dressed in his typical military fatigue, stayed under the canopy. Captain Mahbub, peering through the canopy-window, was able to navigate us towards the market.

Bend-after-bend, we snaked through the winding canal passages that threaded the villages on the canal banks. Like the breeze from a passing wind, before the villagers could make out who we were, we were already gone.

It was a bright sunny day. We traveled for several hours before nearing the market in the late afternoon. As we approached, I was worried that if this were just a small village-market there wouldn't be enough boats for us to hide amongst. Our large convoy could end-up creating more suspicion than we wished for. This situation could invite an enemy attack.

However, we were lucky. It was a large bazaar and many boats were approaching the market. We had no problem blending into the crowd. Nonetheless, when we came close to the bazaar, shoppers noticed that our convoy, instead of anchoring to the market, swiftly passed the bazaar.

This struck their curiosity, and many of the shoppers shouted at us, "Where are you coming from? Where are you going? What's in the boat?"

To placate their quandaries, each boat replied vaguely with their own answer. We were approaching the Patharghata Bridge when we saw that a few Razakars were guarding the bridge.

However, these men were not in combat position. Rather they were standing around casually, gossiping amongst themselves. There were a few merchant boats just in front of us. Hopefully, the Razakars would assume that our boats were merchant boats as well. However, we had to stay alert. We had to be ready for anything.

My boat crossed under the bridge without a hitch. The other boats quickly followed behind. At last, I could take a sigh of relief. However, before my breath could completely leave my chest, my eyes fell upon another bridge just a few hundred yards ahead. This was unexpected. Moreover, there were more Razakars guarding this bridge as well.

Immediately I thought, "Was the lax attitude of the first group of Razakars just a means of trapping us between the two bridges?"

I whispered to Captain Mahbub, "Do you think we're in for some trouble?"

As his vigilant eyes scanned the Razakars from inside the canopy, he responded, "The men at the bridge only have six 303 Rifles. The Razakars are no match for our LMGs and SMGs. We've got them out-gunned."

Commander Karim alerted his platoon. We proceeded as usual and crossed under the bridge. Surprisingly, the Razakars did not react at all. They probably assumed that since we were allowed to cross the first bridge, that we were legitimate merchants.

We were all relieved to have these hurdles behind us. Our boats rapidly moved through the villages. While we had no problems fooling our enemy, we found the local children to be much too clever. It had become obvious to the children that this convoy of six boats had a purpose. Clearly, we were freedom fighters.

As our boat traveled down the canal passages, children ran along side the banks. Excited by our presence, they shouted, "The Mukti Bahini is here!"

Soon, crowds of villagers gathered to the edge of the water, many of which shouted slogans of "Joy Bangla!"

Nevertheless, we remained silent. We needed to avoid encouraging their excitement. We had to maintain our cover.

We proceeded towards Dewanganj. We sailed non-stop until midnight. We hadn't eaten in the last eighteen hours. We were all hungry and tired.

I asked Captain Mahbub to suggest some place for us to rest and get some food. He informed me that we could stop at a village named Mutail, which was coming up. He had once recruited a Mukti Bahini named Badal who was from Mutail.

We stopped at Badal's house at 1.00 A.M. Though it was late night, Badal's parents were quite happy to see us. The first question that Badal's mother asked was "Do any of you know my son Badal?"

Captain Mahbub replied, "I had recruited Badal into the Mukti Bahini personally. Badal is doing just fine. He is fighting the enemy in Roumari under the command of Major Shafayet Jamil."

Badal's parents had lost contact with their son since he left home to join the Mukti Bahini. They were very happy to hear about their son. Badal's mother said, "I am so proud of Badal. He is my only son. May Allah protect him."

It was with that same love and affection that Badal's parents welcomed us into their home. It was as if Badal, himself, had returned from war.

Despite our late arrival, a goat was slaughtered and we were entertained with a feast. Badal's father personally looked over everything so that we were treated well. We ate to our hearts' content.

We bade farewell to Captain Mahbub. He had done his duty and helped us bypass the Bahadurabad enemy position. It was time for him to return to Mankachar. We would now proceed towards the Jamuna River.

We resumed our journey at three in the morning. After an hour, we entered into the Jamuna River. Traveling down a strong current, we sailed at high speeds for most of the day. We arrived near Jaganathganj Ferry Station just after sunset. Our timing was perfect.

We had one more hurdle to cross. Jaganathganj Ferry Station was on the eastern bank of the river and it was swarming with Pakistani forces. It was only under the cover of night that we could cross this passage. Just like Bahadurabad Ferry Station, the enemy used gunboats and searchlights to comb the water. However, we eluded the enemy by navigating alongside the western bank behind a "char", a sand-island, which jutted out off the edge of the bank.

At midnight, on July 7th, we reached our camp at Bhuapur Bazaar. Commander Gafur and his company received us warmly. They were excited to see the large quantities of arms and ammunitions. It was beyond their expectation.

Tired and exhausted, we desperately needed some rest. I asked Commander Gafur to take over the security of the boats and we went to bed.

They say good news travels quickly. After hearing the success of my mission, Moazzem Hossain Khan and other leaders of the Mukti Bahini could not wait for me to wake up to express their joy. They rushed into my room and woke me up. Moazzem nearly tossed me in the air and began dancing with joy.

The excitement of our success was dampened a bit when Commander Karim whispered into my ear. One of our boats was lost while crossing Jaganathganj Ferry Station and still had not arrived.

As we were making our detours, the boat had fallen behind the convoy and lost its way. We waited several hours for its return, but the boat never arrived. It had been swallowed by the darkness of the Jamuna. We prayed for their safety. We prayed that the enemy did not capture them.

The report of our successful return was sent to Kader Siddiqui immediately who was then staying at Sehrabari in the Eastern Zone.

Apart from bringing arms and ammunitions, my mission to India opened up much needed contact with the governments of India and Bangladesh. Many subsequent events during the war attested to the fact that this mission was a turning point for the Tangail Mukti Bahini, as well as the liberation of Dhaka.

Dr. Nuran Nabi

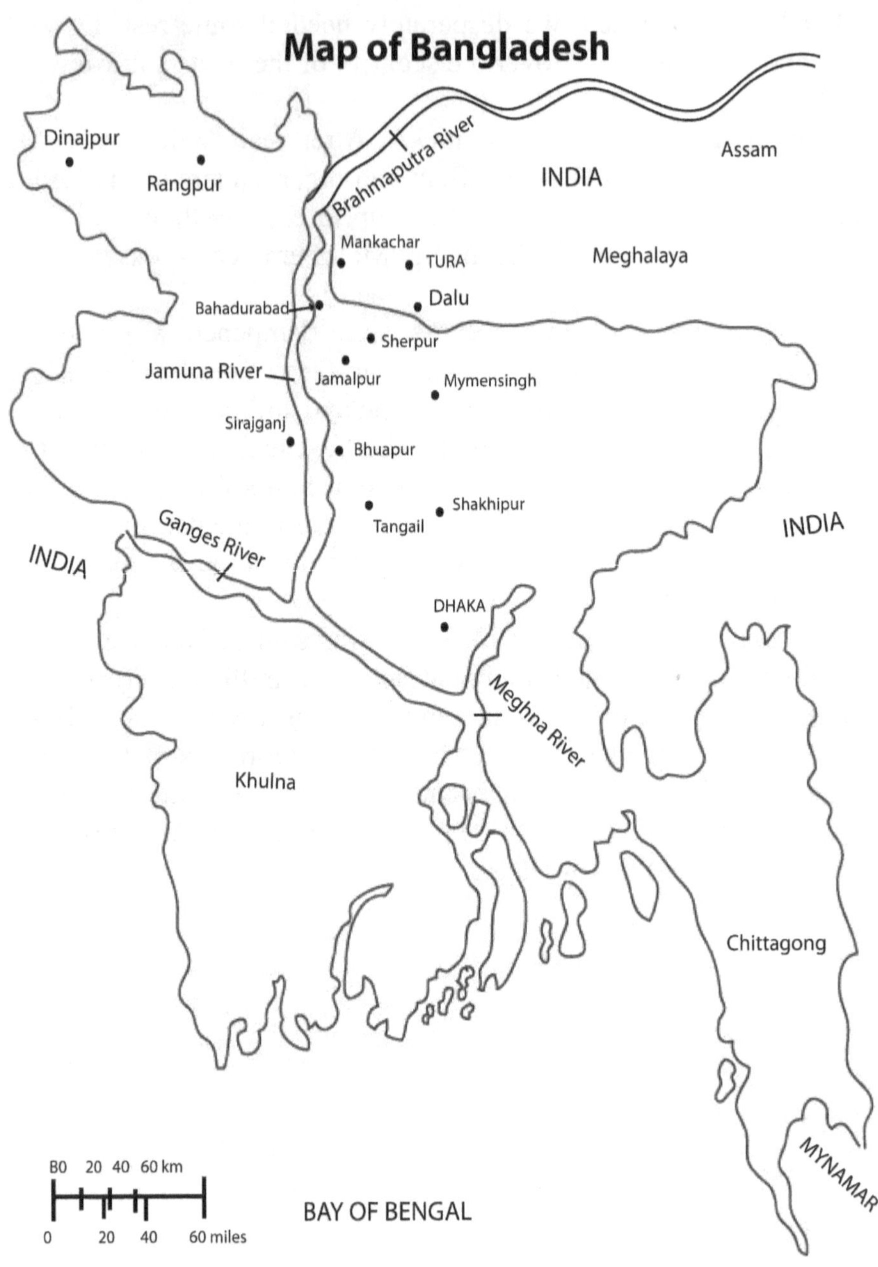

Map of Bangladesh

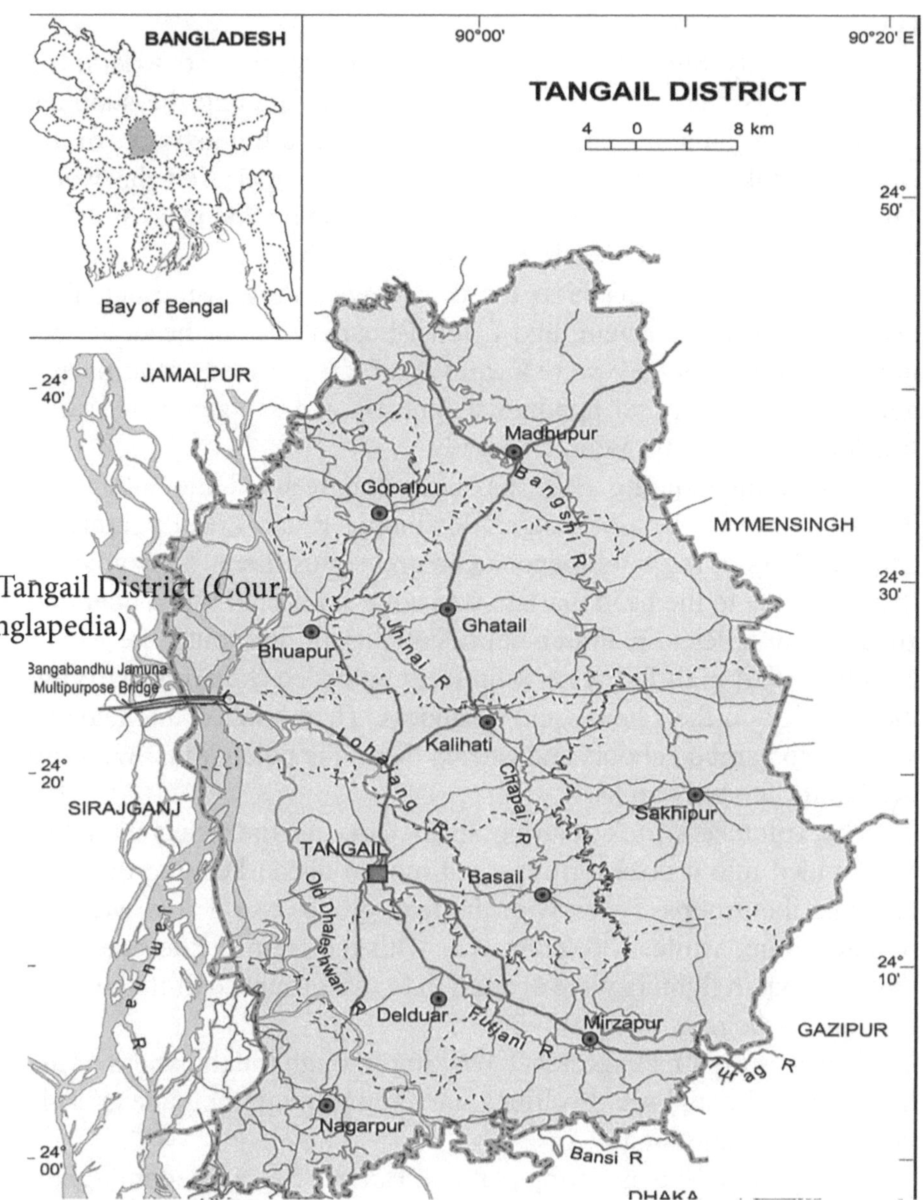

Map of Tangail District (Courtesy, Banglapedia)

Halt!

It was July 8th. About two hundred volunteers had assembled at Bhuapur Bazaar. They were enthusiastically loading the supplies brought from India into small boats. The civilian administrators of the Bhuapur Mukti Bahini, Enayet and Moazzem supervised the work. They were assisted by volunteers: Alim, Bhola, Shamsu, Mahfuz, Motahar, Bulbul, Dudu Miah, Bari Miah, and Zia.

Like a well-oiled machine, the work flowed in perfect order. That evening, Nurul, Moazzem, and I, left Bhuapur for our headquarters in the Eastern Zone. We were a caravan of ten boatloads of arms and ammunition, about two hundred volunteers and a platoon of armed freedom fighters from Benu Company.

Navigating winding river passages, we reached the village of Pakutia Porabari, west of Tangail-Madhupur Road. Local volunteers and members of the intelligence team greeted us there. They advised that this route to the headquarters was quite safe. This was a liberated zone, but in order to maintain confidentiality of this route, we would not cross until nightfall. The volunteers unloaded the arms, carrying the supplies on their heads and shoulders. They hooked the heaviest supplies to bamboo shoots and carried them like palanquins. We were headed for the hilly areas.

The volunteers took rotating shifts carrying the heavy bundles. We divided into a dozen groups and moved ahead keeping distance amongst the groups. I was with the lead group. Nurul was with the middle group, while, Moazzem was with the team at the rear. The armed freedom fighters were divided in to two groups, half in the front and half in the rear.

This was my first experience walking through the thickness of the hilly jungle. I could see dwellings scattered through the plateau. This was not a typical village.

The leader of the escorting platoon, Hatem, was a freedom fighter of no more than sixteen-years old. He knew this area very well. Our group wasn't carrying any of the heavy supplies. We had been walking swiftly.

It was a moonlit night. Under the glow of the luminous sky, the landscape seemed to come alive. Nonetheless, the middle group carrying the heavy arms was lagging so far behind that we could no longer see them. Some of these men were not accustomed to carrying such heavy loads. As we walked deeper into the thickness of the jungle, it was apparent that exhaustion had set in. Nonetheless, none of these men had to be there. They volunteered their energy and time out of a sense of patriotic duty.

As we approached a house, we heard someone scream the word "Halt!" from the front yard. Instantly Hatem grabbed my arm and said, "Sir, follow me".

Hatem left the path and entered the forest. He took position under the cover of a tree and whispered to me that only Pakistani troops and Razakars use the term "halt". Our volunteer groups usually say more colloquial things like "Who are you?" or "Where are you from?"

We weren't expecting the presence of any Pakistani or Razakar forces in this area. Rather, our volunteers were supposed to be there. But then why did someone say, "halt"?

Hatem wanted to be assured. He sent three of the freedom fighters from our group to the party carrying the heavy arms. Immediately, the freedom fighters ran through the forest to inform the other volunteers that they should not move ahead without clearance from Hatem.

Hatem told me and another freedom fighter to move towards Chankhola Bazaar and wait for him there. He said he would go back towards the house and investigate what was going on. I insisted that I accompany him, but he resisted. He turned to me and said, "If anything happened to you, Mukti Bahini Commander, Kader Siddiqui and my commander, Commander Benu, would surely shoot me."

I was carrying the letter from General Gill for Kader Siddiqui. If I got caught with it, my whole mission would turn into a huge disaster.

I understood Hatem's concern. I heeded his word and ran for almost half an hour. The freedom fighter and I reached Chankhola bazaar, where the local volunteer groups greeted us. I told them about what had happened. They assured me that those in that house were in fact, our volunteers. Maybe one of them got excited and decided to take this opportunity to practice some English. I felt reassured by their confidence and good humor.

After an hour, around five in the morning, Hatem arrived at Chankhola Bazaar with his team. He told us what had happened after we left.

Hatem, accompanied by some freedom fighters, slowly advanced through the woods towards the house. As he approached the house, he was met with an eerie silence. Cautiously, he instructed his soldiers to take tactical combat positions around the house. He then attempted to probe the identity of the dwelling by sounding the agreed password into the air. Luckily, those from the house recognized the code and responded accordingly. Thus, the misunderstanding was ended and a potential catastrophe was averted.

Sadly, it was just five weeks later that this same Hatem, who did not hesitate to take risks and acted so courageously to protect me, died heroically in a battle against the Pakistani Army.

Pleased By Our Success

At that time Kader was stationed at Sehrabari, five miles away from Chankhola. He was anticipating my arrival. I sent him a message from Chankhola Bazaar, reporting our location.

It was time for the volunteers of Bhuapur, who carried the arms up to Chankhola Bazaar, to return to their homes. These volunteers assisted the Mukti Bahini part-time. Some of them lived close to several pro-Pakistani Muslim League leaders. They had to help the Mukti Bahini secretly, to ensure their own safety. Additionally, many of the volunteers who helped us transport the arms had work the next morning, and so their livelihood depended on a safe return home.

The volunteers of Chankhola Bazaar hosted breakfast for us with puffed rice and molasses. I sincerely thanked the volunteers and bid them a safe return to Bhuapur.

From Chankhola Bazaar we moved onward to Sehrabari. Some of the local volunteers from Chankhola carried the cargo and accompanied us. As we had decided previously, we offloaded half of the arms and ammunition at Angarkhola Bazaar for storage.

At about six in the morning, we arrived at the residence of Abdul Basit Siddiqui, a member of the Provincial Assembly. We had about seventy-five volunteers with us. Kader greeted us warmly. The modern arms and ammunition we had brought with us excited him and the other freedom fighters. In his book Shadhinata 71, Siddiqui writes:

After about two weeks, I saw Nuran Nabi and Nurul Islam again at six in the morning on July 9th. Overjoyed, I embraced them. I was so moved by their safe and successful return that I repeatedly said, "With such committed and brave colleagues, victory was certainly ours." (p. 262)

I handed over the letter from General Gill to Kader. In the letter General Gill congratulated Kader on his success in fighting the enemy within the country. He went on to assure Kader that the Tangail Mukti Bahini would receive as much support as possible from the Indian Army. He concluded by expressing his desire to see Kader in a liberated Bangladesh very soon.

Arrangements for lunch for the volunteers were made at Basit Siddiqui's house. Kader himself supervised the luncheon. After we ate, Kader thanked the volunteers.

The supplies I brought from India included several light machineguns, rifles, thousands of grenades, bullets of various calibers, hundreds of mines, several wireless sets, and a large quantity of explosives. Unfortunately, we had no detonators.

As stated earlier, on our way from India to Bhuapur, one of the six boats accidentally went off-course in the darkness. At a huge intersection on the Jamuna River, near Jagannathganj Ferry Station, the boat lost its way and ended up in the opposite direction, rather than following us to Bhuapur. Unfortunately, all of our detonators were loaded onto this one boat. Overall, we had a very successful mission, but this one setback disappointed me a little.

Conspiracy in Aschim

The arms and ammunition were properly stored and concealed in secret places. Then Kader proceeded with his team to Aschim Bazaar under the Phulbari Police Station in the Mymensingh District. I accompanied him along with Basit, Nurul, and Moazzem. The journey was on foot. At about eight in the evening, we reached Lahorer Baid Village, some five miles on the east of Sagardighi and there we stopped at the camp of Commander Laltu and Commander Idris.

About four hundred freedom fighters, trained in India, had arrived to Aschim with explosives and detonators. Kader sent a group of four freedom fighters from the communication company, lead by Commander Abdul Khaleque to Aschim Bazaar. Their mission was to establish contact with these freedom fighters in order to obtain detonators.

Khaleque was a very ambitious person. After arriving at Aschim, Khaleque relinquished his responsibilities and conspired to instigate the freedom fighters to rise against Kader. Kader got wind of Khaleque's mutinous-intent and betrayal through his own intelligence sources. So, he proceeded to Aschim in order to further investigate the problem.

He sent a message conveying that he would meet the freedom fighters from India on July 10th. By then Kader had deployed about a thousand freedom fighters around Aschim.

We ate dinner at the camp of Commander Laltu and Commander Idris. After dinner, we convened for a meeting to review the situation at Aschim. At the meeting were Commander Abdul Hakim, Monirul Islam, Golam Sarwar, Laltu, Idris, Basit Siddiqui, Nurul Islam, Moazzem, and I.

The meeting began with the deliberations of three reputable intelligence personnel, namely Bachhu, Sabur and Kashem. They cautioned that they had information from reliable sources that Khaleque had been engaged in a conspiracy against Kader. Khaleque would try to kill Kader in order to become the leader of the Mukti Bahini. This news instantly sparked angry reactions amongst the attendees of the meeting. However, elaborate discussions soon followed.

We all agreed that any conspiracy should be handled swiftly and promptly. In a war, the prerequisite for success is to uphold strict discipline and maintain the chain of command. Indiscipline could not be tolerated. Moreover, Aschim was a very strategic location, northeast of the liberated Eastern Zone. The area was tactically significant in maintaining the safety of the Kader Bahini headquarters. Allowing the presence of any opposing or untrustworthy groups in this area posed a great risk that we were simply not willing to take.

In spite of unanimity on this point, we were divided on whether or not Kader himself should go to Aschim the next day. Though we had good reinforcements around Aschim, many thought that there was too much at risk, and felt that Kader should cancel his visit. Instead, they felt the better move was to allow the freedom fighters to find a military solution to Khaleque and his mutiny.

Despite these sentiments, some of us, including me, disagreed. We felt that conflicts among freedom fighters should be avoided and addressed peacefully.

Quoting information from one of the intelligence sources, I said that the four hundred soldiers trained in India were very simple men, but patriotic in nature. They were most probably, not even aware of Khaleque's conspiracy. Moreover, they should be informed of our connection with the governments of Bangladesh and India. If they came to know and experience the personality of Kader Siddiqui, they would most likely shun any plot of Khaleque's.

Kader listened to our suggestions and said we must try to avoid any conflict within the Mukti Bahini itself. He must try to resolve the crisis, even if it meant, risking his own life. And so, he had no choice, but to proceed to Aschim the next morning. We accepted his decision, but mentioned the importance of moving cautiously. He reminded us of the responsibilities of each commander and instructed them to go back to their respective camps. He asked them to be prepared to face any situation.

The next day, at eight in the morning, Kader sent a team to Aschim, led by Commander Idris, to inform the freedom fighters there that Commander Kader Siddiqui was on his way. This was done, so as not to take them by surprise.

Idris visited the freedom fighters at Aschim Bazaar camp in the morning. He had tea and breakfast with them before returning to our camp. Soon after, hundreds of freedom fighters from various camps made their way to Aschim Bazaar under the leadership of commanders Laltu, Munir, and Sarwar. The commanders showed the freedom fighters that had returned from India a great deal of warmth and respect. They established a solid foundation of camaraderie.

At 9 A.M., Kader proceeded to Aschim Bazaar, accompanied by Basit, Nurul, Moazzem, and I. For our safety, a handful of courageous freedom fighters were specially selected to accompany us. They were: Abdus Sabur, Saidur Rahman, Arif Ahmed Dulal, Abdul

Halim, Moqbul Hossain Khoka, Shamsu, Ferdous Alam Ranju, Abdul Quddus, Amjad, Masud, Kashem, and Rafiq. They were all equipped with automatic weapons.

Under the tight security of these freedom fighters, we reached the Aschim Bazaar camp at nine-thirty. There, Commander Abdul Mannan, and his deputy, Mozammel Huq greeted us warmly. They, along with other commanders, received Kader.

There was an assembly of nearly fifteen hundred freedom fighters at Aschim Bazaar. We ourselves were about eleven hundred. The remaining four hundred were those who had recently returned from India.

We met with the commanders of the freedom fighters in a room. They insisted that we have breakfast with them. They served us parata, a fried flat bread, and meat curry, which they prepared fresh in their mess hall.

A special security force lead by Commander Sabur was assigned to protect Kader Siddiqui. Two layers of defense always surrounded Kader Siddiqui. Moreover, several freedom fighter platoons were positioned around the bazaar area.

Though at first glance, our freedom fighters seemed relaxed and just part of the scenery, these soldiers carefully scoped the perimeter and were prepared to react to any situation.

Khaleque, the man we suspected to be a defector and betrayer was nowhere in sight. While, we were all drinking tea, he suddenly appeared.

It was just two weeks ago, that he was a loyal freedom fighter who invoked Kader as "Sir" and always showed his respect to military rank. However, on this morning things were very different. He was not his respectful-self. He didn't even say good morning to us. He was not the man we thought we knew.

Khaleque unexpectedly approached Kader and introduced himself as the commander of the Aschim Bazaar Mukti Bahini camp. Kader did not respond to his audacity and arrogance.

Rather he calmly remarked, "I am pleased to see that you are leading these men, but I would have been prouder of you had you simply completed your original mission."

Kader continued to state that his primary reason for coming to Aschim Bazaar was to establish contact with the new freedom fighters from India. Furthermore, he ensured that he would provide assistance in times of need.

He said, "During these tumultuous times, unless we each seek to help out one another, we would be sure to face serious problems."

Kader went on to say, "By now, we have in our possession, a large quantity of explosives. However, without detonators, these explosives are useless. I sent you here to get detonators. I would have been happy if you had simply done just that."

Khaleque replied, "Well, we don't have any detonators!"

However, unbeknown to Khaleque, engineers from his camp had already informed us that they, indeed, had detonators. By lying to our faces, his betrayal became evident.

Khaleque was quite unnerved by the assembly of so many armed freedom fighters at Aschim Bazaar. Furthermore, I was sure that he felt the presence of even more soldiers, beyond the perimeter of Aschim Bazaar.

Despite the negative image Khaleque's lies had painted of us, the freedom fighters from India found us to be very warm and friendly. In no time, they had changed their minds.

Kader called the freedom fighters to assemble at the bazaar grounds. As a measure of security, members of our troops lined up in front of the Aschim Bazaar freedom fighters. Sabur's team positioned itself at the rear.

Kader made a passionate speech by extending his friendship to the freedom fighters from India.

He introduced me to the crowd and told them how I had established contact with the Indian government and the Bangladesh government in Mujibnagar. He ensured that both governments were committed to assisting us in anyway possible.

As a token of goodwill from the Kader Bahini, Kader donated a box of LMG magazines for the Aschim Bazaar camp. The freedom fighters responded with applause. They showed their support for Kader by chanting slogans into the air.

After seeing the strength we had established in-and-around Aschim Bazaar; after seeing the camaraderie forged between the two camps; and after seeing the leadership of Kader Siddiqui, it became abundantly obvious to the cunning Khaleque that his conspiracy had failed.

Upon this new epiphany, Khaleque quickly changed his tune. He reverted to his old self and overtly expressed his loyalty to Kader. But it was too late; he had lost our trust.

The freedom fighters from India expressed their allegiance to Kader and reciprocated Kader's promise to provide assistance in times of need. Backing up this statement, the freedom fighters secretly provided us with detonators. By doing so, these freedom fighters were successful in completing Khaleque's once failed-mission.

Returning to Sehrabari

We were all relieved to see that the encounter at Aschim Bazaar went so smoothly. We left Aschim Bazaar for Laltu and Idris's camp. It was just a few miles away.

We ate lunch at Laltu's camp and left for Sehrabari. The presence of more than one thousand freedom fighters greatly encouraged the people in the area. Along the way, people spontaneously gathered around us and Kader was asked to address several impromptu meetings.

At four in the afternoon, we arrived at Sagardighi where a public meeting was organized. A large number of people had assembled. Before the start of the meeting, a contingent of uniformed freedom fighters lead by Commander Sarwar conducted an honor guard for Kader.

Moazzem, Basit, and I addressed the audience. It was my first time speaking in a public meeting. I was incredibly nervous and anxious. My throat was dry. I was trembling. Slowly, my mouth opened and I addressed the crowd.

I spoke about my mission to India and its success. I tried to mention Bangabandhu's name as many times as possible. I knew that it would please the crowd. Nonetheless, it was a very brief speech. As I closed, I shouted one last time, "Joy Bangla!"

As I finished, Kader Siddiqui stepped forward. It was his turn to address the crowd. A remarkable orator, he moved the crowd with an eloquent and emotional speech. He sought the help, cooperation, and blessings of the public. He reiterated to them that our battle was their battle. Our victory was their victory.

After the meeting we proceeded to Sehrabari. Basit Siddiqui, a middle aged man and a member of the Provincial Assembly, challenged the rest of us to a race. Surprised by his challenge, we skeptically accepted. We thought to ourselves, "How was a man in his mid-fifties expecting to keep pace with those of us who were nearly half his age?"

Two hours and nine miles later, we arrived at Sehrabari. Amazingly, Basit Siddiqui was right in the middle of the pack. The whole way through he never fell a step-behind.

We spent the night at Basit Siddiqui's house in Sehrabari. The next morning, I accompanied Kader to the headquarters of the Mukti Bahini. Nurul and Basit were also with us. At eleven-thirty in the morning we reached the headquarters.

For Nurul, Moazzem, Basit, and I, this was our first visit to the headquarters. We had been traveling from July 5th to July 11th.

On the 5th, Nurul and I began our trip from Mankachar and crossed a distance of about one hundred miles by boat to reach Bhuapur. From Bhuapur to the headquarters we had traveled another hundred miles by foot. In total, we had traveled more than two hundred miles in just under six days. It was an extraordinary journey.

Looking back, it all seems unbelievable.

Mukti Bahini Headquarters

After we reached the headquarters, Shaheed gave me a bear hug and started dancing in joy. The extraordinary success of the Indian mission had moved everyone. They treated me like a hero. I modestly mentioned that I had only performed my duties.

I was introduced to everybody at the headquarters. I had met some of them earlier at Bhuapur. Later that day around noon, Kader had a meeting with all of us and provided some new guidelines regarding the day-to-day operations of the headquarters. He also reviewed some organizational issues. In the afternoon, he went out for a quick visit to the Mukti Bahini camps at Hateya, Bashkhali, Hatubhanga, Kalikoir, Phulbari, Kachina and Katamore. I stayed behind at the headquarters.

The headquarters of the Tangail Mukti Bahini was housed in a primary school at Mahanandapur. This was a remote fortress, deep in the jungles between Madhupur and Bhawalgar. It was difficult to access by foot, and completely impossible by vehicle.

Ditches protected three sides of the school. Even the slightest bit of rainfall transformed them into formidable moats. The building was engulfed in thick jungle. To the west, there were two dwellings. To the east, there were four houses at least a mile away. It was a truly difficult place to reach. A stronghold such as this needed only a simple defense to hold off even the most powerful of attacks. It would be impossible for an enemy to occupy it.

The headquarters looked like a well-organized office. There were designated chairs and desks for Kader, Shaheed, and others. There was an iron safe in one corner. A large portrait of Bangabandhu Sheikh Mujibur Rahman was hanging on the wall. The maps of Bangladesh and Tangail District were hanging adjacent to it. Red and blue pins indicated the positions of the Pakistani forces and the Mukti Bahini, respectively.

The headquarters were responsible for: coordinating the activities and communication of the Mukti Bahini and the volunteers; recruiting and training of the Mukti Bahini; public relations; collecting information on the enemy as well as maintaining the discipline of the Mukti Bahini and the management of the accounts of the income and the expenditure of the Mukti Bahini.

Anwar-ul Alam Shaheed

Shaheed was in charge of coordinating all activities of the Mukti Bahini from the headquarters. Additionally, he was responsible for the civil administration of the liberated zone.

Before the war, he was the general secretary of Salimullah Muslim Hall Student Union of Dhaka University and a member of the Central Committee of the Student League. He was also a leader of the Student League at Karotia Sadat College and Tangail District. As a member of the Boy Scouts, Shaheed had traveled to several foreign countries.

Shaheed was quite popular and respected amongst the Mukti Bahini for his unique background. Kader Siddiqui himself treated Shaheed with respect and entrusted him with the responsibility of running the headquarters.

Shaheed utilized his experience in student politics to perform his duties skillfully. He was known for his organizing abilities, his modesty, friendliness and genteel manner.

He never misused the powers at his disposal. Shaheed's great organizing ability complemented Kader's extraordinary military leadership. This was one of the reasons for the success of the Tangail Mukti Bahini.

After the independence of Bangladesh, Shaheed became the Deputy Director of the Rakkhi Bahini. Later, he served as the Bangladesh ambassador to several countries, including Spain.

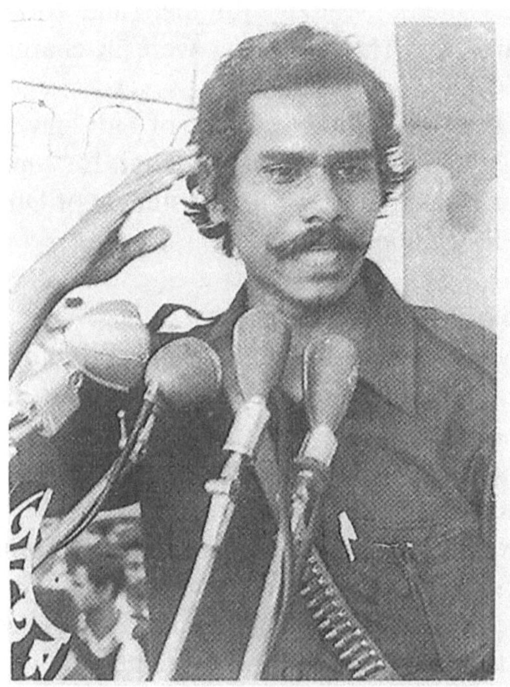

Anwar-ul Alam Shaheed

The Mukti Bahini Hospital

The day after my arrival to the headquarters, Shaheed and others took me to visit the Mukti Bahini Hospital. The Mukti Bahini had converted a house into a hospital. It was just a few miles away from the headquarters, in Andhi Village.

Dr. Shahjada Chowdhury, a fifth year student of Mymensingh Medical College and Dr. Sisir Ranjan Saha, provided medical treatment. Amjad, a former schoolteacher, coordinated the operations.

When we reached the hospital, we found six wounded freedom fighters undergoing treatment. Habibur Rahman Khoka of Tengpuria and Anwar Hossain of Rampur were among them. Enemy mortar shells had seriously wounded these two brave freedom fighters during a battle in Kamutia. The other four had sustained minor injuries.

Additional people who were also involved in the activities of the hospital were: Dr. Amal Krishna Sarkar, Ratan, Bimal, Nizamuddin, Abdul Majid, Mostafa, Sirajul Islam, Belayet Hossain, Shukur Mamud, Osman Ghani, Mofizur Rahman and Motaleb. Shawkat Momen Shahjahan and Hamidul Huq were in charge of collecting medical supplies.

One West Pakistani Pathan, a trader of bidi and tobacco leaves, also extended his help in running the hospital. He supplied medicine from Tangail and Dhaka. Osman Gani, a student of Dhaka University looked after the food supply.

Training Camp of Mukti Bahini

The next day we went to inspect the Mukti Bahini training camp. The camp covered about a square mile and was located four miles south of the headquarters. An open field surrounded by heavy forest was used for training. To the unknowing eye, it would not appear obvious that this was a training camp.

The camp was tightly secured and carefully monitored. Several freedom fighters were perched on the canopies of trees as they maintained surveillance over the surrounding area. Subsequently, there were several checkpoints positioned throughout the encompassing lands.

I was amazed to see the training camp operate so efficiently.

I had read about the Vietnam War and was intrigued by the ability of the Vietcong to fortify their positions. However, visiting the camp I realized, we too, held an advantageous position against our enemy.

As we reached the training site, the commander of the camp, Swapan Bhattacharyya, a policeman in his early twenties, welcomed us. He gave us a thorough tour of the facility.

About one hundred freedom fighters were being trained on-site. Small tin sheds were erected under the trees to provide sleeping accommodations for the freedom fighters. Commander Shahjahan spearheaded the establishment of this training camp and from what I could see; he had done a commendable job.

Wireless Station

The wireless station was installed about two miles from the headquarters in the house of a woodcutter named Ingraj. Wireless-sets were captured during the raids on Pakistani police stations. The Mukti Bahini used these sets to create an improvised system for wireless communication.

Anisur Rahman of Bakbajan was in charge of the wireless station. He was a wireless operator by trade. He performed his duty very diligently to repair, maintain, and operate the wireless station. The wireless operators of Tangail and its surrounding occupied areas had helped the liberation war by passing information to the Mukti Bahini via secret codes.

Mohu Sardar

The next day, I stepped out from the headquarters with Shaheed, Nuru, and Faruk.

As we walked, Shaheed says, "In the last two days, I have shown you the training camp and the hospital. Today I will introduce you to someone special. I am taking you to a special place."

I was curious about our destination and the identity of whom Shaheed wanted me to meet.

However, despite my efforts, Shaheed would only smirk and say, "Wait a little, you will find out soon enough."

We came to a compound about a mile away from the headquarters. Two freedom fighters welcomed us at the entrance. As we stepped into the yard of the house, a tall bulky man came out. He was about six and half feet tall with the physique of Mr. Universe. He was a middle-aged man with a thick beard. He greeted us with a military salute. Shaheed introduced him to us as Mohu Sardar, the jailor of the Mukti Bahini. In fact, the outer house of the compound was, in actuality, the prison-house of the Mukti Bahini.

In order to maintain law and order in the liberated zones, criminals were imprisoned in this jail. Freedom fighters accused of misconduct were also temporarily imprisoned here. Mohu Sardar had an assistant. His name was Ansar Ali. During our visit, there was only one ordinary criminal imprisoned in the jail.

Eventually, I came to know more about Mohu Sardar in detail. His life story was quite fascinating. Before the war, Mohu was known throughout the area as a notorious bandit. He was the perpetrator behind several robberies across the country and even across the border in Assam, India. He had a network of more than three hundred bandits all over the country working for him.

In order to take part in the liberation war, he voluntarily went to Kader Siddiqui.

In an attempt to test Mohu's integrity, Kader said, "Look, if I shoot you now presuming that you are a Razakar, what would you do?"

Mohu replied, "Though I admit I am a criminal, I want nothing more than to repay my debt by fighting the enemy and liberating my country. And if, after all that I've said, you still want to kill me, do so, but know that arresting me isn't an option. There hasn't been a prison built that I can't escape from"

Despite Mohu's criminal history, when we met him, he did not give off the impression that he was a man that we could not trust. Mohu Sardar performed his duties for the Mukti Bahini with absolute dedication.

After the liberation of the country, Kader Siddiqui entrusted Mohu as his personal bodyguard. For many years Mohu was Kader's shadow. He was the perfect person for this particular responsibility.

Commander Khalilur Rahman

The company commander, Khalilur Rahman was in charge of security and defense for the headquarters. Khalilur Rahman defected from the Pakistani naval forces. He was a local. His house was located in a nearby village called Saira Baid, just a mile away from the headquarters. He knew the forests, roads, and alleys of this area like the palm of his hand. Those who assisted him were: Abdur Razzak of Hamidpur, Muniruzzaman Sanu, a student of Dhaka College, Abdul

Mannan and Biren Barman of Kalihati Lalmohan, "Junior" Abdullah of Kachua, and many others.

The Commanders of the Mukti Bahini

At the start of the Tangail Mukti Bahini there were only about one thousand freedom fighters. However, by July of 1971, this number rose to more than ten thousand and eventually grew to seventeen thousand. In order to conduct a disciplined war, this huge number of freedom fighters was divided into several companies. The commanders of different companies were as follows: Manirul Islam, Lokman Hossain, Abdul Gafur, Labib Rahman (martyred), Laltu, Sarwar, Fazlur Rahman, Nabi Newaz, Shawkat Momen Shahjahan, Habibur Rahman (Bir Bikram), Abdul Hakim, Sabur Khan, Matiur Rahman, Mokaddes, Azad Kamal, Habi, Afsaruddin, Abdur Razzak, Benu, Golam Mostafa, Bayezid, Saidur Rahman, Humayun, Angur, Fazlu, Moqbul Hossain, Khorshed Alam, Rezaul Karim, Amanullah, Idris, Ferdous Alam Ronju, Halim, Shamsul, Taser Ali, Solemen, Gazi Lutfor Rahman, Tara, Anis, Yunus, Arzoo, Nurul Islam, Chand Miah, Riaz, Shah Alam, Sultan, Moin, and Mozzamel.

Commander Abdur Razzak

The Mukti Bahini commanders represented different strata of society. They came from various professional institutions. Some were military men, but many others were teachers, industrial laborers, politicians, students, and even farmers. Abdur Razzak was a student leader of Mymensingh Agricultural University. Gentle, polite, and always smiling, Razzak performed his duties as a commander with the utmost dedication. After the war, he earned a Ph.D. from the United States and then returned to Bangladesh to become a high government official. Now he is the Minister of Food and Disaster Management for the Bangladesh government and a Member of Parliament.

Volunteers' Groups

Arranging food for the seventeen thousand freedom fighters of the Tangail Mukti Bahini was an enormous and crucial task. Thousands of volunteers worked to ensure that these men were always fed. Every village had established a group of volunteers dedicated to this responsibility. The total number of volunteers rose to about seventy thousand before the end of the war. The volunteer-leaders whose names I still remember were: Hamidul Haq, Khorshed Master, Awal Siddiqui, Khorshed Alam in the Eastern Zone, and Abdul Alim, Bhola, Moazzem Hossain Khan, and Dudu Mia in the Western Zone.

Shawkat Momen Shahjahan

The secret of the Tangail Mukti Bahini's success lay in the hills of Tangail and the courageous hearts of the patriotic people who lived there. The people of the hilly area played a critical role in the organization of the Mukti Bahini, the establishment of the headquarters, and the implementation of other essential activities. Those who played important roles in these activities were: Hamidul Haq, Shawkat Momen Shahjahan, Commander Idris, Awal Siddiqui, Abdul Barit Siddiqui, Amjad Master, Commander Khalil, Khorshed Alam R. O., Khorshed Master, Ali Pagla, and Khoka.

Of them, Shawkat Momen Shahjahan was a distinguished character. Before the war, he was a student leader of Mymensingh Agricultural University. Aside from his contribution to the formation of the Tangail Mukti Bahini in its early stages, another anecdote surrounding Shawkat comes to mind.

Shawkat's father was the chairman of the local union council. The Mukti Bahini had arrested him on accusations of collaborating with the Pakistani Army. At the time, Shawkat was a commander of the Mukti Bahini.

Despite being very anxious and concerned for his father's wellbeing, Shawkat, at no point, sought favor to have his father released.

Ultimately, after a thorough investigation, the Mukti Bahini released his father. Subsequently his father worked to help the freedom fighters in every way possible.

Shawkat, much like his father, was confronted with a similar test of character. One day Shawkat was blind-sided when a few of the local villagers filed complaints against him. As a result of the accusations, Shawkat was relieved of his duties and temporarily imprisoned.

Despite this, after serving his term in prison, Shawkat rejoined the Mukti Bahini and performed his duties with valor and commitment.

This patriotic freedom fighter passed two difficult tests in the nine months of the liberation war.

Later, in the 1980's, Shawkat Momen Shahjahan was elected to the Bangladesh Parliament on the Awami League party ticket. Currently, he is a member of the Bangladesh Parliament and chairman of the parliamentary committee of the ministry of agriculture.

Fighting All Around

Our headquarters was situated in a dense forest stretching some sixty to seventy miles, north to south and some twenty to thirty miles, east to west. The forest was known as Madhupur-Bhawalgar.

As a first-line of defense for the liberated Eastern Zone, several permanent defense posts had been established. In the west, posts were located at Deopara against the Kalihati Pakistani Police Station and in Dhalapara against the Ghatail Police Station.

To the southwest, posts were located at Ballah and Pahartali, against the Basail Pakistani Police Station. To the north, defense was located at Rangamati while posts at Aschim and Bhaluka provided coverage from the east. Lastly, a southern post, located at Patharghata, provided additional support against the Basail Police Station.

These units had been located strategically to counter attacks from the enemy-occupied police headquarters. Regular attacks were conducted on Pakistani forces from these posts.

As a second-line of defense for our headquarters, Commander Khalilur Rahman's company was specifically deployed to ensure security.

Initially, the Mukti Bahini had adopted a "hit and run" strategy. However, by July we had obtained a large reinforcement of weapons and ammunition from India. The Mukti Bahini was ready to do more than just safeguard its own position. We were ready to engage in aggressive offensives attacks against the enemy. The Pakistani Army could no longer rest on its laurels.

Irritated by our new tactics, the Pakistani forces retaliated with stronger counterattacks. From July 11th to the 24th, the enemy attacked several of our frontal-posts. Many of these attacks were very intense and resulted in fierce battles with our forces.

On July 18th, the enemy attempted to probe our strengths and attacked our outpost at Deopara. We had already gathered information on enemy movement from Kalihati. In response, Commander Lokman moved some of his forces a few miles ahead and re-positioned them at Birbasunda. There they ambushed the enemy.

As a result, the enemy was forced to stop. However, when they attempted to retreat, the Mukti Bahini ambushed them again at Birbasunda, Kosturipara, and Deonaghat. Commander Lokman orchestrated this valiant counter attack.

More than one hundred Pakistani soldiers and Razakars were killed or injured in the attack. Armed with the automatic weapons brought from India, we were finally fighting on an even ground. At last, the enemy had gotten its first taste of what we, the Mukti Bahini, were capable of.

Meanwhile, at the headquarters, we were alerted of an imminent attack by Pakistani forces. Accordingly, we took cautionary measures to defend our headquarters. However, by evening we came to learn of the Mukti Bahini's victory on the battlefield. We were overjoyed.

The next morning we awoke to the sound of heavy gunfire. Our headquarters trembled in the quaking-sounds of exploding mortars shells. We were alarmed. In a report briefing we learned that in response to the previous day's defeat, Pakistani forces moved ahead ferociously towards Deopara with six-pounder-mortars and 120 mm machineguns. The Mukti Bahini forces were waiting for them inside their bunkers.

At about 11 AM, a mortar shell fell near the bunker of Commander Lokman. It was nearly a direct hit. His gun was destroyed and the bunker was completely devastated. Commander Lokman was partially buried under the rubble of the bunker. The freedom fighters rescued their commander by pulling him out from under the debris.

Commander Lokman strategically retreated to Dhalapara and reconstructed new bunkers on the bank of the Bangshai River.

In the evening we were informed that our Deopara outpost had fallen to the enemy. However, Commander Lokman narrowly escaped to safety. Kader Siddiqui was then stationed at Kalamegha, some fifteen miles away from the headquarters. We informed him of the events of the day. He quickly arrived at the Mukti Bahini post at

Dholapara the next morning. Every one was reassured and enthused by the sight of their commander.

Kader Siddiqui instructed the freedom fighters to use guerilla tactics to intensify our offensives strikes on the enemy. That same night, he returned to the headquarters.

The enemy continued its assault on other fronts. On July 19th, they attacked Bhaluka post in the east. Commander Afsar put up a heroic resistance. The enemy was forced to retreat after an entire day of ceaseless fighting.

On July 22nd, a team of freedom fighters, under the leadership of Commander Motiur Rahman, ambushed a patrolling Pakistani contingent near Basail police station. In the span of just a few minutes, five Pakistani soldiers were killed, and the Mukti Bahini seized their weapons.

The next day, the Pakistani Army retaliated. Desperately, they deployed two companies armed with heavy mortars and attacked Commander Motiur Rahman's position.

Commander Matiur Rahman and Commander Mokaddes were forced to retreat and reestablished their outposts at Banshtoli and Ratonpur, three miles away.

Attack on Shutrapur Bridge

On June 29th, the Mukti Bahini achieved an important victory under the leadership of Commanders Khorshed Alam, Pulak Sarkar, and Mohendra Ghosh. That night, the Mukti Bahini executed an attack with lightening speed and captured the Shutrapur Bridge located thirty-miles from Dhaka on the Dhaka-Tangail Road. The Razakars guarding the bridge were taken prisoner by freedom fighters.

Habib and Bari of Jamalpur were Mukti Bahini explosive experts. In just a few minutes, they had blasted the bridge. These two were among the freedom fighters that had initially visited my house in June upon their return from India. Together we joined Kader Siddiqui at the Bhuapur Mukti Bahini camp.

The blast was heard across the surrounding area. Its tremors spanned north of Dhaka to Tangail, including our headquarters. This was the first blast of this magnitude felt in this area. The people were frightened.

Unfortunately, the freedom fighters were not equipped with enough explosives. Only part of the bridge actually collapsed. However, it was enough to disrupt the movement of Pakistani forces.

This event generated an enormous amount of publicity. The blast took place only about thirty miles from Pakistani military headquarters.

On June 30th and July 1st, the BBC, the Voice of America, Akashvani, and Free Bangla Radio broadcasted this news across their bulletins. This blast echoed far beyond the ears of the Pakistani military cantonment. The whole world now knew of the resistance brought forth by the freedom fighters of the Tangail Mukti Bahini and their leader, Kader Siddiqui.

A Black Chapter

At the end of June, a shameful incident took place at Kedarpur under the jurisdiction of Nagarpur Police Station. This was a black chapter in the annals of the liberation war.

On June 25th, a team of freedom fighters took over Nagarpur Police Station headquarters in a rapid assault. Commanders Labib Rahman, Sarowar, and Laltu led the operation. After the police surrendered, the Mukti Bahini captured their arms, ammunition, and wireless sets.

Soon after, Commander Labib Rahman learned of a group of freedom fighters in the area under the leadership of Commander Abdul Baten. He was informed that Baten's group was interested in joining his company. However, Kader had previously warned Labib of the existence of splinter groups. Despite this, Labib was encouraged by the possibility of expanding his company.

The next morning, two of Baten's deputies, Shahjahan and Shahjada, came to Labib's camp with two other commanders. They handed over a letter from Baten. The letter was an invitation to Labib asking him to come to Baten's camp. There, Commander Baten would announce that his group would join Commander Labib's company.

Commander Labib was an honest and simple person. He was not the type of man to suspect foul play from such an invitation. And so, the following day he proceeded towards Baten's camp accompanied by two of his co-fighters. Baten's camp was one and a half miles away.

As Labib and his companions neared the camp, shots came at them from hidden alleys between nearby dwellings. Commander Labib and his co-fighter Jahangir were killed instantly. The third soldier who accompanied Labib kept a distance from Labib and was luckily unscathed by the ambush.

He then opened fire in the direction of the attack. After a brief counterattack, the soldier retreated and ran back to the Mukti Bahini camp to report the killing of Labib and Jahangir.

Commander Sarowar and Laltu rushed to the ambush location with their troops. They found the bloodstained spot, but could not find the bodies of their dead comrades. The villagers reported that they had seen some armed individuals flee from that vicinity. The freedom fighters combed the area for the bodies of these two valiant sons of Bangladesh for two days. Unfortunately they were never recovered. This event deeply shocked Kader and everyone else.

I heard the story from Faruk, a staff worker at the headquarters. He wiped his tears as he narrated the tragedy. Jahangir was a close friend of Faruk from his boyhood days. They grew up together and developed a loving and faithful friendship.

I was also deeply hurt by this incident. We lost two of our valiant freedom fighters, not to the Pakistani enemy, not to traitorous Razakars, but to some miscreants masquerading as freedom fighters.

Eventually we learned that Baten was not present in the area at the time of the incident. He was across the border in India. The letter sent in Baten's name was a forgery. Nonetheless, there was no doubt that Shahjada and Shahjahan, the men who brought the letter were a part of Baten's group.

Guerilla Operation at Tangail Town

By August, almost all of the pro-Pakistani Bengalis had left their homes in the areas liberated by the Mukti Bahini. They took shelter in Tangail town, which was still occupied by Pakistani forces. At that time, Tangail town was the location of training sites for Razakars.

In order to intimidate the Pakistani soldiers and their collaborators, a commando force was formed to launch a grenade attack on the enemy. Some young and gallant residents of the town were recruited to join this special freedom fighter group. They were fully aware of the risks that they would be taking, but joined the group anyway.

Some of the freedom fighters in this group were Baku, Salauddin, Abul Kalam, Minu, Abdul Sabur, and Helu. By the end of June, they had received their supply of grenades and left the headquarters to take their positions at Tangail town. They took shelter at different hideouts. Some hid in their own houses, while others took cover in their relative's homes.

On July 2nd, commando Baku threw a grenade at the jeep of a Pakistani Colonel, but unfortunately he missed his target. However, the sound of the blast shook the entire town. Baku was captured by the enemy and was taken into police custody. Before the enemy could proceed with an interrogation, Baku requested the use of the lavatory. With the guard's attention directed to leading Baku to the bathroom, Baku quickly struck the guard rendering him unconscious. Baku was able to flee from captivity. Baku saved himself from certain death.

On July 14th, commando Minu threw a grenade at a bus running towards Tangail town. This attack was enough to cancel the final examination for the Secondary School Certificate scheduled for that day. It was common for the occupation forces to create the appearance that life was normal in Bangladesh. This included scheduling school examinations in battle zones. Minu's grenade attack disrupted the "normalcy" that the enemy foisted upon the Bengali people.

On July 23rd, Baku was involved in another valiant guerilla operation. This time commando Kalam was with him. Kalam was riding a motorcycle while Baku sat in the rear. As they came in front of a Tangail power station, Baku threw a grenade at a group of five Pakistani guards. Plumes of smoke followed a loud explosion. The five guards were killed, but the eruption alerted other Pakistani soldiers. The soldiers attempted to follow the commandoes, but Kalam and Baku adroitly escaped using the narrow alleys and lanes, which they knew like the backs of their hands.

The next day, about three hundred trained Pakistani collaborators had been enjoying a film at Rupbani cinema hall. Commando Minu and Anis Junior were also among the audience members. It was an Urdu film show. During a fighting scene, Minu and Anis threw grenades inside the hall, which resulted in twelve Razakar casualties and more than one hundred Razakar injuries. Fortunately, Minu and Anis escaped safely during the commotion.

On July 30th, two commandoes, Haider and Bachchu launched yet another commando grenade attack. This time it was on a truck carrying Razakars. These two commandoes were adolescents, no older than sixteen. They noticed that every morning, Razakars were brought in and out from their camp in trucks as a part of a routine change of shifts.

In the early hours of the morning, Haider and Bachchu saw two trucks on the move. They positioned themselves on a banyan tree and threw two grenades at them. Both trucks were destroyed with shards of metal splintering from the truck cabins. Fortunately, Haider and Bachchu had hid themselves so high on the branches of the tree that they were unhurt. They climbed down at an opportune moment and then returned to headquarters.

These repeated grenade attacks by the commandoes not only killed a number of Pakistani soldiers and their collaborators, but it greatly frightened the supporters of Pakistan who had taken shelter at Tangail town. The occupation army once felt quite safe in Tangail town. However, with the execution of these attacks, the enemy began feeling insecure. They were haunted by the thought of potential freedom fighters lurking around every corner.

While the grenade operation brought us some success, it came at a hefty cost. In a subsequent operation, the Pakistani Army captured Baku and Kalam. However, this time Baku wasn't as lucky as he was before. He had to pay the price for escaping from Pakistani captivity. In enemy custody, Baku was tortured to death. The fearless commando, Baku became a martyr for his country.

Kalam was put to unbearable physical torture in order to force him to divulge information on the Tangail Mukti Bahini and their leader Kader Siddiqui. His statement was aired on television and radio in an attempt to mislead people. However, Kalam was very intelligent. He carefully chose his words in such a way that he did not compromise the security of the Mukti Bahini.

The Pakistanis kept Kalam alive because they wanted to use him as an agent for propaganda. Nonetheless, Kalam was too clever to fall to such exploits.

After the independence of Bangladesh, Kalam was released from prison.

I had some memorable experiences at the headquarters from July 11th to the 21st. Kader returned to the headquarters again on July 21st and discussed with us the latest situations on the frontlines.

Pakistani forces were growing desperate day-by-day and began mounting continuous pressure on us. We were greatly in need of additional arms and ammunition, particularly mortars and rocket-launchers. Once again I would have to go to India to garner more supplies. This time Nuru and Basit would accompany me.

Second Mission to India

On July 24th, I left for India from Mohanadapur headquarters. The next day, Basit, Nuru, and I arrived at Bhuapur, our main outpost in the Western Zone. On July 26th, in accordance with Kader's instructions, I convened over an important meeting of the Mukti Bahini commanders, civilian administration officers, and volunteer groups. Among the commanders who attended the meeting were Habibur Rahman, Abdul Gafur, Khorshed Alam, Rezaul Karim Tarafdar, Humayun, Benu, and Amanullah. Enayet Karim, Moazzem Hossain Khan, and Nurul Islam represented the civilian administration. Basit and I represented the headquarters.

At the meeting, we decided that we needed to fortify our defense at Bhuapur in the same way we had done in the Eastern Zone. Strategically, Bhuapur was a very important location. It allowed us to bring supplies directly in from India, via the Jamuna River.

It was further decided that from then on, grenade strikes on enemy bases in Tangail would be conducted from our Bhuapur outpost as well.

On July 29th Basit, Nuru, and I boarded a small boat and set sail for India. We headed upstream through the Jamuna River towards Mankachar, India. Our goal was to follow the same route that I had traversed during my return from India to Bhuapur on July 7th.

Refugees had been using this route to flee to India since the military onslaught on civilians began.

The wind was in our favor. We were nearing Bahadurabad Ferry Station. It had been a productive day's journey.

The Jamuna River was quite wide in these parts. Once again, we were sailing alongside the west bank of the river to hide from the public. Unlike the eastern bank, the western side of the river was completely barren. There were no inhabitants, only the many sand-islands.

It was a sunny morning. However as the afternoon crept in, dark-dense clouds suddenly appeared across the horizon. Within a few minutes the wind started bellowing. We found ourselves amidst a torrential downpour of what looked like the beginnings of a violent tempest.

The boatman was struck with fear. He struggled to speed up and get us to shore. However, the storm only seemed to move faster. At one point, a strong gust of wind tore our already worn-out sail into several pieces. The constant thrashing of waves cracked the bottom of our boat and before we knew it, water began leaking in. It was a terrifying situation.

The boatman was on the brink of exhaustion. He used every ounce of his strength, but was overwhelmed by the storm. Nuru and I joined the boatman and started rowing as well. Basit looked to the sky and started crying for God's mercy.

The water was rising quickly in the boat. It was a race between us reaching the bank and our boat sinking to the bottom of river. It wasn't looking good. The boat was nearly filled with water, yet we kept on going. We rowed with all of our might.

As the muscles in our arms pulsated like pistons of an engine, the boat rocked forward. Suddenly, the rain had let up. The intensity of the storm attenuated. It was just a passing storm.

With our boat severely damaged, it was clear we were about to sink, but fate had drifted us near the riverbank.

We were lucky. The boat sank and we swam just a few yards to shore. Though we were tired and drenched, we had avoided drowning and escaped the grasp of the mighty Jamuna River. Finally, we were safe on shore, but our boat was lost.

We were stranded in no-man's land. The only means of transportation in this region was boat. Where were we going to find another boat?

Boats weren't readily available in remote places like this. We might have to wait till morning before another boat would pass by. This meant we'd have to find shelter. Granted, we could spend the night under the open sky, but if another storm came, how were we going to survive?

In spite of all of this, my main concern was still getting to India as quickly as possible. I had a very important mission to complete. Being delayed was not an option. As I struggled to come up with a solution, Nuru suddenly pointed to the sky and said, "Look, to the north!"

He was pointing to the top of a pole, which resembled the mast of a boat. However, from our vantage point we could see no boat. A huge sand-hill stood right in front of us.

We climbed the hill and rushed towards the pole. As our eyes peered over the hilltop, we saw two boats with canopies, anchored to the shore. These boats likely took shelter on the shore during the storm. These passengers were lucky as their boats were still intact.

With thoughts of our mission still fresh in my mind, I saw these two vessels, not as boats, but rather as rescuers. This was our only hope. We thought that given our circumstances, we had only once choice. We had to seek help from these two boats.

We approached the boats. They were refugee boats packed with men, women, children and their few meager belongings. They had absolutely no extra room. The passengers were members of the Hindu community. They were fleeing Bangladesh on their way to Mankachar, India.

Pakistani forces and their pro-Pakistani allies especially persecuted the Hindu-minority of Bangladesh for not only their support of the Awami League, but also because of their religion. The Pakistani authority often alleged that Bangladeshi Hindus were more loyal to India than to Pakistan. This sentiment coupled with individual prejudice fueled the heinous acts of Pakistani soldiers against innocent Hindu lives.

This family had become victims of such atrocities perpetrated by the enemy. They had fled their homes to protect their lives and the honor of their women. These people were scared. They had every reason to be skeptical of strangers. They had every reason to be suspicious of us.

We carefully thought about how to approach these people. How would they react to the four of us? Would they believe us? Even if they were sympathetic, would there be any room for four more passengers on their already overcrowded boats?

As our voices stuttered with hesitation, we introduced ourselves to the passengers.

"We are the Mukti Bahini," I said.

We explained our mission and asked if there would be room for us on their boats. To our dismay, they said no. However, we continued to plead for reconsideration.

The passengers of the boats consisted of two families who were fleeing Sirajganj Town. The people of Sirajganj particularly infuriated the Pakistani forces. After the March 25th crackdown, the people of Sirajganj organized a resistance against Pakistani forces. By the end of March, Pakistani forces found themselves in a fierce battle to reoccupy Sirajganj. The Pakistani Army suffered heavy causalities.

In retaliation the Pakistani forces took a heavy-handed approach to Sirajganj. They indiscriminately carried out acts of carnage, arson, and rape.

Naturally, the families on the boat had no reason to trust strangers.

In a moment of empathy, the head of one family called his brother from the other boat for consultation. Wet and hungry, we anxiously waited for their decision. A few minutes passed like several hours for us.

It was getting dark. If they didn't take us, our fate would lie in the hands of the stormy night sky. The chance of us finding another refugee boat was remote.

Basit was reciting verses to himself from the Koran. He was confident that some way, somehow, we would be saved.

After a few minutes, we were called back to the boat for further inquiry. Finally they returned to us and said, "You are the Mukti Bahini. Please board our boats."

They had heard of Kader Siddiqui and the Tangail Mukti Bahini. They were especially honored to meet Basit Siddiqui, a member of the Parliament.

Continuing, they said that they did not consider our presence an inconvenience. Rather, they wanted to make sure that we were comfortable. They wanted us to feel at home with them, as if they were our family.

We were overwhelmed by the respect, sympathy, and cooperation that these refugees showed us. We were relieved.

They transferred some of their family members from one boat to the other to make room for us.

We sat at the front of the boat while the women and children nestled inside the canopy. There were a total of thirteen people on our boat. Six men, and the rest women and children.

As I was about to speak with the boatmen about our journey ahead, a young man came out from under the canopy. The head of the family introduced him to us as his elder son, a student of Rajshahi University. He was about my age.

Basit asked, "If this is your older son, where is your younger one?"

Suddenly, the man's eyes flooded with tears as he struggled to speak. The man's elder son responded and told us of how Pakistani forces had brutally killed his younger brother. We were speechless. Despite all the bloodshed the three of us had witnessed, no experience could give us the right words needed to console this family.

It was for this loss that the elder son had been hiding under the canopy until now. Fearful of losing another child, the father was unwilling to let his son take any risks.

I tried to ease the gloomy atmosphere by changing the subject. I mentioned that I had used this route about a month ago as I returned from my mission to India. Based on my experience, there were a few things I wanted them to know.

The Pakistani forces had a garrison at the Bahadurabad Ferry Station on the east bank of the river. We would have to cross it in the middle of the night to avoid the watchful eyes of the enemy. Therefore, it was imperative that we navigate along the west bank of the river. For our timing to be correct, we would have to begin our journey now. And so, the boatmen set sail.

We hadn't eaten all day. After our perilous journey, we were tired and hungry. As our boat sank to the bed of the Jamuna, so did our rations. The refugee family invited us to share in their meals. We ate Chira, fried flattened rice, and Gur, molasses candies.

Basit was an articulate conversationalist. He thanked them again for their food and hospitality. He entertained the families with the success stories of the Tangail Mukti Bahini. They shared with us their tales of suffering. Within an hour, we had established mutual trust and friendship. The women and children were no longer hidden under the canopy. They came to the front of the boat and joined us in the discussion. After many worry-filled days, this was the first night that they had felt at ease.

We continued our discussion until midnight before we went to sleep. However, we did not all sleep simultaneously. We took turns. At all times, there were two men awake to assist the boatmen.

We came to know that for several generations this family had owned a business in Sirajganj Town. The two sons of the family were student activists. They were participants in the March non-cooperation movement against the Pakistani government.

After the fall of Sirajganj Town, Pakistani forces went on a killing spree, burning everything in sight. The shops and houses of Sirajganj were looted by pro-Pakistani elements under the protection of Pakistani forces. The family's business was left in ashes.

Rumors had circulated that the neighborhood in which they lived was next. With whatever meager possession they could carry, the family immediately left their home. However, as they tried to escape, the Pakistani Army killed their younger son. Sadly, they were not able to recover his body.

Many of their neighbors and relatives failed to escape in time. Pakistani forces targeted and killed the able bodied men and raped the young women left in the neighborhood. Though the family lost one of their sons, they felt fortunate that their wives and daughters had escaped such horrific fates.

After escaping, the family hid in a rural area for few days. However, even in remote locations, hiding from Pakistani forces was difficult. Razakars aided the Pakistani military in these areas to smoke out any and all refugees. It is with great dismay and agony, that they were forced to flee their motherland and become refugees in India.

Though they knew exactly what they had left behind, they were anxious to know what lay ahead. They were apprehensive about their journey to India. Questions flooded their minds. Once they got to India, where would they stay? Would this be a one-way journey? Would they ever return to their motherland? After all, Bangladesh was their home.

As they came to know that I had visited Mankachar earlier, they eagerly bombarded me with questions. Were there any facilities for refugees? Was there a refugee reception center? Were there camps or housing facilities for the refugees? I did not want to disappoint them. So I answered their questions diplomatically.

I asked the young man if he was interested in joining the Mukti Bahini. I told him that I knew the commander of the training camp and that if he wanted, I could recommend him. The young man was non-committal and told me that his first responsibility was to take care of his family.

After the loss of one son, his parents were reluctant to let him take such a risk. We understood their situation. This was a heartbreaking story, but it was typical of the experiences of millions of families across Bangladesh.

We reached Mankachar the next evening without any problems. We thanked the refugee family again and wished them all the best.

Major Binder Singh, the Commander of Mankachar BSF received us at his camp. He was pleased to see me again. He transmitted the news of our arrival to Major General Gill and Brigadier Sanat Singh of the Indian Army.

Meeting with Major General Gill

The next morning, Basit and I left for Tura with an Indian Army escort. Nuru stayed back at Mankachar. We arrived at Brigadier Sant Singh's camp near Tura. I had been here once before. I exchanged greetings with many officers whom I had met during my previous visit. Brigadier Singh was happy to see me again. He immediately took us in his jeep and drove us to an Indian Army camp near the border where Major General Gill was waiting for us.

This was a frontal outpost for Brigadier Singh's Brigade. It was situated on a small hilltop behind a mountain on the border of Meghalaya and Mymensingh.

The brigadier told us that his men had established this camp recently. The camp was situated opposite to Kamalpur, a fortified Pakistani Army outpost on the border. Its purpose was to support the Mukti Bahini during attacks on the Pakistani Army at Kamalpur.

While driving up to the top of the hill, we saw Indian soldiers training in an open field at the base of the hill.

Major General Gill sat in his camp situated on the top of a hill overlooking the valley. From there he kept an eye on his soldiers in training. He was happy to see me again and greeted us warmly. After an exchange of pleasantries, we got to business. I handed over a letter from our commander, Kader Siddiqui. He opened the letter and smiled. I realized my mistake. The letter was written in Bengali and obviously, a Sikh officer was not expected to read Bengali. I apologized. He handed me the letter and I began to translate the letter into English:

Dear Major General Gill,

I am sending my representatives Nuran Nabi and Basit Siddiqui, a member of parliament, to you. At this hour, whatever they say should be treated as my word. You have asked me to come to India once, but at this moment it is not possible. I feel that Allah has imposed on me the responsibility to protect the three million people in the areas we have liberated. I fight this war not to save myself, but to save others. We can defeat the occupation forces with your cooperation. The situation here is fairly good. On behalf of my countrymen and myself, please accept these greetings.

Sincerely,
Kader Siddiqui 23.7.71

Major General Gill had a profound love and respect for Kader. He said, "Initially I didn't believe it was possible to confront a very well-equipped army with just a few old and ordinary weapons. Moreover, to do this in Tangail, only thirty miles from Dhaka, was even more incredible. I couldn't believe that these offensives could be made without a supply line, without experienced and trained soldiers. But, as I know from the intercepted Pakistani Army radio messages, the enemy is facing a tough fight from the Tangail Mukti Bahini. And now, after meeting with you, I am further convinced of the Mukti

Bahini's resolve. I salute Kader Siddiqui for the heroism that he has displayed."

This was our opportunity to ask our Indian friends for some much needed help. We explained to Major General Gill and Brigadier Singh that unless pressure was mounted from across the border, the occupation forces would intensify their assault on us. External assistance would be our best hope.

A series of attacks on Tangail-Mymensingh Road could potentially threaten the enemy's supply line and reduce their movement. This, in turn, would alleviate some of the pressure on the Mukti Bahini.

We continued our plea for help and explained that we urgently needed long-distance wireless sets to improve communication within the Mukti Bahini camps, as well as with the Indian forces.

Major General Gill and Brigadier Singh gave a patient hearing. The general promised us all the help he could give. He instructed Brigadier Singh to give us as much arms and ammunitions as we could carry into Bangladesh. He also reminded us of the importance of the personal safety of Kader Siddiqui.

By the end of our meeting, night began to approach and the skies had opened to rain. As we were leaving the tent, an army officer wrapped in a raincoat, slowly entered. As he made his way inside the tent, he removed his rain soaked army cap and saluted the general. Even amidst the dim surroundings of the tent, the officer never removed his black-tinted goggles. He wore a reserved look on his face.

Brigadier Singh introduced him to us. He was a Bangladesh Army Officer, Major Zia. We greeted him with enthusiasm. However, he remained reserved and did not reciprocate our warm greetings. We said good-bye to all and left the camp. An Indian soldier escorted us to a tent opposite to the general's and told us that we were to spend the night there.

Attack on Kamalpur Outpost by Z-Force

There were three beds in the tent. Basit and I were quite tired after the long journey we had over the past few days. We laid down to rest.

At about a quarter-to-nine in the evening, Major Zia came to our tent. Packet meals, as used by the Indian Army, were delivered to us. We ate our dinner. Major Zia told us he would rest in our tent until midnight. At 01:00 hours the major was to rendezvous with the soldiers of his brigade, Z-Force, now stationed at the Bangladesh border. To avoid falling asleep, he refused to lie down.

That morning, Z-Force was poised to attack Kamalpur, a strong outpost of the Pakistan Army on the Jamalpur border. Major Zia insisted that we get our rest; however, despite our exhaustion, the major's presence kept us awake.

I recalled Major Zia's historic radio announcement on March 27th. The major's announcement of independence in the name of Bangabandhu Sheikh Mujibur Rahman was a very timely one. It inspired millions of Bengalis like me at a very critical moment in time. My praises seemed to intrigue the major. He wanted to know when, where, and how I had heard his announcement. He wanted to know if his voice was audible. I recounted the moment for him in further detail.

Basit added that the announcement from the clandestine Free Bangla Radio claiming that Bangabandhu was safe and leading the war in person was a risky one. The Pakistani government could have killed Bangabandhu and denied that he was ever in their custody.

Major Zia asserted that unless the name of Bangabandhu was mentioned, the Bengali nation would not have joined the armed struggle against Pakistan. He added, "The announcement of independence with my name alone would not have had any effect."

Basit and I agreed to the major's reasoning. In order to prove that the announcement on Free Bangla Radio was false, the Pakistani authorities boasted that Bangabandhu had been arrested, and were forced to publish a photograph of Bangabandhu under their custody. This showed the Bengali nation, as well as the world, that Bangabandhu was still alive.

Major Zia was eager to learn more about Kader, Basit, and me. He advised us on strategies in leading the Tangail Mukti Bahini. He was pleased to learn that Basit, a member of the provincial assembly, was leading the freedom fighters of his own constituency. He praised Basit for his courageous role.

During our conversation, Major Zia said that his wife and two young sons were still imprisoned in Dhaka Cantonment. He was very worried about them. He admitted that it was a mistake to allow them to go to Dhaka. It would have been wiser had he brought them to India from Chittagong. We could only express our sympathies.

The two of us enjoyed our conversations with the major and soon lost track of time. However, Major Zia kept a vigilant eye on his watch. Suddenly, the major looked up and said, "It's time for me to go."

The clock had struck a half past twelve. The major left the tent and set off for the border.

We wished him and the Z-Force much success and bid him farewell. It was time for us to get some sleep before we too were to set off on our own journey in the morning.

However, before dawn had broken, Basit and I awoke to the sound of gun blasts and mortar shells ricocheting through the air.

Immediately, we realized that the Z-Force was engaged in a fierce battle with the Pakistani Army.

The liberation war started on March 26, 1971. Since then, the members of the East Bengal Regiment, the EPR, the police, and the Mukti Bahini had independently engaged in a war against Pakistani forces. They each waged battles in different places and at different times, without any central coordination.

However, the success of any war is dependent upon the combatant's ability to engage in both conventional battles, as well as guerilla operations. So by the end of July, the Bangladesh government raised three brigades of freedom fighters. Each brigade was comprised of the members from the army, the EPR, the police, and the Mukti Bahini. The recruits in the newly formed brigades underwent rigorous training in conventional battles. Time was of the essence.

Major Shafiullah, Major Khaled, and Major Zia led the brigades respectively. The first initial of the commanding officer's name identified each brigade. Therefore, the brigade under Major Zia was known as Z-Force. Major Shafiullah led S-Force. Major Khaled led K-Force.

The members of the Z-Force underwent two months of rigorous training at Teldela camp near Tura. The blasts that Basit and I awoke to marked Z-Force's first offensive encounter with the enemy.

Kamalpur was a strategically located fortified defense outpost for the Pakistani forces. It was a gateway to Jamalpur, the brigade headquarters for the Pakistani Army. It was constructed as an impenetrable outpost and guarded by two companies of soldiers from the 31st Baluch Regiment of the Pakistani Army. It had concrete bunkers with interlocking tunnels connecting one bunker to another. Mines in every direction secured the outpost's perimeter.

Our meeting with Major Zia was significant with unforeseen historic consequences. It was the first meeting between Zia, the commander of a Bangladesh Army brigade, and us, representatives of the Mukti Bahini, who were fighting the Pakistani Army deep inside the country.

The meeting foreshadowed the days ahead. Major Zia repeatedly reminded us of the importance of Kader's personal safety. However, he added that if the Mukti Bahini's circumstances permitted, Kader should attempt a visit India to see him.

It takes a hero to genuinely convey his sincere respect to another hero. Major Zia's words on that day were a testimony to this effect.

In December 1971, after the liberation of Dhaka, our paths crossed once more. We were both at Dhaka Cantonment. By then Major Zia had been promoted to colonel. My hair had grown long and my beard thick. Regardless, he had no difficulty in recognizing me. The relationship and bond built through the struggles of liberation would not be broken that easily.

Captain Salahuddin Becomes a Martyr

In the early hours of August 1st, Delta Company of Captain Salahuddin Momtaz and Bravo Company of Captain Hafiz positioned themselves northeast of the Kamalpur outpost. The Indian artillery troops were ready to offer their support. The Mukti Bahini launched the attack exactly at three-thirty in the morning. However, Pakistani forces answered with heavy mortar shells, which inflicted a few casualties on the Mukti Bahini.

The initial casualties slowed the advancement of the Mukti Bahini. However, Captain Salahuddin, a valiant freedom fighter, led his team from the front. The freedom fighters were inspired by his leadership and followed him.

They gradually encroached on the enemy bunkers. After the offensive was mounted, the Pakistani forces retreated and took shelter inside the concrete bunkers of the outpost. From this vantage point they regrouped and let loose a barrage of machinegun fire on the advancing freedom fighters.

The fierceness of the battle gradually intensified. The freedom fighters continued their advancement under the leadership of Captain Salahuddin. His men cautioned him to slow down, but Captain Salahuddin, determined as he was, continued the aggressive attack.

Captain Salahuddin responded defiantly to his soldiers' warnings, "The enemy has not yet made a bullet that can kill me."

Just as these words were uttered from his mouth, two mortar shells landed in front of Captain Salahuddin. Before he took his last breath, Captain Salahuddin said, "If you have to die, die after killing the enemy. Die on the soil of Bangladesh!"

The captain had become a martyr.

Salahuddin's team had gotten too close to the concrete bunkers of the Pakistani camp. Three of his men tried to rescue his dead body, but they too followed the path of the martyr. Captain Salahuddin's body was never retrieved. All that was recovered of this war hero was his Sten gun, his watch, and some documents.

The battle had taken a new turn. Mukti Bahini casualties were on the rise.

On the other hand, Bravo Company leader, Captain Hafiz escaped death just marginally. A Pakistani mortar shell damaged his Sten gun and he was severely injured. Rabiul, one of his soldiers, rescued him. In doing so, Rabiul was mortally wounded.

After reviewing the causalities, Major Moinul Hossain Chowdhury, the battalion commanding officer ordered the withdrawal of his forces.

In addition to the casualties, the Z-Force lost several weapons, which included: heavy machineguns, LMGs, Sten guns, rifles, and rocket launchers.

As morning broke, the Indian officers in Brigadier Singh's camp briefed us on the details of the battle. There were thirty-five freedom fighter casualties and many more wounded. The bodies of the martyrs and wounded soldiers were brought to a nearby community center. Brigadier Singh ordered his medical team to rush to the spot. The news of this loss was devastating.

However, Pakistani forces also suffered serious casualties. Moreover, their morale was shaken. They were left stunned by the ferocity with which the freedom fighters attacked.

This battle was a glorious event in the history of the liberation war. Moreover, for many of these soldiers, this was their first experience on the front lines. This confidence helped them in winning many subsequent battles.

Captain Salahuddin's courage and heroism is an example of the patriotism of the East Bengal Regiment and the rest of our armed forces.

Before the war broke, Captain Salahuddin was posted in Quetta, West Pakistan. Fully aware of the risks involved, he escaped and crossed the Pakistan border into India. Soon after, he joined the liberation war in July. Prior to the battle of August 1st, he led numerous daring missions, including several secret reconnaissance missions that preceded the battle itself.

Though the attack on Kamalpur was not a victorious one, the occupation forces became intimidated by the strong offensive of the freedom fighters. For the first time, the enemy at Kamalpur outpost experienced the deadly fighting prowess of these freedom fighters. They learned first hand that the Mukti Bahini was determined to win the freedom of Bangladesh.

From that night on, the Pakistan Army remained confined within its bunkers. Even the slightest rustle of leaves in the night was answered with a ceaseless and fruitless onslaught of gunfire. The Pakistani soldiers were scared.

The August 1st battle of Kamalpur remains a testament to the heroism of the soldiers of Bangladesh. Martyred Captain Salahuddin Momtaz lives on in our memories as a legendary war hero.

After the independence, schools and landmarks were named after Captain Salahuddin Momtaz in Dhaka Containment, as well as in his native town, Feni to commemorate the bravery of this martyred native son.

Fall of Kamalpur

The battle of Kamalpur marked a significant chapter in the history of Bangladesh's liberation war.

The border outpost at Kamalpur was a gateway to Dhaka. If the Mukti Bahini could take this outpost, their attack on Bakshiganj-Sherpur-Jamalpur to the south would pick up momentum. This made Kamalpur an attractive target for the Mukti Bahini.

The first attack in August was a probe to test the strength of the enemy. Though we suffered heavy losses, the attack struck fear in the hearts of our enemies.

For the next two months, the Mukti Bahini regrouped. In October, another attack was launched. However, both sides suffered heavy losses once again.

On November 14th, another heavy offensive was launched. The attack took place in front of the Kamalpur outpost. However, the specific mission objectives were to navigate past the outpost and occupy the Bakshiganj-Jamalpur Highway. The primary goal of the mission was to cut off the outpost from the 31st Baluch Regiment stationed in Jamalpur.

The Mukti Bahini was largely successful in this mission, but yet again, we suffered heavy losses.

Major Taher, commander of Sector 11, was seriously injured. A Pakistani mortar shell blew away the upper part of his left knee.

The strategy behind the November 14th attack was not merely to capture this outpost. Our goal was to demoralize the enemy. We wanted to turn the outpost from a Pakistani military vantage point into a death trap.

Since Kamalpur was of such strategic importance, the enemy predictably mobilized reinforcements to defend the outpost.

Soon after the November 14th attack, a group of Pakistani soldiers moved from Bakshiganj into Kamalpur with 120 mm mortars to strengthen their defense of the outpost.

However, the Mukti Bahini was ready. The Mukti Bahini ambushed the Pakistani soldiers en route. The trap resulted in ten Pakistani soldiers killed, seven injured and one machinegun seized. Most notably, these Pakistani casualties included an officer.

The enemy was nearing defeat. They had been completely isolated. Captain Ahsan Malik, the desperate Pakistani commander of the outpost, requested immediate reinforcements from Jamalpur Battalion headquarters.

On November 23rd, Captain Malik sent out a team of Razakars to Bakshiganj on patrol. But his men never returned. They were captured by freedom fighters.

Soon after, another team of Pakistani soldiers was sent to find the Razakars. They too vanished into thin air, never to be seen again.

As anxiety crept through the captain's mind, Captain Malik radioed the battalion headquarters for help. Col. Sultan, Commander of the 31st Baluch Battalion responded to Captain Malik's request and sent a group of soldiers on a rescue mission in search of the missing men.

The Pakistani rescue team traveled with an extra vehicle in case the missing men had fallen to injury. Once again, the Mukti Bahini attacked. The Pakistani soldiers lost their vehicles, but this time they managed to escape with their lives and return to Bakshiganj.

Pakistani forces made three more attempts, each effort resulting in retreat. The Pakistani Army became desperate.

On November 27, three enemy teams were instructed to move north along the Bakshiganj-Kamalpur Road, while maintaining a safe distance between each other. Simultaneously, another team from Kamalpur moved south toward Bakshiganj. Their goal was to reconnect in the middle.

However, once again, the Mukti Bahini was ready. Like a tiger crouching amidst the grasses, the Mukti Bahini vigilantly watched its prey migrate down the roadside.

As soon as the first enemy team came within range, the Mukti Bahini opened fire. The enemy team was completely wiped out. The enemy's attempt to reinforce the outpost was foiled yet again.

That same night, the Mukti Bahini attacked the Kamalpur outpost. However, this time the enemy resisted the offensive from its fortified-concrete bunkers. The Mukti Bahini and Indian forces lost twenty soldiers in total, including one officer.

Despite continuing attacks, the Pakistani forces continued to reestablish contact with their isolated outpost.

On November 29th, Major Ayub led a team of Pakistani soldiers and Razakars to Kamalpur. The Razakars carried arms, ammunition, and food supplies balanced on their heads. Cleverly, this time they did not travel through the highway.

Rather, the enemy took an unconventional route through the villages. Major Ayub himself somehow managed to reach Kamalpur. However, when he arrived he noticed that his soldiers and the Razakars had not.

Once again, facing an attack by the Mukti Bahini, the rest of Major Ayub's entourage was forced to retreat to Bakshiganj. Fleeing for their lives, they eagerly threw down their arms, ammunitions, and food supplies. The major was lucky to return to Bakshiganj the next day.

Soon after on December 4th, Major Ayub attempted another trip to Kamalpur. However, this time fortune was not in his favor.

The Mukti Bahini surrounded the enemy outpost. It was quite a difficult and depressing situation for the enemy. The Pakistani forces had no scope for medical treatment. There were no drugs. There was no doctor.

The enemy soldiers rationed one chapatti per day. Their stock of arms and ammunition was nearly exhausted. In the face of repeated attacks by the Mukti Bahini, the enemy had grown extremely scared. At night the mere croak of a frog or the howling of a fox sent shivers through the enemy camp, ending in a nervous fusillade of gunfire into the air.

Under these circumstances, the Mukti Bahini and Indian Army proposed a surrender to avoid further bloodshed. A freedom fighter was sent to deliver this message to the enemy.

However, the Pakistani commander, Captain Malik rejected the proposal with a profane and invective response.

Perhaps to protect Pakistan and its self-professed Islamic faith, Captain Malik thought it best to fight to the bitter end. Perhaps, he dreamt of going to heaven as a martyr. Perhaps, he just had a death wish for himself and his men. Regardless, he made it clear that surrendering was not an option.

By December 3rd, an all-out war had broken out between India and Pakistan at both the eastern and western fronts.

On December 5th, the Mukti Bahini and the Indian Army launched a ferocious attack on Kamalpur. Reeling from the intensity of this attack, Captain Malik and his men were forced to surrender.

At last, the mighty Pakistani outpost of Kamalpur had fallen!

It was here at Kamalpur that a glorious chapter of Mukti Bahini heroism was written. It was here that the arrogance and false-pride of Pakistan was crushed to dust.

Major Siddiq Salik, a Pakistani Army officer, has narrated the Pakistani Army's defeat at Kamalpur in his book titled, Witness to Surrender.

The Wicked Monsoon

On August 2nd, Basit and I left Tura for Mankachar with two truckloads of arms and explosives. Major Bindar Singh of the BSF would provide additional supplies just as he did earlier. Basit and I rode in two different trucks.

The driver of my truck was a young Sikh. He was tall and slim, with a turban on his head. He looked like a teenager of fourteen or fifteen. A thin grey hair subtly peaked above his upper lip forming what was yet to be his moustache.

He drove the truck through the curvy hills, quite rapt within his own thoughts. It was a huge truck. Sitting beside the driver, I stared out the window. Unfortunately, we were moving so fast that the beautiful landscape appeared as if it was coming through an out-of-focus lens.

His driving made me nervous. I was uncertain as to whether the driver even possessed a valid license. However, this was not a question I could ask, nor was this the appropriate time. He maneuvered the vehicle through this rough terrain with such confidence that I had to trust his skill.

However, Basit's truck could not keep up. His truck was so far behind that it had vanished in the horizon behind us.

The Sikh driver continuously sang a chorus from a Hindi song. He sang, "Very wicked, this Monsoon is".

I said to the driver, "you must love this song?"

He emphatically replied, "Yes! I do. It is a love song from a Hindi film."

I said, "Does it remind you of a girl back home?"

The driver blushed. Then he quickly changed the subject.

He told me that he was from Ludhiana in Punjab. His family had a road transport business. His father, his three elder brothers, and he drove trucks to various parts of India. They were in fact contractors to the armed forces.

I asked him if he liked his job.

He replied, "Very much so. I drive trucks from one border of India to the other. My job takes me to exciting new places. I move from town to town, meeting new and interesting people. It's great. However, I miss my mother very much. She lives in Ludhiana all alone."

Reminding him that he never answered my previous question, I asked him if he missed his girlfriend.

He replied, "I have wanted to write to her for a long time, but if her father were to find out about me, he would be furious. As much as it pains us, we've kept no communication while I've been on the road. I miss her terribly".

He then added, "It's not just the memory of those I miss that makes me love this song. In my line of work, there has always been one constant enemy – the monsoon. That's why I love this song so much. It's as if this song was written just for me."

As the driver and I conversed, I was reminded of my own life back home. It had been three months since I was last home. I've had no contact with my family whatsoever.

I wondered how they all were: my father, my brother, my uncles, and my aunts. I missed them all.

My father must be worried about me. He was probably wondering what I was doing and whether or not I was eating. He was probably praying nightly for my safety. And yet, he didn't even know that I was in India.

I pondered how I had affected him. Had my decision to join the Mukti Bahini jeopardized my family's safety? This question in particular replayed in my mind.

Fortunately, our home was within the liberated zone. It was unlikely that the Pakistani forces or Razakars would dare move into the region. Regardless, I was concerned.

I was reminded of my mother. Her thought brought tears to my eyes. I could barely hold it in. I knew she was watching me from above, praying for me from heaven.

As my eyes swelled with tears, the driver looked to me and asked, "Have you been reminded of someone?"

This time, I was the one who changed the subject.

"Let's break for tea," I suggested.

Two Hundred Mile Tea

We crossed a few more miles and stopped at a tea stand. It was a thatched-shed on the side of a hilly road. We could see water boiling in a country oven. There were benches to sit on. However, they were covered with scat and did not seem very strong.

We looked around. The surrounding area was desolate. There were no dwellings. Even in the distance, there was no village in sight. All we saw was this lone-shed, stooped on the side of the road. It was obvious that this stall was meant to serve people like us.

As we pulled up to the shed, we saw that we were the only customers. An old gentleman from one of the indigenous tribes was the shopkeeper. He greeted us and asked, "What kind of tea would you like?"

I asked for a regular cup of tea, while the truck driver asked for a cup of "Two Hundred Mile Tea."

Curiously, I inquired, "What is that?"

The driver said, "Truck drivers who drive long distances, usually asked for extra strength tea for every hundred miles they have left to drive. I have to drive another two hundred miles, so I have asked for two hundred mile tea". Unperturbed, the shopkeeper handed us our tea.

The driver's anecdote reminded me of one of my own experiences. It was in Dhaka during the mass uprising of 1969 and the non-cooperation movement of 1971. Back then we would go out late at night to write our political slogans across the walls of various buildings.

In order to keep our activities going, we would need insomnia-inducing fuel to keep us awake.

Just opposite the Secretariat Building on Topkhana Road there was a row of several restaurants that we would frequent. These restaurants were open late and played old, mostly Hindi movie songs over loud speakers.

While silence crept through most parts of the sleeping city, rickshaw pullers, scooter drivers, and student activists like ourselves were drawn to the melody that resonated through the air.

As we entered the restaurant, a waiter would ask, "How much patti tea do you want?"

If we were trying to stay awake for the whole night, the waiter would cry out our order, "Table one - four cups of tea, tin patti (triple strength)!"

Mystic Mankachar

On the afternoon of August 2nd, our trucks arrived at Border Security Force (BSF) camp in Mankachar. Major Bindar Singh received us.

Basit left the camp to stay with Shamsur Rahman Khan, a leader of the Awami League and a Member of Parliament. At the time, Mr. Khan was staying in Mankachar. My accommodations were at a BSF guesthouse where I spent that night.

Major Singh briefed me on the arrangements that he had made for my departure to Bangladesh the next day.

I had been to Mankachar twice before. However, thus far, I had only seen Mankachar at a glance. What I had seen intrigued me. This time I would have to make the most of my opportunity.

On the morning of August 3rd, while eating breakfast, I told Major Singh, "I'll be leaving Mankachar for Tangail this evening. Before I go, I'd like to see Mankachar Bazaar".

Major Singh provided me with a guide who accompanied me to Mankachar Bazaar.

Mankachar was an old river port situated on the borders of Bangladesh and the Assam province of India. It was situated on a narrow offshoot of the Jamuna River.

Mankachar had been an important port of commerce between Northern Bangladesh and Assam for over a hundred years.

However, in the last few months it had become much more. Millions of refugees from Bangladesh came over to Mankachar through this port. One could see thousands of boats scattered for nearly a square mile around the port of Mankachar.

Without pause, refugees arrived, while goods were loaded and unloaded like clockwork. Hundreds of refugee camps sprouted throughout the area.

It was almost noon, when my guide and I reached Mankachar Bazaar. There were swarms of people in every direction. The storefronts, while small and crowded, efficiently utilized every inch of the market. It was an amazing feat to imagine that while these shops, crammed in every alley and crevices fostered millions of dollars in the trade of such commodities and services as jute, rice, and money laundering. With so many refugees, the market looked less like a bazaar and more like a village fair. Before the war, Mankachar was known to attract smugglers. However, the war had allowed this business to thrive. Mankachar had become a smugglers paradise.

The roads and shops were covered with a thick dust. Most of the people gathered at the bazaar were refugees. Their faces were marked with fear, uncertainty and tension.

Although they were now beyond the reach of the Pakistani Army, the refugees had left their lives and all that they knew behind. They had lost their loved ones and experienced the atrocities of the enemy first hand. Their lives were forever changed.

Mankachar was not prepared for the massive overflow of refugees. There were no organized refugee reception centers. These people stepped off the boats and arrived in a foreign land, unaware of what lay next for them. The local administration was simply overwhelmed.

In spite of such uncertainties and confusion, the refugees could find consolation in knowing that they had escaped the enemy's deadly grasp.

Major Taher and Major Manzur

After I came back from the bazaar, I took a bath at the guesthouse. After seven arduous days, the bath was quite refreshing. The guesthouse sat high along the roadside, overlooking the river. As I sat on the veranda soaking in the view of the harbor, I pondered the situation on the frontlines.

By evening I would be off for Tangail. However, doubt and uncertainty plagued my mind. What perils would lie ahead? Would we make a safe return?

At that moment, Major Singh stopped by. A gentleman dressed in civilian clothes accompanied him. Major Singh introduced the man as Major Taher of the Bangladesh Army, Commander of Sector 11.

After Major Taher and I had a brief exchange of greetings, he told me that he had come from his camp in Dhalu to see me. He was recently appointed Commander of Sector 11. The major knew of our successful guerilla operations under the leadership of Kader Siddiqui. As soon as he had heard that I was at the camp, he made it a point to come and see me.

I briefed Major Taher on our encounters with Pakistani forces in Tangail. When I told him that we would be leaving that evening for Tangail through the Jamuna River via Bahadurabad Ferry Station, he offered some important advice. He warned that I be especially alert while crossing Bahadurabad Ferry Station. A few days ago, a platoon of Sector 11 freedom fighters attacked the Pakistani Army camp at Bahadurabad Ferry Station. The platoon was able to inflict substantial damage and the Pakistani camp suffered many causalities. After such a skirmish, the enemy was likely to be extra vigilant around Bahadurabad Ferry Station.

As we continued speaking, our conversation grew more informal. Major Taher inquired of my life before the war. I obliged and told him about my student life in the department of Biochemistry at Dhaka University.

He immediately asked, "Do you know Anwar? He is my younger brother."

Anwar and I were classmates, but more importantly, we were both student activists in the liberation movement. However, after March 25th, I had lost all contact with him.

Before the war, Anwar had mentioned that his older brother was a major in the Pakistani Army, stationed in West Pakistan.

Now that Major Taher had mentioned Anwar's name, I could see the family resemblance. Given their dark complexions and thick mustaches, I really should have recognized him.

I asked Major Taher, "I had heard that you were in West Pakistan. How did you end up making it here and joining the liberation war?"

Major Taher's story unfolded like the plot of an action movie.

On March 25th, Major Taher was stationed at Baluch Regimental Center in Abbottabad, West Pakistan. He was an officer of the elite commando unit of the Pakistani Army. He received special training in the United States.

Initially, he was unaware of the situation in East Pakistan (Bangladesh). However, his suspicion was aroused by certain activities in his camp. Entire commando units from the camp were sent to Bangladesh. However, Major Taher was not selected, nor was he briefed on the unprecedented move. Major Taher was sure that something was wrong in Bangladesh.

A few days later, at the officer's canteen a West Pakistani officer cursed Bangabandhu Sheikh Mujibur Rahman as a traitor. Major Taher vehemently protested and asked the West Pakistani officer to withdraw his comment and apologize. The officer refused. Major Taher became enraged. He pulled the officer's collar and shouted, "You must apologize. Apologize for cursing the leader of the Pakistani Parliament. You should not forget that Bangabandhu is the supreme leader of Bangladesh."

Major Taher was arrested and jailed for this altercation with the West Pakistani officer. However, this courageous patriot was determined to liberate his motherland from the clutches of Pakistan. He decided to flee from West Pakistan to join the liberation war.

However, escaping from a Pakistani military jail was no easy task. Major Taher would soon find that he had a very risky adventure ahead of him. It was a matter of life and death. He was already under the watchful eyes of several West Pakistani soldiers. Guards followed his every step. However, his determination and love for his motherland kept him going. He told himself, "I am a commando officer. I must use my training. My country needs me. I cannot stay here at this critical juncture in history."

He made three attempts to escape. Unfortunately, each one ended in failure. Pakistani intelligence remained vigilant in tracking his every move. Nonetheless, he could not give up.

He had learned of other Bengali officers who also tried to escape from West Pakistan to join the liberation war. However, they had no direct contact with each other. With so much at risk, it was impossible to trust one another.

Under these circumstances, Major Taher came in contact with Major Ziauddin, a Bengali officer, stationed at Rawalpindi Cantonment. They found that they shared a similar goal. A few days later, Major Taher came to know that two other officers, Major Manzur of Sialkot

Cantonment and Captain Patwari of Jhilam Cantonment were also trying to escape West Pakistan.

Major Taher and Major Ziauddin finalized their plan. They used the last of their money to buy an old Volkswagen, their only means for escape.

It was nearly the end of July. Around noon, Major Taher, Major Ziauddin and Captain Patwari arrived at the residence of Major Manzur in Sialkot Cantonment.

Major Manzur realized why his comrades were at his door. He knew they had to escape that night.

This was a very critical decision for him. Unlike the other officers, Major Manzur lived in the cantonment with his family. He had his wife Rana, a three-year old daughter, and a four-month-old son. If he were to leave his family behind, they were sure to be arrested and tortured. He had no choice, but to flee with his entire family. This was the most important decision of his life. If their mission failed, his family would be in deep waters. If they stayed, their fate would be worse.

The decision Major Manzur's wife had to make was also serious. After all, the lives of her children rested in her hands. However, this patriotic mother had made her decision. She was ready to take the risk and decided that she and her children would accompany her husband.

After dark, they all crammed themselves into the old Volkswagen. There were a total of eight passengers in the car. It was jam-packed. Major Manzur's Bengali orderly also accompanied them.

Mrs. Manzur wore a long veil, which was typical of West Pakistani women, to avoid suspicion. Major Taher and Major Ziauddin wore scout uniforms and carried golf clubs.

In spite of their efforts, they were still afraid of being found by the guards. Additionally, their car made them apprehensive. A car this old was likely to break down at any moment.

Fortunately, the eight travelers were very lucky. They left the cantonment without a hitch and fled the town heading towards Jafarwall.

Nature was also in their favor. It was raining, so only a few people were out on the streets.

They safely arrived at a village near the India-Pakistan border. They abandoned their Volkswagen and walked towards the border into the darkness.

Mrs. Manzur had given her four-month-old son and three years old daughter sleeping pills. It was quite a risk that she was willing to take. Any doctor would have hesitated to prescribe such a dangerous narcotic, but Mrs. Manzur, the courageous and patriotic mother, did so without a second thought. She did what was necessary to ensure that her husband, Major Manzur could escape and join the war. The safety of her children was overshadowed by the call for the liberation of her motherland.

Few mothers could make this same patriotic decision.

It was the darkest of nights. The group bypassed a Pakistani border outpost and walked silently and cautiously toward the international border.

Though the border was an open area, the international borderline zigzagged. Major Taher and the group had to walk through muddy and slippery irrigation canals.

It was difficult for Mrs. Manzur to follow the officers. These were trained and experienced soldiers and commandoes that she was trailing. This was her first experience in such dire circumstances.

They had no compass and no star in the night sky to guide them. After an hour of treacherous walking, they found themselves back near the Pakistani outpost, which they had passed earlier. There is a saying in Bengali, "night falls where there is the fear of tiger."

Pakistani forces were alerted by the sound of their steps. A powerful torchlight was aimed in their direction. The group quickly fell to the ground and escaped detection by the enemy.

However, when Major Manzur dropped to the ground, he fell on something solid. In the darkness he couldn't make out what it was. Luckily, he felt around and recognized he was lying on top of the milepost for the international border. They quickly started for the Indian Territory.

At about two o'clock in the morning, the group arrived near an Indian border outpost named Debighar. However, at the risk of being mistaken as the enemy, they did not contact the Indian forces in the middle of the night. They had no intention of getting shot. As the night sky continued to drizzle, they searched for shelter away from the Indian outpost. Finally, they found a dry canal where they spent the night.

At dawn, Major Taher and Major Ziauddin reported to the Indian border outpost and introduced themselves. The news of their arrival was transmitted to the intelligence branch of the Indian Army and Bangladesh Army.

The Indian forces gave the officers a royal reception at the outpost. Indian villagers from the neighboring area had come to see the heroes who had risked everything for the liberation of their country.

Major Taher and his team were sent to the eastern border of India to join the Bangladesh liberation war.

It was an amazing story. I listened to Major Taher with fascination.

I told Major Taher, "The Pakistani military junta chose the wrong enemy. With heroic soldiers like you and patriotic mothers like Mrs. Manzur at our side, victory is sure to be ours."

Major Taher smiled.

I further inquired about Anwar. Major Taher told me that Anwar and all of his brothers had been fighting in sector eleven under his command.

Very soon I would be moving out of Mankachar towards Bangladesh. Regrettably, I had no time to see Anwar. I asked Major Taher to convey my greetings to his brother.

The major and I talked some more, before he wished me a safe trip across the border.

The two highlights of my second visit to India were my meetings with Major Zia and Major Taher. These two freedom fighters played very significant roles in changing the political climate in post-liberated Bangladesh.

Major Zia later became Major General Zia, before eventually becoming president of Bangladesh. While serving in office he was tragically assassinated in a military coup d'état in 1981. This was an ironic twist of fate, as Major Manzur who by then was a major general, was the one who had orchestrated the takeover.

Immediately after the death of President Zia, Major General Manzur was killed in a counter coup.

Major Taher went on to become a Colonel. In another ironic twist, after a failed coup attempt, a kangaroo military court found Colonel Taher guilty, while Zia was still president. Colonel Taher was tragically hung in 1976.

Meetings with members of the Parliament

Most of the members of Parliament took shelter in India. Those who did not were quickly arrested and some were even killed.

Those parliament members in India formed the Provisional Government for an Independent Bangladesh. They were assigned to stay close to their respective borders from where they encouraged the freedom fighters' efforts.

At Mankachar, Basit and I met with Latif Siddiqui who was a member of the provincial parliament and the elder brother of Kader Siddiqui.

When Latif had heard that his younger brother, Kader was leading many of his own followers in the war against Pakistan, he was eager to return to Tangail.

For Latif to return to the liberated areas of Tangail was a major decision. We told him that we couldn't advise without first checking with Kader.

Moreover, Kader had emphasized to us that Latif's presence in India would reinforce the Mukti Bahini mission.

We conveyed this to Latif and reminded him that the letter Kader had sent to him only reiterated this truth.

By this time, several of Latif's followers moved into leadership positions in the Tangail Mukti Bahini.

At the Mukti Bahini camp in Tura, Basit and I met two more members of parliament. Principal Humayun Khaled was a member of the national assembly and Fazlur Rahman Khan Faruk was a member of the provincial assembly. In order to promote unity and nationalism, they offered political training to the freedom fighters at Camp Tura.

They suggested that Basit stay in India. However, Basit was quick to turn that notion down. In a firm tone, Basit said, "My place is not in India. My place is at Kader Siddiqui's side in Tangail."

We met freedom fighters from various regions of Bangladesh at Camp Tura. They included Habibullah Khan of Netrokona, Ratan of

Kishoregonj, Mahbub of Rangpur, Munshi of Bogra, Abul Kalam Azad of Jamalpur, and Ajoy of Mymensingh.

We described the barbaric atrocities perpetrated by the Pakistani occupation forces in different areas of Bangladesh.

However, as they learned of our success in liberating a huge area of Tangail, they burst into joy. They had seen the carnage of the enemy first hand, but they had yet to exact retribution.

When they learned that one of the world's most organized militaries was losing ground to the Tangail Mukti Bahini, these men were invigorated. Our success had encouraged them and strengthened their resolve to liberate their motherland.

The freedom fighters of Camp Tura earnestly requested we convey their regards to Kader.

From then on, news bulletins of the liberation efforts in Tangail were disseminated through Camp Tura. These bulletins were prepared from intercepted messages from the Pakistani Army and reports directly from the Tangail Mukti Bahini.

Crossing the Border with Arms Yet Again

In the evening, we left Mankachar and began our journey home.

Seven large boats had been loaded with arms and ammunition and were ready for departure. Major Singh had made all the necessary arrangements.

That evening Basit and Nurul joined me at the harbor. We waited for darkness, before we set sail. Major Singh bade us goodbye.

A team of freedom fighters accompanied us for our defense. They were divided into seven groups and were posted accordingly in each boat. This time we were carrying large quantities of arms and ammunition, which included a number of long distance wireless sets, several thousand arms, large quantities of explosives, and several thousand grenades.

Thus far, I was pleased with the success of my mission. However, I was still very nervous. I knew the rest of our journey would be filled with danger. Reaching our destination safely with our arms and ammunition was my number one priority. Before we left the harbor, Basit said his prayers.

Evenly spaced, our boats set off in a linear formation. It was midnight when we came near the Jamuna River. We took a break for some light snacks. Unfortunately, a light snack was all we had to fill our stomachs. Nonetheless, it was welcomed sustenance.

As we ate, nervousness wafted through the boats with the river breeze.

We asked ourselves, "How would we cross Bahadurabad junction in the dark hours of the night?"

Unfortunately, crossing Bahadurabad junction during the day was no option either. Regardless of night or day, we knew that the vigilant eyes of the Pakistani Army were watching. We could not sit idle.

We only had a short window to make our move. We knew that our journey home would be riddled with peril and uncertainty. We had no choice, but to rise to the challenge. After all, we were freedom fighters. We were the Mukti Bahini.

In the thick of darkness, we were ready to make our way across Bahadurabad junction.

As we proceeded, it felt almost as if nature had extended her hand of friendship. The tide moved in our favor and the wind grew stronger from the north with clouds hovering above us. With the current and the wind behind us, we "flew" down the river. We were still fifteen miles from Bahadurabad junction, but we traveled swiftly and safely.

About four miles from Bahadurabad junction the wind finally let up and our boats consequently slowed.

I had to ensure that under no circumstance would we lose our cover and risk our mission. We gave clear-cut instructions to the freedom fighters that for no reason whatsoever should we reveal our identity. We had to ensure a safe passage at all cost.

The men understood that even if one of our boats were to fall under enemy attack, the remaining boats were not to engage the enemy. It was clear that even if two of our boats got lost, the others were to proceed to safety.

Our boats neared Bahadurabad junction. We moved quickly along the western bank. It was almost dawn. The first and second boats crossed the Bahadurabad junction quite safely. Each boat maintained a good distance from one another, but kept within sight.

As the third boat traveled about one mile west of Bahadurabad junction, it came under enemy fire.

Hundreds of bullets rained around the boat. The boatmen got scared, stopped hauling the boat and fell to the deck for cover.

Simultaneously, the fourth boat got within the firing range of the enemy. The freedom fighters sought my permission for a counter attack. I refused and reminded them of our strategy. I asked them to hold fire.

Basit recited his morning prayers on the canopy of the fourth boat. Bullets hit the mast of his boat and broke it in two. Basit jumped down and miraculously escaped unharmed.

The firing continued for fifteen minutes. Since there was no counter firing from the other boats, the enemy was convinced we were amongst the many merchant boats, which typically traveled up and down the river. The enemy stopped firing.

No significant damage was done to our boats. As we crossed Bahadurabad junction, we found that our excitement would be short lived. When we came near Changalier Char near Jagannathgonj junction, we encountered our next threat. Pakistani Army patrol boats were moving towards Shariakandi in Bogra. We found an alternative route on the west bank. We diverted into a secondary channel behind a sand island. As the patrol boats sailed out of our sight, we proceeded towards our destination, Bhuapur Mukti Bahini camp.

We docked at Camp Bhuapur at about noon. The freedom fighters and commanders were thrilled to see us with several boats loaded with arms and ammunition.

In addition to me, the others commanding the boats were Nurul, Lutfur, Basit, Badsha and Zia.

Basit Siddiqui

There were several important participants who led to the success of my missions to India. One of them was Basit Siddiqui.

In 1970, Basit was elected to the provincial assembly as an Awami League candidate. Prior to the election, Basit worked as a government servant. After retirement from government services, he became the headmaster of Dhalapara High School.

While both men shared the surname, Siddiqui, Kader and Basit shared no blood relation. However, fate would ensure that their paths would cross nonetheless.

When the liberation war began on March 26th, Basit did not flee to India like many parliament members. Instead, he went underground and soon joined the freedom fighters led by Kader Siddiqui.

I first met Basit at his old house in the second week of July. I had just come from India with the first consignment of arms. A middle-aged and bearded man, Basit seemed to be a very gentle and modest person.

The next day, Basit and I accompanied Kader on a short tour to Aschim. This is when I discovered his human qualities and energy.

Though he was a member of the parliament, Basit spent his days with us like an ordinary freedom fighter. On our way back from Aschim, he proposed that we speed up our journey. Although, he was over fifty years old, Basit had as much spirit and energy as any freedom fighter, half his age.

It was on Kader's instruction that Basit accompanied me on my second mission to India. Basit, Nurul, and I were on a small boat.

During this journey, I discovered some extraordinary qualities in Basit. I already knew that Basit was a former teacher, a member of parliament, and as old as my father. I, on the other hand, was only twenty-two years old, and still only a university student. And yet, Kader made me the leader of this mission. I wasn't sure how Basit would take this.

This was not to mention that Basit was very large in stature, almost reminiscent of my father. I had not seen my father in months. As I saw Basit, I was repeatedly reminded of my father. I never conveyed this to Basit, as I didn't want to give him reason to start acting like my guardian.

On the first day, the mood on the boat was monotonous and serious at the same time. The boatmen rowed continuously. We did our best to pass the time by taking turns sitting on top of the canopy and lying underneath it.

Basit brought about a change to this pattern. He challenged us to a competition in poetry recitation.

Nurul Islam was a trade union leader and likely had no prior interest in poetry.

Although I enjoyed listening to poetry recitations, I was a student of science and had never cultivated interest in reciting poetry myself. At best, I could probably recite no more than few lines of some arbitrary poem from my high school days.

However, Basit surprised us, reciting one poem after another. He was not limited to the works of popular Bengali poets, such as Rabindranath Tagore and Kazi Nazrul Islam, either. Basit eloquently recited even the most complex soliloquies of Shakespeare. What an extraordinary memory he had! Basit was truly a cultured person.

From that day on, the age gap between Basit and I was gone. Throughout the liberation war, we remained friends. Our shared goals bridged the differences in age, education, wealth, and social hierarchy. We became comrades.

In our nine-month long liberation war, I saw many comradeships hatched in the same way.

The Team of Unarmed Fearless Freedom Fighters

Another significant contribution to the success of my missions came, not at the hands of armed soldiers, but rather through my paddle-carrying boatmen. These men helped us bringing arms from India.

I did not know their names. However, I went to India three times. That is six trips by boat. Each time my boatmen and their assistants risked their lives for the mission just as any freedom fighter would have.

These men were masters of the river routes. Every bend in the river, every turn, was an extension of their paddle. The boatmen skillfully evaded the enemy while keeping us safe.

The boatmen were wiry in appearance. They would often go without food for long periods of time, but they never stopped rowing. They were men of great stamina and resolve.

Their goal was to take us safely and swiftly to our destination. These men were not motivated by their wages. Nor did our guns persuade them. These boatmen carried out their duties fueled by their unwavering sense of patriotism.

The boatmen labored endlessly. Their commitment went unrivalled. They faced the perils of great risk and adversity. And yet, nothing deterred them from taking us to our destinations. I cannot express the gratitude I have for them in words.

While traveling by boat we ate once a day. The other soldiers and I often ate a meal of crisp-puffed rice with a small piece of molasses. However, the boatmen needed something more convenient to eat while they rowed. The boatmen ate their rice in glasses filled with water, salt, and green chilies. We called this panta rice.

Although it wasn't a glamorous fare, the rice and water brew was quite a tasty meal amidst the warmth of the bright sun of the summer.

To this day when I think of panta rice, I instantly return to those moments on the Jamuna River. I return to moments sitting on top of the canopy of the boat as we sped down the waterway, swerving by other boats as we passed whole villages in just seconds. I can still feel the wind blowing through my hair and the river mist splashing against my skin.

People of all walks of life took part in the liberation war. This was a people's war. There were restless young men like us. There were middle-aged individuals like Basit. There were political leaders and workers like Nurul. And of course, there were working people like the boatmen, the fearless soldiers of the armed forces, women, and patriotic Bengali expatriates all over the world. We were all freedom fighters of 1971.

The Valiant Volunteer Group

The Mukti Bahini had an outpost at Bhuapur in the free zone just west of the Tangail-Modhupur Highway. The Pakistani Army was trying incessantly to recapture Bhuapur. It became apparent that storing our arms and ammunition at Bhuapur was no longer safe.

Kader instructed us to carry the new supplies from Bhuapur to the forests of Ghatail-Kalihati, where our headquarters was located. However, we could not carry the entire stockpile by ourselves.

The Mukti Bahini camp at Deopara had fallen to the Pakistani Army. As a result, we were forced to take a detour, which added an extra fifteen miles to our journey. Moreover, there was no direct river-route between our headquarters and Bhuapur.

From Bhuapur we would have to go by boat for about four miles and then lug the arms and ammunitions through the jungles of Ghatail. This required the labor of hundreds of volunteers.

Enayet Karim and Moazzem Hossain were the civilian administrators for the Mukti Bahini in Bhuapur. They had alerted the volunteer groups.

On the evening of August 7th, about six hundred volunteers assembled at Bhuapur. We left Bhuapur for our headquarters by boat in the darkest hours of the night. Basit, Moazzem and Nurul also accompanied the team.

By midnight we arrived at Pakutia Porabari, west of the Tangail-Modhupur Highway. The local intelligence department and volunteers received us.

The volunteers unloaded the arms and started carrying them by shoulder. They carried the heavy containers on strong sticks like palanquins.

Commander Benu and his platoons escorted us. The members of the local Intelligence group briefed us on the security of our route.

Our plan was to cross the highway at a walkway alongside a madrasa. However, Pakistani forces were stationed at Ghatail Police Station only a mile south of the madrasa. They were only a few minutes away by jeep.

We had to take extraordinary precaution to keep the enemy from smelling the presence of more than six hundred freedom fighters and volunteers. Although the moon was hazy in the dimly lit night sky, we took off any white clothing. Even the softest reflection was more than we were willing to risk. We could not allow anything to alert the enemy.

We divided ourselves into three groups and moved forward silently. Basit was leading the first group. Moazzem and Nurul led the group in the middle and Commander Benu and I led the group at the rear.

Before we started, the two platoons set up lines of defense to the north and south of the highway crossing.

I observed the operation from the madrasa. Six hundred people moved along the village roads and paddy fields in a number of small groups. One by one they crossed the highway with caution and in a disciplined order. And yet with all this activity, the silence was still deafening.

I was reminded of the Vietnam War. On one end of the battlefield there was one of the world's most powerful armies equipped with the most modern weapons and communication systems imaginable. On the other end, there was the undersized and ill-equipped Vietcong. Yet it was the Vietcong who organized themselves into a united and indomitable army. They, like us, were a people's army.

The Mukti Bahini was motivated by a patriotic zeal and devotion to preserving the freedom of their people. This is why they risked their lives and fought the Pakistani forces.

Politics aside, it became obvious that the Vietcong and the Mukti Bahini shared a common thread.

The number of Tangail Mukti Bahini volunteers soon rose to about fifty thousand. They lived in their own homes, in their own villages or towns. But when the Mukti Bahini needed them, they were there. Each village's volunteers worked in groups organized by a designated volunteer leader.

The liberation war had a wonderful effect on village societies. People from all walks of life came together as equals working for a common cause.

We entered the forest two miles to the east of the highway. The entire forest was under our control.

In the early hours of August 8th, we arrived at Chankhola Bazaar with the load of arms. The volunteer groups of Bhuapur broke for food and rest.

They then divided into small groups and proceeded back towards Bhuapur.

The volunteer groups of Chankhola made arrangements for their breakfast. The local volunteers helped us to carry the arms and ammunition to Basit's house in Sehrabari.

Kader welcomed us. I briefed him on my meetings with Major General Gill and Brigadier Singh of the Indian Army, and with Major Zia and Major Taher of the Bangladesh Army. I shared with Kader my experiences of the second Indian mission. Basit kept busy by hiding the arms and explosives in different locations throughout the free zone. In the evening, Kader, Basit, Nurul, and I went to the headquarters.

I can hardly give credit to each volunteer who contributed to the success of the Mukti Bahini, but of the names that come to mind are: Siraj Talukder, a student leader; Rahim Mia, a school teacher; Sadek Mia, a retired policeman; Khoka, a day laborer; Karim Ali, a farmer; Abdus Sattar, a professor of Kumudini College; and Shamsul Alam, a high-ranking government official.

A Great Success

On August 9th, seven Pakistani Army ships were anchored at Sirajkandi on the Dhaleswari River. They were about six miles west of the Mukti Bahini headquarters at Bhuapur.

Commander Habib, the commander of Bhuapur Mukti Bahini Camp, prepared for an all-out resistance against the likely enemy attack. However, Mukti Bahini Intelligence, with the assistance of the volunteers, reported that two Pakistani ships loaded with arms were moving towards Phulchori in Rangpur.

The intelligence report stated that additional ships were moving along for added protection. These ships were carrying soldiers as well. The arms were to be unloaded at Phulchori and then delivered to the Pakistani cantonment at Syeedpur in Rangpur.

Equipped with this valuable information, Kader instructed Commander Habib to explore an opportunity to attack the ships.

The next day, a strong contingent of Mukti Bahini soldiers moved from Sirajkandi to Matikata under the leadership of Commander Rezaul Karim. This was the same platoon that was trained in India and accompanied me on my mission when I transported the arms from India. However, this would be their first time actively engaging in battle.

On August 11th, the ships slowly sailed north. Commander Habib consulted with the Intelligence Division and planned a series of ambushes at different points on the riverbank.

Commander Habib himself moved north and took position between two rural dwellings. The platoon sat on the east side of the river where the water was deepest and easiest for boats to navigate. Slowly, the ships began moving within range of the freedom fighters. The freedom fighters held their fire waiting for direction from their leaders, but Commander Habib and Rezaul Karim patiently waited for their prey.

Two small ships passed the awaiting freedom fighters. However, Habib didn't open fire. Another ship sailed by and still Habib's guns did not discharge.

The freedom fighters had been waiting in utter excitement. Their hearts pounded. Sweat dripped from their brows, their fingers itching at the trigger, but the freedom fighters waited. They would not fire without Commander Habib's order.

Finally, two large ships loaded with arms came into sight. Commander Habib pulled the trigger on his machinegun and Manzur fired his rocket launcher. Then like a chain reaction, the rest of the Mukti Bahini joined in on the offensive.

The attack was so sudden and intense. The first three ships that had just sailed by lacked the courage to turn around for a counter-attack. They fled and continued heading west. The other two defensive ships that followed did the same.

Under the intense strike of the Mukti Bahini, the cabins of the ship's officers and the position of Pakistani forces were completely destroyed.

Pakistani Captain Amanullah Khan managed to flee. However, Assistant Lieutenant Ataullah and Subedar Rahim Khan, along with another fifteen enemy soldiers were killed. The enemy soldiers who survived left the dead bodies of their comrades and fled away in two speedboats.

Three freedom fighters became martyrs on this day. Seven others were injured.

There was a Bengali sailor onboard the Pakistani ship by the name of Gulam Mustafa. He was an informer for the Mukti Bahini.

Nearly a month prior to the attack, Gulam had established contact with Kader. It was he, who informed us of the Pakistani ships' movement.

Though the battle lasted for less than an hour, its consequences proved to be much more significant. The two wrecked ships were stuck on the western bank.

Habib rescued Gulam who had jumped into the river. Once, safe and dry, Gulam briefed Habib on the kind of ammunition and artillery onboard the two ships.

Commander Habib decided that we would unload all the cargo, but take only those items that could be utilized by the Mukti Bahini. Within an hour the volunteers were alerted and the unloading began.

Nearly five hundred members of the Mukti Bahini and volunteers unloaded and carried the arms by hand and by boat to nearby villages. The arms needed to be hidden. However, even with the help of so many able bodies, we only salvaged forty percent of the military stockpile.

Major Habib anticipated an all-out counter attack by the Pakistani Army to rescue the ships. He decided his safest course of attack would be to set the ships ablaze.

Volunteers Zia, Jamshed, and Gulam started on setting the ships on fire. Suddenly, a fierce chain of blasts resonated down the river as the arms and ammunitions began to explode. The scene was reminiscent of a fireworks show. All of Bhuapur cheered with joys of victory.

It was a great triumph for the Mukti Bahini.

In the nine-months of the liberation war, the destruction of ships at Matikata was a seminal event. News of this event was broadcasted throughout the world on the BBC, the Voice of America, Indian Radio, Free Bangla Radio and other foreign media outlets.

There were more than one hundred and twenty thousand boxes containing arms and ammunition of Chinese, British, and American origin. The value of this stockpile was more than five million dollars. The majority of this was destroyed in the fire, but of more concern to the Pakistani Army was the fact that much of the ammunition was in our possession.

In the early morning hours of August 12th, Kader was informed of the event at Sehrabari. Kader and some of his comrades, myself included, proceeded to Bhuapur. We walked quite a distance and then traveled by boat for another fifty miles before we reached the village of Panchtikri.

Even from our vantage point, blasts were heard at a distance of seven or eight miles. While resting that afternoon at Faldarbazar, a mortar shell exploded just three or four hundred yards away from us.

Kader began reviewing the situation on the basis of the report furnished by the local commanders. The commanders reported that a brigade of the Pakistani Army had started moving towards Bhuapur via Elenga and Palima, from Tangail.

The companies of Khorshed Alam and Humayun had put up a tough resistance. However, the Pakistani Army continued to mount massive-pressure on the Mukti Bahini. Their aim was to rescue their ship.

In the morning of August 15th, we understood that the enemy was proceeding to Bhuapur from every direction. From the north, one unti was moving from Gopalpur via Hemnagar. From the east, another unit was moving from Kalihati by motor-launch. From the south, another group proceeded from Tangail, straight to Bhuapur. The enemy had us surrounded.

Humayun and his company were holding off enemy forces that attacked via river routes. Unfortunately, the push of the Pakistani commando brigade from the south had created severe pressure and forced the Mukti Bahini to retreat.

This regiment was equipped with heavy arms. They could reach Bhuapur by road within a very short time. Something had to be done.

Kader selected a special squad and marched south. They destroyed a bridge on the Bhuapur-Tangail Highway. This halted enemy movement by road. Unfortunately Kader sustained some minor injuries during this operation.

By noon, two saber jets flew over Matikata unleashing a violent machinegun and rocket attack. This air raid resulted in significant civilian-property damage, including the destruction of several village dwellings and the loss of cattle. One freedom fighter was also injured.

As the air raid ended, five Pakistani motorboats, anchored behind the ship wreckage, attempted to land at Matikata. Just then the Commander Habib and Gafur and their companies came out of the trenches and attacked the Pakistani soldiers, forcing the enemy to retreat.

Enemy pressure intensified through the day. The freedom fighters and the volunteers had been engaged in a continuous battle for a number of days.

By now the men were tired, hungry and weak. Kader assessed the situation and ordered the units to leave the outpost at Bhuapur and seek refuge amidst the forests of the free Eastern Zone.

Throughout the afternoon, we prepared to leave Bhuapur. The information was passed to each Mukti Bahini unit. We had to protect our positions till dark, at which point we would proceed to our headquarters. Arrangements were made to remove the arms and ammunitions stored at Bhuapur Girls' School.

Those who played very important roles in this battle were Motahar Hossain, Zia-Ul-Huq, Jamshed, Akbar, Samad, Gama, Samsur, Lutfur Rahman, Lutfor, Saidur, the policeman, Salam, Alim, Bhola, Abdul Bari, Dudu Mia, Enayet Karim, Moazzem Hossain, Rezaul Karim, and above all, a valiant freedom fighter—Commander Habib.

It was just two days prior to the battle that all of Bhuapur danced in joy. But now, the situation was tense. Since the Mukti Bahini had retreated, the villagers became apprehensive of an attack by the Pakistan Army. People began leaving Bhuapur. There were still about forty freedom fighters including Kader and I at Bhuapur.

At about nine in the evening, a report came to us that all units had left Bhuapur. With great dismay and anguish, we too proceeded towards the headquarters.

Commander Habib who destroyed Pakistani cargo ships

Commander Habibur Rahman Bir Bikram

Prior to the war, Habib was a member of the Pakistan Army stationed at Jessore Cadet College. Soon after the start of the war, he left the army and came to Tangail to join the Mukti Bahini.

Within a short period of time, he was promoted to the rank of a commander. This daring freedom fighter became a legend after proving his valor by heroically capturing an enemy ship loaded with arms.

After the war, Habib would receive the second highest gallantry award for living-war heroes, "Bir Bikram."

Habib played an important role in our success in the liberation war. However, despite his military success, his personal life was riddled with misfortune.

Unfortunately, an independent Bangladesh did not provide him with a good job or a viable business opportunity.

The press had reported that his finances were in such dire straits that he had trouble marrying off his daughter.

Finally, in the winter years of his life, Habib fell ill. With no money, or other means for medical treatment, Habib was left to die alone.

In a desperate move, he rode his bicycle to the office of the district commissioner to seek help from the government.

Unfortunately, on his way to the office he had a massive heart attack and his lifeless body fell to the roadside.

To this day, Habib's family suffers from economic hardships. Soon after his death, a social organization in Tangail donated a bicycle to the son of Habibur Rahman "Bir Bikram".

How futile? How shameful?

The Traitor

By four o'clock in the morning, we arrived near the village of Garjana. We were east of the Tangail-Modhupur highway.

The sunlight peeked just over the horizon and the enemy was already on patrol. Without cover of darkness, it was unsafe to cross the road.

Kader decided that we should take a day for rest and continue after sunset.

We dispersed in different groups through various houses in the village. The owner of the house in which Kader and I took shelter was a member of the local council.

Our host expressed how fortunate and honored he felt to be able to render services to the Mukti Bahini. He immediately served us some crisp puffed rice and molasses. Our host then ordered his men to prepare some hot meals.

The men slaughtered three goats to prepare a feast for us. We were tired and hungry. The anticipation of our first sumptuous meal in months made our mouths water. We were excited!

However, the cooking process moved slowly. While we waited, we received reports that Commanders Benu and Khorshed and their companies could not cross the highway the previous night. They had taken shelter on the other side of Garjana. Kader asked the commanders to join him for consultation.

Garjana and its surrounding areas were inundated by water during the rainy season. Each house looked like an island. You needed a boat to go from one house to another, let alone, from one village to the other.

It was already eleven in the morning, but still there was no sign that our meals were ready.

Kader became suspicious. We noticed that the women and children of the house were leaving with small bundles. This further heightened our suspicion.

As our local intelligence and volunteers learned of our whereabouts, they informed us that our host was a staunch supporter of Pakistan.

From the start of the war, Pakistani authorities had put a price of one hundred thousand takas on Kader Siddiqui's head.

It would seem that our host was quite greedy and was quick to report to the Pakistani camp in Ghatail that Kader Siddiqui was at his home.

By noon, Kader looked through his binoculars and saw ten Pakistani Army boats moving towards Garjana from the direction of Brahmanshashon.

Immediately, Kader ordered a counter-attack. He instructed Commanders Khorshed and Benu to return to their respective units.

Quickly, Kader left the house and moved to the next one. He was accompanied by twenty freedom fighters. They set up an ambush behind a raised earthen base covered in heaps of straw.

The other freedom fighters and I strategically took position in another house. We were to provide cover-fire to protect Kader's position.

The enemy boats divided into two groups and proceeded toward the position of the Mukti Bahini on the other side of Garjana.

As the enemy approached the Mukti Bahini's position, a fierce battle erupted before Commanders Khorshed and Benu could return to their respective units.

The gun blasts resonated across the water. The village was caught off guard. The quaking grenade explosions terrified the villagers. As machinegun shells and smoke scattered through the air, frantic women and children made their escape to neighboring villages.

The enemy was also taken back by the ferocity of our counterstrike.

At one point, the enemy got off the boat and took a defensive position at a house adjacent to the freedom fighters.

Benu's company was under attack. However, his unit was fighting back.

The firing went on ceaselessly. The tide of the battle turned steadily in favor of the Mukti Bahini.

Suddenly, Commander Khorshed noticed two Pakistani soldiers crawling to the east of their house. Commander Khorshed jumped out from behind his cover and opened fire on the two soldiers.

Just at that moment two enemy bullets pierced through Khorshed's hand and the right side of his belly. A nearby freedom fighter, Jahangir, was able to drag Khorshed to safety.

In the face of a fierce counter-attack by the Mukti Bahini, the enemy soldiers retreated to their boats and headed towards Ghatail.

During this hour-long battle, Kader never had the opportunity to ambush the enemy. They never even made it into his firing range. However, Kader's luck began to change.

Enemy boats then headed towards his position. He immediately alerted his squad for action.

As the enemy boats came within range, Kader pulled the trigger of his LMG. Causing a chain reaction, nineteen other machineguns roared simultaneously behind Kader's.

The battle lasted for only five minutes. As the smoke cleared, five enemy boats sank into the water.

Our unit's role was to cover Kader and his squad, but with such a brief battle, we had no opportunity to open fire.

The remaining five boats retreated to Ghatail behind cover-fire.

We recovered seven dead enemy bodies. The number of enemy soldiers who drowned was unknown.

In the meantime, Kader instructed all of his units to assemble at a village to the west of Golganda and Ratanpur.

While Commanders Khorshed and Benu's companies fought a fierce battle with the enemy, six freedom fighters were lost in action.

Their names were Aslat, Sriti, Moti, Anis, Kamal and Mintu. Although they fought gallantly, they ran out of ammunition and jumped into the water to save their lives. They were listed as missing.

Khondoker Nurul Islam was a middle-aged man and the general secretary of Kalihati Thana Awami League. He volunteered to lead a rescue mission to find the missing freedom fighters.

Khondoker took a small boat and combed through the paddy fields. Finally, he found the men hidden amongst the tall stalks of the paddy.

In the mid-afternoon, we went to Ratanpur to check on Commander Khorshed. We found that he had not yet received any medical treatment. The volunteers' communication network had broken down and, therefore, the medics could not be contacted.

I was a student of biochemistry, and thus, had seen my share of rat dissections. However, I never imagined what it would be like to see the open wounds of a comrade.

Commander Khorshed was groaning in pain. Kader assured him that we would do everything possible to provide him medical treatment and security. Kader entrusted Bulbul Khan and me with this responsibility.

Meanwhile, Kader decided that we would cross the highway that night and instructed us all to be ready.

We were all waiting in a village on the west of Porabari Pakutia. We were tired and hungry. Since we had left the headquarters, we had not had a regular meal.

Kader's personal squad had a reputation of enduring hardships. However, we were all exhausted from the non-stop fighting. Having gone the last forty-eight hours with hardly any food, we grew weak. We had to survive on water alone.

Our host's treachery not only jeopardized the lives of five hundred Mukti Bahini, but his false promise of a feast was evermore agonizing for us now.

Moreover, the threat of further enemy attack was still very real. Only now, we lacked the strength to fight back.

We counted the minutes waiting for sunset, but the wait seemed eternal.

On the other hand, since August 15th, the enemy was on a round-the-clock patrol of Tangail-Modhupur Highway. They were particularly vigilant near the madrasa.

In order to mislead the enemy, we leaked a message indicating that as before, we would cross the highway near the madrasa at night.

However, Kader sent a secret message to all units asking us to reconvene at Pakutia Porabari, a few miles north of the madrasa.

Our intelligence department informed us that the enemy was pacing back and forth every fifteen minutes, from north to south along the highway near the madrasa. This would give us a window of exactly fifteen minutes to cross the highway.

In the evening, we divided ourselves into small groups and waited in the jungle about three hundred yards west of the highway. We prepared to cross the highway at ten o'clock.

As enemy patrol cars went away, two platoons from Benu's company set up barricades at the north and south sides of the crossing.

At first, three large groups crossed the highway cautiously and quickly.

I was in the second group with the wounded Commander Khorshed. He was lying-flat on a makeshift stretcher improvised from a level piece of wood supported by two bamboo poles. He was carried by four freedom fighters.

While crossing the paddy field, the freedom fighters raised Commander Khorshed's body up so that the paddy stalks did not exacerbate his injuries.

We, too, crossed the road very carefully. However, because of the wounded Commander Khorshed, we couldn't move as swiftly as the unit in front of us.

After crossing the highway, I took position in a paddy field near the highway in order to guide the units that followed me.

Kader stayed on the adjacent side of the crossing where he directed the units across the highway.

After all the freedom fighters had safely crossed the highway, Kader made his way across as well. He then shouted my name to find my location and joined me.

After we successfully crossed the highway, the two defense units who had barricaded the road, crossed and joined us.

At midnight, we reached a village four miles east of Porabari. Once again, we took shelter in the house of a local council member. Unlike our previous host, this council member was on our side. He cordially welcomed us into his home.

Kader instructed our convoy to spread ourselves among ten houses. Though this was a free zone, a strong contingent of Mukti Bahini guards was posted for our defense.

Despite the hospitality of our host and his village, we were still unable to arrange medical treatment for Commander Khorshed. We were only able to provide some fresh bandages and hot milk.

Despite our late arrival, our host graciously prepared a quick meal. After three long and arduous days, this was our first hot meal. We ate to our heart's content.

Our meal consisted of steamed rice with split-pea soup. I never knew that the simple combination of rice and soup could be so delicious and satisfying.

Kader reminded Bulbul and me of our responsibility. Attending to Commander Khorshed's medical treatment was our first priority.

In the early hours of August 15th, after three long days and nights, we finally had the opportunity to lie down. With so many of us in one house, we were sprawled across the veranda and the courtyard of the house. Kader and I were among the lucky few who got a bed inside.

I reflected on the extraordinary help and cooperation that the volunteers had given us. I thought of the great courage and sacrifice displayed by the freedom fighters. I also remembered the treachery of the Bengali traitor whose actions jeopardized the lives of five hundred freedom fighters. As I absorbed the events of the last few days, my weary body gave into sleep.

The Treatment of Khorshed Alam

August 15th, 5:30 AM.

I woke up to the painful groans of Commander Khorshed. He had already gone twenty hours without medical treatment. Unfortunately, we were still without any medical supplies. My words were all I had to offer him in consolation.

Kader ordered us to move out of the village at six-thirty in the morning. With only an hour to spare, we hurried but were punctual with our departure.

We were fortunate to get a few hours of sleep and some food. Our host's hospitality was refreshing, but fatigue continued to take its toll.

There were about four hundred of us. We divided ourselves into groups and started moving towards our headquarters.

Our journey led us through the hilly areas. All of our outposts to the west had fallen. Therefore, we were open to an attack from the rear.

Kader ordered us to keep marching. At a slow pace, we moved forward towards the east.

Bulbul, Nurul, and I led a team of one hundred freedom fighters. The wounded Commander Khorshed was also with us, groaning in pain.

Four freedom fighters carried Khorshed in his improvised stretcher. We held his hand, taking turns trying to comfort the wounded commander. However, his cries of pain indicated that our efforts were futile.

Khorshed, a middle-aged man, was the leader of Ghatail Thana Awami League before the war broke out. Only a few civilians became commanders of the Mukti Bahini. Khorshed was one of the rare few.

Since I frequented the eastern zone on my way to India, I became closely acquainted with the commander. I was given the responsibility of getting medical care and treatment to my wounded comrade. Unfortunately, there was nothing I could do.

I felt utterly helpless and frustrated. However, some things were simply beyond my control. Against the backdrop of pain-riddled screams, all I could do was mumble a prayer and ask for Allah's blessings.

At about ten o'clock in the morning, we reached Chaankhola Bazaar. A group of volunteers welcomed us. Kader instructed them to go ahead to Pecharati Bazaar, arrange food for four a hundred freedom fighters and facilitate medical treatment for Khorshed.

Sometime during the last few days, our communication system had been cut. We were on the edge of desperation, but the presence of these new volunteers was encouraging.

After half an hour, as we neared Pecharati Bazaar, a leader of the local volunteers came running with medicine in-hand.

He said, "We have no doctor here. The best I could do was to collect these basic medical supplies from the general store." He added that several houses, just a half a mile ahead, had arranged lunch for us.

We immediately stopped to take care of Commander Khorshed.

Kader washed the wound with Dettol, an antiseptic, and re-bandaged the commander. He then administered a penicillin injection and some painkillers. Bulbul, Nurul, Khoka, Dulal, and I helped Kader in this process.

We resumed our journey. After half a mile, we arrived at Pecharati Bazaar and stopped for lunch.

Our team was first to be fed, since the commander's life was still in our hands. We had to get Commander Khorshed to the Mukti Bahini hospital as quickly as possible.

After a quick bite, our group continued walking, carrying the commander as before.

As we were about to leave, Commander Khorshed suddenly broke into tears as he said his goodbyes to his commander, Kader.

Kader embraced Khorshed and said: "Nabi and Bulbul will take you to the hospital. Don't worry. Soon, you'll be as good as new."

Kader handed me the rest of the medical supplies and reminded us of our duty to Commander Khorshed's medical treatment.

We directly proceeded to the Mukti Bahini hospital, and dropped off Commander Khorshed. We then made our way to the Mukti Bahini headquarters.

Kader Wounded

At noon of August 15th, Kader arrived at Basit's house in Sehrabari. Only four days ago, he left for Bhuapur from this very house.

However, in those four days, the state of the war had taken a dangerous turn. The enemy lost several ships loaded with arms. They lost a fierce battle at Garjana. And now they were extremely desperate.

Two Pakistani brigades began mounting simultaneous offensives, from all sides.

The enemy was attacking every defensive outpost of the Mukti Bahini. They attacked the eastern sectors at Baid, Fulbaria, and

Bhaluka. In the north, they attacked Rangamati. In the south, they attacked Patharghata. In the southwest they attacked Baharatul. In the far west they attacked Dhalapara. Fierce battles continued in these areas for several days.

Two days earlier, we were forced to abandon Bhuapur and the liberated zones of the west. Now, the enemy took the battle to the east.

Kader reassessed the state of the war and contemplated leading his troops to where the enemy's attack would be most intense.

However, he did not have to contemplate for long. While he was at Sehrabari, Kader got the enemy's attention. He was up for the challenge.

Kader penned his experience in his book <u>Shadhinata 71</u>:

> Dhalapara was two miles west of Sehrabari. As the sounds of firing reached my ears, the earth began to tremble.
>
> I was contemplating asking someone to fetch me an updated report. Just at that moment I was informed of the enemy attack on the Mukti Bahini defense outpost at Dhalapara.
>
> I quickly outlined my plan. There were about two thousand freedom fighters at the defense outpost at Dhalapara. This was the largest number of freedom fighters to have ever participated in any single battle.
>
> Commanders Habib, Gafur, and Humayun joined the forces at Dhalapara on the afternoon of August 14. Earlier I had instructed Commander Lokman to hand-over the command of Dhalapara outpost to Commander Habib.
>
> I strongly believed that it was impossible for the enemy to cross over the Bangshai River. There was no way that they could pierce through a defense-line of two thousand freedom fighters.
>
> Moreover, I thought an attack on the enemy position fortified with heavy artillery would be futile. However, if the enemy were prevented from crossing the Bangshai River, they would not dare stay overnight

on the riverbank. They would have no choice. They would have to retreat before sunset.

Furthermore, if we were to setup an ambush on the other side of the river while the enemy retreated, we could really teach them a lesson.

With this plan, I left Sehrabari with Commander Benu and moved west. We crossed the Bangshai River, north of the enemy's position. We then moved further west behind the enemy position and then moved southwest near a road that the enemy was likely to utilize in retreat.

I then instructed Commander Benu to take his team two miles farther west to ambush the enemy on the road to Ghatail. As Benu left, I scouted the area and then found a tactical location on the south of Ghatail-Dhalapara road. I set up my ambush here.

Twenty-five yards to my right, Quddus, Khoka, and Selim were guarding the road. On my left were Halim, Dulal, and Kashem. Samsu, Saidur, Fazlu, and I were in the middle.

I had instructed both groups to hold their fire unless we were attacked. We were about fifty yards from the road. We got into firing-position and waited for an opportune moment.

August 16th. 1:15 PM.

The first enemy group retreated west. They walked briskly, but stayed in file, keeping some distance from one another.

Earlier in the day, they faced stiff resistance from the companies of commanders Hakim, Habib, Gafur, Lokman, and Humayun at Dhalapara ferryboat dock. They abandoned their plan to cross the river. They were forced to retreat to Ghatail.

We were waiting for our enemies. Our ambush was ready. We were thoroughly prepared to attack.

There were about twenty Pakistani soldiers in the first group that walked by us. They seemed unconcerned.

Then several groups, one after another, followed walking westward. I observed their movements and waited for the right moment. Like a wet crow on a rainy day, I sat fixed and firm, waiting for enough of the worm to peek through the mud.

I did not wait long. The anticipated moment arrived. It was twenty past one. About fifty soldiers were running out of formation. It was as if they were running for their lives. They appeared desperate to retreat.

Without hesitation, I fired at them. The soldiers didn't see the attack coming. They were in an open field with no place to hide.

Saidur, Samsu, and I fired on the enemy soldiers, who all fell to the ground. A few enemy soldiers tried to take cover under the mounting piles of dead bodies and return fire. However, the situation was not in their favor. They were in no position to counter-attack. They had no choice, but to receive our bullets.

A few Pakistani soldiers tried to move in on us from the east, but Khoka, Quddus, and Selim opened fired on them. During the battle the chain on my Chinese LMG jammed, so I grabbed a British LMG from Saidur and went on firing.

Every moment was precious. But once again, the chain jammed. I took a Sten gun from Samsu.

The enemy still returned fire, but their blasts became less and less frequent. They were so confused and disoriented that they could not figure out which direction our shots were coming from.

I had started firing the Chinese LMG again. As I fired twenty-five or fifty rounds, the gun jammed, yet again. I fixed the jam and started firing again. After about ten or twelve rounds, it got stuck again.

Frustrated, I opened the gun and very carefully realigned the bullets.

Meanwhile, Saidur, and Samsu continued firing on the enemy. As I was lining up the last bullet, I felt my LMG tremble. I felt something in my palm. I felt a flash rush through my leg.

It all happened in seconds. I couldn't make sense of it. I looked up to fire the LMG again. Blood squirted from right hand and splashed against my face. I was blinded.

I used my left hand to wipe my eyes and face. I pressed down on my wound and fired my LMG again. After some more rounds, the chain got stuck again. The handle of the LMG was now all covered in blood. I never realized that my body could carry so much blood.

Samsu and Saidur repeatedly asked me to retreat.

I replied, "Yes, you two are right. Samsu, give me your gun and you bring the LMG."

I came down a twenty-foot slope. Samsu bent down to pick up the LMG, but the bi-pods of the LMG were embedded into the ground. After several heaves, Samsu pulled out the LMG and rolled down the slope with it.

Coincidentally, when I got hit, the enemy stopped firing and quickly retreated west. We pulled back about fifty yards to a safe place.

The battle only lasted ten minutes. The three of us were able to take out thirty Pakistani soldiers. Our comrades to the left and right of us, Khoka, Quddus, Selim, Dulal, Halim, Amzad, and Kasem also inflicted heavy casualties on the enemy.

The only loss that the Mukti Bahini suffered was my injury. An enemy bullet had broken the sight-knob of my LMG. When the knob had splintered, it shattered and hit my palm and at a spot one inch above my knee.

We moved south from Makrai to Baid where we found an empty shed. The blood was still oozing from my wound.

Dulal and Khoka tore their shirts and bandaged my hand tightly. However, blood was still flowing profusely from my foot. Slowly, I rolled up my trouser leg and found the wound above my knee. As I washed the wound carefully, I could see that the bullet was still lodged in my leg.

Using my left hand, I put my finger about an inch into the wound until I felt something solid. I removed my finger and repeatedly pressed hard on two sides of the wound until the bullet came out.

Selim Siddiqui, overwhelmed by the situation, looked at me and cried, "What will happen to us now?"

I asked him to be calm and said, "Look, nothing has happened to me, I am alright".

But my words did little to ease the tension. I looked around and saw that my other comrades were also very worried.

It was very painful to keep my trousers on. We bought a coarse lungi from a local villager with which I was able to substitute for my trousers.

Even in this situation, I had to send written instructions to Commanders Habib and Hakim who were stationed at Dhalapara post.

I wrote, "Cross the river and move ahead to Makrai. There, you will find the scattered dead bodies of our enemies and their weapons. I sustained a minor bullet-wound to my hand, so I was unable to write this letter myself. However, I am signing it with my left hand so the signature may look a bit different."

A freedom fighter delivered this letter to Dhalapara. I left Makrai and went to Chambaltala.

I realized that the wounds had taken their toll and my body had gotten weak. I felt as if I could collapse at any moment. It was imperative that I get to safer grounds as soon as possible.

I stopped at the house of a volunteer named Tula. With wounds to my hand and leg, I somehow walked nearly two miles.

By the time I had arrived to Tula's house, I had a very high temperature. I had lost so much blood that I began to feel dizzy. I was getting nauseous.

My comrades carried me to a large table in the outer courtyard of the house.

Lying on the table, I felt as if the room was spinning and I was sinking. My body was burning up.

I closed my eyes. Against the darkness of my eyelids, I saw the fireflies dance. I became senseless.

Hatem the Martyr

The enemies who survived the battle at Dhalapara most likely used wireless communication to report their precarious condition and the events of the battle to their headquarters at Ghatail.

As a result, a regiment of Pakistani Army soldiers started moving in to rescue them. A group of freedom fighters under the leadership of Commander Benu had been waiting on the roadside with spying eyes. Hatem, Aslat, and Junior Fazlu had Chinese rifles with them, while the others had Sten guns.

The enemy soldiers came quite close to commander Benu. Benu pulled the trigger on his Sten gun, but there was no fire. Helpless, Benu cried out, "Fire! Fire!"

Before the freedom fighters could react, the enemy started firing their automatic weapons.

Seven freedom fighters including Hatem were too close to the enemy to retreat. If only Benu's gun did not malfunction, the battle would have been in our favor.

Commander Benu instructed his team to retreat. However, Hatem and Fazlu could not hear his command, as they were detached from the main squad.

Hiding in a bush, Hatem fired ceaselessly at the enemy. He killed four Pakistani soldiers and wounded seven more. Just as he emptied the last round from his Chinese rifle, three enemy bullets hit him and he fell to the brush. The enemy scurried around looking for him. However, despite their efforts, they could not find him. His wounded body was still hidden behind the bush.

The rest of the Hatem's squad retreated to a safe place. However, they did not know that Hatem was wounded. Fazlu looked everywhere for his comrades. When he found Halim and Dulal, they retreated to a safe place. Unfortunately, they too were unaware that Hatem was wounded and left behind on the battlefield.

When the enemy retreated, the volunteers brought Hatem to Sehrabari. Even Commander Benu was uninformed of Hatem's condition. He assumed that with his instruction to retreat, all of his comrades had returned safely.

At Sehrabari, Hatem was given first aid, but his condition still deteriorated. Hatem said, "I may not live long, but before I die I want to see Kader, my leader. I passed exhaustive tests before he allowed me to join the Mukti Bahini. I want to tell him that I upheld his trust."

As his voice quivered with increasing pain, Hatem repeated himself over and over again, "I want to see Kader. This is my dying wish…my final will."

Three bullets had hit Hatem. Two pierced through his right shoulder and a third bullet hit his lower chest and was still lodged in his back peeking through his skin.

Hatem was a rare example of a patriot. He was a teenager. When he came to join the Mukti Bahini, the recruiting officer rejected him because he looked too young. In fact, he had always looked younger than his age.

Hatem was infuriated by the rejection and cursed the recruiting officer. He was detained and beaten up for his misconduct. He was given money for his treatment and sent home. To our surprise, he came back to join the Mukti Bahini again.

He was given several physical tests. Surprisingly, he passed each one with flying colors and was admitted into the Mukti Bahini. He was given several difficult assignments, but he never complained. He became one of the most reliable freedom fighters in the Mukti Bahini.

Hatem was the only child from a poor family. Today, most Bangladeshis may not know of Hatem's sacrifice to the liberation struggle. However, thousands of freedom fighters in Tangail will always remember him. He was a hero who fought the enemy and sacrificed his life to liberate our motherland.

Future generations deserve to know his story.

Seized by the Enemy

Shaheed, Dr. Chowdhury, Faruk, Syed and others welcomed me at the headquarters. They were all waiting eagerly for my return. I told them what I had gone through over the past few days. I covered everything from the captured enemy ships, the fall of Bhuapur, the traitor, the battle with the Pakistani Army in the village Garjana, and the injury of Commander Khorshed.

Around eleven at night, as we were preparing to go to sleep, two freedom fighters from Kader's squad arrived at the headquarters. They delivered a note to Anwar-ul Alam Shaheed.

The note read, "Please send Dr. Shahjada Chowdhury with the bearer of this letter".

Dr. Chowdhury obliged. The rest of us were anxious.

What might have happened? Who was Dr. Chowdhury called to see? These questions began eating at us.

Dr. Chowdhury returned after two hours. He had a very serious look on his face.

On our repeated insistence, he disclosed, "Sir is seriously wounded."

The freedom fighters greeted Kader with "Sir." Dr. Chowdhury told us, "Sir has forbidden me to tell others. But, this is a serious matter and I must share it with you."

We were informed that Kader was wounded around noon and soon after became feverish. Amidst tremendous pain, he became senseless and was taken to a house. The women of the house were able to nurse him back to his senses, before he had set off for Mohanandapur headquarters by boat. However, in the midst of his journey, his condition had worsened and he stopped at the house where his family was hiding. From there he had called for Dr. Chowdhury.

Everybody in Kader's family was worried at the sight of his wounds. Dr. Chowdhury washed the wound and applied a fresh dressing. He administered the necessary injections and arranged for medication.

It was a matter of sheer luck that Kader was alive. If the bullet had not hit his LMG's scope and veered off course, it would have gone straight through Kader's chest.

Dr. Chowdhury informed us of more bad news. Hatem, the great freedom fighter had died. I shivered in pain.

The night of July 8th, during my journey from Bhuapur to the headquarters, Hatem was appointed to be my personal guard. Along our journey there was a moment of threat, at which point, Hatem got me to safety, while he risked his life and confronted the danger head on.

Now, this brave young freedom fighter was no more. He had become a martyr.

This news was so shocking that I thought I had lost my own brother.

Only two days ago, Kader looked after the medical treatment of Commander Khorshed. And today he himself was seriously wounded.

As I pondered the fates of the wounded Commander Khorshed, Kader Siddiqui, and the martyred Hatem, I asked myself, "What else could lie ahead? What will the next moment bring?"

I suppose this is life, and life is unpredictable.

The next day, anxiety pulsed through the headquarters. We received news of fighting in every sector.

Desperate, the enemy continued their all-out attack against every Mukti Bahini post in the free zone. However, the outposts of the Mukti Bahini held their ground and resisted the Pakistani Army's onslaught.

Yet, even against the backdrop of such good news, we were apprehensive as our commander-in-chief's health remained uncertain. We had to know what really happened to Kader. Was Dr. Chowdhury keeping something from us?

Later that evening, Kader called for Shaheed and me to meet him at Shurirchala. Kader was staying with his family at a farmhouse there, owned by Justice Abu Sayeed Chowdhury. Justice Chowdhury was serving as a roaming-embassador of the Provisional Bangladesh Government. He was stationed in London. His farmhouse was close to our headquarters.

Still befuddled with concern and worry, Shaheed and I made our way to see Kader at once. Unfortunately, it was immediately evident that our concerns were warranted.

Kader's condition was more serious than what Dr. Chowdhury had previously led us to believe. Kader received us from his bedside, tightly wound in a blanket. We greeted him and anxiously inquired, "What happened to you, Sir?"

Slowly, Kader extended his right arm from underneath his blanket and revealed his hand. The bandages were still soaked in blood. His hand was red and swollen to the size of a goalkeeper's glove. He then pulled back his blanket from over his knee and exposed a second bullet wound just above the joint. As sweat dripped from his brow, we touched his forehead and found that he was running a high fever.

Despite what his body revealed, Kader's spirit told a much different story. His voice never showed signs of worry. Rather, he was extremely upbeat and buoyant. Even while bed-ridden, Kader proved that he was still the commander-in-chief.

It was clear to us that Kader's wound was very serious. In order to recuperate completely and rejoin the war, Kader would need at least a month of rest.

We were stuck in a Catch-22. On one hand, Kader's health was of the utmost importance. On the other hand, his absence on the battlefield would dishearten the freedom fighters during a critical juncture of the war.

Shaheed argued, "The war is in our favor right now. If we can hold our resistance for a few more days, it is likely that the enemy would abandon their thrust into the free zones. However, news of Kader's injuries could weaken the freedom fighters' psyche. We need to be careful about how we approach this situation."

Kader agreed with our concerns.

As a cautionary measure, Kader asked Shaheed to move some important documents from the headquarters to a more secure location.

He then instructed me to proceed to India on a third mission. He advised me to convey the state of the war in Tangail to the Indian authorities. He instructed me to solicit their help in pressuring the Pakistani Army at the border outposts in order to ease the pressure on us.

The next morning, Nurul and I left the headquarters for India. At midday, we arrived at the house of Kasem, a freedom fighter from Rosulpur Village.

In order to safely cross the Tangail-Mymensingh Highway and get to Bhuapur, we would have to travel at night. Bhuapur was the gateway to the Jamuna River.

However, unlike our previous missions, it would seem this time, luck was not on our side. Kasem told us that each route out of the forest was closed. Enemy soldiers had placed blockades along the forest paths in order to limit the mobility of the freedom fighters. We immediately changed our plan and returned to the headquarters.

On our way back, we stopped at Basit's house in Sehrabari. But little did we know, there was more shocking and significant news waiting for us further ahead.

Earlier that day, a very strong Mukti Bahini outpost at Dhalapara had fallen. It was a serious blow for our war strategy. The fall of Dhalapara meant that the key to infiltrating the free zone had been snatched by the enemy.

Over the previous two days, enemy soldiers had suffered substantial losses in Dhalapara. In desperation, they launched long-distance mortar attacks from Ghatail and intensified their offensives against the Mukti Bahini.

After two weeks of continuous fighting, our freedom fighters were exhausted. They had little or no food. There was no time to rest. They had no choice, but to retreat. To defend the outpost any longer would have been suicidal.

We hastened back to the headquarters and informed Kader of this shocking development.

That night Kader called us to Shurirchala again. It was here that a very important meeting took place - a meeting that would prove to be of great consequence to the history of the Tangail Mukti Bahini.

Kader, Shaheed, Faruk Ahmed, Syed Nuru, Khorshed Alam, Dr. Shahjada Chowdhury and I conducted a comprehensive review of the prevailing war situation. With the fall of Dhalapara, the momentum had shifted in favor of the enemy. The Mukti Bahini outposts to the east were now vulnerable to attack. Moreover, we no longer had a strong position in the west. We each expressed our thoughts and waited for Kader's input.

He mulled over the situation and stated, "We have to slow the momentum of the war for the time being. We cannot risk great losses for the sake of protecting just a few outposts. While it is our duty to resist the enemy's advances, our primary mission is to destroy the enemy using hit-and-run guerilla tactics which minimize our casualties."

Kader then added, "I know our freedom fighters are tired. They have been fighting for nearly twenty days without pause. In the last few days, we have lost more than fifty freedom fighters to death and injury. If this pace continues for another two weeks, we are sure to run out of arms and ammunition. While we have been fortunate in the past, we cannot rely on the off chance of capturing enemy supplies. We will need to enact a self-imposed ceasefire for the time being."

Kader then continued, "The enemy wants to get to the hills. Let them do that. If they do so, we can attack them from the rear. We can anticipate that if they infiltrate the liberated zones, they will burn our villages. They will rape and torture our wives and daughters. They will kill our people."

"Sadly, we have no other option. In order to avoid impending destruction, we will have to accept some losses. We would have to leave our people at the mercy of the enemy," Kader concluded.

We agreed with Kader. It was time to make a strategic decision. We would have to bite the bullet. We decided to withdraw our outposts in the free zone.

Instructions were sent out to close down the outposts controlled by commanders Golam, Laltu, Idris, and Monirul at Aschim, Lahore Baid, and Rangamati.

After some elaborate discussion, we decided that Kader would go to India to establish contact with relevant authorities. He also still needed to receive medical treatment.

The Mukti Bahini headquarters would be closed down. The freedom fighters would leave the permanent outposts and disperse into small groups in various hideouts throughout the greater-Tangail District.

Our meeting adjourned at midnight. I returned to the headquarters with a heavy heart. I tossed and turned through night. In just seven days, the war had taken a turn for the worse.

The government of Independent Bangladesh was located in Calcutta. There were a few small pockets along the Indian border under the control of the Mukti Bahini. However, since May, the free zones of Tangail represented a truly independent Bangladesh. Tangail was only forty miles from Dhaka and about a hundred and fifty miles from the Indian border. It was an area covering forty to sixty miles and entirely under freedom fighter control.

The enemy was fully aware of the free zones of Tangail. There were frequent battles at every outpost bringing us face-to-face with the enemy. The people of Tangail moved without any fear. The flag of Bangladesh proudly fluttered above market places.

Alas, after tomorrow, this long-standing free zone of Independent Bangladesh would fall to the occupation forces. This thought was intensely painful to me.

Just one week earlier, Bhuapur had fallen. Soon after, the Pakistani Army adopted a "kill on sight" policy. They set many of the shops and commercial establishments at Bhuapur Bazaar on fire. The army cruelly tortured many civilians.

We were shocked by this news. The possibility of such unspeakable torture being inflicted upon the people living in the hilly areas only made us more worried.

Shaheed tried to console us. He recounted historic tales of war and said, "Sometimes a retreat is your best strategy. Sometimes we must accept defeat in a battle in order to win the war."

The next morning, Kader asked to see Dr. Shahjada Chowdhury and me in his quarters.

When we reached Shurirchala, we found that Kasem of Rosulpur was with Kader. It was this morning that Kader introduced us to his family for the first time.

As the war broke out, Kader's parents and his younger brothers and sisters were all brought to this farmhouse.

Kader looked much better than he did when we saw him last. His fever had finally ceased and his injuries had begun to heal. However, he was still in a worried state of mind.

He asked the three of us to sit by his bedside. Even in the heat of battle, I had never seen Kader with such a serious demeanor.

I was concerned for him. I anticipated his next word, as it was clear he was about to divulge something of great significance.

Just last night, we decided to withdraw from our position in the hilly areas. But, was there something more serious than this bothering him?

Had he changed his plan? Would he not leave the headquarters and proceed to India? And if he had now changed his mind regarding last night's decision, why would he invite only the three of us here? Why was Shaheed not invited?

It didn't take long for me to get my answer.

Kader looked up and told us that he had been pondering his decisions all night long.

He said, "I need to give you three some important responsibilities. But today, I speak not as your commander, but rather, as your brother."

We were all taken aback by these words.

Abul Kasem was a simple and innocent villager. He immediately assumed that Kader's injury had led him into depression.

Abul Kasem assured Kader that the three of us were all fit and willing to carry out his orders.

Shahjada and I continued in the same reassuring tone.

But Kader replied, "No. This has nothing to do with this depression of mine. This is something much more personal. This is why I hesitate so."

Shahjada responded to Kader, "Sir, with all due respect, the lines between personal affairs and the duties of battle have long since been blurred."

I added, "We all fight because we share a personal sense of duty. Each battle we have fought, each mission we have carried out has been in the name of liberation, but has also affected us personally. There is nothing that you can ask of us that is too personal in nature."

Kader's reaction was astounding. For the first time, we found Kader in tears.

As he wiped the freshly cut rivers from his cheek, he regained his composure and said, "I have decided that I will proceed to India within the week. However, my mother would not be able to withstand such a long and difficult journey."

Moreover, Kader told us that he could not justify removing his entire family from Bangladesh. He decided to divide his family members in two groups. God forbid that something happened to one group, there would still be hope for the other.

Kader would take with him his father and Babul and Belal, his two younger brothers.

He decided that his three sisters and two of his younger brothers would stay behind with his mother.

Kader looked at our eyes and earnestly vowed, "I place the lives of my mother and younger siblings in your hands. Please escort them to my aunt's house in Dhaka."

While under different circumstances this would be a simple chaperon mission, but we all knew that we would be taking Kader's family across enemy lines and into Dhaka, the heart of occupation forces.

Shahjada noted that his relatives had a house in Narayanganj, just on the outskirts of Dhaka.

I added, "As a student of Dhaka University, I also had some friends in Dhaka."

I assured him that we could take his family to the city and provide safe shelter there.

Chapter 3

A Serious Setback

Escorting Kader's Mother to Dhaka

On August 19th, Kader's mother, three sisters, and two brothers were placed in our hands. A heartbreaking scene unfolded as Kader's family said their goodbyes.

The valiant freedom fighter, "Tiger" Siddiqui, the very mention of whose name struck fear in the hearts of Pakistani soldiers, was now weeping profusely as he embraced his mother and younger siblings. The last two days provided a rare window into an emotional side of Kader seldom seen on the battlefield.

Despite his stature and well-known heroism, Kader's mother still saw him as her child. It was not easy to separate the family, but at the time of an ongoing war, this was a necessary decision.

As we were about to leave, Kader avidly said, "Take care of my family at any cost. In the name of Allah, I leave my dear ones at your disposal."

We swore to protect Kader's family with our lives.

After the family finally said their farewells, Shahjada, Kashem and I left Shurirchala for Boheratoli with Kader's mother, his sisters Rahima, Shushu and Shahana, and his brothers Murad and Azad.

Rahima was a college student. Shushu and Shahana were in high school. Murad and Azad were seven or eight years old.

The last few days were fraught with heavy rains, which turned the yellowish clay-rich soil of the hills into a thick cement-like mud.

Kader's mother had great difficulty treading through these muddy paths. But after a long and arduous journey, we finally arrived at the camp of Captain Fazlur Rahman in Boheratuli.

It was late afternoon when we arrived. Captain Fazlu took good care of us. However, he had no clue as to why we were there and to where we were to go next.

It occurred to me that I could not return to Dhaka in my current appearance. Over the last several months, my hair had grown long and my beard thick.

A haircut and shave were long overdue. If we were to cross enemy lines successfully, I would have to look more like a normal civilian and less like a freedom fighter.

It was a market day in Boheratuli, so I decided to try my luck in finding a barber at the bazaar. Fortunately, I found one.

The barber had no shop. He simply conducted his business in an open area in the corner of the market. He had two pieces of "furniture" - two red bricks - one brick for him to sit on and another for his customer. The barber immediately knew who I was. He favored me and took me immediately ahead of his other clients. I sat on the brick in front of him as he lathered my face with soapy foam.

With his blunt razor he began to shave my face. It was so painful! It felt as if he was plucking my bristles, one by one. The pain brought tears to my eyes. But still, I sat patiently. Little did I know - the worst was yet to come!

The barber washed my face with dirty water from a small bowl and then rubbed a transparent cube, some sort of antiseptic, on my face. The burning was excruciating. It was as if someone was pouring salt on an open wound!

In spite of this horrible experience, when I saw my reflection in the barber's broken mirror, I was pleased to see the face of a gentleman.

Back at the camp, I spoke to Kashem and Shahjada and finalized our plans. We decided that we would leave Boheratuli by boat in the middle of the night. From there, we would go to a bus station on the Tangail-Dhaka Highway to get to Dhaka.

As planned, Kader's family and we boarded a boat. Captain Fazlu and other's had inquired of the details of our plan. However, we were careful not to divulge our destination and compromise the safety of Kader's family.

Our strategy was to get on an early bus towards Dhaka. In the early hours of August 20th, we arrived at a culvert between Dhalla and Shuvalla.

In the near distance we saw a bus headed towards us. Quickly we got off the boat and approached the bus.

We did what we could to appear as if we were simply members of a family traveling together.

We tried to contain our relief when the bus driver opened the door and welcomed us in. The bus driver hit the gas and we were off.

As we crossed Mirjapur, I noticed the curious glare of the bus driver in his rearview mirror. He gave me a wink and a smile. He asked me to sit next to him. After a few moments, when the coast was clear he leaned over and whispered, "Don't say anything at the military checkpoint ahead. I know exactly who you are. Just let your auntie know that there is nothing to be worried about. We will take you to Dhaka without any trouble. Don't bother getting off at the bus stop either. Just give me directions in Dhaka and I'll take you directly to where you want to go."

I had mixed feelings about the bus driver's comments. I was disappointed that we lost our cover; however, it was also reassuring to know that the bus driver was eager to help us out.

We were apprehensive as we approached the first checkpoint just before Kaliyakaur. Fortunately, the military guards and the Razakars did not interrogate any of the passengers. With just a cursory glance, they let us go.

After a long night's duty, it's more than likely that the soldiers were still groggy in these early morning hours.

I left the driver's side and returned to my seat in the back beside Dr. Chowdhury.

I waited for an opportune moment to tell auntie that the bus driver and the conductor knew what we were up to. Before I could finish my sentence, I could see the look of fear paralyze her face. In a murmuring voice she recited a Qur'anic phrase and asked for Allah's protection.

I quickly assured her that the driver and the conductor were both on our side and have promised to take us to our destination. With her prayers answered, the life returned to her face and she humbly thanked God.

We arrived at another checkpoint near the Kodda Bridge. However, the reception here was not quite the same.

At gunpoint, military guards ordered the passengers to get off the bus. We all obliged. However, the driver asked Kader's family to stay on the bus. The military guards angrily inquired as to why the woman and four children were not getting off.

The driver shrewdly replied, "This is the family of the malik, the owner of this bus. I can't allow them to get down or else I risk losing my job."

In the Pakistani language of Urdu, the word malik has an authoritarian connotation. It literally means owner or boss. It is also one of the one hundred names of Allah. After hearing this word, the soldiers were unwilling to push the matter any further.

They boarded the bus and searched every corner. Finding nothing, the soldiers ordered the passengers back onto the bus, one by one, checking each traveler's identification. With fake IDs in hand, the three of us boarded the bus and easily fooled the unsuspecting soldiers. Satisfied, the soldiers asked the driver to move on.

There were more checkpoints at Chowrasta, Tongi and Kurmitola. But only at Kurmitola, was the security as thorough as it was at Kodda. The rouge worked here as well. The bus driver was able to protect Kader's family under the guise of his boss's wife and kids.

When the bus arrived at the final destination at Gulistan, the other passengers got off.

The driver continued towards Narayanganj Road. Once we got near Tikatoli, we got off the bus.

When I offered to pay the fare, the bus driver and the conductor refused to accept my money. They said, "We know what you and your commander, Kader, are doing for our motherland. May Allah be with you."

Later, we came to know that the name of the driver was Najar Ali and the conductor was Shushil Rajbangshi.

From Tikatoli, we took a rickshaw to Sarat Gupta Road where one of Kader's aunts lived. But, there was not enough room for all of us.

After a few days, we went to Narayangonj to stay at the house of Dr. Shahjada Chowdhury's in-laws. The house was located in town on the bank of a river.

Here, there was enough space for all of us. I liked the house very much. It was away from the main road and in a quiet neighborhood – the ideal place for a hideout.

A special feature of the house was the guest room, which stretched out of the main building and hovered over the water on stilts. This was my room.

Over the course of the last few months, I found myself sleeping in many different places. Some not so comfortable, like the jungle floor, in barns with beds of hay, and of course, my least favorite, the bamboo cot in the VIP tent at the Mukti Bahini camp in Tura, India.

But tonight's accommodations were special. It was as if I was spending the night sleeping cozily in a luxury resort bungalow on my own private island. And all the while I was still in the industrial city of Narayanganj.

Unfortunately, Kashem was not as comfortable as I was. He was a villager from a small hilly area and wasn't fond of the city environment. He was homesick. It was time for him to go back to the open air of his rural village He apologized and bade us goodbye.

Dr. Laila Chowdhury was the wife of Dr. Shahjada Chowdhury. Both were students of Mymensingh Medical College. They had courted during their student days before getting married. Dr. Laila Chowdhury and her parents were very hospitable and took good care of us.

Our Aunt

Kader's mother and I became very close right from the beginning. Usually people call me Nuran Nabi or affectionately, just "Nabi."

But at our first introduction, Kader's mother immediately began calling me by my new nickname, "Nuru." "Nuru, I have some food for you," she would say.

There was always a deep affection in her tone. She reminded me of my mother whom I had lost only a few months ago.

While engaged in battle, my mother's memory passed through my thoughts periodically. But when Kader's mother would call me "Nuru," I felt deeply touched.

It only took a few days, but very soon, Kader's mother became dear to me. She became my aunt.

To those who have never had the pleasure of meeting her, it is very difficult for me to convey the nature and extent of her affection. Her love as a mother extended far beyond her own children and touched the hearts of all who were near. To put it simply, she was a magnificent mother.

Operation Thunder

It was planned earlier that Dr. Shahjada Chowdhury and I would go to India after we arranged a safe hideout for Kader's family. But our plan took a sudden twist.

I told Shahjada that since we were in Dhaka, we should try to execute a guerrilla operation.

Shahjada inquired about my plan. I told him that it was simple:

"In an attempt to create a sense of normalcy during war time, the military has forced the doors of Dhaka University open and strong-armed some students and teachers into returning to class. Many of these students and teachers weren't Razakars."

I explained to Dr. Chowdhury that I knew Dhaka University's science complex, Curzon Hall, very well.

By simply distributing pro-liberation fliers through the campus, we could bring the spirit of the liberation war back to the campus and incite a panic amongst the anti-liberation forces.

I went to New Market and bought some stationery to get started on some posters and fliers. The only question was how to get them printed.

Shahjada had an idea. When he was a student of Mymensingh Medical College, he befriended an engineer named Salam.

Salam had been working as a contractor to install the elevator at the Mymensingh Medical College. But now he was back living in Dhaka and Shahjada knew his address. There was a good chance that Salam might be able to help us get our posters and fliers printed.

We went to Salam's home. When Salam opened the door it was clear that he was excited to see Shahjada.

During our conversation we probed Salam to uncover his stance on the liberation war. Once we had confirmation, we shared our plan with him.

Without giving it a second thought, Salam happily agreed to what we proposed and asked us to return at his place the next day.

Shahjada and I were relieved to see that our plan was beginning to come together.

The next evening, we arrived at Salam's place a little ahead of schedule. To our surprise, Salam had a new proposal for which we were not ready.

Salam told us that he was currently installing a lift in the office of the Central Meteorological Department in Mirpur.

There were several Pakistani Army offices and officer's residences located in the surrounding area. Salam added that a command centre of the Pakistan Army was also nearby.

Nobody without a pass issued by the army could enter the zone. Fortunately for us, Salam not only possessed such a pass, but he had special authorization to stay in the meteorological office over night.

I was excited. An opportunity like this could not be wasted.

I was eager to go to Salam's office and survey the place. However, Salam told me that I needed to wait until he checked the matter with the building guards. He'd let us know the outcome by the next day.

Once again, we returned to Salam's the next day. We waited at the door for quite some time. But, Salam never came to receive us.

Disappointed, we headed back. I had so many questions. Had something happened to him? Should we have really trusted him in the first place?

Despite my reservations, Shahjada assured me that Salam was a trustworthy person. He was a supporter of the liberation war.

The next night, we tried our luck again and returned to Salam's place. He was happy to see us and said that we would be able go to his office the next morning.

He apologized for his absence the previous evening, and explained that he had to wait late into the evening to speak with the guards.

Salam had fooled the guards into believing that Shahjada and I were just relatives of his who were eager to see where he worked.

Salam looked at us with scrutinizing eyes. He said to me, "Nabi, you need to buy some new clothes. Your outfit might create some problems."

I had a worn-out shirt on and a pair of ill-fitted trousers that I picked up in India. Unfortunately, this was all I had in my current wardrobe.

Shahjada was a little more fortunate. His fair skin, pointed nose, and long moustache helped him resemble a typical West Pakistani Punjabi.

Later that evening, I had to go shopping to find some more suitable clothing. In those days, it was something of a rarity to find clothing shops that sold ready-to-wear outfits.

I headed to Jinnah Avenue to try my luck. I went from shop to shop, but could not find clothes that fit. Finally, I found a pair of trousers at one shop and a nice dress shirt that fit at another store.

Dressed to impress, I looked down in the store mirror and realized that my shopping was still incomplete. I still had the same worn-out pair of sandals that I got in India. Luckily, I was able to get some new shoes from yet another store.

The next day, the three of us headed to the meteorological office.

As we entered the second capital area, the military guard stopped our auto-rickshaw. He examined Salam's pass and allowed us to move on. However, we had to ditch the auto-rickshaw after a few blocks when we approached a sign that read, "Only Military Vehicles Allowed".

We continued on foot towards the office. Salam had a briefcase with him. There was no mistaking where we were – the center of a military zone.

Military jeeps criss-crossed around us. Soldiers rushed from one office to another. The entire area was fortified with anti-aircraft cannons and machine guns. I was excited to see the enemy so up-close. However, I had to keep my cool and appear relaxed.

On our way to the office, there were several military checkpoints where we had to stop. Fortunately, between Salam's military pass, Shahjada's Punjabi-like appearance, and my new clothes and small stature we did not arise any suspicion.

The last checkpoint was at the meteorological office itself. Everybody there knew Salam very well. It didn't hurt that he also spoke Urdu fluently. More importantly, I noticed that none of the guards checked the briefcase that was clenched in Salam's fist.

We rode Salam's elevator to the top floor of the high-rise building. The installation was almost complete. Salam told us that his work order would end in a few months. The top floor resembled the observation deck at the Empire State Building. You could see all of Dhaka city from this one vantage point.

As I took a look around, I finalized the plans in my mind. I could have never imagined a more perfect place to conduct a guerrilla operation from.

I remembered Kader Siddiqui. If he were still in Tangail, I would have headed there by daybreak to take further steps to execute the operation. But he was in India for medical treatment. So instead I'd have to wait.

Since this area was now reclassified as a military zone, the routine activities of the meteorological office had been suspended. Only contractors, like Salam, were allowed to visit the site for construction and maintenance matters. This situation favored the implementation of our plan.

Once we got back to Salam's home, I disclosed my plan to Salam and Shahjada.

Back in July, I brought some explosives from India during my first mission. Unfortunately, in the middle of the night, the boat carrying the detonators broke from our fleet and vanished into Jamuna River, never to be seen again.

Without detonators, the explosives I had brought were useless. The fruits of my mission sat idle in our camp.

However, on my second mission to India, I was extra careful and carried the detonators in my own boat.

My plan was to assemble the explosives and detonators at Salam's house in Dhaka.

We would then bring Salam back to our camp and train him in the detonation of explosives.

Every morning, as usual Salam would go to work. And every morning, Salam would take a small piece of explosive with him in his briefcase and store it inside the tower.

Salam was an engineer, so he eagerly agreed to carry out my plan. He volunteered to take a few days off from work to get the necessary training from the Mukti Bahini Camp.

The importance of this operation would have far-reaching consequences. The meteorological office was located inside the military zone. A new high command was now in operation there. So a blast, of any capacity, in the heart of their military operation would be certain to panic the enemy.

Moreover, this incident would find its place in the news bulletins of every agency in Bangladesh. Even the foreign media would have to report on such an incident, attaching even greater importance.

A Mukti Bahini operation inside the Pakistani military camp in Dhaka would be seen as a serious blow to the enemy. Salam and Shahjada enthusiastically supported the plan and promised to take any risk to implement the operation.

We decided to postpone our trip to India for the time being. We also suspended our plan to distribute posters and fliers around the Dhaka University campus. Instead, we chose to return to the liberated zone in Tangail and put forth efforts to implement "operation thunder."

A Wrong Turn

My new clothes had already given me an extra bounce in my step. But with the recent developments of our new plan for the meteorological office, my confidence had reached new bounds. I decided to get around and see more of Dhaka city before I returned to Tangail.

One day, I hired a rickshaw to see how the civilians of Dhaka led their lives, while we were engaged in a war of "do or die."

Dhaka seemed different. There were fewer people around. The usual crowds in the shops of New Market, Baitul Mukarram, and Jinnah Avenue had thinned since the days before the war.

There was no way for me to tell what these people were thinking. There was no way I could know who was for and who was against the liberation war.

As I passed Curzon Hall campus, I could hear the familiar chatter of students. Instantly, without thinking, I asked the rickshawalla to head into campus.

I got off the rickshaw on the east corner of Curzon Hall, in front of the Biochemistry department, my home for last three years.

As usual, the teachers' cars were parked in front of the building. I was both anxious and thrilled. I ran quickly up to the first floor. There I found Golam Hossain, the custodian of the animal house of the Biochemistry department. He embraced me and wanted to know where I had been and how things were going with me. He told me that all my classmates were now in the classroom upstairs.

From Golam Hossain, I came to know that the Pakistani military authority had issued a military decree to keep all educational institutions and all government and non-government offices open. Again, this was to show that everything was still normal in East Pakistan. With the exception to Solaiman, Amin, Bokul and I, all of my classmates had returned to the University.

They had completed the last part of their B.Sc Honors practical examination and were now enrolled in M.Sc classes.

No sooner had I finished my conversation with Golam Hossain had the period ended and the students rolled out of their classes. As my classmates hurried down the stairs, I found myself suddenly surrounded by my peers.

However, none of my classmates showed any interest in me. No one even thought to approach me.

I was invisible to all, but one student. He was a student of the M.Sc class, in the preliminary group. He quickly embraced me. This was strange.

As a student of the honors class, I did not have much of a rapport with the students of the preliminary class. While, this particular student was an activist, he was a member of the Islamic Student Association, a group opposed to the liberation of Bangladesh.

While my classmates were indifferent towards me, the students of the Islamic Students Association were quite enthusiastic to see me. The situation made me sick. Initially, I returned to campus on a whim. I came here without a thought. I didn't consider what to tell people. I didn't know how to explain why I was here.

Based on my presence of mind, I decided to explain why I was here.

The leader of the Islamic Students Association was from the district of Noakhali. He repeatedly asked me why I hadn't returned to the University on time. He asked why I had missed the final examination.

While other classmates were already on their way to their next class, his interrogation continued.

I had no alternative, but to lie to him.

I told him that the fighting had progressed into our area. The Mukti Bahini was in control of our area. However, the Pakistani Army had the area surrounded. Therefore, it was too dangerous to return to Dhaka. It was only in the last month that the Mukti Bahini had left our area. This was my first opportunity to return to the University.

I did my best to keep my composure as I fabricated this farce.

Before I went further, I looked him in the eyes and asked, "How could I get back to school in the midst of all of this?"

Worried he had already heard about my whereabouts, or didn't believe my story; I anticipated his reply with misgivings.

With a smile and an arm on my shoulder, he said, "It's not a problem. I will take care of everything."

And right there and then, he drafted an application addressing the Vice-Chancellor conveying all that I had told him.

He dragged me to the office of my teacher, Professor Kamal Ahmed, Chair of the Department of Biochemistry. Before I even had an opportunity to say something, he had already announced me to Professor Ahmed's secretary.

Prior to the war, I had always known this Islamic student activist to be a low-key guy. However, his overzealous response to my story frightened me.

Clearly, he was showing off his power and influence because his party was collaborating with the Pakistani Army. His behavior would have me to believe that he was the one who called the shots in the department, not Professor Ahmed.

The secretary went inside the professor's office. When he returned, he announced that I was permitted to meet with the chair.

It wasn't until this moment that the Islamic student activist handed over the application he wrote on my behalf.

As the chain of events had unfolded so quickly, I had no time to think. I quickly regurgitated the same fabricated account to my professor.

Professor Ahmed listened to me sympathetically. He told me to write an application to the Vice-Chancellor and if necessary he would talk to the Vice-Chancellor on my behalf.

Before the war broke out, I was the leader of the department student body, which put me on good terms with Prof. Ahmed.

Despite this, I responded to the professor's suggestion by handing over the application drafted for me by the Islamic student activist.

I hadn't even taken a moment to glance it over.

Prof. Ahmed took the paper from my hand and immediately got irritated.

He looked at me and asked furiously, "What is this? What have you written?"

"Get a new application and I will recommend that to the Vice-Chancellor," the professor demanded.

As I left the professor's office, I found the Islamic student activist still waiting at the door with his still troubling enthusiasm.

He immediately asked me how the meeting went.

Still a bit perplexed, I said to him, "Everything was alright, but Professor Ahmed wants me to rewrite the application. This time, I think I will do it myself."

I thanked him for all of his help and reminded him that he was late for class. As I walked away, I added that I'd be back again in the morning and if needed, I would seek his help.

As soon as he was out of sight, I made a dash down the staircase and headed toward Fazlul Haq Hall. I figured I could find a rickshaw at the hall gate.

As I walked, I looked over the application. I quickly understood why Prof. Ahmed was so upset with the original application.

My application read like a legal document. Every paragraph began with the word, "That..."

It was hardly appropriate correspondence between a student and a teacher.

I balled up the application and chucked it in the pond between Fazlul Haq Hall and Dhaka Hall.

As I came to the gate of Fazlul Haq Hall, I felt a sense of nostalgia come over me again. On the evening of March 25th, I stepped out of my dorm room just like I did any other day. Of course as history would have it, the war started later that evening. It would not be until today, five months later that I would have a chance to return to my room.

I left all my belongings inside. Naturally, I was curious to see my room, so I went inside the hall.

It was noon and so most of the students were still in class. From inside, the hall looked empty. I quickly walked to my room and found that it was locked from the outside.

The dormitory doors were so old and warped that I was able to steal a peak by pushing my weight against the door. Unfortunately, my belongings were not in sight. What I saw were the effects of someone else: a suitcase, a bed, books, and clothes.

Already, my room had a new occupant. I couldn't help but feel a little sad.

Next door, I found my classmate Moqbul Hossain, a student of the M.Sc class. He was feeling a little under the weather and decided to stay in bed.

He had always been something of an introvert, always keeping to himself, while the rest of us were engaged in student activities. He seemed astonished to see me, but glad nonetheless.

Again, I told him the tale I that had concocted earlier on campus. I wasn't sure if he believed me, given he was all too aware of my activities in the Students' League and my participation in the liberation movement.

As I had him alone, I decided to find out about the war efforts in his home district of Rangpur in the northern part of Bangladesh.

Moqbul replied stoically, "There are no war activities in Rangpur as far as I am aware. I haven't seen anything and haven't heard otherwise from anyone else."

I was quite disappointed to hear this. Just one month ago, I was in Mankachar, a river port in Rangpur where I was engaged in military activities. Rangpur, like any other district along the Indian border, was a hot spot for Mukti Bahini activity. I couldn't help but feel pity for him.

I asked him again whether he had ever seen a freedom fighter before. But again, he said no.

I didn't have the courage to tell him that a freedom fighter was sitting in front of him this whole time. I just told him another lie and promised to see him the next day in class.

What if?

I was relieved as I took a rickshaw out of the hall gates. I was headed toward Narayanganj bus station, trying to recapitulate everything that happened in the last few hours. It was foolish and irresponsible of me to go to my class. Why did I go to Curzon Hall?

There was no reason for it. My emotions had overtaken my judgment. As reality set in, I began to shiver. Had I been discovered as a freedom fighter, the consequences I would have had to face would have been grave, to say the least.

Not to mention, the insult and neglect of my classmates had been eating away at me. Why didn't they show any enthusiasm upon seeing me? Was it because I had left the university and they were now students of the M.Sc class?

In the previous six months, I was only preoccupied with the liberation war. I never considered the ramifications of victory or defeat. It was all war, nothing else. But my experience over the last few hours, transformed my mood from excitement and pride to a grim state of depression.

If the country did not become free, what would happen to me? All of my classmates were now M.Sc. students. Those who had done well in the examination had already been admitted in the thesis group. I had once also nurtured the idea of becoming a student of the thesis group. Many of my classmates would complete their thesis, go abroad, and would eventually earn PhDs. As for me, I would remain in limbo as a B.Sc Honors student.

If Bangladesh failed to gain its freedom, I would not be able to stay in the country and I certainly would not be able to return to my hometown.

I would be forced to leave the country as a traitor, a miscreant of India. I would have no home. Worse yet, what if I was wounded and the country remained a colony of Pakistan? I would be left to beg at the holy site of Ajmeer Sharif in India.

If the country did not gain its independence, if I became disabled, what would I do in India? If I were lucky, maybe I would have a chance as a teacher in a primary school and marry an otherwise undistinguished daughter of a wealthy Muslim farmer. At best, I would live a life of mediocrity.

I would not be the only one to suffer for my involvement in the war. As relatives to a traitor, my father, brothers and other family members would also suffer dire consequences for my decisions.

However, nothing hurt me more than the thought of my mother. She always prayed that her son would be a very successful person and would go abroad for higher studies. Even on her deathbed, her priority was ensuring that news of her illness did not get to me. She wanted nothing to interfere with my studies.

Failing my country would mean failing my mother.

My thoughts came to a halt as the rickshaw pulled up to Narayanganj bus-stand. Once on the bus, I tried to regain my courage and composure. I reminded myself that I was a freedom fighter. I joined the war at the call of Bangabandhu to make my country free.

Thousands of freedom fighters, like me, risked their lives in this war. Millions of people have helped us in this struggle. This was a duty that went beyond personal glory. This was my responsibility and I was fortunate to have it. I was fortunate to be a freedom fighter.

Remembering all the people who were a part of the liberation war, I was able to escape the horrors of last few hours when I came back to Narayanganj amongst Shahjada, aunt and others.

Out of shame I could not tell anyone of my stupidity.

The next day, Shahjada and I decided to return to Shakhipur, our headquarters in the liberated zone. However, "Operation Thunder" was still on my mind.

September 4th

After spending about two weeks in Dhaka and Narayanganj, on September 4th, Shahjada and I proceeded for Shakhipur via Tangail. We went to Karotia in Tangail by bus.

It was a market day at Karotia and the streets were bustling. The risk of being identified by someone was high. We quickly made our way to the dock and hired a boat to Kauljani, Shahjada's home.

Shahjada's family members were very happy to see him back at home. From them, we came to know that Shaheed and some other freedom fighters were still at our headquarters in Shakhipur.

The next day, we went to Shakhipur by boat. However, once we arrived, we found that our headquarters had been relocated from Bhabanipur to Bagarchala.

Shaheed, Syed, Faruk and others were excited to see us. We informed them that Kader's mother and other family members were safe at Shahjada's in-laws' house.

The Atrocities of the Pakistani Army

Kader Siddiqui left for India on August 20th. Before his departure, he instructed the commanders of all free zones to dismantle their permanent outposts and go into hiding.

Shaheed also gave similar instructions to his fellow fighters. After a couple of days, he headed towards India with some of his most trustworthy associates.

In the mean time, Pakistani occupation forces had surrounded the free zones in the hilly areas. By August 24th, they had already installed an outpost at Sagardighi. The Pakistan Army had recaptured almost all of our outposts. But despite this uncontested shift in control, the occupation forces were perplexed by the sudden disappearance of such a huge number of freedom fighters.

The Pakistani soldiers were apprehensive. They kept their eyes on the treetops. At any moment they expected us to jump out of the trees and ambush them. But with no sign of our whereabouts, and with the help of some deliberately misleading information from the locals, the jungle had become haunted with the ghosts of the Mukti Bahini.

The frightened Pakistani Army cautiously proceeded out of Sagardighi towards our former headquarters in the south.

However, along the way, they burned the dwellings in which we used to stay. They tortured and killed everyone they encountered. They slaughtered the livestock and left the corpses to rot in the humidity of the jungle. As for the few locals who were able to save themselves, they too found their homes burned to ashes. The stench of rotting flesh and ashes blanketed the hills.

For one whole week, the enemies tortured the people of the hilly area around Sagardighi and Shakhipur. The Pakistani Army returned to Tangail with a false sense of victory.

Disorder

In order to cross over to India, Shaheed and his group - Syed, Faruk, and Commanders Sabur and Idris arrived at a village bordering India. They needed to rest as they had been walking for three consecutive days.

However, unbeknownst to them, the house in which they took shelter belonged to a person who was a member of the Peace Committee, a pro-Pakistani group.

This person informed the Pakistan Army of their whereabouts.

Immediately, the Pakistani Army attacked Shaheed and his group. Commanders Sabur and Idris were able to put up enough of a resistance to allow the group to escape and return to Sakhipur. This episode was kept a secret.

With the absence of Kader, the commanders had lost communication between themselves. The command structure amongst the freedom fighters began to disintegrate. Discipline was at an all time low. It was alleged that some freedom fighters were becoming involved in illegal activities. The reputation of the Mukti Bahini was at risk.

Shaheed's Lie

September 7th, Shaheed convened over an emergency meeting of the commanders and headquarters' staff to discuss the prevailing situation and our next move. Commanders Sarwar, Laltu, Nabi Newaj, R.O. Hamidul Haq, Khorshed Alam, Shahjada, Nuru, Faruk and I were all present.

Shaheed expressed his deep concern about the lack of discipline amongst the freedom fighters in the absence of our commander, Kader Siddiqui.

He discussed the need to restore the chain of command and reestablish discipline and coordination among the freedom fighters. However, Shaheed knew that only Kader would be able to restore order amongst the freedom fighters. Shaheed had no choice, but to drop Kader's name.

Shaheed concealed the truth and said that he had met with Kader in India and had returned to Tangail with Kader's instructions.

He further reported that Kader would come back to Tangail on September 20th. However, until Kader's return, Shaheed's decisions should be treated as Kader's order. We all agreed to go along with Shaheed's plan.

The commanders present at the meeting pledged their allegiance to Shaheed. It was also decided that a cyclostyled bulletin on behalf of Kader would be distributed amongst the freedom fighters. The news of Kader's return to Tangail on September 20th restored discipline and confidence amongst the Mukti Bahini.

This historic, yet, risky decision by Shaheed was a very important episode for the Tangail Mukti Bahini.

Our New HQ

Our new headquarters was established at the house of a woodcutter in Bagarchala. The house was built on stilts. This was an essential security measure to protect the residents from tigers and wild bears.

The open area below the house doubled as a kitchen and grazing area for cows and goats. Our living quarters were upstairs accessible only via ladder.

Shaheed, Nuru, Faruk, Shahjada, and I slept in one room. We had a wireless set by which we could maintain contact with the operator in Tangail. We gathered information regarding the liberation war at different parts of the country. We also used the wireless to maintain communication with various informants throughout Tangail. In order to do this safely, we utilized a series of cipher codes.

A young man from one of the local tribes, named Burman, was our 24-hour bodyguard. In addition, the roads leading to our headquarters were fortified by a series of freedom fighter camps.

We all had a proclivity for tea. Unfortunately, tea was a rare commodity during these times.

Pakistani forces had ravaged the shops and tea stalls in the area during their most recent strike.

One morning, Burman woke us up. He came up with a mug and said "Sir, have your tea."

The mug was filled with a light green hot water.

Immediately I asked, "What kind of tea is this?"

Before he would answer, Burman insisted that I had a sip. Intrigued at the thought of a hot cup of tea, I took his advice. What I found was the leafy and slightly sweet taste of a local fruit referred to as bel or wood apple.

Until local tea supplies were replenished, Burman's bel tea would have to suffice.

Things were quiet for a few days. Several commanders regularly came to meet with us to discuss some of their problems. They inquired about Kader's return. We did our best to provide satisfactory answers.

One of their immediate needs was medicine for the wounded Mukti Bahini. However, Dr. Shahjada Chowdhury didn't have the necessary medicine in stock at the headquarters. Worse yet, the Pakistani Army's recent attacks had totally disrupted our network of medical supplies.

A West Pakistani Freedom Fighter

Shaheed and Shahjada gave me the responsibility to procure adequate medical supplies for the Mukti Bahini.

We had a particular pharmacy in Tangail town, which we had previously used to meet our medical needs. Unfortunately, now, the Pakistani Army and members of the Peace Committee kept a vigilant eye on that pharmacy. I had no choice, but to go to Dhaka.

My visit to Dhaka last month was quite hasty and risky. However this time, I would be traveling alone. I decided that it would be necessary to get the appropriate documentation should my mission be threatened. I would need a pharmacist's identification card.

One of Shahjada's relatives owned a pharmacy. He arranged a photo identification card for me, which stated that I worked in his store as a pharmacist. A photo studio in Tangail helped us with the rest.

My beard and moustache had grown, so after a quick shave and a change of clothes, I set out to Dhaka with the ID card tagged to my breast.

Once in Dhaka, I arrived at the house of a West Pakistani named Mumtaz Khan on Agamasi Lane.

Mumtaz was from a Pakistani tribe from the Northwest Frontier Province known as the Pathans. The tribe spanned from the Northwest Frontier Province of Pakistan to its border with Afghanistan.

I carried a letter that bore the name of Kader, which I handed to Mumtaz. He read the letter. Just before leaving the room, he assured me that he could help. I waited in the living room.

Suddenly, I heard the unmistakable sound of military boots.

I became alarmed. A few moments later, I found two West Pakistan military officers entering the living room.

I did not know what was happening. Was I being set up?

I began praying. I asked Allah to protect me and keep me from getting arrested. To die by a bullet was one thing, but being arrested meant an end far more torturous and painful.

I didn't know what to tell these officers should they begin to interrogate me. My Urdu wasn't fluent and speaking English would raise doubts regarding my credentials as a pharmacist, as most pharmacists were not fluent in English.

Just at that moment, Mumtaz Khan entered the room and introduced me to these two military officers. They were his relatives.

I was introduced as Mumtaz's business client. He asked me to wait, while he took his relatives inside. I felt relieved as I wiped the sweat from my brow. I thanked God.

Mumtaz Khan was a businessman who traded tobacco leaves at Sakhipur. Kader arrested him early on in the liberation war as he was obviously from West Pakistan. However, we soon found that he was a supporter of our cause.

Many of the Pathan community knew firsthand what it felt like to be discriminated against; as the Pathan were oppressed by the Punjabi ruling clique of West Pakistan. Mumtaz and his people were sympathetic to the plight of Bangladesh.

Needless to say, when Mumtaz assured us of his help for our cause, he was released. For several months, he had been supplying medicine for the Mukti Bahini. As a West Pakistani, Mumtaz was able to travel with medical supplies to our old Headquarters without raising the suspicion of the Pakistani forces.

This is why I came to him.

I planned to return to Tangail later in the day. That afternoon, Mumtaz brought me the medical supplies. With the supplies in hand, I got on a bus for Tangail. The bus was stopped twice along the way, but I easily passed each checkpoint by showing my ID card. I planned to reach Kouljani by boat from Karotia before nightfall. But by the time I arrived in Karotia, the last boat was gone. I would have to spend the night in Tangail. This was an added risk for my mission.

I had to find a safe place to stay in Tangail. In those days, travelers from different parts of Tangail would stay in hotels. Many of these travelers came from rural areas in connection with on-going civil and criminal litigation in the district courts.

Staying in a hotel would put me at risk of being recognized by someone from my village area.

Suddenly, I remembered the postmaster at Hemnagar from six years ago. I had become very close to him and his family, while attending high school in Hemnagar. The post office and the postmaster's residence were next door to my high school. I had become like an extended family member to them.

I recalled that he had recently been transferred to Tangail as the postmaster-general. However, I wasn't sure if he was still at this post. Nonetheless, I had to take a chance and visit the post office.

The night watchman at the post office informed me that my friend was still the postmaster general. Luckily, the watchman was able to provide me with his home address.

Late in the evening, I stepped on the porch of the postmaster general. The postmaster answered the door as if he had just seen a ghost. He could not believe it. There had been no contact between us in more than six years.

His children had grown up so quickly that I could not recognize them. His two young girls had now blossomed into young women.

Trusting him, I told him the purpose of my visit. He reassured me of my safety in his home. Like many government officials, he was also a supporter of the liberation war.

Before we went to sleep, we reminisced of our old days in Hemnagar. The postmaster was an organizer of cultural activities in Hemnagar and a fixture on the badminton and volleyball courts. These were some of my favorite pastimes at Hemnagar.

The postmaster told me about the activities of the Pakistani Army in Tangail. Though he worked for the government, he was still afraid for the safety of his teenage daughters. The lustful bite of Pakistani soldiers was known throughout Tangail for preying on innocent young women. While many young women were able to leave Tangail for a safer climate, the postmaster's duties made such an escape impossible.

Early the next morning, I reached the headquarters with the medical supplies.

Kader Siddiqui in India

Kader Siddiqui left for India on August 20th. His father Abdul Awal Siddiqui, Babul and Belal, his two younger brothers, and some trusted freedom fighters including Dulal and Khoka accompanied him. Before he left the headquarters, he asked the commanders to go underground, and if necessary, to cross over to India for a few days.

Hamidul Haq and a recruiting officer were entrusted to secure the arms and ammunition of the Mukti Bahini in the hilly areas. Amjad Master was ordered to arrange the medical treatment of the wounded freedom fighters and to ensure their safety.

Kader instructed Shaheed and his followers, including Professor Rafiq Azad, Professor Mahbub Sadik, Professor Shariful Islam, and Bulbul Khan Mahbub to go to their respective villages or to find a safe place to hide out.

Kader's group walked for three days at a stretch. Their trek took them through perilous jungles and rainy nights. The absolute blackness of the jungle was interrupted by the sound of branches and vines crunched under heavy boots. The bats fled, the snakes slithered, and the howling foxes were silenced. Kader and his men continued their journey.

On August 23rd, Kader crossed the border and reached Dalu in India.

The wounds on his hands and legs had become swollen, and he had a temperature of 104 degree. But none of this seemed to slow Kader's stride. His only objective was to get his family and his group safely across to India. He would not rest until his goal was accomplished.

Along the journey, Kader's elderly father Awal Siddiqui also showed his vigor by walking at the same spirited pace as the young freedom fighters accompanying him.

During my two missions to India, I had painted a good picture of Kader to the Indian authorities. They had also corroborated my depiction of Kader by intercepting radio messages from the Pakistan Army. The Indians already knew about Kader's injury and the objective of his visit to India. They were waiting for him.

As soon as Kader reached the Indian border outpost in Dalu, Brigadier Sanat Singh got the news.

During my visits to India, I had meetings with Brigadier Sanat Singh, Major General Gill, and Lieutenant General Aurora. I expounded to them the heroic activities and war strategies of Kader Siddiqui.

So, as soon as Brigadier Singh saw Kader Siddiqui, he embraced him. The twenty-two freedom fighters that accompanied Kader were accommodated at Rawshan Ara camp near Tura.

Kader was given medical treatment immediately. In a couple of days, the wounds on his hands and legs showed signs of recovery. In the meantime, more freedom fighters had crossed over to India from Tangail. Another camp was constructed alongside Rawshan Ara camp for their accommodation.

While in India, Kader met several Indian military leaders including Lieutenant General Aurora, Major General Gill, Brigadier Klair and Brigadier Sanat Singh. He also met Lieutenant Colonel Ziaur Rahman and Major Taher of the Mukti Bahini. Among the members of the Bangladesh Parliament whom he met with were Latif Siddiqui, Humayun Khalid, and Fazlur Rahman Khan Faruk.

Kader discussed the liberation war efforts in Tangail as well as his future war strategies.

Additional training arrangements for the Tangail Mukti Bahini were made inside the camp.

The freedom fighters of Tangail were given an opportunity to meet a large number of freedom fighters that came from different parts of Bangladesh. This boosted their morale further.

Kader's Return to Tangail

Immediately after his arrival in India, Kader Siddiqui had told the Indian authorities that he would return to Tangail as soon as his wounds had healed.

Accordingly, along with his team of trusted freedom fighters, Kader Siddiqui left India on September 20th. He instructed the other commanders to go back to Tangail with their teams through different border outposts.

Kader's team safely entered Jamalpur district. They traveled by boat via the Jamuna River near Bahadurabad. On the way, he encountered only one skirmish with the enemy.

It took them a week to reach Shashuachar on the bank of the Jamuna River via Jhawail of Gopalpur. For three days, incessant rainfall continued and his team was confined to a house in the Shashuachar Village. Unfortunately, the area surrounding Shashuachar was incredibly poverty-stricken. While a home elsewhere might have had the means to sustain such a large party, such a daunting task was outside of the capacity of such a poor village. The freedom fighters were left without food for three days. They were hungry and tired.

Bahauddin, one of my classmates at the university, was the commander of the volunteer group of that area. On the fourth day, the rain finally stopped. Bahauddin had finally managed to get some food for the freedom fighters.

By then, the other commanders had also entered Tangail following Kader's instructions. Kader re-organized the groups and asked them to launch an attack against the fortified enemy posts at Gopalpur and Bhuapur.

The Martyrs of Bhuapur

On October 8th, a team of freedom fighters led by Commander Habib attacked the enemy camp at Bhuapur Bazaar. Commander Arzu, Angur and Rafiq and their respective teams joined Habib's team. Habib had become famous for destroying enemy ships.

Two of Habib's bravest soldiers were Quddus and Salam, both from the Bhuapur area. Quddus was a student leader of Bhuapur College and a local of the nearby Chabbisha village. Abdus Salam was also a local from nearby Borolokerpara village.

Quddus and Salem had sworn to themselves that they would give their lives to make Bhuapur free of the enemy.

With some help from India, the Mukti Bahini was now equipped with modern weapons. The freedom fighters were now armed with light machine guns, mortars, Sten guns, grenades and rocket launchers.

At midnight, Habib's team swiftly moved in on the enemy posts at Bhuapur Bazaar.

As Kudus and Salam were locals, they were very familiar with the network of alleys, which made up Bhuapur Bazaar. Kudus and Salam guided the team to strategic vantage points throughout the bazaar. Once in position, Habib initiated the attack by firing mortars. The freedom fighter's guns roared through the marketplace, raining down upon their enemy targets.

The intensity and firepower of the Mukti Bahini attack had caught the Pakistani Army by surprise. As fortified as their position was, the occupation forces were unable to defend themselves against such a fierce freedom fighter attack.

By dawn, the Mukti Bahini had defeated the enemy. Many Pakistani soldiers were killed. Those who survived surrendered along with the local Razakars.

As the early morning sun washed over the mortar-scorched earth of the bazaar, the Mukti Bahini celebrated their victory. Sadly, their celebration was short-lived.

While scavenging the battlefield for the dead, some of Habib's men came across two dead bodies. The bodies were of Quddus and Salam.

Quddus and Salam had bravely stormed into the heart of the enemy's position. Unfortunately, as bullets pierced through each of their chests, destiny had called them to fulfill their promise to their hometown. The sacrifice of their blood made Bhuapur free from then on.

Meanwhile, a team of freedom fighters under the leadership of Commander Hakim launched their attack simultaneously on Gopalpur police station. The teams of Commander Humayun, Commander Tara, and Commander Benu joined the attack.

They intensified their strike to capture the enemy camp at Gopalpur police headquarters. However, in spite of all their heroic attempts, they did not succeed. Later, freedom fighters assembled from all directions and created a siege around the enemy soldiers.

During the first week of October, Kader entered Tangail. We received news of his safe arrival immediately. We at the headquarters were overjoyed. Kader's return to Tangail was a huge morale booster.

The news of recapturing Bhuapur came to us shortly thereafter. Unfortunately, this victory was tainted with the news of Quddus and Salam's death. Shaheed and I were particularly close to Quddus, as he too was once a student leader like us.

A Setback at Nagarpur

After the dust at Bhuapur had settled, Kader mobilized his forces south towards the enemy's position at the Nagarpur police station.

Commanders Sabur and Humayun joined Kader's strike on the police station. The plan was that Humayun's company would attack the enemy position with a mortar launch led by Samad Gama. Their objective was to shut down the road so that the enemy could not move. This would allow Kader's squad to attack Nagarpur from the other side.

Unfortunately, Humayun's team failed to cut off the road and the enemy attacked Kader's squad from the rear. With an enemy fortified position in the front and enemy forces from behind, Kader's team was sandwiched. Under direct fire, they had no choice but to save their lives by jumping into a canal.

Sabur lead the retreat. He made it safely across the water hyacinth-covered canal finding a shallow path. However, Kader's path across the canal was not as smooth. The water level of the canal where he crossed was quite deep. Needing one hand to clear the water hyacinth, Kader struggled to swim with his favorite LMG. He was drowning.

This LMG had been with Kader since the beginning of the war. It was his lucky charm. He did not want to lose it. However, the weight of the LMG was pulling him down into the water.

Commander Sabur saw the dilemma of his commander and shouted, "Sir, leave the LMG. Swim to the bank".

Kader had no choice, but to drop his gun.

The Mukti Bahini repositioned and returned fire at the enemy. One hundred yards apart, they were face to face with enemy.

However, the Pakistani Army had good cover. They shot at Kader's squad from higher grounds behind Nagarpur-Tangail Road.

On the other hand, the Mukti Bahini had no cover. They were fighting an uphill battle from an open space. Moreover, as Kader and Sabur's teams had been detached from the main squad, the enemy had heavily outnumbered them. It was only a matter of time before Kader and his men were killed.

Suddenly, Commander Sabur, risking his life, took position with absolutely no cover in the middle of an open space and began firing. He continued his barrage for two minutes.

Meanwhile, Kader and his men quickly ran and took cover. They retaliated from a new position behind a nearby house. The Pakistani Army soldiers were forced to retreat to their camp at Nagarpur police station.

Sabur then dived deep into the water, rescued Kader's LMG and returned it to his commander. Had Commander Sabur not risked his life, Kader and his squad would have been gunned down. The history of the Tangail Mukti Bahini would not have been the same.

Commander Sabur had no prior military training. Prior to the war, he was a young construction worker. However, he rose to the occasion. He was a ferocious fighter with a rare combination of wit and courage. He had great agility. During the nine-month war, he displayed his heroism repeatedly.

Kader's Return to Headquarters

At the headquarters we were all eagerly awaiting news of Kader's arrival. Finally, we had received a message that Kader would arrive on October 15th.

Captain Fazlur Rahman was assigned to escort Kader to the headquarters. We arranged a mass reception for Kader by organizing a public meeting at Sakhipur. Shaheed took on the responsibility of organizing the event.

While in Kedarpur, Kader had inquired of me. As he had not heard from me since I had left to escort his family to Dhaka, Kader was eager to know of their whereabouts.

Several of us left the headquarters for the ferry station at Sangrampur where we waited to receive Kader.

As his team approached in a convoy of five boats, a crowd had gathered at the dock chanting patriotic slogans: "Joy Bangla, Long live Kader Siddiqui!"

I could see Kader standing at the front of his boat, carefully scanning the crowd. He looked so intently, as if to drown out the cheers of the crowd.

Suddenly, his eyes gleamed brightly and he began to wave. The boat had merely kissed the shore before Kader jumped out and began shouting, "Nuran Nabi! Where is my mother? Where are my brothers and sisters? Are they safe?"

I pushed through the crowd, making my way to greet Kader. I responded, "Sir, your mother and siblings are all safe in Dhaka."

Kader immediately embraced me. From the look on his face it was clear that two months of worry and concern were finally over. Kader was at ease.

Kader walked down to Sakhipur. Hundreds of freedom fighters and local people followed him.

Shaheed, Shahjada, and Basit received Kader at the public meeting. There were thousands of people in attendance making it the largest public meeting in the liberated zone ever.

The return of Kader Siddiqui created a festive atmosphere. In his public address, Kader expressed his sympathies for those who had been victimized by the occupation forces during his absence. He also commended Shaheed and other leaders for the maintaining discipline within the Mukti Bahini in his absence. Above all, he swore to the people that the enemy would be driven away and the country would soon become free.

Kader met with us in the evening. We briefed him on everything that had happened in the last two months. However, as we reminisced, a secret was revealed.

For the first time, Kader disclosed to the other commanders that Shaheed did not actually meet with him in India. In fact, Shaheed never even made it to India.

Shaheed's story was fabricated in order to restore discipline within the Mukti Bahini. Everybody was surprised except for the few of us who knew the secret.

This was just one instance of quick wit amongst millions during the liberation war. If not for Shaheed's guile, the reputation of the Tangail Mukti Bahini would be different.

The next morning, Kader met the commanders again to redistribute their responsibilities. The Mukti Bahini outposts were again installed at different locations. A new plan of attack was chalked out for the eastern zone.

Martyrs Momen, Hanif, Rocket and Amir

Commanders Fazlu and Mustafa lead an attack on the enemy camp at Balla. A fierce fight continued for two grueling days.

There were four young freedom fighters in particular who fought courageously during this battle. Their names were Momen, Hanif, Rocket, and Amir. They were teenagers, but they fought like grown men.

Sadly, these four heroes fell victim to the treacherous actions of a Razakar. The Razakar had revealed their position to the enemy.

Momen, Hanif, Rocket, and Amir were gunned down by enemy machine guns. Another six freedom fighters suffered injuries.

The enemy had also sustained heavy losses. Twenty enemy soldiers were killed. Though Fazlu and Mustafa's teams were unable to occupy the enemy camp, they were able to keep the Pakistani Army under siege.

Meanwhile, Kader left the headquarters. Just as he did before sustaining his injuries, Kader began his usual lightening tours. His squad was always on the move. They traveled ten to fifteen miles every day on foot and by boat from camp to camp.

Kader visited a number of camps in the hilly areas and then went to the western zone near the Jamuna River.

He called a meeting of the commanders of the western zone. Kader had reorganized their troops and drafted a new war strategy for the region.

The Fate of Operation Thunder

I briefed Kader on Operation Thunder. He approved this operation with enthusiasm. He instructed us to bring Salam to the free zone in order to train him in the handling of explosives.

Salam came to the free zone and was trained for a couple of weeks and then went back to Dhaka with explosives.

When I first met Salam, he carried a briefcase. Our plan was to have Salam smuggle a small amount of explosives in his briefcase everyday and store them at the meteorological office. Once he had gathered enough explosive material, he would put his training to use.

Unfortunately, in apprehension of a possible war with India, the Pakistani military authority revoked all civilian passes to the area before Salam could smuggle enough explosives.

Suddenly, Salam's entry into the office was prohibited, and thus, Operation Thunder was silenced. Regardless, the heroism and efforts that Salam displayed are not to be forgotten.

Freedom Fighters are moving freely in the liberated zone. (L-R) Engineer Salam, Author, Dr. Choudhury, Shaheed, Faruk and Nuru in the front and others in the back

Chapter 4

The Signal for Victory

My Third Mission to India

I spent the month of October at the Mukti Bahini headquarters. On October 24th, I received a message from Kader that I would have to go to India to discuss important matters with the government of Bangladesh as well as with the Indian Army.

This would be my third visit to India. This time Shaheed, Shahjada, Nuru, and Faruk would accompany me.

On October 25th, we left Sakhipur. We crossed about forty-five miles on foot and by boat. We reached Arjuna on the western side of the Jamuna River on October 27th.

Kader was waiting for us inside a worn out cottage. We had a meeting to discuss our responsibilities in India. Kader decided that this time, Shaheed would lead our team. Shaheed would meet the leaders of the government of Bangladesh in Calcutta in order to exchange ideas regarding the state of the liberation war.

Before the war broke out, Shaheed was the general secretary of Salimullah Hall Students' Union at Dhaka University, and a member of the central committee of the Students' League. This experience made him personally known to some of the leaders of the Bangladesh Government.

Nuru and Faruk were responsible for visiting the refugee and training camps of the freedom fighters along the Indian border. Their job was to publicize the successes of the Tangail Mukti Bahini.

As before, I was entrusted with the responsibility of meeting with the military authorities of both of Bangladesh and India, in order to discuss our future war strategies in detail.

In the afternoon of October 27th, we left for India by boat. On October 30th, we arrived at Mankachar on the Assam border. My previous trips to and from Mankachar were filled with danger and peril. However, this time we were better organized and equipped with a larger network of volunteers, making our journey efficient and smooth.

On the way to India (L-R) Author, Dr. Choudhury, Shaheed, Nuru, Faruk & Barman

The officials of the Bangladesh Army and Indian border security forces received us in Mankachar. However, we had no time to spare. There was much to do in a very short amount of time. We immediately began working on our responsibilities.

Nuru and Faruk stayed behind at the camps on the border. The Indian Army escorted Shaheed, Shahjada, and me to the training camps of the freedom fighters near Tura, the capital of Meghalaya.

After a full day of traveling by jeep, we reached the Indian Army camp near Tura. Major Mukherjee and Captain Bose received us. I introduced Shaheed and Shahjada to them. Just as my previous visits to India, arrangements were made for me to stay at this camp.

The next day, Shaheed and Shahjada flew to Calcutta.

General Aurora

On the morning of November 3rd, I went to see Brigadier Sant Singh at his office. This was our third meeting.

Through my previous two meetings with Brigadier Singh, we had established a strong personal bond.

Once again, he greeted me with the same warm spirit that I had come to know.

I handed over a letter from Kader and discussed the activities of the Tangail Mukti Bahini. We also reviewed the movement of the enemy forces.

At the end of the meeting, Brigadier Singh told me that the following day, I was to meet Major-General Gill, G. O. C. of the 101 Communication Zone of the Indian Army.

During my last visit, there were approximately a thousand freedom fighters receiving training at the Indian Army camp. Hundreds of Indian Army personnel were also present in the camp.

However this time, the number of both Mukti Bahini and Indian Army soldiers were much less. The camp seemed quite empty to me. This would be good news for the Liberation War. The freedom fighters I had met previously had since been trained and deployed throughout Bangladesh to fight for our cause.

The next day, Brigadier Singh picked me up from the camp. He drove himself, while his driver sat in the rear. I sat beside the brigadier.

We arrived at the headquarters of the Communication Corps of the Indian Army, which was located just outside Tura. Major-General Gill was waiting for us in his office.

I had barely saluted him before he stood up from his chair. He looked at Brigadier Singh and asked, "Is this the same Nuran Nabi?"

His smile peeked through his mustache as he came towards me. He quickly lifted me up in his arms, as a father would welcome his child home from school.

This was also my third meeting with General Gill. In my two previous meetings, my hair was long and I had a thick beard. I had worn a lungi and a shirt with sandals on my feet.

This time I was a clean-shaven Mukti Bahini with trimmed hair, wearing the trousers and dress shirt that I had bought in Dhaka.

General Gill asked me to take a seat.

After an exchange of greetings, General Gill said, "From your new look and attire, I can tell that the liberation war in Tangail must be going in your favor."

I nodded my head in affirmation and then handed him a letter and a cassette tape with a recorded message from Kader.

General Gill smiled again and said, "Yes, there is no doubt about it. There must have been some positive developments."

General Gill recalled our last meeting in August and how I had delivered Kader's letter to Brigadier Singh. Last time, I had no pockets in which to hide the letter. So I rolled my sleeves, hiding the letter within the creases.

Smiling, I said, "You are right, General. We are much stronger now than we were before. Since our last meeting, we have liberated additional areas of Bangladesh."

I then handed Kader's letter to the general. However, upon seeing his perplexed face, I realized that the letter was written in Bangla. I took the letter back and read it aloud, translating Kader's Bengali into English.

Fortunately, Kader's speech was recorded in Hindi. In his letter and recorded message, Kader had conveyed his sincere thanks and greetings to the Indian Army for their help and co-operation.

In regards to the Mukti Bahini's future plans he added, "Nuran Nabi's word would be as good as mine."

As per Kader's instructions, I discussed our progress, challenges, and future plans for the war. I answered the General's queries regarding the enemy's movement.

As the General had observed, we were more organized and disciplined than before.

At Kader's request, I presented General Gill with two important questions. First, I asked if he thought that the Bangladesh Liberation war would last long.

I then added, "If so, we are apprehensive that the enemy might launch a final strike to annihilate the sixteen-thousand freedom fighters that were now only forty miles from the Pakistani military headquarters in Dhaka. In this scenario, what kind of assistance could we expect from the Indian Army?"

At the end of our discussion, General Gill told me that he could not say anything at the moment, but he would meet me again after a few days. He then invited me to join him for lunch in the officers' mess hall.

As we sat for lunch, General Gill and I discussed a broad range of topics. He was particularly interested in knowing Tangail's landscape: its trees, its plants, its rivers, and the terrain around the Modhupur-Tangail Highway.

He inquired further, asking if there were tall bamboo forests or large trees along the highways. He was particularly interested in knowing whether the areas along Modhupur-Tangail Highway were under our control and whether the people of these areas were supporters of the liberation war.

While answering General Gill's questions, it never occurred to me to ask where his sudden curiosity had come from.

I stayed in the camp for another three days. I shared a room with Captain Bose, a Bengali captain of the Indian Army.

I was still anxious as I had yet to hear General Gill's response to Kader's two questions. These were very important issues, which concerned the life and death of sixteen thousand freedom fighters and fifty thousand volunteers stationed within enemy clutches. Our forces were more than one hundred miles away from the Indian border. If the Indian Army was going to help, we would need to know now.

Seeing that I was clearly stressed, Captain Bose did everything he could to cheer me up. As he knew that I loved the songs of Rabindranath Tagore, he managed to find some cassettes of Tagore's songs, which he played for me. He showed me around Tura. He also shared with me the story of his forefathers who migrated to India from Bangladesh. Captain Bose knew quite a lot about Bangladesh.

On November 7th, Brigadier Singh drove me to the office of General Gill for a meeting. General Gill received us, and without asking us to sit down in his office, took us to his car and drove us directly to the heliport.

A little taken back, I asked him "Are we going somewhere by helicopter? Where are we going?"

General Gill answered, "We aren't going anywhere. We are just going to receive a VIP at the heliport."

Then he added, "The meeting would take place at the heliport waiting room upon the arrival of our guest."

He and Brigadier Singh escorted me to the waiting room located next to the helipad and asked me to wait there. They both returned to the helipad.

As I saw General Gill and Brigadier Singh standing at the helipad, I pondered the identity of our VIP.

Moments later, an army helicopter landed and a Sikh military officer came out of the helicopter. General Gill and Brigadier Singh saluted him. Ducking their heads, the three men rushed to the waiting room.

I stood up and saluted the VIP. I introduced myself and then made a gesture to shake hands with the Sikh officer.

Suddenly, I felt a momentary sense of awkwardness come over me. At five feet two inches, I found myself standing before three bearded, turban-wearing Sikh officers who were much taller than me. I tilted my head to the sky just to look the third officer in the eyes.

He said, "I am Lieutenant-General Jagjit Singh Aurora."

He shook my hand. I had heard of General Aurora from Kader. He was the G. O. C. of the Eastern Command of the Indian Army. I never thought that I would meet him in such dramatic fashion.

I had to remind myself that I was not just a twenty-two year old university student. I was the representative of sixteen thousand freedom fighters. My word was as good as Kader's, the leader of the Tangail Mukti Bahini. I regained my confidence and was ready to engage in discussions.

I had a feeling that General Gill had already apprised General Aurora of the agenda of our earlier discussion. So I went straight to the point and raised those two issues.

While, General Aurora did not address my two questions directly, he did give me a hint.

As our meeting ended, we decided that I would return to Tangail very soon. Once there, I would make contact with General Gill. Upon my signal, several officers of the Indian Army would come to the free zones of Tangail and stay with us. We would be responsible for their security.

Our next assignment would be to secure an area of ten to twelve miles near the Tangail-Madhupur Highway by the end of November or early December so that Indian paratroopers could be dropped. Lastly, we would have to collect as much secret information about the enemy in Dhaka as possible.

At the end of the meeting, General Aurora cautioned me about the importance and secrecy of our discussion. He warned me that under no circumstance, should I share this information with anyone other than Kader Siddiqui.

He further mentioned that I was the first Bangladeshi person privy to the details of this top-secret military operation. He reminded me repeatedly of the importance of this message and asked me to comply accordingly. I swore to him on my life.

General Gill understood General Aurora's concern. However, to reassure General Aurora of my trustworthiness, General Gill mentioned that when Kader Siddiqui came over to India for medical treatment, he gave the responsibility of looking after his mother, brothers, and sisters to me. I was Kader's most trusted comrade.

General Aurora blushed. He stated that he had not questioned my trustworthiness. Nonetheless, maintaining the secrecy of this mission was of paramount importance.

Our meeting lasted for about half an hour. As we shook hands, General Aurora mentioned, "This is the Liberation War of your motherland. I am certain you will be able to make good on your promise to your country. I hope to see you in liberated Tangail."

Major General Gill and Brigadier Singh followed General Aurora to the waiting helicopter to see him off. As the helicopter took off, General Gill and Brigadier Singh walked towards the waiting room.

I stepped out of the waiting room and waited for General Gill and Brigadier Singh.

As he approached, the smiling General said, "I hope that you have now gotten answers to your two questions."

I smiled back. As I boarded Brigadier Singh's jeep, General Gill asked that I see him once more before I return to Tangail.

A Signal for Victory

In December, Indian paratroopers would land in Tangail. I asked myself repeatedly if this was a sign of our impending victory. As I returned to the camp, I felt my heart throb with joy and excitement.

Captain Bose received me at our tent and inquired into the subject matter of my discussion with General Gill. I did not mention General Aurora, but said that we discussed the state of the war in Tangail.

The next day, Brigadier Singh told me that I had to see his colleague Brigadier Klair. He was the commander of the 95th Mountain Brigade of the Indian Army. His office was situated on a hilly road about thirty miles from Tura.

This was my second meeting with Brigadier Klair. I met him once in August. As our conversation proceeded, I realized that he knew of the details of my discussion with General Aurora. He wanted to know the positions of the enemy camps at Bahadurabad ferry station, Jamalpur, and Modhupur. He inquired as to whether the Tangail Mukti Bahini could organize attacks in conjunction with the Indian Army at these locations, with the Indian Army coming from the north and the Mukti Bahini from the south.

I replied in affirmation. We then discussed some strategic matters.

While saying goodbye, this bearded and turban-headed Sikh officer smiled and said, "See you soon in Tangail!"

The next day I went to see General Ovan of the Indian Army. He was in charge of recruiting and training a special Mukti Bahini group known as the Mujib Bahini. The Mujib Bahini was an ideological force created to uphold the ideals of Bangabandhu Sheik Mujibur Rahman.

My visit with General Ovan was simply a courtesy call. The members of the Mujib Bahini were trained at a camp far from Tura. I met General Ovan near their camp. He was particularly interested in gauging the sincerity and loyalty of the Tangail Mukti Bahini to Bangabandhu Sheik Mujibur Rahman.

He also wanted to know how many freedom fighters in our group were from leftist political parties.

With my discussion with General Ovan, I had finally completed my responsibilities as planned.

I had become restless to return to Tangail. However, Shaheed and Shahjada still had not returned from Calcutta.

On November 12th, I again went to see General Gill. He instructed me to communicate with the Indian Army through long-distance wireless sets. He added that Brigadier Singh and I should choose cipher codes to communicate and coordinate the landing of paratroopers in Tangail.

I told him that I would see him soon in Tangail and said good-bye.

Shaheed and Shahjada Meet with the Prime Minster

Shaheed and Shahjada met the leaders of the Bangladesh Government in Calcutta and apprised them of the various activities of the Tangail Mukti Bahini.

Shaheed called on acting-president Syed Nazrul Islam, Prime Minister Tajuddin Ahmed, Captain Mansur Ali, Minister of Finance and Commerce, A. H. Quamruzzaman, Minister of Home and Rehabilitation, and Khondoker Moshtaque Ahmed, Minister of Foreign Affairs.

In his discussions, Shaheed covered different topics including the accomplishments and requirements of the Tangail Mukti Bahini.

Shaheed submitted the accounts of income and expenditures of the last few months of the Tangail Mukti Bahini. Minister Captain Mansur Ali expressed his satisfaction and complimented Shaheed for maintaining such neat accounts amidst such difficult circumstances.

The civil administration of the Tangail Mukti Bahini printed some cyclostyled copies of deeds and documents for the sale and purchase of properties with the monogram of the Government of Bangladesh.

Shaheed showed the documents to Moshtaque Ahmed, Minister in charge of Law and Parliamentary Affairs. Minister Ahmed conveyed his appreciation of our efforts as well.

Syed Nazrul Islam and Tajuddin Ahmed instructed Cabinet Secretary Toufiq Imam to issue an appointment letter to Shaheed as the Civil Administrator of the free zone of Tangail.

Shaheed also met two of the great sons of Tangail. One of them was Abdul Mannan, Member of the National Assembly. He was in charge of Free Bangladesh Radio. Abdul Mannan used a pseudonym for his on-air commentary on the war to protect his relatives.

On November 11th, an interview of Shaheed was aired on Free Bangladesh Radio. Mr. Mannan introduced Shaheed, but the interview was conducted by famous radio personality M. R. Akhtar Mukul.

The other important personality of Tangail was Khondoker Asaduzzaman. He was the Finance Secretary of the Bangladesh Government. Prior to the war, he was the Joint Secretary of the Finance Ministry of Pakistan.

During the non-cooperation movement, he defected to Bangladesh. On the 25th of March he was appointed the Principal Secretary of the Tangail Action Committee. Soon thereafter, he organized the first resistance against the Pakistani Military forces in Tangail. However, the Mukti Bahini was defeated and Tangail fell into enemy control. Pakistani forces retaliated by dynamiting Secretary Asaduzzaman's home.

Secretary Asaduzzaman was a high-ranking bureaucrat who dedicated himself to creating an independent Bangladesh.

Despite his personal loss and relocation to Calcutta, his heart was with the Tangail Mukti Bahini. He helped us in any way he could and conveyed his sincerest greetings to the Tangail Mukti Bahini through Shaheed.

Shaheed also met Col. Osmani, the Chief of Staff for the Bangladesh Liberation Forces. They discussed the current affairs of the war in Tangail.

In the office of Col. Osmani, there was a map in which the positions of the Mukti Bahini and enemy forces had been identified with red and blue markers. Most of Tangail was now shown as a liberated land.

Shaheed also met other high profile Bengali intellectuals such as Ghaziul Huq, a leader of the language movement, Quamrul Hassan, a famous artist, Zahir Raihan, a famous film producer.

Shaheed told them of the activities of the Tangail Mukti Bahini. He also met Captain A. K. Khondoker, Col. M. A. Rob, Major Salahuddin and Lieutenant Sheikh Kamal. Kamal was the oldest son of Bangabandhu Sheikh Mujibur Rahman and was the ADC to Col. Osmani.

Additionally, Shaheed met the representatives of foreign news agencies and shared with them his account of the war from an area inside the country only forty miles from Dhaka.

Among the reporters he spoke with were Lionel Limb of the BBC, Arnold Zeitlin of the Associated Press, Mr. Hersein of German Television and a representative of Radio Australia.

Shaheed also met four youth leaders of the Awami League, namely Sheikh Moni, Abdur Razzak, Serajul Alam Khan, and Tofael Ahmed. They were very close to Bangabandhu Sheik Mujibur Rahman prior to the war.

Meanwhile, Shahjada met with the Bangladesh Government Health Secretary, Dr. T. Hossain with whom he discussed the health situation and medical supplies of the Tangail Mukti Bahini.

Shaheed and Shahjada came back to Tura on November 17th. In the meantime, two of my companions, Nuru and Faruk were engaged in public relations activities with freedom fighters around Mankachar.

Conspiracies against the Tangail Mukti Bahini

Initially, Shaheed's meeting with the Bangladesh Government was not an easy task. He heard complaints against the Tangail Mukti Bahini including allegations of extortion. However, he knew exactly who was behind it.

Before the war broke out, there were some rivalries between two student leaders of Tangail, namely Shahjahan Siraj and Latif Siddiqui. This conflict spilled over to the liberation war. Latif was Kader Siddiqui's older brother.

When Kader organized the Tangail Mukti Bahini, Baten, one of Shahjahan Siraj's followers, organized a separate group of the Mukti Bahini at Nagarpur.

In June, Kader sent a group of freedom fighters to Nagarpur to capture the police station. It was alleged that some members of Baten's groups in the Nagarpur area killed Commander Labib and his associate, Jahangir. This sad event created some animosity between the two factions.

Some fabricated complaints were lodged against the Tangail Mukti Bahini and reported to the Bangladesh Government. Various groups hatched these complaints to undermine Kader's reputation. In addition to the past conflict, these accusers were motivated by selfish interest, jealousy and above all, the prospect of future influence in a post-independent Tangail.

Though the Indian Army warmly greeted Kader during his August and September stay in India, the members of the Bangladesh Government snubbed him. Not a single member of the Bangladesh Government chose to contact Kader during his stay in India.

Shaheed took the opportunity to counter the allegations and explained the situation to the Bangladesh Government officials during his meeting with them.

He pointed out that there was neither government financing, nor arrangements of food supplies for the Tangail Mukti Bahini. However, we needed to feed and support the seventeen thousand freedom fighters in the Tangail Mukti Bahini.

Spontaneous and unsolicited help from various people kept us going. They gave us food and shelter. Those who could afford it, donated money to support the Mukti Bahini. It is through this generosity that we had been able to survive.

Shaheed and I had earned the respect of Bangladesh Government officials and the Indian Army Generals, respectively. We were Kader's closest and most trusted associates. Our reputation helped to clear the name of the Tangail Mukti Bahini.

Shaheed was the General Secretary of Salimullah Muslim Hall Student's Union of Dhaka University and a central leader of the Student League. The post of General Secretary of Salimullah Hall was a very prestigious one in those days. Acting President Syed Nazrul Islam was once the Vice-President of the Student Union of the Salimullah Muslim Hall.

I was also a student of Dhaka University and known to some of the Bangladesh Government leaders. However, I had also become personally acquainted with Lt. General Aurora, Major General Gill, Brigadier Sanat Singh, and Brigadier Klair.

I was able to present a very positive image of the Tangail Mukti Bahini to the Indian Army, and they had graciously reported their findings to the Bangladesh Government officials.

In spite of the impact of our reputations, Shaheed's meeting was very necessary to settle the misunderstandings between Kader and the Bangladesh Government.

Shaheed was able to dispel the air of suspicion. He apprised acting President Syed Nazrul Islam, Prime Minister Tajuddin Ahmed,

Commander-in-Chief of the Mukti Bahini, Col. Osmani, and others of the activities of the Tangail Mukti Bahini. Finally, they appreciated our contribution to the liberation war and sent their personal greetings to Kader Siddiqui.

Back in July, when I first came over to India, I had also sensed some suspicion towards the Tangail Mukti Bahini. Though Major General Gill and Brigadier Sanat Singh received me cordially, Captain Bose had asked me some rather embarrassing questions.

Captain Bose asked me how much cash and gold I had been carrying.

Literally, I came to India empty-handed. I had a lungi, a pocketless-shirt, and a pair of sponge flip-flops on my feet. The only item I carried was a note from Kader Siddiqui that was hidden within the folds of my shirtsleeve. I had nothing else with me. I was visibly embarrassed by his question. Captain Bose apologized and said, "There is a rumor that Kader had extorted quite a bit of cash and gold."

I explained to Captain Bose the constraints under which we arranged food and other supplies for seventeen thousand freedom fighters.

The Indian Army was also able to corroborate this information. They knew of the success of our military operations against the enemy, as they were able to intercept Pakistani Army radio messages.

My meeting with General Gill was also very meaningful in establishing the Mukti Bahini's reputation. When I first met the general, I told him that the only purpose of my visit to India was to secure arms and ammunition.

He assured me of the supplies and proposed that I should go to Calcutta to relax for a few days.

However, I modestly declined the proposal. I explained that the liberation war was gaining momentum inside the country. At that juncture of time, the sooner I had returned with arms the better our chances would be for winning the war.

General Gill was astonished by my response and expressed that he was encouraged by my dedication to the liberation war.

My response on that day certainly helped to create a positive image about Tangail Mukti Bahini and to undo some of the false allegations against the Tangail Mukti Bahini.

Bullets of '71: A Freedom Fighter's Story

Shaheed and my efforts put the conspiracy against the Tangail Mukti Bahini to rest.

Conspiracy against Prime Minister Tajuddin

In the absence of Bangabandhu, Prime Minister Tajuddin successfully led the liberation war. Though his family lived nearby, during the nine months of war Prime Minister Tajuddin slept in the Prime Minister's office and personally washed his only shirt by hand. He established a standard of discipline and became the role model for others. Unfortunately, Prime Minister Tajuddin faced a myriad of challenges, some of which came from within his own circle.

Khondoker Moshtaque Ahmed, a minister & colleague of Prime Minister Tajuddin was the first to conspire against him.

Khondoker Moshtaque established a secret meeting with an American diplomat in Calcutta to prevent the complete independence of Bangladesh. Instead, he intended to keep Bangladesh within a loose confederation with Pakistan. Such an alignment would have rendered the efforts of the liberation war useless.

The second conspiracy took place with the provocation of a parliamentary group of the Awami League. A few parliamentarians moved for a no-confidence motion against Tajuddin Ahmed in the meeting of the parliamentary group.

Fortunately, Tajuddin thwarted these conspirators with patience and dexterity, and was able to lead the liberation war.

Tajuddin Ahmed was a veteran, a selfless and a dedicated leader, who was trusted by Bangabandhu Sheikh Mujibur Rahman. However, when it became apparent that there were people lurking in the shadows waiting to conspire against a leader of such noble stature as Prime Minister Tajuddin's, it became obvious that the Tangail Mukti Bahini would be an easy prey to such conspirators as well.

History is littered with such stories and has proven that patriots and traitors often coexist side by side.

An Atrocity at Bhuapur

On November 21st, we left Mankachar by boat for Tangail with the secret message from General Aurora. However, this time we had a new companion, Abdul Latif Siddiqui, a member of parliament. Kader asked that we request Latif to join us in the free zone. He was Kader's older brother and our former student leader.

We were on the boat for two days and two nights. During this journey, Latif recounted various anecdotes of the past including his experiences in Calcutta. Everyone listened attentively - everyone except me.

I had other thoughts spinning in my head. I was restless.

I began counting the days until I would return to Tangail.

Shaheed tried to engage me by asking me about the status of my mission. I told him that the army authorities of India had asked us to collect secret information on the enemy. However, I couldn't share with him the information I was entrusted with regarding the paratroopers landing in Tangail.

Fortunately, we had wind and tide in our favor. We safely reached Bhuapur on November 23rd. As I got off the boat, I expected to meet Kader at Bhuapur and share the top-secret information with him right away. However, when we got to shore, we were met with some rather unfortunate news.

Bhuapur headquarters had been under Mukti Bahini control. On November 17th, a battalion of Pakistani forces launched an attack on the Mukti Bahini at Bhuapur.

A company of freedom fighters led by Commander Major Abdul Hakim put up a strong resistance. There were no freedom fighter casualties. However, while retreating, the enemy set fire to the nearby village of Chabbisha. They killed several villagers by brush fire and threw a number of old men, women, and children into the flames.

We heard the rumor that Pakistani forces also raped several women. However, people were reluctant to talk about it out of shame.

The messenger carrying this horrific news to Kader was caught and killed by enemy forces as well. Kader and others in the headquarters were unaware of the atrocity perpetrated by the retreating Pakistani forces.

Immediately after our arrival at the village, we began rehabilitation services. As the village was near my hometown, I knew the locality fairly well.

In the early months of the liberation war, Shaheed and I had visited this village a number of times. I knew many of the victims personally. We were deeply moved by the suffering of the surviving villagers.

Luckily, we had with us some medicine, winter clothes and cash, which we brought with us from India. Not to mention we had Dr. Shahjada Chowdhury with us who was able to provide his services.

We worked around the clock for five consecutive days. Local freedom fighters and volunteers came forward to help the victims. We were able to boost the morale of the people of Chabbisha.

However, despite the buffer gained by getting to Bhuapur so quickly, I was now running out of time. Again, I was getting restless. I needed to get General Aurora's message to Kader. Time was no longer on my side.

Fortunately, our diligence and that of the volunteers allowed us to proceed towards Kedarpur to meet Kader.

Secret Message

We arrived at Kedarpur on November 29th. Commander Sabur and his platoon received us at the landing station on the river. They informed us that Kader was on his way to welcome us. However, waiting for Kader in an open area near the river was a bad idea. Instead, we walked towards Kader's camp. By now it had gotten quite dark.

As we advanced some distance, we met Kader. He was extremely glad to see us and warmly embraced his elder brother Latif Siddiqui. He then embraced each of us - me, Shaheed, Dr. Shahjada Chowdhury, Nuru and Faruk.

As we reached Kader's camp at Kedarpur, a platoon of freedom fighters led by Col. Fazlur Rahman received us with a formal guard of honor. We were accommodated at Kader's camp.

After dinner, we sat in a room and indulged ourselves in a discussion of the events that happened during last nine months. Latif was the central attraction in our meeting.

Everybody present enjoyed the deliberation, as we all had been involved in student politics of Tangail under the leadership of Latif. This was the first such occasion since the Liberation War began that Latif, Kader, Shaheed and others met in the liberated zone. Our discussion continued long after midnight.

However, I was growing restless. I still had not gotten the chance to pass the secret message to Kader. He was always with someone.

In the meeting, Kader, Latif, and Shaheed sat next to each other. If I asked Kader to come out to speak with me, it would look odd. Such a gesture would be noticed and could possibly affect the mood of the meeting. I had no choice, but to wait for the right moment.

At about two in the morning, when everybody was asleep, I whispered to Kader that there was something secret I had to discuss with him.

Kader said, "Let's go outside."

It was dark, so as we came out, the guards stopped us and asked whether they should follow us. Kader declined their offer and asked that they stay behind.

We moved to the other end of the courtyard and sat on a bench. I talked in a very low voice. I laid out the details of my conversation with General Gill and General Aurora to Kader. I emphasized the pending arrival of the Indian Army officers in Tangail. I especially mentioned the landing of the paratroopers at the free zone near Tangail-Madhupur Highway in the first half of December. We talked almost for an hour about our future plan.

Kader told me that the following morning, he would send messages to General Gill using a secret password to allow Indian officers to come to the free zone, and he would also take the necessary measures to facilitate the landing of the paratroopers.

We knew the significance of Indian paratroopers landing on the Tangail-Madhupur Highway. It was a clear sign that our long-cherished victory was pending. We embraced each other.

It was decided that the war strategy must be kept between the two of us. I felt a great relief after disclosing the top-secret information to Kader. I felt as if a huge burden was taken off of my shoulders. For the first time since November 7th, I went to bed with some peace of mind.

Setback at Nagarpur

On the morning of November 30th, the security guards woke me up. I saw that Shaheed and Latif were already dressed.

Latif said, "Hurry up. Get ready. Kader is waiting for us."

Bullets of '71: A Freedom Fighter's Story

I got ready quickly and the three of us started walking along the bank of the river. After half a mile, we saw that Kader was ready with about a thousand armed freedom fighters to attack Nagarpur enemy headquarters.

He was briefing his commanders with detailed instructions for the offensive against the enemy position. We wished them success in the attack and said good-bye.

Author (extreme right) with Shaheed, Kader and other Mukti Bahini before Nagarpur attack

The freedom fighters divided themselves into various groups and marched towards the enemy positions.

Around noon, we heard the first sounds of battle. Our freedom fighters were equipped with automatic machine guns and mortars. The whole area trembled from the blast of our two three-inch mortars. The firing continued for the whole day.

The enemy was stationed at the police station headquarters at Nagarpur. They had a fortified position around their perimeter. They were firing defensively from concrete bunkers, waiting for reinforcement from the Tangail enemy garrison.

Our plan was to capture the enemy position before sunset. We received information in the night that our offensive had failed and several freedom fighters were wounded in the battle. However, the freedom fighters were able to surround the enemy. They would attack again in the morning.

The next day, on December 1st, Shaheed and I proceeded towards Nagarpur to get the latest updates from the battlefield. Three Mukti Bahini soldiers escorted us along the elevated village road.

We approached the enemy position from the east, behind the frontline of the Mukti Bahini position. We thought we were safe. However, we were suddenly greeted by enemy gunfire. We were sitting ducks!

From the security of their concrete bunkers, the Pakistani Army scoped us with their binoculars. As a barrage of gunfire rained down on us, we jumped down from the road and took cover behind the wall of a nearby home. The frontline Mukti Bahini forces counter-fired on the enemy position.

For the third time, I narrowly escaped death. Maybe it was luck, or maybe divine intervention, but someone was looking out for me. I knew I had yet to serve a higher purpose.

We took a detour walking below the road and behind the houses. Finally, we reached the camp of Commander Fazlu.

Fazlu briefed us on what had happened the previous day. The Mukti Bahini attacked the enemy positions as per our original plan. They made a surprise lightening attack on the enemy position from three sides, keeping the western side open. The Mukti Bahini continued their fierce thrust for two hours.

Pakistani forces were shaken by the ferocity of the attack from the three sides. Moreover, they were intimidated by the mortar attack. At about sixteen hundred hours, the enemy started to escape to Tangail through the Western flank. This was all part of Kader's original plan. They were falling into our trap.

However, an overenthusiastic platoon of freedom fighters attacked the fleeing Pakistani soldiers from the west and thus, blocked their escape route. The Pakistan soldiers then retreated to their well-protected bunkers and resumed their firing in self-defense. From here, they dispatched an S.O.S. to the Tangail garrison for reinforcements.

Fazlu told us that Shamsul Huq of his platoon was seriously wounded at a distance of twenty to twenty-five yards from the enemy bunkers and was confined to the ground for several hours.

Freedom fighters could not rescue him since there was no cover in between the freedom fighters' position and that of the enemy forces.

However, it was against the freedom fighter oath to leave a wounded soldier behind. Abul Kalam of Fazlu's platoon volunteered and took the challenge. At the risk of his own life, he slowly crawled to Shamsu and dragged his body to a safe place. Immediately, Shamsu was given medical treatment.

Meanwhile, a contingent of Pakistani forces had been moving toward Nagarpur from Tangail garrison to rescue the soldiers under-siege by the Mukti Bahini.

After receiving the information, Kader immediately marched towards Elasin Ferry Station on the Dhaleshwari River with a company of freedom fighters to resist the enemy's movement.

Commander Fazlu warned us that it was not safe for us to stay. We came back to Kaderpur.

In the evening, Commander Rabiul reported that the Mukti Bahini was in jeopardy at Elasin. The Pakistani forces launched a sudden attack and captured several freedom fighters including Commander Sabur and Commander Fazlu. Kader was positioned away from them and therefore, was unaware of their predicament.

Everyone stationed at Kedarpur camp became very worried. We were anxious to know more about this set back. Both Fazlu and Sabur were valiant freedom fighters. Their valor was known all around. It was hard to believe that they had been captured alive by the enemy.

We were shocked and worried for all of them. If something happened to Kader, what would be the future of the Tangail Mukti Bahini? We were bothered by such thoughts.

Latif was so worried for his younger brother that he began to weep in front every one.

Shaheed and I got very worried as well. However, we tried to maintain our composure. We were all too aware of how the chain of command had broken down within the Mukti Bahini in Kader's absence. We did our best to find out about Kader's whereabouts.

A little later, Col. Fazlu Rahman came back and told us that Kader was safe. A few moments later, Commander Fazlu showed up to confirm the report. We were all relieved.

However, at about midnight, we became anxious again. Commander Fazlu confessed that he never had information on Kader's safety. Under the insistence of Col. Fazlu Rahman he lied to us. Once again, anxiety gripped us throughout the night.

In the morning, a messenger, named Bachchu showed up to report that Kader was all right and he would arrive at Kedarpur in two hours. He would carry the dead bodies of two freedom fighters with him.

They had become martyrs yesterday at Elasin. Kader instructed us to prepare graves for the burial of these fallen soldiers.

At noon, Kader arrived with the dead bodies. The presence of Kader was very heartening for us. However, the dead bodies made us sad.

We had already arranged for their burial. We had purchased land in front of the mosque at Kedarpur.

We conducted a Janaja prayer, led by the imam of the mosque where hundreds of villagers were in attendance. Their caskets were adorned with the Bangladesh flag. We then followed with a twelve-gun salute, before finally laying our comrades to rest.

After the burial rituals, Kader told us the truth about yesterday's unfortunate chain of events.

Before Kader could reach Elasin, Pakistani forces had already made it to the other side of the river.

Kader instructed Commander Moinuddin to establish a defense at the bank of the river, while Kader's company moved northwest along the river.

There was a possibility that the enemy would move to Nagarpur from a position on the river where the water level was low. This assumption was the basis for Kader's strategy.

Commander Rabiul followed Kader. Nearby, Commander Razzak's company was positioned to help resist the Pakistani forces.

Kader continued along the river passing Commander Razzak's position. Suddenly, a shower of LMG bullets came down on Kader and his men.

Kader and his team jumped down into a ditch to save their lives. The enemy fired from the other side of the river. Luckily, the enemy was positioned too far away to pose much of a threat.

Kader moved further north to get a better idea of the enemy's location. As he walked, he found that the companies of Sabur and Rabiul were positioned nearby waiting for the enemy.

Kader instructed them to follow him while maintaining a safe distance as he advanced farther northwest.

Kader was looking for a dry sandy surface in the middle of the riverbed, from which his men could find cover.

Before Kader could move two hundred yards, he faced yet another barrage of bullets. There was no place to hide. With such shallow grass, even lying on the ground would not help. So Kader began running as fast as he could. Luckily he found a channel to the west, where he could hide. Only seven freedom fighters were able to join him. Commanders Sabur and Rabiul and their men were nowhere to be seen.

Kader quickly took a defensive position, but found that a team of Pakistani soldiers was already on the same side of the river. They were only twenty-five to thirty yards away. They were moving towards Kader's position under the cover of a sand strip.

Kader did not waste a minute to fire on the enemy. The enemy returned fire. An enemy bullet hit a freedom fighter named Sanowar. Kader and Abdullah continued firing without pause and succeeded in keeping the enemy from advancing. As Kader and Abdullah provided cover, Kader instructed his men, including Sanowar, to retreat to safety. After his men were safe, Kader and Abdullah continued firing, while back-pedaling to a safer position.

Kader later came to know that Commander Rabiul was positioned at a comparatively high position on the riverside. The Pakistani soldiers noticed Rabiul's position. Hiding behind the sand strip, the enemy attacked Rabiul's company from the side. Rabiul was caught off-guard by the enemy's side attack. Panicking, Rabiul and small group of his men fled for safety.

However, he left behind a small group of his company who bravely resisted the attack and fired back on the enemy. They were able to kill several enemy soldiers, but unfortunately, two of their comrades were wounded. Under intense enemy fire, the freedom fighters were forced to leave the wounded behind and retreat for safety. Sadly, as soon as the freedom fighters had retreated, the enemy advanced on the two wounded soldiers. They brutally stabbed the wounded men several times with their bayonets and killed them.

Although they were unable to save two of their fellow soldiers, the bravery of this small group of men, who without their commander, were able to put up a fight, which ultimately allowed Kader and his one-hundred freedom fighters to disperse and retreat to safety.

Kader took shelter in a house with a wounded Sanowar, who was given some medical treatment. In the morning, Kader rescued the dead bodies of the two comrades and arrived at Kedarpur.

The Pakistani Army arrived at Nagarpur to rescue their fellow soldiers, before leaving for Tangail garrison.

Finally, Nagarpur was liberated forever. However, the cost was quite high, two freedom fighters were wounded and another two had given their lives to the liberation of Nagarpur.

As soon as Kader finished his narration, our trusted messenger, Badsha, arrived. He reported that one officer of the Indian Army had arrived at Bhuapur last night. He wished to see Kader and me as soon as possible.

Though I was eagerly waiting for the arrival of the Indian Army, I didn't expect that he would arrive so soon. Kader instructed me to go to Bhuapur to take care of the security and hospitality of the Indian officer.

Badsha and I left for Bhuapur on bicycle to meet the Indian Army officer.

Landing of Indian Paratroopers in Tangail

On December 3rd, Badsha and I reached the village of Baroiotol on the Dhaleshwari River near Bhuapur. The Indian officer was waiting for us in a house at that village.

When we met him, he introduced himself as Peter, a Captain of the Signal Corps of the Indian Army. He was a Bengali from Calcutta.

As we exchanged greetings, I came to understand that the captain had detailed information about Kader and me. He carried our photographs with him, as well.

We exchanged passwords, as predetermined by Brigadier Sanat Singh, and established confidence with each other. He conveyed the greetings of General Gill, Brigadier Sanat Singh, and Brigadier Klair to me, as well as, to Kader.

Captain Peter explained that he had been waiting at Mankachar on the border of Assam for a week in anticipation of our signal. I told him that because of the disaster at Chabbisha, we could not send the signal in time.

With time running out, he had no choice but to set off for Tangail District. He couldn't continue to wait for a signal from our side. Fortunately, he received our signal in the midst of his journey.

Captain Peter arrived in the free zone just last night. He was escorted by five freedom fighters, three of which were trained wireless set operators.

I wanted to apprise him of our activities. However, he declined to listen.

He politely said, "That's not necessary, I received a detailed briefing from Brigadier Sanat Singh and Brigadier Klair."

Captain Peter was arguably the first Indian Army officer to infiltrate more than one hundred miles within the Bangladesh free zone before December.

We had dinner together and spent the night on two boats on the Dhaleswari River.

The next morning, I came to learn that Kader was on his way to meet us. When Kader arrived, he and Peter greeted each other warmly. Immediately after Kader's arrival, the three of us sat down for a discussion inside one of the boats.

Peter informed us that he had already established contact with the Indian High Command through the use of a long distance wireless set.

His primary mission here was to select the strategic locations for the landing of the Indian paratroopers and send any relevant information to Indian High Command.

Peter then reiterated the details of my discussion with General Gill at Tura the previous month. He also requested that we plan an attack on the enemy at Bahadurabad Ferry Station, Jamalpur, and Modhupur to stifle enemy communication.

As I had already discussed these matters with Kader, he had instructed Commander Anis to attack the enemy position at Bahadurabad Ferry Station.

After the meeting with Captain Peter and me, Kader worked feverishly to organize the deployment of the entire Mukti Bahini for a final offensive against the enemy. He instructed the seventy commanders on their specific targets.

Captain Peter, my team, and I started testing the wireless sets.

After dinner, Kader met with Peter and me for further discussion on the boat. With the help of a kerosene lamp, we examined the Indian Army's map of Tangail District. We examined possible safe-pockets in which the paratroopers could land.

By then, Kader had already instructed some of his most trustworthy men to inspect the spots personally and report back to him.

We had established that the first criteria for picking a safe landing zone was to ensure that the spot was in close proximity to the Tangail-Madhupur Highway so that the paratroopers' heavy guns and vehicles could easily get to the highway. The other criteria we chose for a safe-spot was that the freedom fighters would be capable of protecting the paratroopers under any circumstance, during and after their landing.

After a long discussion, we selected three spots for the landing of the paratroopers: 1) Gourangighat on the West of Ghatail Police Station, 2) the wide open ground of Bangra-Sholapura on the West of Kalihati Police Station, and 3) the Pathan ground on the south of Ichchapur-Sahdevpur of Kalihati police station.

The map-points of these locations were determined and the coordinates were sent via radio messages to Indian High Command. Additionally, Badsha would deliver this information to India by hand.

The next morning, Kader left to oversee the massive preparation for the impending attacks.

On December 7th, Captain Peter and I left the boat and camped by the side of Nikrail School.

While Peter and I were busy testing the wireless sets, Kader showed up. He formally put me in charge of communication regarding all subsequent attacks.

Additionally, one hundred fifty freedom fighters were placed under my command to coordinate communication among the different companies, to maintain constant contact with Kader, and to help Peter in his work.

Additionally, I had ten military and four civilian wireless sets at my disposal. This equipment complemented the long-distance wireless connection with India, which was already in place.

Lastly, half of the members of Kader's team were connected directly to me via wireless communication sets.

Kader ended by formally attaching Captain Peter to my group.

After reorganizing the communication group under my command, Kader met with the commanders present at Nikrail School again for a final briefing of the battle strategies.

Amidst our hectic activities at the Nikrail School, came some uplifting news: India had finally announced its formal recognition of independent Bangladesh.

This news was widely publicized through radio stations such as Free Bangladesh Radio, Akashvani, and the BBC. We quickly arranged to spread this exhilarating news through our messengers among the villagers.

The two pieces of rousing news: India's recognition of an independent Bangladesh, and the presence of Kader Siddiqui at Nikrail created a feverish excitement amongst the people. Thousands of people assembled at Nikrail School. They wanted to see Kader. They wanted to hear him speak.

At about three in the afternoon, while I was busy supervising the radio equipment with the operators, Kader called me in for a meeting with him.

In the meeting, we decided to organize a public rally. He asked me to arrange the construction of a stage and a microphone for the rally.

We made arrangements for the public meeting before nightfall. After the evening prayers, thousands of people assembled at the school ground.

Kader gave a passionate speech. He spoke of the sacrifices made by civilians and volunteers. He thanked them for all of their help and cooperation. He concluded his speech by saying that victory was certain for us. Bangladesh's liberation would be a reality.

Captain Peter was deeply moved by the rally of thousands of freedom fighters and common people. He could not believe that we were such an organized and disciplined force, and that the people had so much love and support for us.

After the meeting, Kader bade good-bye to the commanders of the Eastern Zone, as they prepared to proceed to their various positions.

By then, we made contact with Brigadier Sanat Singh through secured wireless communication. He replied with a simple message, "Wait for my next instruction."

Kader left Nikrail at about eleven at night, but before he left, he had another meeting with Peter and me. We informed Kader of the series of information that we had already collected regarding the Mukti Bahini, the enemy position, and the Indian Army.

He set off for Jhawail to organize the attack on the Gopalpur enemy position.

He instructed us to leave Nikrail. He said, "After such a mass rally. It isn't safe to stay here any longer."

We started packing right away. However, it became apparent that we needed help carrying so much equipment. In addition to the one hundred fifty armed freedom fighters, I was able to recruit an additional fifty volunteers to help us transport our equipment.

Very late that evening, Peter and I proceeded with a caravan of two hundred men for Ghatail carrying all of our equipment. We were on foot all through the night and into the very next day.

In the morning of December 9th, we reached a village named Dighalkandi, which was situated near Gourangichawk to the west of the Ghatail enemy garrison.

Peter and I set up a temporary camp at the house of Abdul Halim Chowdhury. The freedom fighters took positions at various locations around the house and along the perimeter of the village.

It was almost noon when we finished setting up the communication system. From the radio communication as well as from messengers, I came to know that about ten thousand freedom fighters had taken their positions since last night and that some armed skirmishes had already taken place at some battlefields.

The team led by Commander Anis had launched an all-out attack on the enemy to capture Gopalpur and Madhupur enemy garrisons. The fierce fighting continued.

In the afternoon, news reached us that Commander Anis' team had taken over Madhupur enemy positions. The Pakistani forces were fleeing.

The capture of Madhupur was a very important victory, since Madhupur was the conjunctive link of Jamalpur, Mymensingh, and Tangail Highways. Now that Madhupur was free, the Indian Army could easily reach Tangail from Jamalpur without any enemy interference.

Captain Peter communicated this news immediately to Indian High Command through radio messages. News also reached us that the Pakistani forces had been able to defend Gopalpur. Anis did not succeed there, but the battle was still ongoing.

Our camp was near the first Indian paratroopers' landing site. Commander Hakim's team had already secured the area. Additionally, a group led by Commander Habib was on high alert on Tangail-Madhupur Road to ambush enemy soldiers.

At night, Kader showed up at our camp. He called for Major Hakim and Major Habib. Kader and the commanders decided that they would launch an attack on Ghatail garrison very early the next morning. Kader and Commander Sabur's team would lead the frontal attack on the enemy at Ghatail garrison.

As part of the plan Commander Hakim would launch a three-inch mortar attack. Meanwhile, Commander Mostafa and Commander Habib would respectively launch an attack on the two bridges to the south and north of Ghatail Police Station. Their goal was to dislodge the Pakistani soldiers on guard, before destroying the bridges.

At two in the morning, Kader and other commanders moved to their respective positions. We were all awake. As per our plan, fierce fighting began two hours later. Then, after about thirty minutes, we heard the rippling sounds of tremendous explosions.

Habib's team had captured the bridge on Baliapara. It was completely destroyed. Sounds of shelling and ferocious gunfire could be heard till late in the morning. The inhabitants of the Ghatail area started fleeing to the west as the battle gained momentum.

Meanwhile, Commander Hakim launched his mortar attack on Ghatail Police Station at six-thirty in the morning. Soon after, we received a message from Kader that Ghatail police station was now free.

About three hundred enemy soldiers including regular army, militia, and Razakars had been captured by the freedom fighters. Eighteen dead bodies of enemy soldiers lay scattered in the police station and bunkers.

While trying to capture Kalidaspara Bridge, one freedom fighter of Commander Mostafa's platoon was killed and two others were injured.

The two wounded freedom fighters were brought to our camp for medical treatment. Unfortunately, we did not have a doctor. However, time was running out and the situation on the battlefield was moving at a furious pace. We had been working non-stop and responding to an ever-changing battlefront.

I had personally known one of the wounded freedom fighters for several years. He trusted that I would do everything in my power to see to their immediate treatment. I was desperate to get a doctor from anywhere.

I was unable to accurately ascertain the severity of their wounds myself. Only a medical doctor would be able to properly assess their injuries. However, their groans had me worried. I had to do something quickly.

Luckily, that afternoon I learned of a female doctor just a few miles away. She happened to be a distant relative of mine. She had arrived at her village home from Dhaka just a few days earlier.

I sent some freedom fighters to her with a letter requesting her immediate medical assistance. She quickly reported to the camp and provided medical treatment to our wounded comrades.

Meanwhile, the scene on the battlefield in the border area had been rapidly escalating. On the morning of December 10th, a convoy of four hundred vehicles of the defeated Pakistani troops was retreating from Jamalpur and Mymensingh to Madhupur. Commander Anis and Commander Arzoo did not try to resist this large battalion. Rather, they retreated from Madhupur.

A convoy of six thousand enemy forces, consisting of the Pakistani Army and Razakars, started fleeing towards Dhaka.

Brigadier Kader Khan, Brigadier Newaz and Colonel Sultan of the Pakistani Army were leading the retreat. As they passed Ghatail to the north of Baniapara Bridge, Commander Habib ambushed the leading enemy contingent without knowing the strength of the convoy. Sporadic fighting broke out.

However, as Commander Habib came to understand the superior strength of the enemy convoy, he retreated from the bridge under cover of continuous fire.

Three freedom fighters from Habib's platoon were wounded in this counter-attack and they were brought to our camp for treatment.

Meanwhile, even after the capture of Ghatail police station, Kader, Commander Sabur, Commander Khoka, Commander Habib, and their teams chose not to stay at Ghatail. Rather, they moved to Goalgonda to the West of Ghatail.

Kader had been maintaining contact with other groups through me. In the meantime, a contingent of Brigadier Kader Khan's brigade was on the run. Pakistani soldiers stopped at Ghatail Police Station. They intended to regroup and cover the fleeing Pakistani soldiers from any potential Mukti Bahini attacks from the rear.

At noon, Kader sent a radio message instructing us to request Indian High Command to start an air raid on Ghatail and Gopalpur enemy positions. We immediately sent our request. Within an hour, we received the return message conveying affirmation of an imminent air raid.

Kader was informed immediately. He instructed the freedom fighters stationed at the Ghatail and Gopalpur to leave their positions immediately.

At exactly three in the afternoon, 3 MIG-21 fighters began continuous raids on Gopalpur and Ghatail enemy positions.

We could clearly see the MIGs in the sky above Ghatail from our camp. The raid started with the sound of machine guns and rockets, followed by a rolling coil of smoke from behind them.

We were excited to see the air attack on the enemy positions and were overwhelmed with joy. The men at the camp began dancing with exhilaration.

After the air raid, the enemy forces at Gopalpur surrendered. Gopalpur was now under the control of the Mukti Bahini. About three hundred enemy soldiers were captured by freedom fighters.

With the air raid on Ghatail, the Pakistani Army began a quick retreat toward Tangail town.

In the afternoon of December 11th, we received another coded message from the Indian High Command. After decoding it, Peter burst into joy. He warmly embraced me and asked me to contact Kader.

I sent a message to Kader, "They are coming."

Immediately, Kader informed his commanders of the three selected zones, where the paratroopers were supposed to land and asked them to be on alert. At that time, the Pakistani soldiers were fleeing south to reach Tangail town.

Earlier, the Pakistani Air Force had been completely wiped out by the Indian Air Force. The Indian Air Force had absolute control over the Bangladeshi sky. They could fly at ease without the fear of enemy aircrafts.

On December 11th, at five in the afternoon, two Indian Air Force MIGs flew very low over Ghatail and Kalihati. Captain Peter jumped with joy. He shouted, "Look! They are here!"

The two planes began circling over a wide area. We could not tell over which of the three designated spots the paratroops would be dropped.

A few moments later, several cargo planes were seen flying above the circling MIGs. Suddenly, the two MIGs shot up towards the stratosphere as the cargo planes slowly descended.

They were Indian Air Force transport planes, AN-12, C-119, and CD-3. The planes descended in waves. As they approached their lowest point of descent, they came to a slow hover. It was as if they were floating in the air. Suddenly their bellies opened and parachutes began dropping.

Our camp brimmed with passion, joy, and ecstasy. All the inhabitants of Dighalkandi, from the young to the old, both men and women, came out to the open fields to see the spectacle. The southeastern sky, as far as we could see, was covered with what looked like big balloons.

As they initially dropped from the planes, the paratroopers looked like small white leaflets. However, as their parachutes opened up, they looked like huge umbrellas.

On a sunny and breezy afternoon, the blue sky of Tangail was brilliantly recomposed with a spectacular view created by the paratroopers. For those who were lucky enough to watch, this was the scene of a lifetime. It was an unforgettable moment.

It took almost an hour for all the paratroopers to land. The sun had already begun to set. A battalion of paratroopers of the Indian Army landed. They were under the command of Col. Pannu. Under the cover of darkness, the paratroopers began regrouping.

We all rejoiced at the signs of an impending victory.

Dropping of Indian Paratroops in Tangail on December 11, 1971 (Courtesy, Indian Army website)

Liberation of Tangail town

Captain Peter failed to communicate with the paratroopers as they landed. For some reason, our radio communication with the paratroopers had broken down. Moreover, the paratroopers landed on the third spot in Kalihati, the farthest location from us. This made physical contact very difficult amidst the darkness of the night.

Our initial plan was that Captain Peter would join the paratroopers as they landed. This did not happen.

Peter immediately became impatient and restless. He asked me to do something. He wanted to know whether he could go and meet the paratroops right then and there.

I asked him to calm down. I told him that I would contact Kader to see if he could do something about the situation.

At about eight that evening, Kader stopped by our camp. Peter was visibly excited and immediately asked whether the landing of the paratroopers went well. He was eager to know whether contact had been established with them.

Kader reassured Peter that the landing went perfectly and they had been in contact with the Mukti Bahini. The leader of the paratroopers was due to meet with the freedom fighters later that night.

Several thousand freedom fighters, under the direct command of Kader, were engaged in battle for the last sixteen hours. They were all very tired and hungry. We arranged for their meals to be made.

After dinner, Kader rested before reviewing the reports from the battlefield. The reports confirmed that the highways connecting Madhupur, Gopalpur, Kalihati, and Sholakura were now all under the full control of the Mukti Bahini.

The fleeing Pakistani soldiers had been attacked from various positions on the Tangail-Madhupur Highway. They had repositioned themselves further south on the highway between Phultala and Pungli. They were just south of Kalihati Police Station.

About twenty vehicles of the Pakistan Army had been destroyed and more than fifty soldiers had been killed. The Mukti Bahini had been able to capture a number of vehicles as well as a huge quantity of arms and explosives. We were pleased with the outcome of the battles.

In the meeting, we chalked out a strategy to liberate Tangail town. A strong contingent of twenty-five hundred soldiers would be deployed in the form of various platoons and companies.

At four in the morning, Kader sent firm instructions to Commander Habib asking him to build up a strong defense at Kalidaspara. His plan was to prevent the remnants of the enemy forces at Mymensingh and Jamalpur garrisons from retreating and attacking us from the rear.

An hour later, Kader headed out with his troops to Tangail along the Mymensingh-Tangail Highway.

This time, Peter and I also joined Kader's core team. Our journey was smooth. We were welcomed at the liberated Kalihati headquarters by Commanders Nabi Newaz, Riaz, and Samad Gama. They reported that their forces were in full control of the Kalihati Police Station.

They further reported that Tangail Highway was in our control as far south as Sholakura. So we immediately made our way to Sholakura. The teams of Commander Moin, Golam Sarwar, and Abdul Hamid had liberated this part of the highway.

They gave us the exact positions of the paratroopers.

Battle at Pungli Bridge

As we crossed Sholakura Bridge and moved forward to Ichhapur, we came under the attack of enemy forces. We were forced to halt.

The freedom fighters at Kalihati had already told us about the previous night's battle at Pungli Bridge.

After landing last night, the Indian paratroopers took control of Pungli Bridge. Unfortunately, they landed between a convoy of Pakistani soldiers who were fleeing Sholakura and another who were already south of the bridge.

On the other hand, the enemy contingent to the north of the bridge was trapped as well. They were stuck between freedom fighters to the north and Indian paratroopers to the south.

The enemy soldiers panicked and took an offensive against the paratroopers. They desperately tried to pierce through the cordon and move towards Tangail town.

Initially, the paratroopers were puzzled that they had landed in such close proximity to the Pakistani Army. However, the paratroopers fought back with mortars and machineguns.

A fierce battle continued throughout the night. The Pakistani forces suffered heavy losses. Moreover, they had already suffered sizeable casualties in the battles with the Mukti Bahini the day before. They were demoralized.

The spineless nature of the Pakistani Army became apparent in this battle. Rather than rescue their desperate comrades to the north, the convoy of Pakistani soldiers positioned south of Pungli Bridge chose to flee to Tangail town.

After suffering serious losses, the remnants of the enemy contingent north of the bridge abandoned their strategy. They needed to buy time for a new exit strategy. They tried to halt the advance of the Mukti Bahini from the north, so they attacked our position from Ichhapur.

Kader ordered for a strong counter-attack. We were equipped with heavy arms. The Mukti Bahini started its counter-attack from our position at Sholakura with three-inch mortars, light cannons, and heavy machineguns.

Meanwhile, nearly one thousand freedom fighters, under the leadership of Commanders Mostafa, Sabur, Fazlul Huq, Moqbul Hossain, and Tamos advanced towards Ichhapur.

They avoided the highway and marched through the inner roads across the villages. Succumbing to the pressure of a thirty-minute assault by the Mukti Bahini, the Pakistani Army retreated from Ichhapur to Phultala.

We accompanied Kader to Ichhapur. However, as there was no cover between the enemy and us we could not advance farther south. The land between Ichapur and Phultala was wide open. We had no choice, but to maintain our position.

Kader requested an Indian air raid on the enemy position. Captain Peter made contact and informed us that an air raid would take place at nine that morning.

The Indian Air Force launched its attack on the enemy position as planned.

By the first week of December, the Indian Air Force destroyed the entire fleet of Pakistani Air Force fighter planes stationed in Bangladesh.

There was absolutely no chance of a counter-attack. The squadron of Indian fighter planes bombarded their targets with ease. Forty vehicles of the Pakistani Army were set ablaze by the air raid. Hundreds of Pakistani soldiers were killed.

After the air raid, Kader instructed the commanders to move ahead to Phultala. The troops of Kader and Commander Sabur took their positions alongside the house of Amjad Hossain.

Commander Sabur had been trying to assess the situation at Phultala with a pair of binoculars. He bent down alongside the wall of an old mosque to secure his footing. No sooner than he had taken his first glance, had an enemy mortar shell exploded about one or two feet above his head. The mortar hit and broke the wall of the mosque behind him. Commander Sabur was knocked to the ground by the massive thrust of the shell.

His squad immediately rushed to his side to rescue their commander. But surprisingly, he wasn't hurt. With debris shattered everywhere, it was a miracle that he was still alive.

While our attention was with Commander Sabur's miraculous fortune, several volunteers arrived escorting a contingent of paratroopers.

Behind the force of last night's gusty winds, the paratroopers drifted away from their targeted position.

Furthermore, as the battle commenced at nightfall near the Pungli Bridge, they had no chance to join the main contingent.

They made every attempt to contact Kader, but their efforts were in vain. However, as the volunteers knew that Kader was still at Ichhapur, they brought the paratroopers to us.

Captain Peter was very happy to see them. He narrated his experience to his fellow soldiers with excitement.

There was a captain amongst the contingent of paratroopers. He informed us of a minor injury to one of his paratroopers who had gotten stuck in a tree upon arrival. Fortunately, the volunteers rescued him and were able to arrange for his medical treatment.

Kader asked them to get some rest at Ichhapur. He instructed a team of freedom fighters to escort the paratroopers to the main contingent through the Eastern Passage of Tangail-Kalihati Highway.

Local volunteers arranged for their meals. Captain Peter thanked us for our hospitality and accompanied the paratroopers.

As the freedom fighters advanced towards Phultala, the captain of the paratroopers expressed his wish to join us in our fighting. Kader said that the Mukti Bahini was strong enough to face the enemy themselves.

He thanked them anyway for their offer of support. Kader asked them to save their energy for Dhaka.

We bade goodbye to Captain Peter and his team and moved toward Phultala.

The enemy forces were seriously weakened by the air raid, but they were far from annihilated. After a long pause following the raid, the enemy continued firing at us sporadically as we advanced along the right and left trenches of the highway.

Kader instructed Commander Halim to launch a mortar attack on the enemy at Phultala. This strategy provided cover under which, about three hundred freedom fighters moved towards Phultala.

A reconnaissance team of the Mukti Bahini crossed Phultala Bridge unopposed. Up until now, the enemy fire came in intervals from the direction of Phultala. The freedom fighters cordoned off the village. However, after an hour, the enemy gunfire stopped.

We found out that the enemy had fled the village and headed west. Their earlier firing was intended only to slow us down.

In the afternoon, when we took full control of Phultala, I saw about fifty to sixty wounded Pakistani soldiers groaning and lying scattered around. About forty vehicles of the Pakistani Army had been completely destroyed.

The enemy soldiers abandoned their vehicles, left the highway, and fled on foot through the villages. Scattered along the side of the highway were even articles of Pakistani Army fatigue, suggesting that the cowards fled in civilian clothes. It was a desperate move to save their lives.

We established direct contact with the Indian paratroopers positioned at Pungli Bridge.

As we celebrated the liberation of Phultala, we came to learn that Brigadier Klair of the Indian Army was on his way to Tangail with strong convoy of his brigade and additional Mukti Bahini forces.

They had already reached Bamutia to the north. They were eager to meet Kader. Kader immediately left with his squad to head north and welcome Brigadier Klair.

In the meantime, I left with a team of freedom fighters for Pungli Bridge to meet the Indian paratroopers.

Enemy Dead Bodies

As we walked on the road to Pungli Bridge, I came face to face with a bone-chilling scene - the stage of last night's battle between Pakistani forces and the Indian paratroopers.

The corpses of hundreds of enemy soldiers were littered on the road. Their bodies sprawled from one side of the bridge to the other.

These lifeless bodies blanketed our path at every step. We walked with the utmost care so as to respect the dead.

We found limbs separated from torsos. Bodies of enemy soldiers in jeeps were found tangled and twisted. The corpses were amalgamated to their vehicles.

One of our escorts collapsed at the sight of several bodies decapitated from the impact of close range blasts. It was mind-boggling. Never in my life had I seen so much death in one place.

I couldn't help but rhetorically ask myself, "Why had the Pakistani government sent these men to kill innocent Bengalis? Look at them now. They were lambs lead to the slaughter."

These men were fathers, husbands, brothers, and sons. What could the Pakistani military junta say to the relatives of these men? They were told that they were fighting to protect Islam. But, they were mere pawns sent to carry out the dirty work of a despotic regime. There was no honor in the work that these men came to do.

And yet, I could not help but feel saddened by the sight of so many that were sent to sacrifice their lives for an unjust cause.

We crossed the bridge and reached the location of the paratroopers. I introduced myself and asked to see their commander. A paratrooper escorted me to the commander, but before I could introduce myself, Captain Peter came forward and introduced me to the commanding officer.

We exchanged greetings and sat under the bridge. The paratroopers had created a makeshift command control.

As I told them about the liberation of Phultala, a signalman interrupted to inform us that Brigadier Klair and Kader were headed towards Pungli Bridge together.

Kader and Brigadier Klair arrived at Pungli Bridge at about three in the afternoon. We ran up to the bridge to receive them. We greeted each other. The commander of the paratroopers escorted us back under the bridge.

Champagne

When Brigadier Klair and Kader Siddiqui stepped down, five hundred freedom fighters and paratroopers received them with a thundering applause.

Brigadier Klair instructed his officers to assemble and celebrate the victory with bottles of champagne. Within minutes, corks began flying into the air as foam rimmed over the tops of bottles.

Everyone was given a glass. When I was approached, I politely declined and requested that he give Kader and me glasses of soda water instead. We all held our glasses in the air in celebration of our victory.

Brigadier Klair came to me and said hello.

I replied, "Welcome to Tangail."

He thanked me and referred to the help and cooperation extended by the Tangail Mukti Bahini. I smiled and asked him about General Gill.

Suddenly, the celebratory smile adorning Brigadier Klair's face had vanished. He told me that the general was in the hospital. A few days ago, General Gill was seriously wounded in a road accident near Kamalpur.

I was shocked to hear of the accident. I knew General Gill very well. He was very sympathetic and appreciative of my work, and that of the efforts of the Tangail Mukti Bahini.

From the corner of my eye, I saw my old friend Captain Bose. When I first met Captain Bose, he introduced himself to me as an officer in the Signal Corps of the Indian Army. However, as I approached him, his superior officer revealed that Captain Bose was actually an officer of the Intelligence Division of the Indian Army.

In hindsight, Captain Bose was clearly good at what he did. In the time I knew him, he was not only able to gain my trust and extract information from me about Kader and the Tangail Mukti Bahini, but he was even able to gain details about my personal life, and all without ever letting me know that he was an intelligence officer.

The celebration allowed me to reflect on the significance of the recent events of the war.

Captain Peter's entry one hundred miles inside of Bangladesh was a very important and significant moment with respect to war strategies. However, this truth wouldn't be fully understood until the end of the war.

In early October, a strong contingent of joint military forces consisting of the Indian Army and freedom fighters was mobilized on the borders of Comilla, Sylhet, and Jessore. Heavy artillery and tanks were positioned in these sectors. The presence of the joint forces was very visible to the Pakistani Army in these sectors.

However, in the Mymensingh and Jamalpur sectors to the north, the presence of the joint forces was much weaker.

This was an intentional move by the joint forces to mislead the enemy.

Pakistani forces assumed that the Indian Army would move towards Dhaka through the Comilla border. However, General Aurora had a different plan.

On the Mymensingh border, he positioned only two Brigades of the 101 Communication Zone under the leadership of Brigadier Klair and Brigadier Sanat Singh.

These two infantry brigades, equipped with light armory, pressured the Pakistani forces on the borders of Kamalpur and Haluaghat.

Pakistan High Command never thought that India would launch an attack from these locations. Therefore, the elderly Pakistani officer, Brigadier Kader Khan was left alone in charge of this sector.

For Brigadier Khan, this was only the second surrender of his military carrier. During our interrogation, we came to know that he had once surrendered to the Indian Army on the West Pakistan border during the Indian-Pakistani War of 1965.

Wounded General Gill

As I spoke to the other officers, I came to know of two accidents. On December 1st, Brigadier Klair and Brigadier Sanat Singh moved with their brigades and the Mukti Bahini towards Jamalpur and Mymensingh, respectively.

On December 9th, General Gill joined Brigadier Klair and proceeded from Mahendraganj to Jamalpur by jeep. Unfortunately, somewhere between Kamalpur and Bakshiganj, their jeep ran over an enemy anti-tank mine.

The jeep was flipped upside down from the blast of the mine. General Gill was seriously wounded. He lost conscious and both of his feet were badly injured.

He was immediately taken to Tura by helicopter and then to the Shillong Army Hospital for medical treatment.

Miraculously, Brigadier Klair walked away unscathed. He was a lucky soldier. A few days earlier, during a fight in Jamalpur, Brigadier Klair got a little too close to the frontline near the Jamalpur Pakistani Garrison. He came under heavy fire. His bodyguard was killed. The brigadier himself was shot six times. Fortunately, all of the bullets pierced his loose-fitting jacket without ever touching his body. Once again, he was unhurt.

Major General Nagra had now taken over command from Major General Gill.

How ironic? General Gill chalked out the strategies of the last few months. While brigadiers Klair and Singh, along with the Mukti Bahini led by Kader, marched towards Dhaka following his plan, General Gill was confined to a hospital bed thousands of miles away in Shilong, Assam.

Friendly Fire

In the morning, Brigadier Klair occupied Jamalpur Pakistani garrison, which had been abandoned by the enemy earlier. He left some soldiers in Jamalpur and immediately marched to Madhupur on the way to Tangail town.

Since this area was under the control of joint forces already, Brigadier Klair's convoy easily advanced to Ghatail.

However, as soon as the convoy arrived at Kalidaspara, an unfortunate accident occurred.

A company of Mukti Bahini led by Major Habib was stationed at Kalidashpara. The sight of a long military convoy alerted them. They had no prior information about the movement of the Indian convoy at the time.

Unfortunately, the freedom fighters mistook Klair's convoy as the enemy's. The Mukti Bahini opened fire on the convoy. The Indian forces were taken off guard, as well. They knew that the road was clear up to Pungli Bridge where the Indian paratroopers were waiting for them.

Nonetheless, Brigadier Klair's convoy returned fire in self-defense. The fighting continued only for few minutes. However, it was too late. The damage was already done.

Lives were lost on both sides. Four freedom fighters were killed and eleven others were injured. The damage to the joint forces was more significant: seven were dead and another seventeen were seriously wounded.

When the smoke had cleared, Major Habib escorted Brigadier Klair's convoy to Bamutia where Kader welcomed Brigadier Klair.

After talking to Indian officers, I gathered detailed information on the casualties of both sides from the previous night's battle around Pungli Bridge. Three hundred-seventy Pakistan soldiers were killed and more than one hundred were injured. Six Indian paratroopers were killed as they landed in the midst of the enemy forces and fifteen more were injured.

That day, paratroopers captured six hundred Pakistani soldiers. This may have been a disastrous day for the enemy, but for us, it was a day of victory and joy.

After the meeting, Kader and Klair decided to move on to Tangail that same evening. But before they did so, they inquired into the status of freedom fighters at Tangail and the state of the war to the south.

Reports had reached us that after a daylong battle under the leadership of Commanders Fazlur Rahman, Razzaque, Mainuddin, Niyat Ali, and Matiar Rahman, most of Tangail town had finally been taken by the freedom fighters.

To the north, Jamalpur and Mymensingh were liberated. The landing of the paratroopers and the heavy losses sustained by the enemy at Pungli Bridge had left the Pakistan Army shaken and scared.

The enemy's situation was further aggravated by the attack of the freedom fighters on Tangail town. As a result, most of the Pakistani soldiers had fled towards Dhaka.

Meanwhile, the Mukti Bahini had launched an attack on Dhaka Highway. A small contingent of Pakistani forces at the new Tangail town garrison was cut off from all sides. They were virtually surrounded.

Nonetheless, the enemy did not surrender. Rather, they desperately launched a counter-attack on the Mukti Bahini position.

With this in mind, Kader advised Brigadier Klair to wait until he moved into Tangail town and secured it completely. Brigadier Klair was happy to avoid a conflict with the Pakistan Army in Tangail town, as his main objective was to seize Dhaka.

At four in the afternoon, the expedition to Tangail town began. Commander Sabur's team was placed in front with machine gun-ready jeeps. The teams of Commander Mostafa and Kader followed them. There were two hundred freedom fighters moving slowly toward Tangail town. Commander Hakim was instructed to keep pace from the rear with his mortars.

Ten minutes after Kader left, I said goodbye to Brigadier Klair and Captain Peter and joined Commander Hakim's platoon. When we reached Sari Deola near Tangail town, we saw that the Mukti Bahini was busy exchanging fire with the enemy who was now trapped in its new headquarters at Tangail town.

We found that the enemy was firing machine guns perched atop the municipality water-tank. Commander Hakim's team joined the battle and we immediately started firing mortar shells on the enemy position at the water-tank. Within moments Commander Hakim's mortar shells hushed the enemy guns. The Pakistani stronghold was forced to surrender.

On the way to town, Kader stopped at his house. The Pakistani Army had burned it to the ground.

It was an emotional moment for Kader. This was the home his parents had built. It was where he and his siblings grew up. And now only ashes covered the foundation of his home. All of his earthly possessions, all of his family's valuables, accumulated over several decades were looted and burned. All he had left were his memories.

Sadly, Kader had no time to reflect on his personal loss. He had something more valuable ahead to fight for. He had to move on.

Kader arrived at the district Awami League office in midtown Tangail by around seven that evening. Commanders Fazlur Rahman, Razzaque, and the others received Kader. By noon, these commanders had already liberated old Tangail town. After the horrors and joys of battle, we all embraced each other warmly.

By now, tens of thousands of people had begun assembling around the Awami League premises to see Kader and to celebrate our victory. The whole town was dancing with joy.

We sent word to Brigadier Klair that it was now safe to move into Tangail town.

On December 11th, Tangail town was liberated from the Pakistani forces.

Author, Shaheed, Indian civilian officer Mr. Sen and Indian Paratroops Commander Col. Pannu (L-R) in liberated Tangail

Author, Kader Siddiqui & Shaheed (L-R) in a public meeting in liberated Tangail.

Chapter 5

Final Victory: The Liberation of Dhaka

Major General Nagra in Tangail

We received a message that Brigadier Klair was proceeding with his large convoy towards Tangail from Pungli Bridge. He wanted to meet Kader Siddiqui.

We left the Awami League office and marched towards Tangail-Mymensingh Road.

We greeted Brigadier Klair at the bus station near the intersection of Tangail-Dhaka Road. Brigadier Klair congratulated Kader for liberating Tangail town. Brigadier Klair wanted to know the position of the Pakistani forces on Tangail-Dhaka road to the south. Kader told him that his freedom fighters had control of Tangail-Dhaka Highway up to Vatkura Bridge. Kader added that they must not go beyond Vatkura Bridge during the night. Brigadier Klair promised Kader that he would not do so and proceeded to march towards Dhaka with his troops.

We went to the WAPDA guesthouse on Tangail-Mymensingh Road and turned it into a temporary headquarters for Kader.

We had been working ceaselessly for the last five days. Those who worked with Kader, as his personal squad, had to move very quickly from place to place.

For the last nine months, Kader, as the commander-in-chief of our group, was constantly on the move. He traveled from camp to camp and from sector to sector on foot. And on some lucky occasions, he was able to travel by boat.

However, the last five days, from December 7th to December 11th, were completely different. Though we were physically exhausted due to our non-stop activities and fierce fighting, we were mentally replenished and excited from the sweet taste of a hard earned victory - the liberation of Tangail.

Until midnight, we reviewed the current law and order of Tangail town. We further reviewed the strategy for the liberation of Dhaka, as well as, the responsibility of each unit of the Mukti Bahini. A blanket of tight security was established around the building before we went to sleep. For the first time in months, we slept peacefully in the heart of liberated Tangail town.

The next morning we woke up breathing the fresh air of a newly liberated land. The freedom fighters were chanting slogans, "March to Dhaka, Liberate Dhaka." By nightfall, the joint forces of the Indian Army and the Mukti Bahini had already proceeded a significant distance towards Dhaka.

One day earlier, as we were attacking enemy forces to the north of Tangail, our Mukti Bahini forces ambushed the fleeing Pakistani forces on Tangail-Dhaka Road.

Commanders Baijid, Shamsul Haque, Sulaiman, Lutfur, Naik Alam, Azad Kamal, Sultan and their heroic freedom fighters led this operation. Fleeing Pakistani forces suffered heavy casualties at the hands of the Mukti Bahini. In addition, Mukti Bahini road mines blew up several enemy jeeps.

The previous night, after the liberation of Tangail town, Kader ordered our forces to clean up the mines to make Tangail-Dhaka Road safe for the joint forces.

Under the cover of darkness, the joint forces reached Kaliakor without any resistance. Kaliakor was situated about thirty miles south of Tangail and twenty miles north of Dhaka.

The Mukti Bahini and their supporters lead the way for the joint forces at every intersection. Brigadier Klair set up his temporary garrison at Kaliakor.

The next morning, Brigadier Klair led a strong convoy of about five thousand men to Kadda-Mouchak near Dhaka.

Meanwhile, Brigadier Sant Singh led another convoy of joint forces to Mymensingh on December 11th, after routing Pakistani forces in Haluaghat and Shambuganj Ferry Station.

The next day, on December 12th, Brigadier Singh reached Tangail town. Kader and I welcomed him at Kader's headquarters. Brigadier

Singh jumped out of his jeep and opened his arms and bear-hugged both of us. Even his bushy mustache could not hide his smile. His joy and happiness flowed through his face.

There was good reason for this Sikh officer's excitement. During the previous nine months, Brigadier Singh had been in charge of training of about fifty thousand freedom fighters at a camp near Tura in the state of Meghalaya. He trained many of the Tangail Mukti Bahini as well.

Brigadier Singh was known as the Babajee (Father) to the freedom fighters in this sector. He was leading a large contingent of about five thousand joint forces to the south to liberate Dhaka.

The Tangail Mukti Bahini was part and parcel to his core strategy to liberate Dhaka. He took pride in introducing the Tangail Mukti Bahini and me to Indian Army leadership.

And now, for him to arrive in a liberated Tangail town, to meet two of his old friends, he was filled with a sense of accomplishment. He congratulated us, and praised the role of the Tangail Mukti Bahini in liberating Tangail and supporting the Indian Army. He was particularly appreciative of our coordination of the paratrooper's landing.

Brigadier Singh spent some time with us as he rested. After some refreshments, he proceeded to the south to join his colleague, Brigadier Klair, at Kaliakor.

Major General Nagra arrived in Tangail on the night of the 13th. Brigadier Klair and Brigadier Singh were already in Tangail to receive their new commander. We received General Nagra at the WAPDA guesthouse.

At about 9.30 pm, General Nagra sat down in a closed door meeting with Brigadier Klair, Brigadier Singh, and Kader to discuss the strategy for liberating Dhaka. He liberally praised the contribution of the Tangail Mukti Bahini. He particularly appreciated the contribution of our forces in creating an easy passage for the Indian forces up to Kaliakor.

We inquired about General Gill's recuperation. He informed us that General Gill was making good progress in the hospital and his wounds were healing nicely. We asked General Nagra to convey our best wishes to General Gill.

The Capture of a Pakistani Brigadier

The Pakistani forces fleeing from Jamalpur and Mymensingh sectors were completely shattered and demoralized after their defeat at Pungli Bridge and the fall of Tangail town to the Mukti Bahini.

Their command structure had broken down completely. The defeated enemy soldiers were forced to abandon their vehicles and walk through villages to avoid encounters with freedom fighters. The Mukti Bahini was in complete control of Tangail-Dhaka Road.

Some of the enemy soldiers took off their military uniforms and changed into civilian clothing. They were trying to make it on foot to Dhaka. They were desperate to save their lives.

On The 14th of December, the joint forces captured one such group of Pakistani soldiers near Mouchak. There were thirty-one men in the group, none of whom put up a fight. This was surprising given that one of these men was quite a catch. He was the infamous Brigadier Kader Khan of the Pakistani Army, a terror to the people of Jamalpur and Mymensingh.

Brigadier Khan had abandoned his garrison in Mymensingh and came to Tangail around December 10th. After the fall of Tangail, he attempted to flee to Dhaka with a small convoy of about fifty officers and soldiers. The rest of his brigade had been destroyed. They had been either killed or captured by the joint forces.

Given the presence of the Mukti Bahini on the roads, Brigadier Khan and his group, followed suit with the other fleeing soldiers, abandoning their vehicles and walking through the villages.

Though they carried small arms, they lacked the courage and strength to raise their guns to the villagers for food and shelter. This would not have been a problem for them in the past.

But now, they were forced to beg these Bangladeshi villagers for food and water. They were at the mercy of the same people they once murdered, raped, and exploited.

Nonetheless, the villagers thought it best to oblige. Begging or not, these were demoralized men carrying guns who had already shown the kind of atrocities that they were capable of committing.

Under these circumstances, Brigadier Khan began losing control over his subordinate officers and soldiers. Though he wanted to flee to Dhaka, his troops were divided. Some argued that it would be suicidal to continue walking. They were afraid of being killed by the Mukti Bahini. Others were even afraid of the villagers. Several of his soldiers had already deserted the unit and disappeared into the forest.

Brigadier Khan had a dilemma. He had no control. He and his men were hungry, paranoid, tired, and demoralized.

Brigadier Khan, an officer of the so-called heroic Pakistani Army, the self-proclaimed defenders of Islam, finally decided to surrender.

Around noon, while discussing some logistical issues with the officers of the Indian Army at the circuit house of the new Tangail District headquarters, Brigadier Kader Khan and some his fellow Pakistani officers were brought forth to us.

Their mere presence infuriated us. Our emotions were running high. At any moment, any one of us was bound to lose control.

Over the last nine months, these beasts sitting in front of us with their heads down, killed our people, raped our women, and destroyed our homes. Brigadier Kader Khan was even known for personally raping women in his garrison at Mymensingh. On the battlefield, they tortured and killed our wounded comrades. They had no respect for the Geneva Convention. They had no respect for humanity.

Nonetheless, we were aware of our responsibilities. We were not the monsters that they were. We resisted our emotions and vengeful desires. We were victorious and they were defeated. They were prisoners of war. With their tails between their legs, they sat in front of us in humiliation. The guilt of their past sins weighed heavily, not on their conscience, but on their paranoid state of mind.

Somehow, we controlled ourselves. The Indian officers treated them politely and with care. They asked the prisoners what they needed. The captured soldiers, of course, were hungry and asked for food. The prisoners were taken to the next room and fed.

After they were done eating, an Indian intelligence officer interrogated them for an hour. Soon after, an Indian Army helicopter landed in front of the circuit house and took Brigadier Kader Khan and the other prisoners to India. However, many of us still had mixed emotions. Would these war criminals ever pay for their sins?

Meanwhile, on the battlefront at Kodda, fierce fighting had broken out between Brigadier Klair's force and the Pakistani Army. They had been fighting since the morning of December 14th.

The enemy was pounding on the position of the joint forces with mortar and canon fire. They were desperate to stall the advancement of the joint forces towards Dhaka. The joint forces had no long-range cannons. Therefore, Brigadier Klair had no choice, but to avoid a face-to-face battle with the enemy.

With the help of the freedom fighters, the Indian Army crossed the river through left and right flanks attacking the enemy from each side. Pakistani forces could not withstand the attack of the joint forces and were forced to retreat. However, before doing so, they destroyed Kodda Bridge. Brigadier Klair had to stop and camp at the bridge.

Reception of Major General Nagra

On December 14th, we arranged a public meeting in front of Bindubashini High School to receive General Nagra. This would be the first public meeting in liberated Tangail. In the meantime, Shaheed, the chief of the civilian administration of the Tangail freedom fighters, came to Tangail from our headquarters in Shakhipur. Latif Siddiqui and Basit Siddiqui, two members of the Bangladesh Parliament, accompanied him.

A stage was built on the roof of the school building. Just before departing from the WAPDA guesthouse, Kader Siddiqui asked me to call General Nagra to come to the meeting. He was staying at the government circuit house at district headquarters.

I called the circuit house. Col. Pannu, commander of the Indian Army paratroopers, answered the phone. I asked the colonel to convey Kader's request to General Nagra to join us in the meeting.

I left the WAPDA guesthouse after Kader, and reached the meeting in a separate car. The playground in front of the school was packed. Thousands of people already gathered at the meeting. Shaheed, Latif, and Basit were already seated on the dais on the roof.

As I approached the front of the building, I found a ladder hanging from the roof. It was made of rope and bamboo. As the winter chill blew overhead, the ladder would oscillate from left to right making it difficult to climb. I knew that someone as thin as me would have no trouble climbing the ladder. However, such a task might be a bigger challenge for some of the larger, heavier-set men.

I carefully made my way up the ladder. I had no intention of falling off in front of thousands of people and embarrassing myself. At the top of the ladder, I carefully hoisted myself onto the platform and joined the others on the dais.

From the roof, I saw the District Commissioner of Tangail, the chief executive officer of the district, sitting on the ground with the general public. His fellow officers of the district administration accompanied him.

During peace times, the District Commissioner would have been on the dais, and perhaps, would have presided over such a meeting himself. However, the District Commissioner and all of his officers had spent the last nine months working for Pakistani forces. Their guilt had usurped their position.

A little later, General Nagra arrived at the meeting accompanied by Col. Pannu and his staff. They climbed the ladder with ease disproving my apprehension. I welcomed them on the dais and introduced General Nagra to the public. However, Kader had not yet arrived.

General Nagra looked at me and asked, "Where is Kader?"

With a look of embarrassment, I told him that he would be here at any moment.

General Nagra was obviously upset with the absence of his host Kader. He turned to Col. Pannu seated next to him and said in an irate voice: "You made a mistake by bringing me here so quickly. You should have made sure that Kader was here already."

As I stood behind them, I could hear their exchanges. Col. Pannu could do nothing more than apologize. He was visibly embarrassed and shaken. General Nagra retorted to Col. Pannu, "According to the protocol, Kader should have been present here to receive me."

Fortunately, before this episode could continue further, Kader arrived escorted by his bodyguards.

I whispered to Kader and told him about the incident. I explained that General Nagra was irritated that Kader was not there to receive him.

Kader understood the seriousness of the situation. He mentioned in his public address that he was caught in an urgent matter on the way to the meeting and humbly apologized for his lateness. He added that he was sorry that he could not receive General Nagra personally.

Kader then segued into praising General Nagra and the Indian Army for their help in the war.

I noticed General Nagra smile, as Col. Pannu almost immediately let off a sigh of relief.

In response, General Nagra expressed his profound praise for the courage of Kader and his forces. He then exclaimed, "Dhaka will be liberated soon."

The public roared in response.

After General Nagra left, the second phase of the meeting began. First Shaheed, Latif, and Basit addressed the meeting. Kader, in his second speech, thanked the people of Tangail for their help and cooperation in the war. He also vowed that Dhaka would be liberated soon.

Liberation of Savar

The next morning, an Indian Army brigade led by Brigadier Sanat Singh was proceeding towards Dhaka through Nabinagar-Savar Road. About six thousand freedom fighters from our group joined the Indian brigade.

In the evening, the joint forces encountered heavy resistance from the Pakistani Army camp at Jahangirnagar University. This was the last fortified Pakistani Army camp on Savar-Dhaka Highway.

Fierce gunfire continued all through the night. However, enemy moral was at an all time low. They were fighting the joint forces along the outskirts of Dhaka, the capital and their headquarters.

On the other hand, the joint forces fought with a newfound vigor. They had made it all the way to the fringes of Dhaka. They fought with resolve and defeated the Pakistani forces.

However, the battle was costly for both sides. About one hundred-fifty Pakistani forces were killed and about one hundred were wounded. Eleven soldiers of the Indian Army were killed and five were wounded. Luckily, the Mukti Bahini suffered no casualties.

Our schedules were very hectic during the last four days in Tangail. We had captured several thousands of Pakistani soldiers and Razakars. A few Pakistani Army officers were taken prisoner and sent to India.

We had to take care of the rest. It was a logistical nightmare. Shaheed and I were in charge of these activities. Fortunately, several thousand Mukti Bahinis were ready to help us.

Meanwhile, Kader was shuttling between the battlefield and Tangail, coordinating both war and logistics.

Major General Nagra came back to Tangail again on December 15th and stayed at the Tangail circuit house. He called Kader at 11 pm and asked whether it would be possible for us to supply breakfast for thousands of his soldiers on the battlefield by morning. Kader agreed.

Hundreds of Mukti Bahini and volunteers worked all night and cooked breakfast for several thousand Indian soldiers. By 5 AM, the foods were delivered to the joint forces at the Tangail circuit house. From there the food was taken by helicopter to the battlefield.

Victory Day

It was the 16th of December. Kader had arrived at Tangail circuit house at five-thirty in the morning. General Nagra was waiting for Kader there.

An Indian Army helicopter arrived from Mymensingh and landed in front of the circuit house at 6 am. Both Kader and General Nagra boarded the helicopter and headed towards the makeshift headquarters of Brigadier Klair at Mouchak near Kadda.

Brigadier Klair received them warmly. With excitement he exhaled, "I have breaking news! Pakistani General Niazi is expected to surrender today".

He further added that he had intercepted messages of the enemy, which indicated that they were getting ready to surrender. Moreover, the Pakistani Army had not had any activities in this sector since last night. This was peculiar, as they knew that the joint forces were closing in on them.

However, Brigadier Klair added that the Pakistani Army had put up a tough resistance against Brigadier Singh at Mirpur.

General Nagra was visibly happy with this development. He said, "Let's go and find out what is going on with Brigadier Singh."

The helicopter flew west with General Nagra, Brigadier Klair, and Kader. They landed on Dhaka-Manikganj Highway near Mirpur. Brigadier Sanat Singh was there to receive them. Brigadier Singh briefed them on the fierce resistance his troops had encountered from the Pakistani forces the previous night.

The helicopter flew back to Tangail to get supplies for the soldiers on the battlefield.

Brigadier Singh led General Nagra, Brigadier Klair and Kader on to a bridge. Mirpur, the gate to Dhaka city, was only one-and-half miles from the bridge.

The two companies of joint forces marched towards Mirpur on foot from each side of the road. General Nagra, flanked by Brigadier Klair and Brigadier Singh and Kader, also followed the troops towards Mirpur.

They had hardly gone a half-mile before they saw a group of freedom fighters running towards them. It was none other than the famous commanders Sabur and Mustafa along with three other Mukti Bahini soldiers.

The commanders informed Kader that their forces had penetrated Mirpur last night through the arteries of the village paths. They came to ask the Indian Army not to fire on them. They further informed that the Mukti Bahini, under the leadership of commanders Sabur, Mustafa, Bokul and Mozammel, had already reached the left side of Mirpur Bridge.

General Nagra, Brigadier Klair, Brigadier Singh, and Kader were all pleasantly surprised with the news.

General Nagra ordered his forces to occupy and secure Mirpur Bridge immediately.

Ultimatum

General Nagra and his associates arrived on the Hemayetpur Bridge at 8 AM. They were now only a few steps from Mirpur Bridge.

It was here that General Nagra pulled out a pen and a piece of paper from his pocket. He put the paper on the hood of his jeep and wrote the famous note to Pakistani general, Abdullah Niazi:

Dear Abdullah,
I am at Mirpur Bridge. Send your representative.
Yours,
Major General Nagra.

This was a historic moment.

Three Indian soldiers and one Mukti Bahini jumped into a jeep with the note and drove towards the cantonment. They did not forget to hoist a white flag on the jeep.

General Niazi and General Nagra were already acquainted. They were both commissioned in the British Army and were classmates in Deradun Military Training Academy as young cadets. Their friendship further grew when General Nagra was the military attaché for India in Islamabad, Pakistan.

Later, Nagra and Niazi were promoted through the ranks in the Indian and Pakistani armies, respectively. Once classmates, they were now opposing generals at war, fighting for their respective countries.

During the last few days, Pakistani forces were completely defeated at all fronts by the joint forces. Their fate was uncertain and humiliating. Many of them were captured, surrendered, or killed in battle. Those who survived fled to Dhaka. Their last hope was fighting back from Dhaka city.

However, by now, the joint forces had surrounded Dhaka from all sides. Dhaka was a city inhabited by millions of people. If Pakistani forces decided to fight the joint forces in Dhaka, then millions of civilians would die.

To avoid a blood bath, General Manekshaw, Chief of Staff of the Indian Army spent the previous two days broadcasting his message to General Niazi over the radio and by dropping leaflets in Urdu asking the Pakistani Army to surrender. He assured the Pakistani Army of their safety in accordance with the Geneva Convention should they surrender.

However, General Nagra did not know how General Niazi would respond. Even General Nagra was surprised to find himself so close to Dhaka, so soon, and so easily.

Therefore, he took the initiative and sent the personal note. He did not want to miss the opportunity of letting his old friend, Abdullah, know of his presence at Mirpur. Moreover, if General Niazi was going to surrender, General Nagra wanted to give him the chance to surrender to an old friend.

Surrender of General Niazi and the Final Victory

Meanwhile, as General Niazi learned that the joint forces had arrived at Mirpur Bridge, he consulted his commanders at his headquarters at Dhaka cantonment and his superiors in West Pakistan regarding his next move.

General Niazi's last hope was the American Naval 7th Fleet. There was news that the American Naval 7th Fleet was cruising towards the Bay of Bengal to intervene in the war in favor of Pakistan.

This was exciting news for General Niazi. However, it was disturbing news for us. General Niazi expected the American fleet to rescue him and his staff from Dhaka.

Though the U.S. House of Representatives, the Senate, intellectuals, media, and the general public supported Bangladesh's liberation war and condemned the genocide of the Bengali people by Pakistani occupation forces, President Richard M. Nixon and his Secretary of State Henry Kissinger supported the Pakistani military junta.

It was believed that, in addition to the Soviet-U.S. cold war rivalry, Nixon and Kissinger supported Pakistan for personal interests. They yearned to be national heroes by establishing diplomatic relations with communist China through the "good" office of General Yahya Khan, the leader of the Pakistani military junta.

Nixon and Kissinger thought that they needed to oppose the creation of an independent Bangladesh to gain the favor of General Yahya Khan, even though it was against everything that America stood for.

Despite the atrocities committed against Native Americans, The United States was a nation that historically stood against genocide. It was a nation that bravely supported the democratic will of the people. But sadly, for this brief moment in history, American values were compromised by the personal ambitions of two self-serving "statesmen."

With this in mind, it was no surprise why General Niazi became so optimistic about the news of the 7th Fleet's arrival. However, his optimism was short lived. Unfortunately, for Niazi, the Soviet Union threatened to respond to the U.S. naval movement by deploying their own naval fleet to the Bay of Bengal.

General Niazi's hopes were crushed when news came that the American Naval 7th Fleet had diverted its course away from the Bay of Bengal.

General Niazi verified his last stance and asked his commanders if they had any surprises left up their sleeves. The commanders looked around at each other, but each face was blanker than the next.

General Niazi got the message. He had the opportunity to make the most important decision of his career, if not, of his life. His decision would impact the lives of the thousands of his troops and the millions of people in Dhaka. His decision would have a historic impact on his country as well as on the entire subcontinent.

General Niazi ordered the safe passage of General Nagra's messengers to his cantonment.

At nine in the morning, the messengers of the joint forces arrived at General Niazi's headquarters accompanied by a Pakistani Army escort. They handed over General Nagra's note to General Niazi.

Thirty minutes later, a jeep was seen approaching the joint force's position from Mirpur Bridge. But, there was no white flag.

The soldiers of the Indian Army at first defense could not ascertain the jeep's identity from such distance. They were already on highest alert due to the presence of their senior commanders just behind them.

The soldiers would not take any risks preserving the safety of General Nagra, Brigadier Klair, and Brigadier Singh. However, they had no time to think. Having to assume the approaching vehicle was an enemy jeep, the soldiers fired on it with machine guns.

This turned out to be a tragic blunder. In the haste of trying to deliver the news to their commanders, the messengers failed to notice that their high-speed driving blew the white flag off of their jeep.

General Nagra and his colleagues rushed to the location and realized the gaffe. Three messengers were killed and one was wounded. The wounded soldier told General Nagra that General Niazi would surrender and a Pakistani General was on the way to meet him.

This joyous news was tainted with mixed feelings. Arrangements were made to send the three fallen soldiers with the wounded one to Mirjapur Hospital by Indian helicopter.

Minutes later, a Mercedes-Benz sedan and a jeep hoisting a white flag arrived at the location. The passengers of the two vehicles came out. One of them saluted General Nagra and introduced himself as General Jamshed of the Pakistani Army. General Jamshed informed General Nagra that General Niazi would surrender. He further added that General Niazi had invited General Nagra to meet him at his office to discuss and arrange the modalities of the surrendering ceremony. General Nagra wasted no time and said, "Let's go!"

They got into General Jamshed's Mercedes. General Jamshed sat in the front passenger-seat next to the driver. General Nagra, Brigadier Klair, Brigadier Sing, and Kader sat in the backseat of the car.

General Nagra wanted to talk to General Niazi. The General tried several times to call, but his calls did not get through.

The Mercedes was moving quickly towards the Dhaka cantonment.

Just at five minutes past ten, the Mercedes arrived at General Niazi's headquarters. General Jamshed escorted his guests to General Niazi's office and asked them to take their seats. He immediately left the office to fetch General Niazi.

General Nagra arrived at the enemy headquarters with only a few soldiers, but was armed with a tremendous sense of pride.

General Nagra and his colleagues wondered what would happen next. Just an hour ago, such a situation would have been unimaginable. Nonetheless, they now sat in the office of the chief commander of the Pakistani military.

It was ten minutes past ten on the morning of December 16th 1971. General Niazi entered his office. He stood at attention and saluted General Nagra. With formalities aside, they two old friends embraced each other.

At first, General Nagra thanked General Niazi for his decision to surrender and avoid a potential blood bath. They engaged in pleasantries and inquired about each other's families.

Then, General Nagra introduced Brigadier Klair, Brigadier Singh, and Kader to General Niazi. While introducing Kader, General Nagra mentioned that Kader Siddiqui was the sole representative of the Mukti Bahini at the meeting.

As soon as Kader's name was pronounced, General Niazi stood up and saluted Kader and extended his arm to shake Kader's hand.

This moment weighed heavily in Kader's mind. He was perplexed. He saw a monster standing in front of him who terrorized the Bengali nation. General Niazi's hand was sullen with the blood of the people of Bangladesh.

His forces were responsible for killing millions of Bengalis and raping thousands of women. How could he shake the hand of such a war criminal?

General Nagra realized Kader's dilemma. He broke the lull and said, "Kader, you have won. General Niazi has accepted his defeat. Please shake hands."

Kader regained his composure and reluctantly acceded to General Nagra's request.

General Niazi and General Nagra discussed the protocol and logistics of the surrendering ceremony. It was decided that General Aurora, the Chief of the Eastern Command of the joint forces and Group Captain A.K. Khandker, the Deputy Chief of Staff of Bangladesh Armed Forces would arrive in Dhaka at four-thirty that evening to accept Niazi's surrender. The ceremony would take place at the Race Course (now Suhrawardy Park) in the presence of the national and international media.

General Niazi, Commander of Pakistani forces in Bangladesh signs the documents of surrender to Indian General Aurora, December 16, 1971

This moment marked the virtual fall of Dhaka and the demise of East Pakistan. Dhaka was no longer a city of Pakistan. It had become liberated as the capital of Bangladesh.

No one expected Dhaka to fall so abruptly. The city fell like a heart attack victim. It was as if the soul had passed away, while the body was still intact. We would avoid experiencing Germany's fate during the fall of the Berlin in 1945. Dhaka was a vessel now ready to reclaim the spirit of Bangladesh.

After meeting with General Niazi, Kader left for Tangail.

Meanwhile, Shaheed and I had been in the WAPDA bungalow all morning. We had been coordinating the various activities of the Mukti Bahini.

Around ten that morning, we received information that Kader had arrived near Mirpur. We listened to Indian radio reports that stated that Pakistani forces were expected to surrender today. However, we had no clue as to when and how they would go about doing so. Moreover, we did not rule out the possibility of a final battle over Dhaka.

In the meantime, Latif Siddiqui and Basit Siddiqui joined us. We were discussing the role and responsibility of the Tangail Mukti Bahini should Pakistani forces fight to defend Dhaka and inflict damage to the city and its people.

While amidst this brainstorming session, we received a telephone call from Kader. He broke the greatest of news! Dhaka was free! Bangladesh was independent! He added that General Niazi surrendered to Indian commander, General Nagra and himself just moments ago.

Kader further told us that he was going to Dhaka with two thousand Mukti Bahini from our camp at Tangail Cadet College to participate in the formal surrender ceremony that would take place at the Suhrawardy Park that evening.

He asked us to stay in Tangail and oversee the law and order of the district. He further asked us to stand by in case of emergency.

We had been anxiously awaiting this news for the previous nine months. Our office was filled with joy and excitement.

We spread the news of victory all over Tangail and to all of our Mukti Bahini camps by radio and telephone. People flooded the streets shouting victory slogans, "Joy Bangla - Victory to Bangladesh!"

Tangail town erupted in celebration. People from all walks of life came to the streets, playing drums and dancing. Thousands of people gathered in front of our office and congratulated us. Latif Siddiqui and Basit Siddiqui addressed the crowd.

I felt humbled and gratified with the fact that I was intimately involved with a war strategy that allowed two brigades of the Indian Army and the Tangail Mukti Bahini to enter Dhaka. Moreover, I was a trusted comrade of Mukti Bahini Commander, Kader Siddiqui to whom Pakistani General Niazi surrendered. What a feeling!

With great joy and pride, we all shouted from the tops of our lungs, "Joy Bangla!"

Victory Strategy

The fall of the Pakistani military was more than just a matter of luck. Our victory came behind the efforts of careful planning and the precise execution of war strategies.

Firstly, Indian high command used a diversion to mislead the enemy. Joint forces were deployed with tanks and heavy artillery to the east of Dhaka in the Comilla sector and far west of Dhaka in the Jessore sector. Several divisions of the joint forces were positioned in these sectors.

Meanwhile, only two infantry brigades of brigadiers Klair and Singh were deployed in the northern sector in Jamalpur and Mymensingh. They had neither tank, nor artillery support.

This imbalanced deployment was done deliberately to convince the enemy that joint forces would enter Dhaka city from the Comilla sector in the east, which was only about fifty miles from Dhaka city, compared to the one hundred-plus miles from the northern sector.

Secondly, the Indian Army partnered with the Tangail Mukti Bahini to reinforce their war strategy. We maintained the liberation of a long strip of land, which spanned about eighty miles. The liberated strip ranged from an area just thirty miles north of Dhaka to Jamalpur near the northern border. The Indian Army took advantage of our achievement by landing paratroopers in Tangail.

Lastly, to further deceive the enemy, Z-Force, a special Mukti Bahini brigade lead by Col. Ziaur Rahman, was transferred from the northern sector to Sylhet in the eastern sector, where two other special

Mukti Bahini brigades were already stationed; S-Force lead by Col. Shafiullah and K-Force lead by Col. Khaled Mosharraf.

Only Col. Taher and his Mukti Bahini forces were left in the northern sector to attack the fortified garrison of the enemy at the Kamalpur Border Outpost.

By maneuvering in this manner, the joint forces high command was successful in manipulating the enemy into believing that the northern sector would not be a threat to Pakistani forces. Pakistani intelligence was lead to believe that the main onslaught on Dhaka city would come from the eastern sector.

Pakistani high command fell into this trap. They transferred their main fighting forces from Jamalpur and Mymensingh garrisons to Bhairab in the eastern sector.

This move weakened the enemy defense in the northern sector and opened a window of opportunity for the joint forces to gain easy access to Dhaka.

While Pakistani forces were busy defending themselves from the joint forces' onslaught in the eastern sector, the Indian Army, with the help of the Tangail Mukti Bahini, began their march towards Dhaka from the northern sector.

Meanwhile, on December 11th, General Jacob, the Chief of Staff of the Indian Army, Eastern Sector, arranged a press conference in Calcutta. He declared to the national and international press that the night before, Indian paratroopers had landed surrounding Dhaka. He claimed that Dhaka was then, a besieged city, waiting to fall any day.

On the insistence of reporters, General Jacob reluctantly disclosed that a division of joint forces had the capital city surrounded.

However, in reality, the division he referred to was actually only single battalion of paratroopers who had landed, not in Dhaka, but rather some seventy miles to the north, in Tangail District.

This bluff distressed Pakistani command. It placed a tremendous amount of psychological pressure on General Niazi to surrender. The joint forces' strategy worked just as planned.

The inclusion of the Tangail Mukti Bahini in the original war strategy to conquer Dhaka was an important historic event. One of the most significant components to this plan was the landing of a battalion of paratroopers in Tangail.

Arguably, I was the first person from Bangladesh to have had the privilege of knowing this vital secret plan.

I was lucky and honored to be associated with such a clever war strategy. It was also a great testament to Kader, as well as, to the Tangail Mukti Bahini.

(L-R) Author, Kader & Sabur in the Far Eastern Economic Review, May 6, 1972

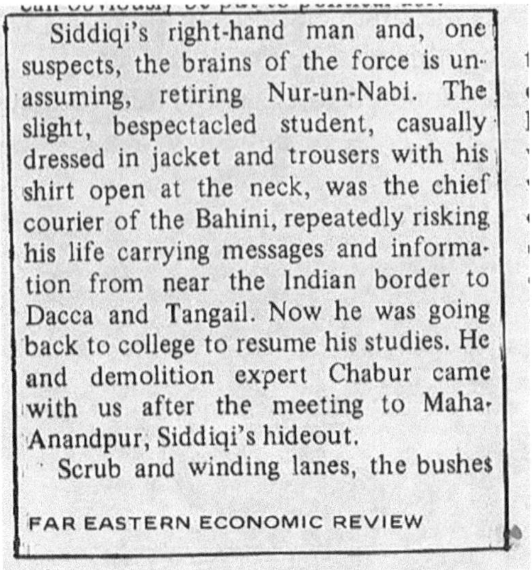

Siddiqi's right-hand man and, one suspects, the brains of the force is un-assuming, retiring Nur-un-Nabi. The slight, bespectacled student, casually dressed in jacket and trousers with his shirt open at the neck, was the chief courier of the Bahini, repeatedly risking his life carrying messages and information from near the Indian border to Dacca and Tangail. Now he was going back to college to resume his studies. He and demolition expert Chabur came with us after the meeting to Maha-Anandpur, Siddiqi's hideout.

Scrub and winding lanes, the bushes

FAR EASTERN ECONOMIC REVIEW

Far Eastern Economic Review, May 6, 1972 recognizes Author as the "the Brains of the forces"

Chapter 6

Arms Surrender

Lt. General Aurora in Tangail

After the 16th of December, Tangail received special attention from the nation and the world. It became a Mecca for national and international press from television, radio, and print. The media was intrigued by the success of the Tangail Mukti Bahini. Every day I entertained hundreds of such visitors as the Tangail Mukti Bahini's media liaison.

But, unbeknownst to us we would receive a new kind of visitor as well – the senior generals of the Indian Army. During the war, we had established personal contact with Major General Nagra and brigadiers Klair and Sanat Singh who had already visited Tangail several times. However, the visit of the senior Indian Army generals was a matter of serious concern, as well as political significance. Their visit raised many questions and spawned many more rumors.

After the fall of Dhaka on December 16, most of the seventeen thousand freedom fighters of the Tangail Mukti Bahini were stationed in and around Tangail town. Instead of sitting idle, we had scheduled regular training and exercise for the freedom fighters. They were also given military uniforms even though there was no formal dress code during the war. By the time the senior Indian Army generals arrived, the Mukti Bahini looked like a division of well-trained and disciplined soldiers.

The presence of the uniformed soldiers coupled with the influx of foreign visitors made Tangail look as if it were a state within state. The Tangail Mukti Bahini administration exuded authority as if it were an autonomous entity outside the government. This appearance of Tangail had created some concern in certain quarters within the newly formed Bangladesh government, and amongst the leadership of the Indian Army.

Though during the war, the Tangail Mukti Bahini was politically loyal to Prime Minister Tajuddin Ahmed, we were not under the direct command of the Bangladesh Army. Therefore, there was concern as to whether we would continue our loyality to the government of Prime Minister Tajuddin Ahmed in Bangladesh's post-war era. Furthermore, the future relationship between the Tangail Mukti Bahini and the Bangladesh Army was still unknown.

Four senior Indian generals independantly visited Tangail to gain firsthand knowledge of the situation in Tangail following December 16th. Each of the four generals had unique credentials.

One of them was Major General Ovan. He was the senior intelligence officer for the Indian Army. He was in charge of developing and guiding the Mujib Bahini. The Mujib Bahini was a special freedom fighter group insituted to protect the leadership of Bangabandhu Sheik Mujibur Rahman, during and after the war.

The second general was Major General Sarkar. He was a Bengali general who was likely in Tangail to understand the psyche of the Tangail Mukti Bahini.

The third General who visited Tangail was Lt. General Jacob. He was Chief-of-Staff of the Indian Army's Eastern Command.

In the beginning of the war, Field Marshall Sam Manekshaw, the chief of the Indian armed forces developed a strategy for the Bangladesh war. The main objective of the strategy was to occupy two regions of Bangladesh: Chittagong and Khulna. However, Lt. General Jacob knew that without occupying the capital, it would be difficult to win the war. He did not see how his commanding officer's plan would lead to the occupation of Dhaka. Therefore, he ignored Field Marshall Manekshaw's directives and designed a new strategy to capture Dhaka. Lt. General Jacob's decision to disobey his commanding officer's order was an unprecidented move in military history.

Lt. General Jacob became the architect behind the "war of movement", a strategy which engaged Pakistani forces in the difficult and swampy terrain of Bangladesh. This went against Field Marshall Manekshaw's plan to implement a "brief incursion into Bangladesh" to capture Chittagong and Khulna. Fortunately, Lt. General Jacob's strategy paid off quickly. Indian forces, with the help of the Tangail Mukti Bahini, were able to capture Dhaka.

With his visit, Lt. General Jacob wanted to make sure that the Tangail Mukti Bahini was not a threat to Prime Minister Tajuddin Ahmed's nascent government. Lt. General Jacob was desperate to discover our motives to remain as a fighting force beyond the Independence of Bangladesh.

The last general to visit Tangail was Lt. General Jagjit Singh Aurora, General Officer Commander-in-Chief of the Indian and Bangladesh forces in the Eastern Theatre. He arrived in Tangail on December 22, 1971.

By then, Lt. General Aurora had become a household name in Bangladesh as well as in India and Pakistan. His acceptance of Lt. General Niazi's surrender had made him a war hero overnight.

We were only given two hours notice that he would be visiting Tangail. Kader, Shaheed, and I received him at the heliport of the Tangail circuit house. Lt. General Aurora was accompanied by Major General B. F. Gonzales and Brigadier Sanat Singh.

It was my second meeting with Lt. General Aurora. We first met in Tura, India on November 7th, 1971 at the army headquarters of Major General Gill. Before ending our first meeting, Lt. General Aurora said that he would meet me in liberated Tangail town. With his arrival he had kept his promise. However, he was not here to celebrate. He came to Tangail with an important hidden agenda.

In the morning of December of 22nd, Lt. General Aurora flew from Calcutta to Dhaka to discuss the situation in Tangail with his senior commanders. Unfortuantely, his commanders were divided. They gave him conflicting advice. He had no choice, but to see what was happening in Tangail for himself. After the meeting, he made his way to Tangail.

It was just before noon that Lt. General Aurora's helicopter touched ground. We stood in line along with several Indian Army officers to welcome him. He and his companions alighted from the helicopter. After a brief exchange of greetings with others, Lt. General Aurora looked at me and said, "How are you Nurandhar? See, I kept my promise, I am in Tangail."

I smiled and thanked him.

General Aurora could not pronounce my name correctly. It had happened even during our previous meeting in Tura. Possibly, he had inadvertantly combined my first name, Nuran with that of D. P. Dhar, an advisor to Indian Prime Minister Indira Gandhi. Dhar had become a famous wartime name as Mr. Dhar was in charge of maintaining liaison with the Bangladesh government.

We led Lt. General Aurora to the Bindubashini School play ground where we had arranged his reception. Thousands of people had already assembled there within hours to greet the famous war hero.

A uniformed squad of Mukti Bahini greeted Lt. General Aurora with an honor guard. After inspecting the parade, he walked on to the stage and asked Kader, "Are these soldiers members of the Bengal regiment?" The Bengal regiments were one of the smartest and toughest regiments in the Bangladesh Army.

Kader replied, "Negative. They are members of the Tangail Mukti Bahini."

In his welcoming address Kader thanked Lt. General Aurora for his role in the Bangladesh liberation war and specially in helping the Tangail Mukti Bahini. In return, Lt. General Aurora praised Kader's bravery and the role of the Tangail Mukti Bahini in liberating Dhaka.

I was the liaison to these generals during their visits in Tangail. As the chief-of-intelligence for the Tangail Mukti Bahini, my responsibility was also to listen to what the generals said, observe their body language, and probe them to find out the purpose of their visit to Tangail.

I noticed that during each of the generals' customary inspection of the parade after the guard of honor, the generals shared one common practice. They each randomly stopped one of the honor guard soldiers and asked them what they did before joining the Mukti Bahini. If the soldier answered that he was in the army, the generals would immediately retort, "What are you doing here now? You should go back to the army." If the soldier said that he was in college, the generals would immediately ask the soldier to return to his studies.

I asked Brigadier Sanat Singh to share with me the hidden agenda behind these visits. He was hesitant, but informed me that Kader had many enemies in the Bangladesh government. Kader's enemies were hatching conspiracies in order to neutralize Kader's increasing political clout as a war legend. The Indian generals were on a mission to find out the Tangail Mukti Bahini's strength and conviction should the Indian Army be asked to neutralize Kader and his soldiers. From Brigadier Singh's comments and my own observations, I could tell that the Indian Army preferred that the Tangail Mukti Bahini simply disintegrate and vanish.

We had finally figured out why the Indian generals were visiting Tangail. They wanted us to surrender our arms. If we would not surrender, the Indian Army would possibly be asked to take military action.

Brigadier Sanat Singh informed me that he had strongly recommended his superiors to refrain from any military action against us as it might lead to civil war and tarnish the success of our mutual victory.

Kader, Shaheed, and I had several meetings to formulate our post-war strategy and response to Lt. General Aurora. We decided that we would not surrender our arms until Bangabandhu was released from his Pakistani prison cell and was allowed to take charge of the Bangladesh government. We also decided that we would continue to support Prime Minister Tajuddin Ahmed and remain on stand by to protect against any threat to his government.

We knew that we were responsible for the future of each member of the Tangail Mukti Bahini. We could not just ask them to surrender their arms and go home. Therefore, we further decided that there must be an acceptable rehabilitation plan for the Mukti Bahini before we could agree to surrender ours arms. Shaheed and I drafted this plan for the rehabilitation of our comrades.

We conveyed our decisions to General Aurora. He was pleasantly surprised to hear of our loyalty to Prime Minister Tajuddin Ahmed. He appreciated the rationale for not surrendering our arms until Bangabandhu returned to Bangladesh. Moreover, he was relieved to know that he would not be asked to take military action against the Tangail Mukti Bahini whom Indian forces had fought side-by-side with.

General Aurora was happy to know our plan and left for Dhaka with great satisfaction.

General Aurora in Tangail. (L-R) Gen Aurora, Kader, Shaheed & Author (behind Gen Aorora & Kader)

Author coordinates the Generals visit in Tangail using walkie-talkie

Author and Shaheed develops plans for the rehabilitation of the Mukti Bahini.

Bangabandhu Sheikh Mujibur Rahman in Tangail

On the fateful night of March 25th, 1971 Bangabandhu was arrested from his residence in Dhanmondi, Dhaka, by Pakistani Army commandos and was taken to West Pakistan.

During the war, the Pakistani military junta tried him in a military court and sentenced him to death for alleged treason.

However, world leaders including Indira Gandhi, the Prime Minster of India, and Leonid Brezhnev, President of the Soviet Union pressured Pakistan to stop the execution of Bangabandhu.

Prime Minister Indira Gandhi even went on a world tour visiting the major capitals of the world in an effort to advocate the release of Bangabandhu, the elected leader of Bangladesh.

Though she found support amongst most leaders of the free world, she received a cold shoulder from the White House. In fact, the meeting between Prime Minister Gandhi and President Nixon went so poorly that Henry Kissinger later admitted that Nixon's post-meeting remarks regarding the Indian Prime Minister were not even printable.

However, on December 16th Pakistani forces surrendered in Dhaka. Bangladesh had finally been liberated. Despite this, Bangabandhu

Sheikh Mujibur Rahman, the father of the nation, was still a prisoner in West Pakistan.

Without the release of Bangabandhu, the liberation of Bangladesh was incomplete. Almost three weeks had passed after the fall of Dhaka, but still there was no news on Bangabandhu's release. Nonetheless, we remained hopeful.

In those days, Kader, Shaheed, and I joined others every evening in our headquarters at Tangail. We reviewed and coordinated the Mukti Bahini's activities as well as maintained the law and order of Tangail District.

On the evening of January 7th, while working in our office, we suddenly heard the sound of tremendous gunfire throughout Tangail town. We were surprised by this unexpected incident. We immediately arranged an investigation of the episode.

We found that some of the Mukti Bahini had heard rumors that Bangabandhu had finally been released from prison. In celebration of Bangabandhu's release, they began firing their guns into the air.

However, the firing went on for several minutes. Kader put me in charge of the office. Kader and Shaheed rushed off to the Mukti Bahini camps. They visited each camp and told the freedom fighters that the news of Bangabandhu's release was premature. The firing stopped.

At noon, January 8th, Indian Radio and the BBC both reported that Bangabandhu had been finally released from a Pakistani prison. Once again the sound of gunfire echoed from the Mukti Bahini camps. However, this time they had cause to celebrate. All of Tangail town was a stage for jubilation.

After being released from a Pakistani prison, Bangabandhu took a special flight from Pakistan to London, a neutral ground for all parties involved. He would arrive in Dhaka on January 10th via New Delhi, India.

We held an emergency meeting to discuss Bangabandhu's homecoming reception. We debated whether we should go to Dhaka to welcome Bangabandhu or meet him at his residence the following day.

We decided not to go to the airport directly. There would be thousands of people at the airport to welcome Bangabandhu. We opted to avoid the crowd. We would wait to greet Bangabandhu at his home.

However, Shaheed and I were assigned to go to Dhaka right away to observe the homecoming reception of Bangabandhu.

Within a few hours we were in Dhaka. So much had changed in the last nine months. Bangabandhu was arrested from this city and taken away to West Pakistan as a prisoner. And now, he had finally returned to the Dhaka as the president of an independent Bangladesh!

Dhaka was a spectacular scene. Thousands of people came to the streets to welcome their beloved leader. Bangabandhu rode in an open jeep and waved to the crowds. He was accompanied by acting-president Syed Nazrul Islam, Prime Minister Tajuddin Ahmed, and other leaders.

Meanwhile, thousands of people were waiting for Bangabandhu at Suhrawardy Park. They were eager just to see him, let alone, to hear him speak.

It took more than an hour just to travel the one-mile between the airport and the public meeting.

When Bangabandhu arrived on the stage, the sea of people in the park roared in applause and welcomed him.

Bangabandhu looked tired. Prison had taken its toll. However, it was clear that he was happy to return to his independent Bangladesh. He thanked the people and especially the Mukti Bahini for carrying out his order and fighting the Pakistani occupation forces. He expressed his deepest condolence and respect for the martyrs and their families.

Just nine months earlier, on March 7th, this was the site where Bangabandhu proclaimed our fight for independence. It was quite fitting to see him here again celebrating our victory.

The next day, on January 11th, Kader led about one hundred Tangail Mukti Bahinis to Bangabandhu's residence at Road 19, Dhanmondi Residential Area. Kader and a few of us entered Bangabandhu's house and found him talking to some other people.

As soon as Bangabandhu looked at us, Kader stood in attention and saluted him in the traditional military style. Kader then immediately bent down and touched his feet to show his deep respect.

Bangabandhu pulled Kader up and embraced him. Then Kader crowned Bangabandhu by laying a garland around his neck.

Bangabandhu looked around at all of us who were present and said, "This is my Kader, he fought against the occupation forces."

He pointed us out to the others and added that we were Kader's co-fighters. Then he embraced each of us one by one.

Bangabandhu asked us, "How did you defeat the monstrous Pakistani forces?"

He then added, "You are the real heroes of Bangladesh. You responded to my call to fight the enemy. Now you have to build this country with me".

Bangabandhu personally knew only two of us before the war: Kader and Latif. However, on that day Bangabandhu behaved as if he knew each of us like his sons.

We were humbled and gratified by his affection.

Bangabandhu was confined in a solitary prison cell and was detached from the rest of the world. He was denied news of the events in Bangladesh over last nine months. It was not until he arrived in London that he was briefed by various sources of the politics of Bangladesh.

However, in just one day, Bangabandhu quickly understood that a power struggle was already hatching within his own party.

Despite this, Bangabandhu's demeanor did not betray whether anyone had lobbied against Kader to him. Instead, Bangabandhu profusely praised Kader and our group for our valor. Bangabandhu escorted us to the gate to bid us farewell.

However, as we approached the gate, we saw a man with a bandage wrapped around his head. He sharply saluted Bangabandhu.

Bangabandhu introduced him to us as Col. Khaled Mosharraf, the Mukti Bahini commander of the famous K-Brigade.

We had heard of this war hero who had suffered a head injury while fighting the enemy. We heard of his many episodes of bravery during the war. One particular story had to do with his ambush of a Pakistani military convoy during the very early stages of the war.

Col. Khaled Mosharaf was a Major in the Pakistani Army before the war. He was the commander of the Bengal Regiment.

He revolted against the Pakistani authority in Brahmanbaria where he was stationed at the time.

He led the Bengali soldiers under his command out of the Pakistani Cantonment and ambushed a Pakistani Army convoy going to Chittagong. Major Khaled's troops destroyed the enemy convoy. The damage to the enemy was unprecedented.

In retaliation, the Pakistani authority sent a larger contingent under the command of a major general to capture Major Khaled, dead or alive.

Major Khaled Mosharraf fought ferociously against the enemy with limited resources. However, once again, the Pakistani Army suffered heavy damages at Major Khaled Mosharraf's hands and the enemy was forced to retreat.

After the battle, Pakistani high command acknowledged the bravery of Major Khaled Mosharraf and admitted, "We have trained Major Khaled so well that even a Major General wasn't enough to defeat him."

We were honored to meet Col. Khaled Mosharraf and were glad to see him alive.

Major Khaled Mosharaf, Bangabandhu, Shaheed, Author, Kader and others (L-R)

On January 15th, we came to Dhaka to meet Bangabandhu again. However, this time we came bearing a complaint.

We planned to publish a special bulletin about the Tangail Mukti Bahini in the Daily Bangladesh Observer. However, four student leaders known as the "Four Khalifa" had interfered and stopped the publication. The Tangail Freedom Fighters were outraged by this insult.

We had decided earlier that Kader would not say a word to Bangabandhu about the matter. So we explained the matter to Bangabandhu personally and submitted our protest to him. We pointed out that one member of the so-called "Four Khalifa" was acting out in jealousy.

Bangabandhu listened to us patiently and consoled us by saying that we should not get upset by these matters. He assured us that he would do something about this.

We still wanted immediate justice. He took a pause and said, "I will arrange something so that one hundred bulletins will be published about you."

Though we had not comprehended the significance of Bangabandhu's promise, we were satisfied and returned to Tangail.

Later we understood what Bangabandhu meant by "one hundred bulletins."

Various quarters were already engaged in a power struggle for post-liberated Bangladesh. They attempted to feed information to Bangabandhu against one another.

Meanwhile, Kader had gained a national and international reputation for his outstanding heroism in the liberation war. He was catapulted to the ranks of legendary war heroes. Many of Kader's political rivals were jealous of him. Some of them even began hatching various conspiracies against him.

One particular conspiracy that was brought to Bangabandhu's attention surrounded the fact that Kader did not go to the airport to welcome Bangabandhu. Kader's rivals alleged that he was not loyal to Bangabandhu.

A second rumor that had been deliberately spread was that Kader would not surrender his arms to the Bangladesh Government.

Still a fledgling government, Bangladesh was struggling to maintain law and order throughout the country. Just after the 16th of December, several groups of youth posing as freedom fighters took to the streets collecting the abandoned arms left behind by the fleeing Pakistani forces.

The criminal activities of these youths defamed the Mukti Bahini. People sarcastically referred to them as the 16th Division of the Mukti Bahini, pointing to the fact that they had become freedom fighters only after December 16th.

Aside from the misguided teens, several hardened criminals had also gotten their hands on some of these abandoned firearms and engaged in other criminal activities.

Bangabandhu was left with no choice. He decided to collect arms from all groups other than police, paramilitary, and military forces.

On January 16th, Bangabandhu invited Kader to his office to discuss the rampant problem.

Bangabandhu said, "The arms scattered all over the country are not safe. They are not conducive to maintaining law and order".

Bangabandhu told Kader that he could put an end to this problem by setting an example and formally surrendering the arms of the Mukti Bahini. He added that by giving up the Mukti Bahini's arms, the other groups would have no choice, but to do so as well.

Bangabandhu looked at Kader and asked, "So, do you think you can help me?"

Kader replied, "You are our leader. We are loyal to you. We will oblige to whatever you ask."

Bangabandhu replied, "You have earned your reputation in the battlefield. Now you will do it once more off of the battlefield."

Bangabandhu was a great politician. He managed to kill two birds with one stone.

By asking Kader to surrender his arms, Bangabandhu would silence Kader's critics. Others would be forced to follow suit, and law and order would be restored.

It was decided that Bangabandhu would visit Tangail on January 24. We chose this date to formally surrender our arms to Bangabandhu. This would be Bangabandhu's first trip outside of Dhaka since his return to independent Bangladesh.

The people and freedom fighters of Tangail were excited by the news that Bangabandhu would be visiting Tangail.

From January 16 to the 20, we had several meetings to finalize the logistics as well as the programs surrounding Bangabandhu's reception.

Bangabandhu specifically asked us to allow the Awami League to organize the public meeting in Tangail. He told us that it would look odd if he did not attend a public meeting under the banner of his own party during his first trip outside of the capital. Otherwise, the dedicated leaders and workers of the Awami League, the party that lead the country to independence, would be disenchanted.

January 23rd was a hectic day. We worked until midnight to finalize every detail of the following day's program. Every facet was scrutinized. Every item was double-checked. This was no small challenge for the Tangail Mukti Bahini.

On the night of January 23, we sat down with Mr. Abdul Mannan, the president of the Tangail Awami League to discuss who would preside over the next day's public meeting. Unfortunately, the matter was disputed all through the night. The meeting ended without any agreement.

After the meeting, Kader met with us to discuss the matter and to find a solution to the problem. It was two in the morning before any of us got to bed. These last two days were as busy as any during the war.

On January 24th, we woke up very early and prepared to receive Bangabandhu in Tangail.

Due to the hectic activities of the previous couple of days, I had no time to shave and had grown a long beard. However, today we would receive the father of our nation. I had to look presentable. I quickly shaved and dressed up before leaving to receive Bangabandhu.

Kader and Shaheed went out at seven that morning towards Tangail-Dhaka Road. They would welcome Bangabandhu at the border of the Tangail District.

Colorful gates were erected at every bus stop on Tangail-Dhaka Road to greet Bangabandhu. Arrangements were also made for the public to hail Bangabandhu from each side of the road.

Almost each day, since the 16th of December, hundreds of media people, from both the national and international press, came to Tangail to cover the story of Kader and the Tangail Mukti Bahini. I was in charge of maintaining a liaison with them on behalf of the Tangail Mukti Bahini.

That day Kader and Shaheed would participate in the formal program with Bangabandhu. So I was assigned again to coordinate with the media.

In the meantime, a mob of journalists from both print and electronic media of the national and international press had already flooded Tangail. They mobbed the streets of Tangail town in anticipation as to whether Bangabandhu would be able to successfully broker the surrender of arms from the Mukti Bahini.

I stood by Shibnath High School located at the entrance of Tangail town. There we built a stage at the high school playground to present Bangabandhu with an honor guard salute preformed by uniformed and well-disciplined Mukti Bahini guards.

We received information that Kader, Shaheed, and the Awami League leaders had received Bangabandhu and his entourage at the Tangail District border. They were on their way to Tangail town.

People from all walks of life gathered on both sides of the road and greeted Bangabandhu chanting slogans, "Joy Bangla, Joy Bangabandhu."

Bangabandhu addressed a few impromptu roadside public meetings. It took almost two and a half hours for Bangabandhu to cross about thirty miles.

Finally, at eleven-thirty, we saw Bangabandhu's entourage approach our location. In the front, a convoy of forty Mukti Bahini motorcycles escorted Bangabandhu. Right behind them was Bangabandhu, standing in an open Toyota jeep flanked by Kader and Shaheed at each side of the jeep.

It was an extravagant scene. Bangabandhu wore his usual attire, a white linen Punjabi and pajama adorned with his trademark Mujib-coat and pipe.

Kader and Shaheed were dressed in their formal military uniforms and stood at each side of Bangabandhu. A military-style motorcycle escort led them. There was a motorcade of about fifty cars behind Bangabandhu's jeep.

I embraced this extraordinary panoramic view from the stage at Shibnath High School. The scene was truly fitting of the honorable reception deserved by Bangabandhu on his first official visit as Prime Minister.

Kader and Shaheed escorted Bangabandhu directly to the stage. Commander Habib led the company of uniformed Mukti Bahini in an honor guard salute to Bangabandhu as another group of Mukti Bahini played the national anthem "Amar Shonar Bangla. Ami Tomay Bhalobashi... - Golden Bengal of mine, my love is for thee..."

Commander Habib requested Bangabandhu to inspect the guards. After inspecting the guards, Bangabandhu came back to the stage and made a short speech to the guards.

Kader and Shaheed remained standing on stage behind Bangabandhu during the ceremony. I stood on the stage next to Shaheed recording Bangabandhu's speech with tape recorder.

Arms Surrender

The next event on Bangabandhu's agenda was the formal surrender of arms at Bindubashini High School playground.

After the honor guard ceremony, Bangabandhu was taken to the venue. Three thousand Freedom Fighters were standing by with their arms ready to be surrendered. We had also arranged the surrender of an additional several thousand arms of various kinds in two rows on the ground in front of the stage.

Bangabandhu was led directly to the stage. As soon as Bangabandhu took the stage with Kader and Shaheed at each side, Commander Hakim called the freedom fighters to attention and rendered an arms salute to Bangabandhu.

We decided that as a symbolic gesture, Kader would be the first to surrender his personal Sten gun to Bangabandhu. Accordingly, Commander Hakim handed over the Sten gun to Kader. This was the gun, which Kader carried with him all throughout the nine months of war.

In typical military style, Kader held the gun with two hands, knelt down and put it in front of Bangabandhu's feet. Three thousand Mukti Bahini followed Kader and laid down their arms on the ground in front of them.

It was a solemn occasion. The once roaring crowd came to a hushed pin-drop silence. All that could be heard were camera shutter clicks from the several hundred photographers.

Bangabandhu bent down and accepted Kader's Sten gun and handed it over to Shaheed and then embraced Kader.

It was a very emotional moment. Every eye was filled with tears.

Bangabandhu was led to inspect the arms. He slowly walked around the rows of guns. Hundreds of journalist followed Bangabandhu.

Display of arms ready to surrender

After the arms inspection, Bangabandhu returned to the stage. Kader came to the microphone and made a brief speech. He said in a somber voice, "Today we are proud. We had raised our arms against the enemy in response to the call of our great leader - Bangabandhu, and today by his edict, we have surrendered our arms to him."

As Kader spoke, Bangabandhu could be seen wiping his eyes with his handkerchief.

Next, Bangabandhu was asked to address the gathering. Bangabandhu started his speech in his soaking voice.

I have seen him speaking in many public meetings. He had a thunderous voice. He roared like lion to protest against the Pakistani Military Junta. However, on this day he was a different person. Tears rolled over his checks. His voice was drenched with emotion and his words quivered with each breath.

It was an extraordinary scene. There he was - Bangabandhu Sheikh Mujibur Rahman, the father of our nation. He was labeled as the greatest Bengali born in a thousand years, the lion-hearted leader who did not blink in the face of death. He spent more than thirteen years of the prime of his life in a Pakistani jail.

And now, he stood before us, wiping his eyes with his tear-dampened handkerchief. He was a proud father given the opportunity to acknowledge the accomplishments of his sons.

Those of us standing behind him could not hold back our tears. Kader and Shaheed stood at attention while I held a heavy tape recorder in my hand, making it difficult for the three of us to wipe the flow of tears from our eyes. All we could do was look down and let our tears drain through the cracks of the stage floor.

Bangabandhu addresses the Mukti Bahini after the arms surrendering ceremony. (R-L) Author, Kader, Bangabandhu & Shaheed

In his speech, Bangabandhu again thanked the Mukti Bahini for liberating the country. He said, "I could not give you arms, but I still asked you to resist the enemy. So you snatched the arms from the enemy and fought back in historical fashion. I am proud of you."

He then added, "Today you have made history once again by surrendering your arms to me. You have created an example for others to follow. I salute you for responding to my order."

After the arms surrendering ceremony, Bangabandhu was escorted to the police parade grounds. Young boys and girls saluted him. Then he laid the foundation for a monument honoring the country's martyrs.

Wearing Bangabandhu's Mujib-Coat

From the police parade ground Bangabandhu was led to the WAPDA Bungalow to get some rest and shower.

During the war, almost every bridge along the Tangail-Dhaka Road was destroyed. Bangabandhu had to travel from Dhaka to Tangail along the grimy service roads near the bridges. To make matters worse, he was traveling in an uncovered jeep. His famous black vest, the Mujib-Coat turned from a vibrant black to an ashy-grey mess soiled by the dust of the road.

While Bangabandhu was taking a shower, a freedom fighter was trying to clean his Mujib-Coat. However, the soldier had difficulty cleaning it. The vest was long and heavy. It was nearly impossible to clean by holding it in one hand and brushing it with the other. The soldier knew that the best way to get the coat clean was to get someone to wear it while he brushed the coat down with both hands.

But, who would dare to wear Bangabandhu's vest? No one! To discourage others even further, Kader was standing right there.

Suddenly Kader looked up at me and said, "You put it on. The jacket has to get cleaned. There is nothing wrong with putting on the vest for cleaning purposes".

Before I realized what Kader had said, the Mujib-Coat was around my shoulders.

Kader recounted the story in his memoirs *Shadhinata 71:*

> Before this incident, Nuran Nabi looked like a young man with normal stature. He was very successful as the chief of the Intelligence Department for the Mukti Bahini. However, it was not until we put Bangabandhu's jacket on him that we realized how small and short in stature Nuran Nabi was. Bangabandhu's waist-length vest came down below Nuran Nabi's knees. We could easily fit another Nuran Nabi within this vest. What a memorable and humorous scene as Nuran Nabi tried to gauge how loose and slack the Mujib-Coat was on him.

After his shower, Bangabandhu got dressed and left for the Tangail Circuit House for lunch. Before, stepping out, we took a group photograph with Bangabandhu.

Recognition by the Soviet Union

Bangabandhu came down to the lobby of the WAPDA Bungalow. Just as he was about to get into his car, Andre Popov, the Consul General of the Soviet Union in Dhaka arrived.

He greeted Bangabandhu and said, "Your Excellency, Mr. Prime Minister, my government has recognized the People's Republic of Bangladesh. I have come here to deliver this good news personally to you."

Bangabandhu thanked Mr. Popov for the good news as well as for coming all the way up from Dhaka to Tangail. He invited Mr. Popov to join him for lunch.

This was the first recognition of the newly independent Bangladesh by one of the world's super powers.

Though the Soviet Union was a staunch supporter of the Bangladesh liberation war and provided strong political and material support during the war, the formal recognition came almost five weeks after the fall of Dhaka.

On the other hand, two other super-powers, the United States and China supported Pakistan and opposed our liberation war. Despite the insistence of world leaders and international organizations like the UNO, which had criticized the Pakistani military junta, the United States and China refused to ask the Pakistan military government to put an end to the genocide in Bangladesh.

President Nixon and Secretary of State Kissinger had both personally taken sides with the Pakistani military junta from the beginning of the conflict.

On March 25th at midnight, Pakistani forces massacred more than ten thousand innocent people including students, teachers, and politicians in Dhaka city alone.

The following day, perturbed by the firsthand account of this genocide, Mr. Archer Blood, the Consul General of the American Consulate in Dhaka sent a confidential telegram to the State Department under the subject heading, "Selective Genocide."

He said in the telegram, "Here in Dhaka we are mute and horrified witness to a reign of terror by the Pakistani military."

He continued, "Moreover, with the support of the Pak[istani] military, non-Bengali Muslims are systematically attacking poor people's quarters and murdering Bengalis and Hindus." *(U.S. Consulate [Dacca] Cable, Selective genocide, March 27, 1971)*

Nixon and Kissinger ignored the telegram and remained silent regarding the genocide in Bangladesh.

Distressed by the continued acts of genocide by the Pakistani military, Mr. Blood and his colleagues in the US Consulate in Dhaka sent another telegram to the State Department on April 6, 1971.

The second telegram was known as the "Blood Telegram." It was seen as one of the most strongly worded dissent channel messages ever written by a foreign services officer to the State Department. Twenty-nine Americans had signed it. This was unprecedented. The telegram stated:

> Our government has failed to denounce the suppression of democracy. Our government has failed to denounce atrocities. Our government has failed to take forceful measures to protect its citizens while at the same time bending over backwards to placate the West Pak[istan] dominated government and to lessen any deservedly negative international public relations impact against them. Our government has evidenced what many will consider moral bankrupt... But, we have chosen not to intervene, even morally, on the grounds that the Awami conflict, in which unfortunately the overworked term genocide is applicable, is purely an internal matter of a sovereign state. Private Americans have expressed disgust. We, as professional civil servants, express our dissent with current policy and fervently hope that our true and lasting interests here can be defined and our policies redirected. (U.S. Consulate (Dacca) Cable, Dissent from U.S. Policy Toward East Pakistan, April 6, 1971, Confidential, 5 pp. Includes Signatures from the Department of State.

Source: RG 59, SN 70-73 Pol and Def. From: Pol Pak-U.S. To: Pol 17-1 Pak-U.S. Box 2535)

Although Mr. Blood was scheduled to stay in Dhaka for another eighteen months, President Nixon and Secretary of State Kissinger, infuriated by the "Blood Telegram" recalled Mr. Blood overnight from Dhaka. Their sole objective was to support West Pakistan in hopes of opening diplomatic channels to China and to counter the power of the Soviet Union. The "Blood Telegram" stood in the way of this agenda.

From their actions it seemed that the two American statesmen were more offended by the threat created by the "Blood Telegram" than by the genocide and rape of thousands of innocent civilians.

Nixon and Kissinger continued their anti-Bangladesh and Pro-Pakistan policy until the very last days of war.

Just before the fall of Dhaka, the United States and China tried one last time to prevent the independence of Bangladesh. They attempted to pass a cease-fire resolution through the Security Council of the United Nations, to prevent the liberation of Bangladesh.

However, this anti-Bangladesh move was thwarted by several Soviet vetoes in the United Nations Security Council.

While we were apprehensive of American and Chinese attitudes regarding diplomatic recognition, as well as post-war help, we were very pleased to receive the timely diplomatic recognition from the Soviet Union.

Public Meeting

After the lunch at the Tangail Circuit House, Bangabandhu arrived at the public meeting in Tangail Park at two-thirty in the afternoon. Mr. Mannan and the other Awami League leaders greeted Bangabandhu. The park was jam-packed. Thousands of people had arrived here from all over Tangail and the neighboring districts. This was Bangabandhu's first public meeting outside of the capital. And of course, this was also the largest public meeting ever held in Tangail town.

Moments before the meeting, there was still no consensus on who would preside over the meeting. When suddenly, Bangabandhu turned to us and asked, "Who is presiding over today's meeting, Mannan?"

Little did he know, but Bangabandhu just made the decision very easy for us.

Mr. Abdul Mannan, president of the Tangail Awami League stood up and presided over the meeting. After a welcome address by Kader, Shaheed and others, Bangabandhu was asked to make his speech.

As he stood in front of the microphone, the crowd greeted him with chants of "Joy Bangla" and "Joy Bangabandhu."

Bangabandhu rose to the podium. But unlike earlier in the morning, Bangabandhu looked like his usual self. Maybe it was the shower. Maybe it was his newly cleaned clothes. Maybe it was the after-effects of a smooth arms-surrender ceremony. Or maybe it was the Soviet's diplomatic recognition of Bangladesh. Whatever it was, it was clear that Sheik Mujibur Rahman had been rejuvenated by the morning's events.

He spoke in his usual thunderous voice as he addressed the audience. He again thanked Kader, the Tangail Mukti Bahini, and the public for their sacrifices in liberating the country.

He mentioned that the enemy had destroyed the country. The economy had been ruined after years of Pakistani exploitation and the stresses of war. But, he reminded the audience that their work was not through. He asked that they continue to make additional sacrifices as they united as people to rebuild their country over the next three years.

He asked that the freedom fighters return to school and finish their education. He asked others to go back to their previous jobs, to join the army, police, or other agencies.

He asked us all to join him in rebuilding the nation.

However, Bangabandhu made a stern warning against corruption. He called for Bangladesh to become a secular nation with freedom for people of all faiths built on a solid foundation of democracy. He added that we now live in the People's Republic of Bangladesh, and this country would be governed by the will of the people.

The public approved his call with a deafening applause and the echoing of patriotic slogans. The meeting ended on a festive note.

After the meeting, we bade farewell to Bangabandhu and his entourage before they headed towards Dhaka.

We noticed that no other dignitaries, such as ministers, chiefs of the armed forces, or senior political leaders accompanied Bangabandhu to Tangail. Only his personal staff and his two young sons joined him.

However, this was no surprise to us. There were far-fetched rumors circulating that Bangabandhu might be taken hostage in Tangail. Conspiracy theorists proclaimed that the arms surrender ceremony was just a ploy to bring Bangabandhu to Tangail. It was alleged that some of Bangabandhu's advisors suggested that he cancel his visit.

Nonetheless, Bangabandhu came to Tangail. He conquered our hearts. And he returned to Dhaka safely.

Once again he proved that he was not only a charismatic leader, but also a confident and courageous one, as well. He defied the concern and advice of his critics and hesitant advisors. He came to Tangail and received the surrender of arms from the Tangail Mukti Bahini. By doing so, he showed the whole country and the world that his freedom fighters were loyal to him. He was their leader.

We thanked all of the freedom fighters and volunteers for their selfless service in making the event such a great success. We worked late as we wound up the final activities of the day. Finally, we got to bed sometime after midnight.

President Abu Sayeed Choudhury in Tangail

On January 12, Bangabandhu resigned as the president of the Bangladesh government and assumed the office of the prime minister of Bangladesh. According to the constitution, in a parliamentary form of government, the prime minister is the chief executive and head of government.

Abu Sayeed Choudhury, former Vice Chancellor of Dhaka University and the roving ambassador of the wartime Bangladesh government was appointed as the president of the republic. President Choudhury was a son of Tangail. The Tangail Mukti Bahini used his farmhouse in the Kalihati jungle as a camp. Coincidentally, from behind the scenes, Shaheed and I observed the process through which Abu Sayeed Choudhury became president of the republic.

Soon after taking office, President Choudhury visited Tangail. It was an honor and privilege for us to receive the new president in Tangail. We accorded him with the same protocol as we did for other dignitaries. He was very pleased with the hospitality we provided to him. He thanked us for our role in the liberation war.

Welcoming President Abu Sayeed Chowdhury in Tangail (L-R) Abdul Latif Siddiqui, Author, President, Shaheed, and Kader Siddiqui

President Abu Sayeed Choudhury in Tangail (R-L) Author, Shaheed, Dr. Shahjada Chowdhury, President, Kader Siddiqui, Dr. Laila Choudhury, District Commissioner, and Poet Rafique Azad

Exit from the Shining Stage

January 25, 1971. I woke up late in the morning. Last night, the news of our arms surrender to Bangabandhu was broadcasted on Radio Bangladesh, Bangladesh Television, Indian radio Akashvani, the BBC, and the Voice of America.

By morning every national newspaper had published our story on the front page marking the success of the event in the headlines and adorning their pages with photos of the arms surrendering ceremony.

We finally understood the extent of Bangabandhu's promise of publishing one hundred bulletins on the Tangail Mukti Bahini.

Yesterday's event would be the last one formally organized by us as the Tangail Mukti Bahini. The curtain had finally dropped on our stage. From today, we would each go our separate ways.

I joined the liberation war on March 7th 1971 at the call of Bangabandhu. That chapter of my life had finally come to an end.

The liberation of a nation only comes once in a lifetime. I was lucky that I had the opportunity to participate in the brightest chapter of the history of my nation. I was humbled and honored.

As I packed my few personal belongings, I realized that I would forever be remembered as a freedom fighter of the Bangladesh Liberation War. I knew that my ancestors would remember me in this way as well. No one could ever take this honor from me.

Around noon, I prepared myself to say my final goodbyes to the hottest and brightest political stage in the nation.

As I rode a Dhaka-bound bus, I reminisced of the events of the last nine months and reflected on the previous day's encounter with Bangabandhu. The memory of my mother kept coming to my mind. I thought of her fondly. She might have been praying from heaven for my victory and safe return from the war. My destination was the F. H. Hall dormitory at Dhaka University. It was time to complete my master's degree.

It was time to do my part in answering Bangabandhu's call once again.

Chapter 7

Bangladesh Genocide 1971*

9 Months

The Bangladesh genocide committed by Pakistani occupation forces began in the early morning hours of March 26th and continued throughout the nine months of the Liberation War (March-December, 1971). Though the Liberation War lasted less than a year, it is estimated that during this time the Pakistani Army and their local collaborators killed three million people. During these months, thousands of Bengali women lost their honor. In response to this carnage, about ten million people fled their homeland to take refuge in neighboring India.

It was one of the worst genocides of the post-World War II era, outstripping Rwanda (800,000 killed) and even surpassing Indonesia (1-1.5 million killed in 1965-66).

Killing of Intellectuals

So that the Bengali nation could not rise, Pakistani occupation forces implemented their sinister blueprint to kill Bangladeshi intellectuals. The first victim was Dr. Shamsuz Zoha of the Chemistry Department of Rajshahi University.

It was the 18th of February 1969. Dr. Zoha, a proctor of the university was escorting a student procession in support of the Non-Cooperation Movement. In the distance, a Pakistani Army platoon, lead by a lieutenant was carefully watching the procession from the side of the road.

Suddenly, without provocation, the lieutenant jumped from his jeep and charged towards Dr. Zoha. In broad daylight, the army officer repeatedly stabbed Dr. Zoha with his bayonet, until the gutted body fell to the street. His students were mortified.

Before the students could rescue their beloved professor, the platoon dragged the still-breathing body across the gravel road and into the back of their military pickup truck. The tires screeched as the truck sped-off from the scene. Dr. Zoha died in the flatbed of the military truck. Since then, Rajshahi University commemorates February 18th as "Zoha Day."

In 1971, Pakistan occupation forces continued their genocide with the systematic murder of Dhaka University intellectuals. Their first Dhaka University victim was Professor Khan Khadem of the Physics Department.

On the night of March 25th, Pakistani forces raided Dhaka University's residential hall, Dhaka Hall, where they killed Professor Khadem, along with many students, faculty, and other employees of Dhaka University. Professor Khadem was my teacher. Because of his quiet and self-reflecting nature we affectionately called him, "our absent-minded Professor." Never could we have imagined that anyone would want to hurt such a soft-spoken and dedicated teacher.

Ironically, while the genocide included people of all walks of life, it ended where it began, with the deaths of several intellectuals across Bangladesh. On the 14th of December, just two days before the independence of Bangladesh, teachers, writers and other professionals were rounded up from their homes, taken to Rayer Bazaar in Mirpur, Dhaka, and summarily executed.

Having lost the war, the Pakistani Army in Bangladesh tried to obliterate the very soul of our emerging nation by killing as many of her finest sons and daughters as possible. Pakistani forces and their local collaborators, Razakars and Al-Badars, armed-cadres of the Jamaat-e-Islami party, kidnapped the intellectuals from their homes. Many of these Razakars even went after their own teachers.

These innocent Bengalis were blindfolded and taken to various concentration camps where they were tortured. Those who survived were taken to Rayer Bazaar where they were mass executed. From this moment on, Rayer Bazaar would forever be known as Rayer Bazaar *Killing Field*.

The mutilated bodies of these innocent martyrs, with their hands tied behind their backs and their blood-soaked blindfolds still fastened around their heads, were found in heaps. Many of these bodies were beyond recognition. In some cases, family members were only able to identify their loved ones by recognizing their personal artifacts.

One of the victims was Dr. Govinda Chandra Dev. He was a professor and Chairman of the Department of Philosophy at Dhaka University. I knew him personally. He often wandered into our dormitory and talked to us about his philosophy on life. Dressed in white-linens and adorning his characteristic bushy-white hair, Professor Dev resembled the philosophers of ancient Greece. His interests were solely the pursuit of knowledge and educating his pupils.

It was unthinkable that anyone would ever raise a voice against such an innocent and peaceful philosopher, let alone murder him. However, Dr. Dev was on the list of Pakistani military strategic targets.

Amongst the other intellectuals and scientists who fell victim to this final wave of genocide were: Prof. Munier Choudhury, Prof. Jyotirmoy Guha Thakurta, Santosh Bhattacharya, Dr. Mofazzal Haider Chowdhury, Prof. Muniruzzaman, Prof. Anwar Pasha, Prof. Giasuddin Ahmed, Dr. Fazle Rabbi of Dhaka Medical College, Dr. Aleem Chowdhury, Dr. Mohammad Murtaza, Dr. Mohammad Shafi, journalist Shahidullah Kaiser, Sirajuddin Hossain, Nizamuddin Ahmed, sports journalist S. A. Mannan (Ladu Bhai), Khandakar Abu Taleb, A. N. M. Golam Mostafa, Shaheed Saber, Nazmul Haq, Altaf Mahmud, Nutan Chandra Sinha, R P Saha, Abul Khayer, Rashidul Hasan, Sirajul Haq Khan, Abul Bashar, Dr. Muktadir, Faizul Mahi, Dr. Sadeque, Dr. Aminuddin, Saidul Hasan, film maker Zahir Raihan and many others.

These great minds were systematically slaughtered as part of Pakistan's strategy to rob Bangladesh of its intellectual leaders.

The magnitude of the genocide committed by the Pakistani Army, the Razakars, Al Badar and Al Shams was unprecedented in the history of mankind, especially because of its intellectualcide component.

Bodies of Bangladesh's intellectuals killed by Razakars at Rayer Bazaar Killing Field

Hundreds of Mai Lais and Lidices in Bangladesh

Not since the extermination of six million Jews by Nazi Germany between 1933 and 1945 has the world witnessed genocide as horrifying in its intent and as wide in its scope.

By many accounts, the magnitude of General Yahya Khan's genocide in Bangladesh is close to that of Adolph Hitler in Eastern Europe.

In 1981, The United Nations Human Rights Commission (UNHRC) reported that the genocide committed in Bangladesh in 1971 was one of the worst in history. It is widely accepted, both in and outside of Bangladesh, that Pakistani troops and their local allies murdered a total of three million Bengalis.

The UNHRC report further assessed that even if a lower range of 1.5 million deaths was taken into account, the Bangladesh genocide would have taken place at a rate of 6 to 12 thousand deaths per day over the course of the 267 days of carnage (Genocide 71: Account of the killers and collaborators, 1988). This made the genocide in Bangladesh one of the most horrendous in modern-history.

Even the international press reported on the magnitude of the genocide. In the June 20, 1971 issue of Newsweek, Tony Clifton, wrote:

> I have no doubt at all that there have been a hundred Mai Lais [Mass murder of 300-400 unarmed civilians by US soldiers in Vietnam village named Mai Lai on March 16, 1968] and Lidices [On June 10, 1942, all 192 men over 16 years of age from the village Lidice in Czech Republic were murdered on the spot by the Germans] in East Pakistan - and I think there will be more... [Speaking of Bangladesh] A much decorated officer with Patton in Europe during World War II, Gallagher, told me: 'In the war, I saw the worst areas of France-the killing grounds in Normandy - but I never saw anything like this. It took all of my strength to keep from breaking down and crying' (Birth of a Nation, P 38).

One of these Bangladesh Mai Lais referenced by Clifton occurred at Mirjapur village in Tangail, my home district. One day in May, Pakistani military forces and their collaborators surrounded Mirjapur village, located next to Kumudini Hospital.

Most of the villagers were Hindus and employees of the hospital. They were taking their usual lunch-break and were busy enjoying their meals. Meanwhile, Pakistani soldiers quietly and swiftly surrounded the village.

Before anyone had a chance to flee, Pakistani forces opened fire with machine guns. They killed five hundred civilians, including women and children, and wounded many more. Some of the Razakars, who conspired in this heinous attack, were locals of the village.

The wounded begged the Razakar traitors for mercy and requested medical attention from the nearby hospital. Instead, these innocent villagers were buried alive along with the dead bodies of their families and neighbors. The bodies were barbarically cast into a nearby construction ditch to rot and be scavenged by rodents.

Another war crime was committed against famous resident of Mirjapur and benevolent founder of Kumudini Hospital, Mr. Ranada Prasad Saha. Mr. Saha was one of the most prominent philanthropists of Bangladesh.

On May 7, 1971, the Pakistani military, with the help of their local collaborators, picked up Mr. Saha and his son Bhabani Prasad Saha from their Narayanganj residence and executed them. Their dead bodies were never recovered.

In 1938, Mr. Saha established the Kumudini Foundation in memory of his mother, Kumudini who died untreated of tetanus when he was only seven years old. Mr. Saha worked very hard to rise from his humble beginnings to become one of the richest businessmen in Bangladesh. His dream was to establish a foundation that would serve the common people.

The Kumudini Foundation established hospitals, schools, and other welfare projects. Its main focus was to provide education and healthcare to women. Mr. Saha believed that education was the foremost requirement to achieve freedom for women and establish their rights.

Mr. Saha was revered as a saintly man who established this hospital in 1947 and employed hundreds of people, all in order to provide free medical care to thousands of poor people in the rural area. Even such a compassionate soul as this was not exempt from the Pakistani military strategy to obliterate Bengali leaders in every field. But, the Pakistan Army's brutality did not end here.

Another Mai Lai occurred in Chuknagar, a town on the India-Bangladesh border, on May 10th 1971.

After the deadly crackdown in Dhaka on March 25th, Pakistani forces continued committing their atrocities throughout the country. First they made their way from occupying the district towns, to the sub-divisional towns, and then finally to the villages.

As news of the massacre and rape trickled down to the people, many of them left their homes and fled to India to save their lives and to protect the honor of their families.

One such group of refugees was on their way to India. They assembled at Chuknagar, a small business town located very close to the India-Bangladesh border in the Dumuria precinct of Khulna District. Chuknagar was located on the bank of the Bhadra River. Through this route thousands of refugees crossed the border to go to Calcutta, India.

On May 10th, more than ten thousand people including men, women and children were waiting at Chuknagar to cross the border. For the refugees, it was a day filled with anxiety as they embarked on an unknown future. Nonetheless, they were relieved to know that they would soon cross the border and would be beyond the reach of the Pakistani Army's cruel hands. Though the town was hectic and crowded, the morning was vibrant bringing with it a sense of hope and security.

Suddenly, two trucks of Pakistani soldiers stormed Chuknagar. The soldiers jumped out of their trucks and showered the refugees with bullets from their LMGs and semiautomatic rifles. There was no warning and no chance to flee or take cover.

The Pakistani soldiers continued firing like hunters taking potshots at birds in a cage. The refugees had no way to escape. Those who ran to flee were followed and killed. Those who jumped into the river were shot like fish in a barrel. The pulsating town quickly turned into a graveyard.

The Pakistani soldiers' barbaric rage continued for several hours until they ran out of ammunition. About two hundred refugees were lucky to survive. Prof. Muntassir Mamun later investigated their eyewitness accounts.

Professor Mamun interviewed witnesses who described bodies of lifeless children slung over the laps of their dead mothers; women who desperately clung to their beloved husbands before both being shot dead; and hopeless fathers who used their own bodies to shield their daughters from an inevitable fate.

Professor Mamun quotes one witness, "Within a flash they all were just dead bodies. Blood streamed into the Bhadra River, it became a river of corpses. A few hours later when the Pakistani bastards ran out of bullets, they killed the rest of the people with bayonets."

(Muntassir Mamun, The Archive of Liberation War, Bangabandhu and Bangladesh Research Institute).

About ten thousand people were killed at Chuknagar. It was 1971's largest single-day, single location massacre.

Remains of Massacre at Chuknagar

International reports on the Genocide

Mr. Hendric van der Heijden, a delegate of the World Bank, who had visited Kushtia in the western part of the nation, wrote that the town resembled "a German town in World War II after Allied strategic bomb attacks."

Ninety percent of the houses, shops, banks and other buildings were totally destroyed. He noted that when he was in Kushtia, the people appeared dazed. He further described, "When we moved around, everyone fled. It was like the morning after a nuclear attack." (Birth of a Nation: Bangladesh Mukti Samgram Sahayak Samity, Calcutta, 1971, P. 38.)

Mr. U Thant, the General Secretary of the United Nations, spoke of the genocide as "the saddest episode in human knowledge, the darkest chapter in the annals of mankind."

Madame Isabella Blum, the head of the World Peace Commission, released a press statement on January 1, 1972, "The shocking sight of these mass graves has horrified and saddened me. This genocide was even more terrible than the Nazis gas chambers." (The Daily Azad, Jan. 22, 1972)

Senator Adlai Stevenson, a leader of the U.S. Democratic Party, visited the mass graves in Comilla and Chittagong. On January 5, 1972, he stated, "I was horrified at the brutality of the Pakistani forces. In the annals of history there is nothing to parallel this genocide. Their inhumanity boggles the mind." (The Daily Azad, Jan. 31, 1972).

Victims of Genocide

Another U.S. Senator, Edward M. Kennedy said, "It is difficult for me to believe that any human being could even think of so much barbaric cruelty." (The Daily Azad, Jan. 31, 1972).

The French writer, Andre Malreaux, said, "I have seen atrocities perpetrated by the Nazis during World War II, but the brutality I have witnessed here is even more terrible..." (The Daily Azad, Mar. 13, 72)

The international press continued its coverage of the Bangladesh Genocide. In its September, 1972 issue, National Geographic Magazine reported:

> Here at Comilla Barracks, Pakistani troops and
> local collaborators - both Bengalis and Biharis - killed
> perhaps 100,000 civilians, burying the bodies in mass

graves that still show as sunken areas in the brown soil…In Dacca's Hindu colony of Shakharipatti, 8,000 out of 30,000 people died…Untold thousands of women were raped, the ultimate dishonor in orthodox Moslem and Hindu societies. A 13-year old girl…was kept for months in a military camp. After the war her father brought her to a women's relief organization that provides abortion and adoption services.

The New York Times, July 4th 1971, also reported the genocide, rapes, and other atrocities perpetrated by the Pakistani Army and their local collaborators.

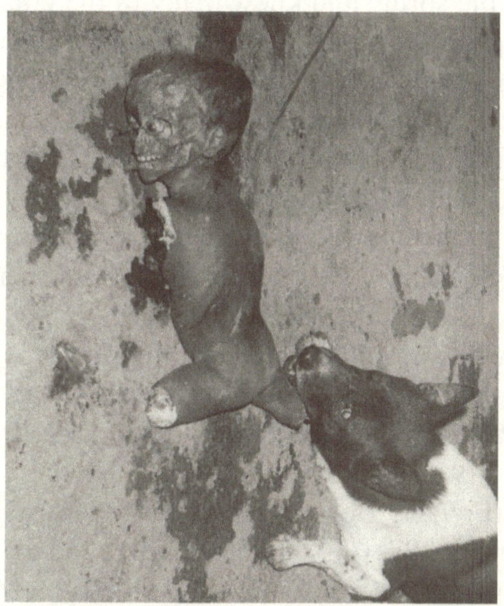

A Child victim of Genocide

Rape of Bangladesh

The atrocities against Bengali women committed by Pakistani forces and their collaborators were despicable. Thousands of women were subjected to methodical brutalization, which included gang rape, confinement, and murder.

The women of Chabbisha village were amongst those who had fallen victim to such atrocities. Chabbisha village was located near our camp in Bhuapur, Tangail. I had just arrived at Bhuapur camp on November 23rd from my third meeting with the Indian generals in Tura. Immediately, I was informed of the massacre at Chabbisha. I was appalled by the actions perpetrated by the Pakistani forces and Razakars.

On November 17th, a battalion of Pakistani forces attacked our camp in Bhuapur. The Mukti Bahini, led by Commander Hakim, resisted the enemy. However, as they retreated, the enemy unleashed its anger on the innocent residents of Chabbisha village.

They began by killing several villagers by brushfire. Then they threw a number of old men, women and children into the flames while they burnt several homes to the ground. I had visited Chabbisha several times in the spring and knew many of the villagers very well.

After hearing the sad news, we rushed to the village with medicine and clothes that I had brought from India for the freedom fighters. When we arrived it was clear that the village had been devastated. Once a spirited village, humming with life, Chabbisha had been transformed into a burial ground in just one week.

While distributing the relief, we came to know of several rapes committed by Pakistani forces. However, out of shame, the victims were reluctant to identify themselves. It was not for another thirty-one years that a few brave women were willing to stepforward to share their stories. One of these victims, Vanu Begam was from Chabisha village. She testified in the fact-finding report: War & Women by Dr. M. A. Hasan (p 149-150).

In the report, Vanu Begam stated that a Razakar named Anis brought eight or nine Pakistani soldiers wearing dark green uniforms to her home. As her husband was not at home, Ms. Begam was frightened at the sight of the military men.

She stated, "They shot at my brother- in- law and killed him. Then they set our house on-fire. After that, they surrounded me and started dragging me to take me inside another dwelling. I fell to their feet and begged for mercy".

Ms. Begam told the men, "I am your mother too, please do not touch me!"

But, her pleading did not sway the men. They attempted to convince Ms. Begam to succumb to their advances. She refused.

Ms. Begam recalled, "When they failed to convince me to their evil desire, they raised my five-year-old son Ranju and attempted to throw him into the flames. I became weak, so to save my son, I was forced to surrender to them. They raped me for an hour until I lost consciousness. After I came to my senses, I found that my body was pulverized, but the animals were still standing over me and laughing through their teeth".

She stated that before they left, they grabbed her gold earrings and necklace, then poured gunpowder on her body and pushed her into the flames. The back of her body was burnt severely. After undergoing treatment for a long time, her burns finally healed leaving severe physical scarring. However, her eyesight would be permanently impaired.

When she was asked what other crimes Pakistani forces committed against her village, she said, "After entering the village, they first set some houses on fire. Two young children were frightened at the sight of the army and hid inside a stack of rice stalks. But, the Pakistani soldiers were not fooled. They set fire to the stalks. The two children were burnt to ashes right in front of my eyes".

Vanu Begam reported several more incidents of rape in the village, including some involving children. She told that Pakistani forces forcibly dragged Jobeda, a twelve-year-old girl, from her home. They surrounded her in her house. They then passed her from one another like a cigarette, each taking turns raping her. Finally, the Pakistani beasts left her stained body while she bled profusely on the floor.

Vanu Begam described another young rape victim. Vaskar, a local member of the union council saw his own daughter raped in front of his eyes. He was held at gunpoint while his innocent young daughter was brutally raped by Pakistani soldiers in the family's open cattle shed.

In addition, she further testified that Pakistani forces also raped several more women. The wives of Shachin, the village gardener and Haidar another local man were both raped.

Vanu Begam stated that while Pakistani soldiers dragged her through the courtyard, she saw several other soldiers chasing Haidar's wife. Fortunately, Haider's wife was able to outrun the soldiers and hide in the village outhouse. However, the Pakistani beasts would not be dissuaded. They broke down the outhouse door and raped her right there in the latrine.

As the soldiers vied for the turn, they began pushing each other in the outhouse. Amidst the tussle, Haider's wife escaped yet again. The despicable men had ripped the clothes from her body. She ran through the courtyard completely naked with blood flowing from her bruised thighs. She ran from the courtyard and hid in the paddy fields.

But, the soldiers were relentless. Four soldiers followed her, tackling her to the ground before raping her once again. With her face buried in the mud and manure of the field she laid senseless long after the men had finished. Eventually, she was rescued by her neighbors, cleaned, and given some clothes. However, no amount of goodwill could ease the pain inflicted on her by these brutal animals.

Vanu Begam further testified that Pakistani soldiers attacked another girl in a neighboring village. The girl was a young mother with an eight-day-old baby. While, she had a pot of rice boiling on the stove, she patiently sat breastfeeding her baby. Suddenly, Pakistani soldiers stormed the house. There was no one else at home at the time.

Having just given birth, the young mother's body was already overwhelmed. The presence of the soldiers only exacerbated her condition. The Pakistani soldiers looked the young body up and down homing in on her breasts like hyenas to prey. They had found what they had come for.

They raped the young mother in-turn until their animalistic desires were fulfilled. Annoyed by its incessant crying, the heartless soldiers threw the newborn baby into the pot of boiling rice just before they left.

Ms. Begam continued her testimony, stating that Pakistani forces killed several other villagers including the mother of another villager named Mansur.

Twenty-five other victims, from across Bangladesh were brave enough to provide their testimony in Dr. M. A. Hasan's report, War & Women (p133-198). These victims shared in gruesome experiences nearly parallel to that of the people of Chabbisha. Their husbands and fathers were killed or arrested. Their mothers, daughters and wives were raped in their own homes and then taken away to confinement only to be repeatedly raped on a daily basis for months. On some occasions these rapes even occurred in public so as to strike fear in the hearts of the masses. These innocent women were deprived of food and medical treatment and subjected to unthinkable forms of torture.

A victim of rape

The atrocities on Bengali women by the Pakistani forces were corroborated by several international reports. Susan Brownmiller, in her ground-breaking book, *Against Our Will: Men, Women and Rape*, likened the 1971 events in Bangladesh to the Japanese rapes in Nanjing and German rapes in Russia during World War II. She reported:

> 200,000, 300,000 or possibly 400,000 women (three sets of statistics have been variously quoted) were raped. Eighty percent of the raped women were Moslems, reflecting the population of Bangladesh, but Hindu and Christian women were not exempt... Hit-and-run rape of large numbers of Bengali women was brutally simple in terms of logistics as the Pakistani

regulars swept through and occupied the tiny, populous land... (p. 81).

Another reporter, Aubrey Menen offered a similar description of one such assault, which targeted a recently married couple. Ms. Brownmiller quoted Ms. Menen in saying:

> Two [Pakistani soldiers] went into the room that had been built for the bridal couple. The others stayed behind with the family, one of them covering them with his gun. They heard a barked order, and the bridegroom's voice protesting. Then there was silence until the bride screamed. Then there was silence again, except for some muffled cries that soon subsided. In a few minutes one of the soldiers came out, his uniform in disarray. He grinned to his companions. Another soldier took his place in the extra room. And so on, until all the six had raped the belle of the village. Then all six left, hurriedly. The father found his daughter lying on the string cot unconscious and bleeding. Her husband was crouched on the floor, kneeling over his vomit. (Brownmiller, *Against Our Will*, p. 82.)

Although there is little evidence, some have argued that gruesome accounts of Droit de Seigneur have existed throughout history. However, the rape in Bangladesh was not limited to the young and fair. Ms. Brownmiller writes, "Rape in Bangladesh had hardly been restricted to beauty."

She adds, "Girls of eight and grandmothers of seventy-five had been sexually assaulted...Pakistani soldiers had not only violated Bengali women on the spot; they abducted tens of hundreds and held them by force in their military barracks for nightly use. Some women may have been raped as many as eighty times in a night." (Brownmiller, p. 83)

These were not isolated incidents. These perpetrators were not only limited low-level soldiers and Razakars. These rapists included the highest level of Pakistani military commanders and members of the Jamaat-e-Islami Party. These vile crimes against women were deliberate and organized in nature. They were carried out in the name of protecting Islam.

Refugees

About ten million people took shelter in India to escape the atrocities of the Pakistani forces and their collaborators. Amongst them was my classmate from Dhaka University, Bokul and her family. Bokul was a student activist of Chatra Union, a left oriented student organization. When Dhaka University was closed in March, Bokul responded to Bangabandhu's call for non-cooperation and returned to her hometown in Dinajpur, a district headquarter in the northwestern part of Bangladesh near the Indian border.

News of the Dhaka massacre perpetrated by Pakistani forces on March 26th had made its way to Dinajpur town. Apprehension fostered rumors that Pakistani forces from the Rangpur cantonment and their Bihari supporters from Saidpur would proceed towards Dinajpur to occupy the town. Biharis were Urdu speaking pro-Pakistani Muslims who migrated from the Bihar province of India to East Pakistan after the partition of India in 1947.

On March 27th, during curfew, sounds of bullets resonated throughout Dinajpur. Bokul's father, Mr. Fahimuddin Ahmed, headmaster of nearby St. Philips High School, grew worried about the safety of his family. His two youngest daughters, Bokul and Nurjahan Talukdar (Kamala) were staying with him. Kamala had been married for a few months, but her husband Karimul Haque Talukdar was in Bangkok, Thailand pursuing his engineering degree.

Bokul's eldest sister, Shamsun Nahar was married to an advocate, Abdul Motaleb who lived in a nearby neighborhood. They had a young boy, Jewel, who was four-years old and a daughter, Shoheli, who was three-years old. They came to know that the people of the town were leaving in apprehension of an impending attack by Pakistani forces.

Mr. Ahmed did not hesitate when making the most important decision of his life. He readied his family to abandon their home and flee to a safer place. It was a very scary and emotional decision. They would have to leave behind all of their memories and personal belongings. They packed only the essential items that they could carry.

They knew that once they were gone, no one could ensure what would happen to their home or to their cherished possessions. Nonetheless, they hired a poor man named Khatir to look after their home.

On March 28th, the curfew was lifted. Before the enemy could infiltrate the town or impose another curfew, Bokul's family, along with her older sister's family, embarked on an unknown destination. They did not know when or if they would ever return home.

There were eight members in the group: Bokul, Kamala, Mr. and Mrs. Ahmed, Shamsun, Advocate Motaleb, Jewel and Shoheli. First they boarded rickshaws to get out of town. While they were passing through the town, they saw dead bodies littered along the roadside at several locations.

At the outskirt of the town, they left the rickshaw and walked on foot for several miles. Finally, they hired an ox-driven cart to take them towards the Indian border.

Advocate Motaleb had some clients who lived in the border area. The family arrived at one of Motaleb's clients' homes where they were graciously received and spent the night.

Unfortunately, the presence of two pretty university-aged girls drew a lot of attention from the villagers. Moreover, there was a pro-Pakistani Muslim League leader in the neighboring village. The host advised his guests to leave his home as soon as possible for their own safety.

Bokul's family left the next morning and continued on their journey towards the Indian boarder. This time, with no roads to travel by, the families could not hire another ox-driven cart. They had no choice, but to walk carrying their belongings on their shoulders. They trekked along narrow aisles of farmland. Their journey was tiresome and fraught with danger. The women and children experienced great difficulty walking. At one point, Bokul and Kamala's sandal-straps snapped. They continued their journey barefoot for the rest of the trip. No one in the family had ever embarked on such an arduous expedition before. They had to take frequent breaks to rest.

Nonetheless, they had to reach their destination before sunset. So they each dug deep within themselves to harness every last ounce of energy.

There was a growing rush to move towards the border. Along their way, they met other families whose paths also converged towards the Indian border.

After spending the day drudging under the blistering sun, they finally reached a village near the border where two of Motaleb's clients lived. Their hosts Moyezuddin and Abdul Hamid cordially received Bokul's family and assured them any help they needed. It was a great relief for the family.

During the last two days, Bokul's family was preoccupied with ensuring their own safety and avoiding the perils of their journey. However, after settling down in a relatively safer place, they had the chance to ask, "Where was the other member of our family, Dalim?"

Bokul's only brother Shamsur Rahman, or Dalim as he was called, was an engineer working for the Bangladesh Railway. He was stationed in Chittagong, a port city in southeastern Bangladesh.

By this leg of the families' journey news of the massacre in Chittagong, as well as the Bengali resistance, had already been aired on Indian radio. The radio news also mentioned that Biharis, with the help of Pakistani forces, had killed many innocent Bengalis in the railway staff quarters in Pahartali, where Dalim lived.

Everyone in Bokul's family was concerned for Dalim. Bokul's mother was desperate to know of her only son's whereabouts. She started crying. There was no way for the family to get in contact with Dalim. With the growing numbers of Bengalis murdered in Dalim's staff quarters, there was no safe way to get information about him. With each day that passed, the families' anxiety grew. All they could do was pray for Dalim's safety.

The family's only consolation was that Kamala's husband, Karimul was still safe in Bangkok. However, Karimul was riddled with anxiety himself, as he had no way of knowing the whereabouts of his wife and in-laws.

The sanctuary of the border village was short lived. Pakistani forces after securing district towns and local towns, moved towards the Bangladesh–Indian border. Enemy forces and their collaborators hunted pro-Bangladesh activists as well as refugees.

Like Bokul's family, many refugees took shelter in the villages near the border. Many had not yet crossed the border to India in hopes that things would settle down, allowing them to eventually return to their homes.

However, by April, an all-out liberation war had begun under the leadership of the Provisional Bangladesh Government. Freedom fighters had regrouped in the border areas and began waging a stiff resistance to Pakistani occupation forces. In response, Pakistani forces did their best to secure the border villages.

Informers would warn the villagers that Pakistani forces and their collaborators were on the way to attack the villages by night. Villagers, particularly women, would flee their homes and hide in the jungles behind the villages.

The house where Bokul's family stayed had no jungle behind it. Instead Bokul and her sisters would hide behind mounds of sand in a dry riverbed. Such hiding places were filthy. During these times, remote villages like this often used the riverbed as latrines for animal and human waste.

Nonetheless, at the first sign of a raid, Bokul and her sisters would run to the back of the house and dive headfirst into the riverbed. These moments were nerve-wracking. Amidst hiding, Bokul and her two sisters would bury their brows in the soil, clenching each other's hands to pray. They prayed to Allah asking that He save them from the Pakistani beast. After each hiding, they had to bathe and wash their clothing just to rid themselves of the stench.

Luckily the informers' warnings had come early; the enemy had not yet raided the village. Mr. Ahmed and his family grew tired of this cat and mouse game. He was no longer willing to put up with such psychological torture. He knew that eventually it would be unsafe to stay here. He had to ask himself, "What would have happened had Pakistani forces raided the village?"

Such quandaries were beyond imagination. He decided it was time to cross the border to India.

In India, Mr. Ahmed had very few options in taking care of his family. The safety and well being of his family were more important than his own life. He could not fathom taking shelter in an Indian government-sponsored refugee camp where thousands of refugees passed their days amidst inhuman circumstances.

Unfortunately, because of the imposed curfew, Mr. Ahmed was unable to withdraw money from his bank account before leaving Dinajpur. He brought with him whatever cash he had at home. Although he did not know how long he would stay in India, he desperately looked for a place to rent for him and his seven family members. But, rural areas like this rarely had spare rooms for rent.

Luckily, Mr. Ahmed found a very poor farmer who was in desperate need of money. Bokul's family rented the hut from the farmer at an affordable price. To allow for the new accommodation, the farmer and his family moved to the cattle shed, while the cattle moved to an open area in the corner of the premises.

A new phase of refugee life began for Bokul's family. Kamala sent a letter to her husband in Bangkok. Karimul replied a month later. He asked one of his Indian friends to mail the letter to his family in India. Then they arranged to deliver the letter to Kamala. She was ecstatic to hear from her husband after so long.

Right after their marriage, Karimul had to leave for Bangkok to attend class. Kamala was scheduled to join him soon after. However, war broke out just before her departure for Bangkok.

Sadly, not all of the family's anxieties were put to rest. In spite of numerous efforts, Dalim's whereabouts were still unknown. To add to their dismay, some more shocking news had filtered to the family. Before the family had fled, they had hired a man named Khatir to serve as the caretaker of the family's home while they were away. But just a few days after Bokul's family had fled, Biharis raided the home, murdered Khatir, and ransacked the house.

In addition, Bokul received some devastating news regarding the family of one of her closest friends, Joyanti. Bokul and Joyanti were classmates in high school, Dinajpur Government Degree College, and then again at Dhaka University. Joyanti's father, Monu Sarkar was part of the administrative staff at Dinajpur Government Degree College and a very popular music teacher in town.

Like most parents of the liberation-era, Mr. Sarkar was very concerned about the safety of his seven boys and girls. He asked them all to flee their home. His children all went to India just as Bokul's family did. However, Mr. and Mrs. Sarkar stayed behind.

One day, after the occupation of Dinajpur Town by Pakistani forces, a few Razakars paid a visit to Mr. Sarkar's house. As the Razakars knocked at the door Mr. Sarkar asked his wife to hide in the chicken-coop behind the house.

The Razakars grabbed Mr. Sarkar by his collar and dragged him out to the courtyard. They cursed at him in Bengali because he was a Hindu and let loose a profane-laden tirade against him. They accused him of sending his children to become freedom fighters.

Before, he could utter a word; they crushed his skull with the blunt end of a hammer. The motionless body fell to their feet. Quivering from inside the sulfurous chicken-coop, Mrs. Sarkar watched as the horrendous scene unfolded.

For all the years that the family had lived in Dinajpur, Mr. Sarkar had always been a revered teacher, respected by the community, Hindu and Muslim alike. But now, hiding in the cramped shack that her husband had built for their chickens, Mrs. Sarkar's tears fell to the straw floor. She was helpless. The fear of death had robbed her of voice. There was no one to hear her scream. She was alone.

She could not believe what had just happened to her husband. Sadly her mental anguish would not end. One of the Razakars then proceeded to cut Mr. Sarkar's throat with the serrated edge of his dagger. Before any more blood could flow from Mr. Sarkar's already dead body, another Razakar brandished a machete. Unable to take it anymore, Mrs. Sarkar fainted.

When Mrs. Sarkar finally came to her senses, she crawled out of her hiding spot and found her husband's body cut into seven pieces. After a somber moment, hysteria had crept in. The widowed Mrs. Sarkar sat in front of her husband's mutilated body for three days and nights.

The curfew had left the neighborhood deserted. There was no one to help her. There was no one to hear her moans. Finally, a neighbor responded to the eerie haunts at the Sarkar residence. The neighbor helped gather the severed limbs and arbitrary body parts from the blood-soaked earth.

Bokul wept at the news of this tragedy. She longed to be with her dear friend to offer her condolences and sympathy. However, Joyanti was one of the ten million refugees living in any one of the eight hundred twenty nine refugee camps in Indian. All Bokul could do was pray for the safety of her friend and remaining family members.

This was not an isolated incident. This was just part of the Pakistani military's master plan. Pakistan had a blueprint to eradicate Hindus from Bangladesh. This was a deliberate message to the Hindu community, urging them to leave Bangladesh for good.

In addition, the Razakars had their own personal incentives. With the Hindus gone, the Razakars would finally be free to seize any abandoned property.

The Ahmed family's new accommodation was a hut consisting of a single twenty-by-sixteen foot room. Its roof was made of straw. With no furniture, the family had to sleep on the mud floor with a layer of straws as a communal bed.

During rainstorms, water leaked through the roof. At night, they would sit in the one corner of the room where the roof had yet to be breached. Meanwhile, pots occupied the areas under the leaks to collect rainwater. As the monsoon season began, the family's life became miserable. Mr. Ahmed had no option, but to spend his last bit of cash to fix the leaky roof.

Another acute problem arose for the women. How would they answer nature's call? They had no choice, but to walk into the nearby jungle and relieve themselves.

As the cash ran out, Mr. Ahmed went to the refugee camps to get weekly rations. Bokul registered with the refugee camp to work as a medical assistant. The solitary hour-long walk to the refugee camp was not easy for Bokul.

Confined to their hut, the family had nothing to do other than sit and listen to the radio and gather the latest news on the warfront. The radio was often glued to Motaleb's hands as he scanned the dial from one station to the next.

Little did Mr. Ahmed know that on that fateful day in March, when he decided to escape with his family towards India, that he and his family would spend the next nine months in this self-imposed prison. Nor would he know that each day would be burdened with the anxiety of not knowing whether his only son was dead or alive. As those nine months passed, all Mr. Ahmed could do was to ensure the safety of his daughters and grandchildren.

Although I did not know it then, this refugee-story would hold special meaning for me. After the war, I returned to the university where my path converged with Bokul's once again. Soon after in 1974, Bokul and I got married. Both Dalim and Karimul attended our wedding.

About ten million people were forced to cross the border into India (National Geography, Sept. 1972) to escape the mass murders, rape, and sheer destruction carried out by Pakistani forces and their collaborators. The Indian government provided eight hundred and twenty-nine refugee camps in the Indian Territory around the Bangladesh border. However, the colossal influx of refugees was a tremendous burden on the Indian economy as well as on the nation's social-fabric.

In places like in Tripura, refugees outnumbered the local population. For the first few months, to cope with the initial thrust of refugees, the Indian government provided logistical support in creating makeshift refugee camps. However, with dwindling resources, many of these refugees were forced to take shelter in subhuman-conditions. Some even took to the abandoned drainage pipes at Salt Lake, Calcutta.

Refugees take shelter in abandoned drainage pipes at Salt Lake, Calcutta

Bullets of '71: A Freedom Fighter's Story

Despite sincere efforts by the Indian government and aid from local and international organizations, many refugees began suffering from malnutrition and diseases, often resulting in death.

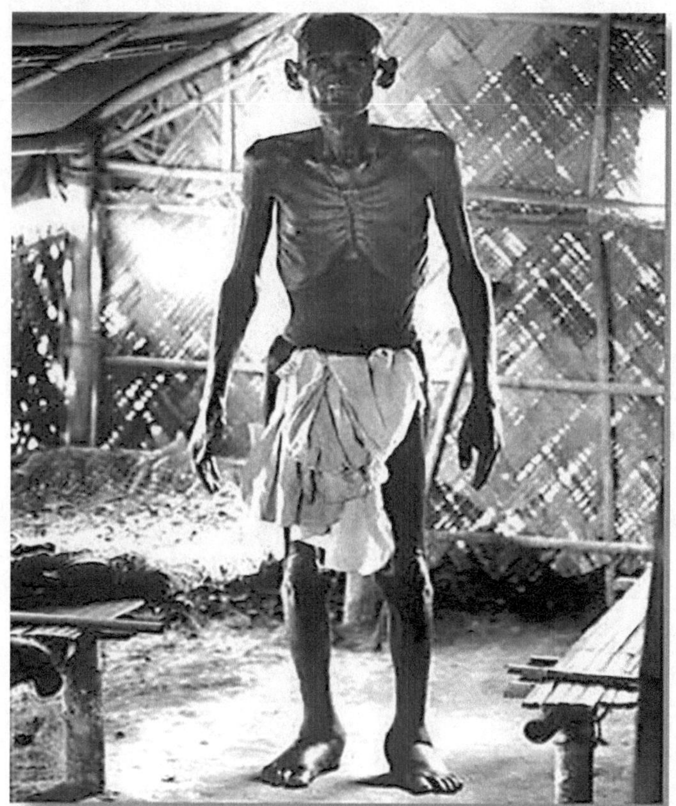

A starving refugee

According to the United Nations office in Bangladesh, in addition to the ten million refugees in India, about twenty million people were displaced within Bangladesh from their homes.

In spite of the suffering of ten million refugees, President Nixon and Henry Kissinger were tilted towards Pakistani President Yahya Khan. Just when hopes for political sympathy were dwindling, one prominent American deviated from the mold of apathy. He was Senator Edward M. Kennedy, a 39-year-old senator from Massachusetts. On August 21, 1971, Senator Kennedy traveled to various refugee camps in India in order to gain firsthand knowledge of the refugees' plight.

Dr. Nuran Nabi

US Senator Kennedy visits refugee camps in West Bengal, August 1971

Senator Kennedy was appalled to see the callous affliction of ten million refugees. Based on his eyewitness account, Senator Kennedy coined the phrase, the "Reign of Terror Which Grips East Bengal" which he detailed in his report to the Senate.

Senator Kennedy's report was so passionate that it shook the world. There was no choice but to take notice. He made it clear that the refugees needed aid.

Senator Kennedy eloquently described his experience:

A traveler today in eastern India cannot help but see, smell, and feel this misery. It is etched in the faces and lives of refugees in countless ways. It is the malnourished child hanging limply in its mother's arms - one child out of a half million who, in a matter of hours or days, can easily die from the lack of protein and adequate medical care. It is a young girl, quivering in a refugee camp in Tripura, still in shock after seeing her mother and father slaughtered by Pakistani troops. It is a 14-year-old boy in Jalpaiguri Hospital, whose face is contorted from the pain and anguish that he has experienced since he saw his family shot before his eyes and since he received a bullet wound in his spine, which has paralyzed him for life. And it is the expression of hundreds of thousands of refugees living in sewer pipes on the outskirts of Calcutta, while overworked relief officials struggle to provide some food and shelter and hope for a needy and hopeless people. (Crisis in South Asia, Report to the Subcommittee Investigating the Problem of Refugees and Their Settlement, Submitted to U.S. Senate Judiciary Committee, Kennedy, November 1, 1971, U.S. Govt. Press, pp.6-7.)

Senator Kennedy stated, "That to drive the roads of West Bengal is to tour a huge refugee camp." Kennedy traveled from Calcutta towards the border through old Jessore Road where he met millions of refugees. On seeing the refugees, Kennedy described, "literally millions of people sat huddled together waiting for food, or lined up in endless queues for refugee registration cards, or simply encamped on the roadside under hastily constructed lean-tos. And each day their numbers continued to grow."

In concluding his report, Kennedy drew on a little known connection between the Hindus of Bangladesh and the Jews of Nazi Germany:

Nothing is clear or more easily documented, than the systematic campaign of terror-and its genocidal consequences-launched by the Pakistani Army on the night of March 25th. Field reports to the U.S government, countless eyewitness journalistic accounts, and reports from international agencies such as the World Bank, and additional information available to the Subcommittee document the continuing reign of terror, which grips East Bengal. Hardest hit have been members of the Hindu community who have been robbed of their lands and shops, systematically slaughtered, and, in some places, painted with yellow patches marked "H". All of this has been officially sanctioned, ordered and implemented under martial law from Islamabad. (Crisis in South Asia, Report to the Subcommittee Investigating the Problem of Refugees and Their Settlement, Submitted to U.S. Senate Judiciary Committee, Kennedy, November 1, 1971, U.S. Govt. Press, pp.6-7.)

It is evident from Senator Kennedy's report that just as the Jews were forced to wear gold stars affixed to their clothing, Hindus during the 1971 war were identified by their own government-enforced markings. It would be hardly a stretch to imagine that the Pakistani military borrowed this strategy from the Nazis.

Systematic racism against Hindus - A Pakistani soldier inspects a man for circumcision to identify whether he is Muslim or Hindu

Senator Kennedy further concluded, "America's heavy support of Islamabad [West Pakistan] is nothing short of complicity in the human and political tragedy of East Bengal." (Crisis in South Asia, Kennedy, pp.6-7)

Leaders of War Crimes

The violence perpetrated against the people of Bangladesh in 1971 was more than a series of random and incidental killings. Rather it was a carefully planned strategy orchestrated by Pakistani military leaders and executed by their professional soldiers and local collaborators. This was a military government-sponsored genocide.

There were several Pakistani military government leaders personally responsible for the genocide in Bangladesh. Topping this list were President General Yahya Khan, Chief of Staff General Pirzada, Security Chief General Umar Khan, and Intelligence Chief General Akbar Khan.

In addition, several military commanders stationed in East Pakistan were responsible for executing this heinous plan. Amongst the many military commanders responsible, General Niazi, General Tikka Khan, and Gen. Rao Forman Ali were amongst the most notable.

The Bengali collaborators of this genocide were the leaders of the Jamaat-e-Islami, an Islamic-fundamentalist political party. There were several perpetrators, but the most notorious of them were Moulana Golam Azam, Moulana Motiur Rahman Nizami, Moulana Ali Ahsan Mohammed Mujahid, Moulana Delowar Hossain Saidi, Moulana Kamruzzam, Kader Mollah, Ashrafuzzaman Khan, and Choudhury Moinuddin.

These leaders established the armed cadres known as Razakars, Al Badars, and Al Shams. These armed cadres were equivalent to Hitler's Gestapo who were responsible for rounding up Jews and sending them to their demise in concentration camps.

Jamaat-e-Islami leaders organized these militant groups for carrying out and aiding in the systematic murder of more than three million innocent people and the rape of more than two-hundred thousand women, all in the name of protecting Islam. Of the women raped, 20% were Hindus and Christians, but 80% were Muslims.

Robert Payne in his book, Massacre, illustrated the mechanical nature of Pakistani forces in carrying out the 1971 genocide of Bangladesh:

> For month after month, in all the regions of East Pakistan, the massacres went on. They were not the small casual killings of young officers who wanted to demonstrate their efficiency, but organized massacres conducted by sophisticated staff officers, who knew

exactly what they were doing. Muslim soldiers, sent out to kill Muslim peasants, went about their work mechanically and efficiently, until killing defenseless people became a habit like smoking cigarettes or drinking wine… Not since Hitler invaded Russia had there been so vast a massacre.

Mr. Payne also described the role of President Nixon and Dr. Henry Kissinger in the Bangladesh genocide. He wrote, "The U.Sgovernment, long supportive of military rule in Pakistan, supplied some $3.8 million in military equipment to the dictatorship *after* the onset of the genocide…and *after* a government spokesman told Congress that all shipments to Yahya Khan's regime had ceased." (Payne, *Massacre*, p. 102)

In the face of documented genocide, the Nixon administration lied to the U.S. Congress regarding the nation's involvement in supporting Pakistan's systematic attempt to obliterate an entire nation of people.

Pakistani generals and their forces, including both higher and lower ranking officers, were "willing-executioners" of the Bangladesh genocide. Their attitudes were fueled by anti-Bengali racism, particularly against the Bengali-Hindu minority. Mr. Rummel in his book, *Death by Government*, attested to this notion:

Bengalis were often compared with monkeys and chickens. Said Pakistan General Niazi, 'It was a low lying land of low lying people.' The Hindus among the Bengalis were as Jews to the Nazis: scum and vermin that [should at] best be exterminated. As to the Moslem Bengalis, they were to live only on the sufferance of the soldiers: any infraction, any suspicion cast on them, any need for reprisal, could mean their death. And the soldiers were free to kill at will. The journalist Dan Coggin quoted one Punjabi captain as telling him, 'we can kill anyone for anything. We are accountable to no one.' This is the arrogance of Power. (Rummel p. 335)

In addition to overwhelming evidence from eyewitness accounts, reports from the perpetrators themselves, as well as reports from international organizations, the post-war Pakistani government also admitted that Pakistani forces perpetrated war crimes in Bangladesh.

The post-war Pakistani government appointed a fact-finding commission on the Bangladesh war headed by Justice Hamoodur Rahman. The reports of the commission concluded that Pakistani forces in Bangladesh committed war crimes in 1971.

Several Pakistani generals also confessed in their memoirs that their forces in Bangladesh committed these war crimes. However, each blamed the other of carrying out the criminal activity without ever taking personal responsibility.

General Niazi once explained that as a military commander he was not responsible for civilian casualties. General Niazi pointed out that General Rao Forman Ali was in charge of the civilian administration. However, when questioned, General Ali stated that General Niazi was the supreme commander of the armed forces, and that General Niazi was responsible for all that had happened in East Pakistan during the war.

About ninety thousand Pakistani soldiers surrendered in Bangladesh and were taken as prisoners of war. The Bangladesh government investigated the accusations of war crimes and filed charges against two hundred Pakistani officers for specific war crimes (List of Pakistani war criminals are shown in appendix A). However, before they were put on trial, the Indian and Bangladesh governments were forced to release the POWs, including the accused war criminals, to Pakistani authorities. The decision came only under pressure from the world's superpowers.

Under the agreement for release of the Pakistani POWs, the Pakistani government promised to put the war criminals on trial in Pakistan. However, they failed to keep their promise.

Rather, the Pakistani government appointed one of these notorious war criminals, General Tikka Khan, as Chief of Staff of the Pakistani Army. Many of the other war criminals were also rewarded with promotions within the armed forces, allowing them to continue their services. Some of these war criminals were even appointed to high-profile government assignments.

On the other hand, most of the leaders of the Jamaat-e-Islami, Razakars, Al Badars and Al Shams fled Bangladesh just before the fall of Dhaka. Right after the independence, the government of Bangabandhu Sheikh Mujibur Rahman had arrested more than 37,000 alleged Razakars, Al Badars and Al Shams under the Collaborators Act of 1972, and the International Crime Act of 1973.

After investigation and scrutiny, 26,000 detainees were found without any criminal charges against them, and they were pardoned under general amnesty. However, about 12,000 collaborators were charged with specific crimes against humanity and were placed on trial under a Special Tribunal Act of 1973.

By August 1975, the Special Tribunal Court completed the trial of a small section of detainees and found 800 guilty-as-charged and sentenced the offenders to prison for various terms. One particular war criminal named Chikan Ali was sentenced to death for his war crimes.

However, on August 15th 1975, Prime Minister Bangabandhu Sheikh Mujibur Rahman was assassinated along with many of his family members, before his government was overthrown in a military coup. The subsequent military government led by General Ziaur Rahman abrogated the Collaborators Act and released all the prisoners including those that were sentenced and those under prosecution.

Soon after these Gestapo leaders were brought back to the country where many of them were reestablished socially and politically by the military government. Some of these war criminals were even elected into the Bangladesh Parliament and became ministers with the backing of a military-sponsored government.

It was an ironic twist of fate that these men whose hands were still stained with the blood of innocent Bangladeshis were now flying the Bangladeshi flag from their homes and luxury government cars.

However, the people of Bangladesh have finally spoken. In the general election of 2008 the people gave mandate to the government of Prime Minister Sheikh Hasina to bring these Bangladesh war criminals to justice. After 39 years, the trial of Bangladesh war criminals has only just begun.

Nevertheless, two hundred Pakistani military leaders who committed war crimes in 1971 have yet to show their faces in court.

The trial of Bangladesh war criminals is not an act of revenge. It is not an attempt to console the relatives of the victims of genocide. It is not even a matter of bringing justice to the people of Bangladesh. Trying these war criminals is an insurance policy for the entire world. The only way to ensure that the world is free from crimes against humanity is to ensure that the precedence for justice remains. Even after sixty years, Nazi war criminals are still being prosecuted.

Bangladesh has paid more than its due share in blood to gain its independence. However, the perpetrators of genocide have yet to pay for their crimes against humanity. As long as these criminals are free, a dangerous precedent will remain preventing the world's future and current victims of genocide from seeking justice.

*This section is written based on my earlier essay, <u>People's Movement in Bangladesh for the Trial of Bangladesh War Criminals of 1971</u>; Nuran Nabi and Jahanara Imam, p.183, <u>Bengal Studies 1994: Essays on Economics, Society & Culture</u>, and 1971 Bangladesh Genocide Archives

Glossary

Ashar: Third month of the Bengali calendar Usually falls between Mid June and Mid July when the rainy season begins.
Azaan: vocal call for prayers of the Muslims
Moulana: Bearded Islamic Scholar
Shirwani: Long Flowing Coat
Madrasa: A religious boarding school for young boys
Atar: Rose Water
Pir: Islamic Saint
Panjabi – Linen or Silk Clothing
Lal - Red
Shemai: A sweet pudding dish
Imam: Islamic figure head
Monojath: Prayer praising Allah seeking his mercy and forgiveness
Chom-Choms: sweet
Rosh O' Gollas: sweet
Jalshaghar: Private theatre
Baize: a professional singer and dancer
Shondesh: Specialty sweet
Puja: A Hindu religious ceremony
Kirton: spiritual Hindu chanting
Jatra: An opera
Dhaka: Capital City of Bangladesh
Hajj: the Muslim pilgrimage to Mecca
Hadhis: Explanation of Islamic Law
Nayeb: local tax collector
Hujur: Islamic religious leaders
Jinnah Cap: Islamic hat worn by Muhamed Ali Jinnah, the father of Pakistan

Polau: Buttered rice
Mughlai parata: fried flat bread stuffed with egg
Haji Biriani (stewed rice and mutton)
Morog Polau (chicken and buttered rice)
Bhagban – Hindu God
Rahman – Islamic word for God
Mohashashan – Hindu graveyard
Gorosthan – Muslim Graveyard
Shahid Minar – Martyr Monument
Padma- Name of a River
Megna- Name of a River
Jamuna- Name of a River
Hujur – Sir
Motijheel – Commercial District in Dhaka city
M. V. Shoat Ship – Name of a Ship
Lungi- Loose Garment worn by men around the waist in Bangladesh,
Pakistan & India
Mukti Bahini- Freedom Fighters
Razakars, Al Badars, Al Shams - Armed cadres of Jamaat-e-Islami
Party who collaborated with Pakistani forces and participated in war
crime activities

Appendix A

List of Pakistani War Criminals

	PA No.	Rank	Name	Unit
1.	PA-477	Lt./Gen	Amir Abdullah Khan Niazi	East Comd.
2.	PA-1170	Maj/Gen	Nazar Hussain Shah	16 Div.
3.	PA-4404	Maj/Gen	Mohammad Hussain Ansari	9 Div.
4.	PA-882	Maj/Gen	Mhammad Jamshed	DGEPCAF
5.	PA-1734	Maj/Gen	Qazi Abdul Majid Khan	14 Div
6.	PA-1364	Maj/Gen	Rao Farman Ali Khan	Adviser to Governor
7.	PA-1674	Brigadier	Abdul Qadir Khan	93 BDE
8.	PA-2235	Brigadier	Arif Raja	HQ SIG
9.	PA-1109	Brigadier	Atta Muhammad Khan Malik	7 BDE
10.	PA-1897	Brigadier	Bashir Ahmed	CAF
11.	PA-100088	Brigadier	Fahim Ahmed Khan	HQ EC
12.	PA-1738	Brigadier	Iftikhar Ahmed Rana	313 BDE
13.	PA-3414	Brigadier	Manzoor Ahmed	57 HQ BDE
14.	PA-3547	Brigadier	ManzooHussain Atif	117 BDE
15.	PA-2111	Brigadier	Mian Mansoor Muhammad	39 Div
16.	PA-1148	Brigadier	Mian Taskin Uddin	91 BDE
17.	PA-2729	Brigadier	Mir Abdul Nayeem	34 HQ BDE
18.	PA-1999	Brigadier	Mohd. Aslam	53 BDE
19.	PA-2103	Brigadier	Mohd. Hayat	107/407 BDE
20.	PA-1044	Brigadier	Mohd. Shafi	23 HQ BDE

21.	PA-1702	Brigadier	N. A. Ashraf	CMD Natore GRN
22.	PA-3430	Brigadier	S. A. Ansari	Rangpur GRN
23.	PA-3548	Brigadier	Saad Ullah Khan S. J.	27 BDE
24.	PA-1880	Brigadier	Syed Asghar Hasan	Sylhet force
25.	PA-2110	Brigadier	Syed Shah Abul Qasim	C.C.ATY ECO
26.	PA-2130	Brigadier	Tajmmal Hussain Malik	205 HQ BDE
27.	PA-1817	Col.	Fazle Hamid	314 HQ BDE
28.	PA-3799	Col.	K. K. Afridi	9 Div
29.	PA-1963	Col.	Mohd. Khan	ISI
30.	PA-100115	Col.	Mohammad Musharaf Ali	14 ADMS Div
31.	PA-2200	Lt/Col.	Abdul Ghaffor	HQ SIGEA
32.	PA-4489	Lt/Col.	Aftab H. Quereshi	33 Baluch
33.	PA-3568	Lt/Col.	Abdul Rehman Awan	CAF
34.	PA-3347	Lt/Col.	Abdul Hamid Khan	ML HQ
35.	PA-4087	Lt/Col.	Abdullah Khan	EPCAF
36.	PTC-4318	Lt/Col.	Ahmed Mukhtar Khan	30 FF
37.	PA-4062	Lt/Col.	Amir Mohd. Khan	7 SEC ML
38.	PTC-4329	Lt/Col.	Amir Nawaz Khan	13 FF
39.	PA-5027	Lt/Col.	Amir Mohd. Khan	34 Punjab
40.	PA-4745	Lt/Col.	A. Shams ul Zaman	22 FF
41.	PA-4608	Lt/Col.	Ashiq Hussain	24 FF
42.	PA-3248	Lt/Col.	Aziz Khan	32 Baluch
43.	PTC-3239	Lt/Col.	Ghulam Yasin Siddiqi	ST HQ Dacca AA & QMG
44.	PTC-3711	Lt/Col.	Isharat Ali Alavi	14 HQ Inf. Div
45.	PA-4441	Lt/Col.	Mukhtar Alam Hijazi	EPCAF

46.	PA-3600	Lt/Col.	Mustafa Anwar	15 Baluch
47.	PA-4100	Lt/Col.	M.R.K. Mirza	33 Punjab
48.	PA-4301	Lt/Col.	Matloob Hussain	18 Punjab
49.	PA-2700	Lt/Col.	Mohammad Akram	Tochi Scout
50.	PSS-2590	Lt/Col.	Mohd. Akbar	EPCAF
51.	PTC-3645	Lt/Col.	Moham Nawaz	15 Baluch
52.	PA-4766	Lt/Col.	Mumtaz Malik	HQ East Comd
53.	PA-4416	Lt/Col.	M. M. M. Baiz	8 Baluch
54.	PA-100207	Col.	Mohd. Matin	72 ADMS MED BN
55.	PA-2917	Lt/Col.	Mazhar HussaiChauhan	ISSC
56.	PA-3610	Lt/Col.	Mukhtar Ahmed Sayed	HQ MLA Cav
57.	PSS-2899	Lt/Col.	Mustafajan	HQ MLA Zone
58.	PA-2821	Lt/Col.	Oman Ali Khan	Survey Sec
59.	PA-5074	Lt/Col.	Reaz Hussain Javed	31 Punjab
60.	PA-4550	Lt/Col.	Rashid Ahmed	HQ EPCAF
61.	PA-4817	Lt/Col.	Seikh Mohd. Naeem	39 Baluch
62.	PA-3932	Lt/Col.	Sarfraz Khan Malik	31 Punjab
63.	PA-4920	Lt/Col.	S.F.H. Rizvi	32 Punjab
64.	PA-4560	Lt/Col.	S.H. Bokhari	29 CAV.
65.	PA-4368	Lt/Col.	Syed Hamid Shafi	DEF Purchase
66.	PA-3817	Lt/Col.	Sultan Badshah	8 EPCAF
67.	PA-5178	Lt/Col.	Sultan Ahmed	31 Baluch
68.	PA-4518	Lt/Col.	S.R.H.S. Jaffari	HQ SIG EA
69.	PSS-3743	Lt/Col.	Zaid Agha Khan	HQ EF LOG
70.	PA-3837	Lt/Col.	M.Y. Malik	14 HQ Div
71.	PA-7059	Major	Abdul Ghafran	East Comd.
72.	PA-5640	Major	Anis Ahmed	205 HQ Inf. BDE

73.	PA-7214	Major	Arif Javed	22 CAV
74.	PA-6736	Major	Atta Mohd.	29 Baluch
75.	PSS-8394	Major	Abdul Hamid	31 Punjab
76.	PA-7299	Major	A.S.P. Quereshi	25 Punjab
77.	PA-7530	Major	Ashfaq Ahmed Cheema	39 Baluch
78.	PSS-8547	Major	Abdul Khaleq Kayani	6 Punjab
79.	PTC-4664	Major	Abdul Waheed Mughal	22 Baluch
80.	PA-3838	Major	Abdul Hamid Khattak	ML HQ
81.	PA-7251	Major	Ahmed Hassan Khan	EPCAF
82.	PRR-4438	Major	Anees Ahmed Khan	15 Baluch
83.	PA-4990	Major	Abdul Waheed Khan	31 Baluch
84.	PA-5868	Major	Ch. Mohd. Jahangir	HQ MLA ZB
85.	PA-4122	Major	Ghulam Mohd.	2 Baluch
86.	PTC-4390	Major	Gulam Ahmed	EPCAF
87.	PA-7439	Major	Ghazanfar Ali Nasir	EPCAF
88.	PA-6959	Major	Hadi Hussain	24 FF
89.	PA-6646	Major	Hasan Mujtaba	8 Baluch
90.	PTC-5733	Major	Iftikhar Uddin Ahmed	33 Baluch
91.	PA-6729	Major	Iftikhar Ahmed	8 Punjab
92.	PA-5250	Major	Shah Muhamad Osman Faruqi	7 Sig. BN
93.	PA-4553	Major	Khursheed Oman	814 FIU
94.	PTC-3947	Major	Khurshid Ali	Survey Sec.
95.	PA-7576	Major	Khizar Hayat	4 FF
96.	PA-7657	Major	Mehr Mohd Khan	31 Baluch
97.	PTC-5911	Major	M. Abdullah Khan	27 BDE
98.	PA-7253	Major	Mohd. Afzal	8 Baluch
99.	PA-7405	Major	M. Ishaq	EPCAF
100.	PTC-3246	Major	Mohd. Hafiz Raja	34 Punjab
101.	PA-6870	Major	Mohd. Younas	32 Punjab
102.	PA-6793	Major	Mohd. Amin	107 HQ BDE

103.	PS-3935/2935	Major	Mohd. Lodhi	Natore Gar.
104.	PA-6554	Major	Mirza Anwar Beg	88 ORD COY
105.	PTC-4157	Major	M.A. K. Lodhi	16 HQ Div
106.	PSS-4245	Major	Madad Hussain Shah	18 Punjab
107.	PTC-3007	Major	Mohd. Ayub Khan	97 BDE
108.	PSS-6110	Major	Mohd. Sharif Arain	33 Punjab
109.	PA-5964	Major	Mohd. Iftikhar Khan	202 HQ BDE
110.	PA-2818	Major	M. Yahya Hamid Khan	6 Punjab
111.	PSS-6150	Major	Mohd. Yamin	ASC
112.	PA-5141	Major	Mohd. Ghazanfar	ISSC
113.	PA-7231	Major	Mohd. Sarwar	33 Punjab
114.	PTC-3016	Major	Mohd. Siddique	205 HQ Inf BDE
115.	PSS-6092	Major	Mohd. Ashraf	HQ EPCAF
116.	PSS-4634	Major	Mohd. Ashraf Khan	53 HQ BDE
117.	PA-5312	Major	Mohammad Safdar	ISSC
118.	PA-6067	Major	M.M. Ispahani	HQ Eastern Cmd
119.	PA-6440	Major	Mohd. Jamil	EPCAF
120.	PA-7559	Major	Mohd. Safi	32 Punjab
121.	PSS-4320	Major	Mohd. Azim Qureshi Qures	ISSC
122.	PA-6460	Major	Mohd. Zulficar Rathore	13 Engr. BN
123.	PA-5962	Major	Mushtaq Ahmed	Det 630 ASC
124.	PSS-7996	Major	Nasira Khan	26 FF
125.	PA-4748	Major	Nasir Ahmed	409 GHQ FIU
126.	PTC-4632	Major	Rana Zahoor Mohyydin Khan	18 Punjab
127.	PA-8655	Major	Rifat Mahmood	31 FD Regt.

128.	PSS-6148	Major	Rustam Ali	314 HQ Bde
129.	ACO-390	Major	R. M. Mumtaz Khan	31 Baluch
130.	A-6063	Major	Sardar Khan	HQ MLA
131.	ACO-2099	Major	Mohammad Azam Khan	12 A.K.
132.	PRR-3389	Major	Saif Ullah Khan	ISSC
133.	PA-6893	Major	S.T. Hussain	734 FIC
134.	PSS-4224	Major	S.M.H.S. Bokhari	24 FF
135.	PSS-8015	Major	Sajid Mahmud	32 Punjab
136.	PA-7415	Major	Sher ur Rehman	29 CAV
137.	PTC-5930	Major	Salamat Ali	EPCAF
138.	PA-6858	Major	Sajjad Akhtar Malik	ISI
139.	PA-5684	Major	Saleem Inayet Khan	57 HQ MLZB
140.	PA-7289	Major	Sultan Saud	EPCAF
141.	PA-6542	Major	Sarfraz Uddin	ISI
142.	PA-5080	Major	Shaukatullah Khattak	36 Sig. BN
143.	PA-7428	Major	Sultan Surkhro Awan	33 Punjab
144.	PA-7076	Major	Sarfraz Alam	EPCAF
145.	PA-6851	Major	Sarwar Khan	Tochi Scout
146.	PA-6272	Major	Tafair ul Islam	HQ Natore
147.	PSS-8124	Major	Zaumul Maluk	18 Punjab
148.	PSS-8464	Captain	Abdul Waheed	30 FF
149.	PA-10202	Captain	Aftab Ahmad	31 Baluch
150.	PSS-8836	Captain	Arif Hussain Shah	ARTY EIZI EMD
151.	PSS-9634	Captain	Abrar Hussain	30 FF
152.	PSS-9959	Captain	Amjad Shabbir Bukhari	31 FDRegt. ARTY
153.	PA-10129	Captain	Ausaf Ahmed	53 Fd. Regt.
154.	PA-10185	Captain	Abdul Qahar	EPCAF
155.	PA-10985	Captain	Ashraf Mirza	12 AK INF BN

156.	PSS-9904	Captain	Abdul Rashid Nayyar	19 Sig BN
157.	PSS-8005	Captain	Aman Ullah	HQ Natore GR
158.	PSS-9363	Captain	Aziz Ahmed	31 FD Regt.
159.	PSS-9440	Captain	Gulfraz Khan Abbasi	22 FF
160.	PSS-8144	Captain	Ikramul Haq	20 CAV
161.	PA-10241	Captain	Ijaz Ahmed Cheema	ISI
162.	PA-8867	Captain	Iftikhar Ahmed Gondal	31 Punjab
163.	PSS-8821	Captain	Ishaq Parvez	24 FF
164.	PSS-9614	Captain	Iqbal Shah	29 CAV
165.	PSS-6910	Captain	Javed Iqbal	33 Baluch
166.	PSS-9765	Captain	Jahangir Koyani	RFT CAMP
167.	PA-7838	Captain	Karam Khan	315 HQ BDE
168.	PA-11554	Captain	Manzar Amin	25 FF
169.	PSS-9387	Captain	Muzaffar Hussain Naqvi	18 Punjab
170.	PA-11551	Captain	Mohd. Sajjad	80 Fd. Regt.
171.	PSS-8820	Captain	Mohd. Zakir Raja (Muhammad Zakar Khan, Arty)	ISSC
172.	PA-7862	Captain	Mohd. Arif	14 HQ Div
173.	PSS-9018	Captain	Mohd. Ashraf	12 Punjab
174.	PSS-8977	Captain	Mohd. Iqbal	12 Punjab
175.	PSS-9927	Captain	Mohd. Rafi Munir	18 Punjab
176.	PSS-10287	Captain	Mohd. Jamill	6 Punjab
177.	PSS-9077	Captain	Naeem Sadiq	409 HQ FIU
178.	PSS-9454	Captain	Sher Ali	39 Baluch
179.	PSS-8093	Captain	Salman Mahmood	26 FF
180.	PA-11009	Captain	Samshed Sarwar	RFN CAMP
181.	PSS-7745	Captain	Shahid Rehman	29 CAV
182.	PSS-10431	Captain	Saleh Hussain	18 Punjab
183.	PSS-9508	Captain	Shaukat Nawaz Khan	6 Punjab

184.	PA-7898	Captain	Zahid Zaman	53 HQ BDE
185.	PSS-11843	Lieutenant	Munir Ahmed Butt	31 Baluch Regt.
186.	PSS-12191	Lieutenant	Zafar Jang	38 FF
187.	PSS-6127	Major	Nisar Ahmad Khan Sherwani	32 Punjab
188.	PSS-8534	Major	Fayaz Muhammad	29 Baluch
189.	PA-4992	Major	Mian Fakhruddin	91 HQ Inf. Bde.
190.	PSS-8880	Captain	Hidayat Ullah Khan	29 Baluch
191.	PSS-10828	Captain	Md. Siddique	27 Sig. BN
192.	10147	Captain	Khalil ur Rahman	COD,Dacca
193.	PA-6726	Major	Nadir Parvaiz Khan	6 Punjab
194.	PSS-10384	Captain	Hassan Idris	EPCAF
195.	P-953	Air Cdre	Inam ul Hoque Khan	PF Dacca
196.	PAF-1069	Gr. Cpt.	M.A. Majid Baig	PF Dacca
197.	PAK-5332	Ft/Lt.	Khalil Ahmed	PAF
198.	P-138	Rear Adm	Mohamed Shariff	
199.	PN-108	Cmdre	Ikramul Haq Malik	Port Trust
200.	PN-219	Cmdre	Khatib Masud Hussain	Base Comd.

Bibliography

1. Shadhinata Ekattur by Kader Siddiqui, Ananna Publisher, 1997
2. Ekattur Amar Shrestha Samoy by Anwar-ul Alam Shaheed, Shahitta Prakash, 2009
3. Liberation Struggle of Bangalees by Aftab Ahmed, Barna-Shagar Prakashoni, 1998
4. People's Movement in Bangladesh for the Trial of Bangladesh War Criminals of 1971; Nuran Nabi and Jahanara Imam, p.183, Bengal Studies 1994: Essays on Economics, Society & Culture
5. 1971 Bangladesh Genocide Archives

About The Author

Dr. Nuran Nabi obtained his Bachelor of Science (Honors) in Biochemistry from Dhaka University, Bangladesh; Post Graduate Diploma from Osaka University, Japan; Ph.D. in Cell Biology from Kyushu University, Japan; and did his Post Doctoral research at New York University, USA.

He was a lecturer of Dhaka University in the early 1970's and a member of the Dhaka University Senate. He has been living in the USA since 1980. He worked for Colgate-Palmolive for twenty-two years and is co-inventor of Colgate Total toothpaste technology. In addition, Dr. Nabi has more than a hundred patents and publications to his credit.

He retired in 2006 from Colgate-Palmolive before deciding to take public office. Dr. Nabi has served as Councilman of Plainsboro Township, NJ, USA since 2007.

Dr. Nabi also currently serves as a Board Member of Applied Research and Photonics, Inc, USA and American Super Specialty Hospital in Dhaka, Bangladesh.

He was the President of Student League's F. H. Hall branch; a dedicated activist during the 1967-1971 Bangladesh Liberation Movement. He was a valiant freedom fighter of the Bangladesh Liberation War of 1971. Based on his heroic contributions to the Bangladesh Liberation War, the Far Eastern Economic Review, referred to Dr. Nabi as "the Brain" of the Tangail Freedom Fighters Forces. He was awarded a special citation by the Commander- in-Chief of Bangladesh.

In the 1980's, Dr. Nabi played a leading role in establishing the "Committee for a Democratic Bangladesh" and later in the 1990's established the "Committee for the Realization of Bangladesh

Liberation War Ideals and Trial for Bangladesh War Criminals." He spearheaded these two organizations from the USA.

He is the Founding Co-Convener and current President of "Bangabandhu Parishad, USA"; Founding General Secretary and Former President of the Bangladesh Society of New Jersey; and a patron of the Bangladesh Association of New Jersey.

Dr. Nabi was also a Founding Member and Former Chairman of the Federation of Bangladeshi Associations in North America (FOBANA); Founding Director of the America-Bangladesh Friendship Caucus; Founding President of the Bangladeshi Americans Against Terrorisms, Inc.; President of the Society to Help Education in Bangladesh International (SHEBI); and Former President and Editor of the Weekly Probashi, New York.

Dr. Nabi was the Publisher of the first Bengali Book "20 Years after Liberation" published in the USA.

Dr. Nabi has been speaking in various forums in the USA including State University of New York, Rutgers University, Kean University, Monmouth University, Montclair University and Philadelphia Community College to make awareness about the Bangladesh genocide 1971and demanding the trial of Bangladesh war criminals.

Dr. Nabi's wife, Dr. Zeenat Nabi is also a research scientist. They have two sons, Mush Nabi and Adnan Nabi. The Nabi Family is now permanently living in NJ, USA.